ULTIMATE BETRAYAL

JOSEPH H. BADAL

SUSPENSE PUBLISHING

ULTIMATE BETRAYAL
by
Joseph Badal

PRINT EDITION
* * * * *
PUBLISHED BY:
Suspense Publishing

Joseph Badal
Copyright 2014 Joseph Badal

PUBLISHING HISTORY:
Suspense Publishing, Paperback and Digital Copy, April 2014

Cover Design: Shannon Raab
Cover Photographer: iStockphoto.com/photo168
Cover Photographer: iStockphoto.com/HamsterMan

ISBN-13: 978-0615972701 (Custom)
ISBN-10: 0615972705

OTHER BOOKS BY JOSEPH BADAL

STAND-ALONE THRILLERS
THE PYTHAGOREAN SOLUTION
SHELL GAME

DANFORTH SAGA
EVIL DEEDS (#1)
TERROR CELL (#2)
THE NOSTRADAMUS SECRET (#3)
THE LONE WOLF AGENDA (#4)

DEDICATION

"Ultimate Betrayal" is dedicated to Trinity Badal, a wonderful granddaughter who right from the start possessed the key to my heart.

ACKNOWLEDGMENTS

"Ultimate Betrayal" is my seventh novel and, as with the others before it, would not have happened without the support, hard work, and guidance from a number of people.

My thanks go to John and Shannon Raab for their work in editing, publishing, and marketing of "Ultimate Betrayal." As usual, Shannon did a masterful job in creating the cover for this novel.

A number of friends reviewed the manuscript and made valuable suggestions that improved the read, corrected my German, and gave me encouragement. They include Stuart & Rosalie Sherman, Inge Taylor, Nick Franklin, and Tom Avitabile.

The inspiration for this book came from experiences I had while serving in the U.S. Army in Vietnam in 1971-72. Although the back story in "Ultimate Betrayal" is based on my protagonist's service in Afghanistan, much of the action and references to activities in Afghanistan were drawn from Vietnam experiences.

Finally, I want to thank all those wonderful men and women who have read my previous books. Your support provides valuable and continuous inspiration.

PRAISE FOR
JOSEPH BADAL

"Crisp writing, masterful pacing, and characters to genuinely care about. This is what top-notch suspense is all about."
—Michael Palmer, *New York Times* Bestselling author of "Political Suicide"

" "Ultimate Betrayal" provides the ultimate in riveting reading entertainment that's as well thought out as it is thought provoking. Both a stand-out thriller and modern day morality tale. Mined from the familial territory of Harlan Coben, with the seasoned action plotting of James Rollins or Steve Berry, this is fiction of the highest order. Poignant and unrelentingly powerful."
—Jon Land, bestselling and award-winning author of "The Tenth Circle"

"Joseph Badal has surpassed his own high standards once again. He pulls out all the stops in his new standalone thriller "Ultimate Betrayal," a tale of crime, espionage, family tragedy, family ties, and ultimately justice and redemption.

"He is the master of the cinematic thriller, in the best sense of the term. His trademark short chapters from multiple points of view take readers on a rocket ride into the worlds of military service, government agencies, law enforcement, family bonds, and organized crime. If you haven't read a Badal thriller before, "Ultimate Betrayal" is a great first step in immersing yourself in his body of work.

"So put on a pot of coffee and fasten your seat belt."
—Robert Kresge, former CIA officer and author of the Civil War spy novel "Saving Lincoln" and the *Warbonnet* historical mysteries

"Joseph Badal has done it again. "Ultimate Betrayal" packs action and revenge into an international conspiracy thriller you won't soon forget. Read it!"
—Steve Brewer, author of "Firepower"

"Joe Badal keeps getting better and better. He knows how to spin a multi-viewpoint thriller without losing the reader, and he knows the international stage so well that he can take us to both exotic and down-home places in a story that flows effortlessly. And uniquely, he can ratchet up the action to a fever pitch without burying us in pages of techno babble. In this tale of "Old World vengeance without New World remorse," you'll love the good guys and hate the bad guys—just as it should be."
—Steven F. Havill, author of the *Posadas County Mystery series*

"Filled with unexpected twists, unconventional allies and a mastermind villain who makes hired killers look like kindergarten teachers. "Ultimate Betrayal" is Joseph Badal's best book yet. A must-read for anyone with a craving for a fast-paced, action-packed, beautifully constructed thriller."
—Anne Hillerman, author of "Spider Woman's Daughter"

ULTIMATE BETRAYAL

JOSEPH BADAL

PART I

JUNE 6, 2001

CHAPTER 1

If someone had asked eighteen-year-old David Hood to define happiness, he wouldn't have had an answer. He couldn't remember what happiness felt like. But he could answer a question about the meaning of life. David knew all about life. Life was hard work, always doing your best, and getting by. Just getting by. He also knew what life wasn't. Life wasn't about the triumph of good over evil.

At 6'2" and 175 pounds, David had the broad shoulders, trim waist, and long, powerful legs of an athlete. He carried himself confidently. Neighbors considered him courteous and respectful—someone who never got into trouble. He was on time for work every day, worked hard, and kept his mouth shut. All qualities that Gino Bartolucci valued.

David rehearsed aloud what he would say to Mr. Bartolucci as he walked down Broad Street. He'd worked in the sprawling Bartolucci Market after school, on weekends, and during the summer for the last four years. Now that he had his high school diploma, he felt he owed Mr. Bartolucci an explanation for what he was about to do. Out of respect. Then he'd have to tell his father.

Gino Bartolucci owned a number of "legitimate" businesses, including Bartolucci's Market. But his real money came from numbers running, bookmaking, loan sharking, and the protection racket. But eighteen-year-old David Hood figured Mr. Bartolucci's mob connections had nothing to do with him. The mob was a part of South Philadelphia—always was, always would be. What really mattered to David was that Mr. Bartolucci gave him a job he badly needed and always treated him fairly. Like a father treats a son.

After he turned down a side street, he walked six blocks of maple tree-lined row houses to the South Philadelphia produce district and stopped across the street from the market. The aromas of frying sausages and peppers reached him and he breathed them in as though his life depended on it. The familiar faces of shoppers as they inspected fruit and vegetables in the sidewalk bins made him sad. Very soon, this would all be part of his past. He already felt homesick.

David crossed the street and entered the market, an open-air affair that could have been transplanted from Sicily. Garlic sautéed in olive oil cut the sweet smell of oregano-laced *salsicci*. Somehow the fragrances of fresh-cut flowers survived the spicy onslaught from the grill. Mr. Bartolucci called this collage of aromas "Italian perfume." The raucous sound of people who argued in Italian and English over prices and the quality of the produce seemed almost melodic.

David watched Mr. Bartolucci come out of his office, his arm wrapped around the shoulders of his fifteen-year-old daughter, Carmela, who was already taller than her five-foot, six-inch father. The girl batted her eyelashes at David, who ignored her. All David ever noticed about Carmela were the rubber band-held braces on her teeth and the maroon and white Catholic school uniform that hung like a tent on her more-than-plump body. She was too young, fat, and silly. Besides, David didn't encourage relationships with girls. They always wanted to know his inner thoughts and feelings. He didn't want them to ask questions. They might not like his answers.

Bartolucci wore his usual blue suit, red tie, and white dress shirt—his tie and shirt open at the neck. Black hair laced with white streaks slicked back. Bartolucci's hands belonged on a giant. They looked almost freakish and damned intimidating on his short, stocky frame.

Gino greeted David with a wave of a ham hock hand and a "*Ciao, Bello!*"

"Mister Bartolucci, could . . . could I talk with you for a minute?"

"*Certo, Michel,*" he responded. "*Uno momento.*" Bartolucci barked a stream of orders in Italian in his sandpaper basso voice to two Sicilian immigrant employees and then told his daughter to get an ice cream cone. He turned to David and asked with the usual rough edge to his voice, but with softness in his eyes, "You need something?"

"Mister Bartolucci, I want to thank you for all you've done for me. You've been great and I appreciate it. But I won't be able to work here after this month."

Bartolucci frowned. "Whatsa matter? Now you a hotshot high school graduate, you gonna leave the wop behind?" He smiled. "You gonna go off to some Ivy League college and chase preppie girls?"

"No, ah, no, Mister Bartolucci." David's face suddenly felt hot. "It's not like that. I enlisted in the Army."

"You did what!" Bartolucci exploded.

David glanced around. Every person within twenty-five yards seemed to freeze in place.

Gino pulled David by the arm into his office, slammed the door behind them, and pushed him into a chair. "Whatsa matter, you get drafted?" he said. "I can fix that. I can make you a free man like that." He snapped his fingers.

"There's no draft anymore, Mr. Bartolucci."

Bartolucci's face flushed and his eyes narrowed to slits. The veins on the sides of his neck bulged. "You enlisted? What'd you finish at South Philadelphia High? Last? You stupid or somethin'?"

"First." David looked at his shoes and quietly said, "I finished top of my class."

"First!" Gino growled. "First! You gonna waste that on the goddamn Army? Get your ass shot off in some goddamn foreign country?"

David sat silently, momentarily met Mr. Bartolucci's eyes, then looked away to avoid the man's blistering gaze.

"Look at me, kid! Look at me!"

David steeled himself. Raised his head.

"You sure you want to do this? You made up your mind?"

David dropped his gaze again.

"I asked you a question, boy. You sure you want to do this?"

David looked up again. He licked his lips and swallowed. "It's not a matter of *want*, sir. It's something I gotta do."

"That's bull. You . . ." Bartolucci stopped and stared hard at David. Then he nodded and said, "What did your father say about this?"

"I haven't told him yet. He doesn't get home from work 'til 8:00."

With a sigh, Gino fell into his chair. "He ain't gonna like it."

"He won't care one way or the other."

"You couldn't be more wrong."

David closed his eyes and rubbed his forehead. He had no interest in arguing with Mr. Bartolucci about his relationship with his father.

"Okay, if it's gotta be, it's gotta be. *Che sera, sera.* Now I'm gonna tell you what to do." He pulled an enormous wad of cash from a pants pocket and peeled off ten one hundred dollar bills. "You take this money and you go party like crazy until you gotta go to the Army. And if you ever need anything at all—ever—you gonna call Gino Bartolucci."

CHAPTER 2

Carmela Bartolucci practiced moving her hips like a runway model, while she walked back to her father's office. She pushed the remainder of the ice cream cone into her mouth and thought about David Hood. Daddy didn't like it when she looked at boys. But David acted as though she didn't exist. She wished he'd pay attention to her. She had every detail of his face memorized: black hair combed straight back; high forehead; dark, well-shaped eyebrows; long, dark lashes; blue eyes; straight nose; sensually-full lips.

"Carmelita, come over here."

Gino's loud voice shocked her out of her daydream. She smiled and said, "*Si, Papa, che volete?*"

"*Venga, Carina,*" he shouted.

Carmela blushed. She followed him into his office. "Why did you yell at David, Papa? I could hear you through the door."

Gino frowned at his daughter. But his face quickly softened. He blew out a stream of air and said, "He just told me he enlisted in the Army. That boy is *molto intelligente*. He should go to college, not the Army."

"He's awfully quiet," Carmela said. "It's like he's . . . you know, kinda sad."

Gino turned his gaze back to her and smiled. "You're a smart girl, Carmelita."

She smiled. "Why's he like that, Papa?"

Gino hesitated, sat down behind his desk, waved a hand at his daughter to take a seat. "You're probably old enough to hear this."

Full of anticipation, she sat forward in her chair.

"Patience, *Carina.*" He leaned back in his chair and folded his arms across his chest. "One evening when David was twelve, he and his older brother, Tommy, were on their way home from the movies. Tommy was maybe sixteen. Nice boy, just like David. Tough, too. It was just after dark and they were only a few blocks from their house when a gang of hoodlums jumped them."

Carmela knew her mouth had dropped open. Her heart raced, but she didn't dare move. She sat transfixed by the sadness in her father's eyes, the grim set of his jaw. The thought of someone hurting David made her feel sad and angry.

"There were five of them against Tommy and David. Tommy fought like a *lupo* and beat up three of the gang. Then one of the others pulled a knife on David. Tommy went after that guy." Gino paused, as though he expected Carmela to ask a question.

"What happened?" she obliged.

Gino's mouth turned down and he closed his eyes for a moment. When he opened them again, he said, "Tommy died right there. The one with the knife stabbed him in the heart. The word is David has always blamed himself for his brother's death. He was just a kid. There was nothin' he coulda done." Gino shrugged. "To make matters worse, David's mother went *demenziale*, crazy, over Tommy's death. She died a couple years ago. And David and his father don't have much of a relationship. You understand now, Carmelita, why David seems so sad."

"But it wasn't his fault that gang attacked them. They were just in the wrong place at the wrong time."

"Yeah, that's true, Carmelita. But I heard Tommy didn't want to go out that day. David kept pestering him. Their parents wouldn't let David go out alone; he was too young. So, Tommy finally agreed to go."

"You think he's going into the Army because of what happened to his brother?"

Gino's mouth dropped. "You're too damned smart for your age." He smiled. "Get outta here so I can do some work."

Carmela nodded, stood up, and walked to the office door. She tried to wipe away the tears from her eyes before Papa noticed. She didn't know what to do about the ache in her heart.

DECEMBER 12, 2002

CHAPTER 3

Lieutenant James Ross crawled up the side of a natural trench in the Nad-e Ali District of Helmand Province, Afghanistan and peeked toward the sun, which now rested on the horizon. He blew into his gloved hands and tried to warm his fingers. "Damned cold!" he muttered. He turned to his right and looked at Sergeant David Hood. "There's supposed to be a Taliban unit out there somewhere, but I haven't seen or heard a thing."

"With these mountains, a thousand snipers could be fifty yards from us and we wouldn't know it, Lieutenant," David said.

Ross peeked over the top of the trench once again. "Sergeant, have the men check their ammunition and supplies. I'm going to call for a resupply drop."

"Already done, sir. We're down to three magazines per man and a day's worth of water and MREs."

"How're Peterson's feet?"

"Not good. He's got blisters on blisters."

"I'd better call for a medevac. Between the cold and the terrain, I'm surprised all of us aren't crippled. Damned coun—"

David saw the lieutenant's skull explode, felt warm, wet spray hit his face, heard the distinctive sound of an AK-47 rifle. Then the *whump, whump, whump* of launched mortars. The bullets and mortars seemed to come straight from the setting sun.

"Sonofabitch! Sonofabitch!" David panicked, felt the urge to run. But there was no place to run. He forced himself to stay under control. "Incoming!" he shouted into his headset. "Incoming!" He looked left and then right. The eighteen men in his unit were arrayed in a depression, which meandered off to the left on a relatively straight line and on the right curved in an arc that ultimately turned west into the now half-set sun. He grabbed Lieutenant Ross's boots and pulled his body down into the trench.

On the radio communications net, David ordered the men on his right to only fire at clearly visible targets. "Conserve ammo," he told them.

The first mortars impacted twenty-five yards short of and to the left of his position, damned close to his men in the left side of the trench. He ordered those men to move past him to join up with the right side of the unit, where the trench was at its deepest. This left David alone, a good thirty yards from his closest team member. He unslung his grenade launcher and "walked in" rounds in twenty-yard increments, beginning about fifty yards in front of his position. At about the one hundred-yard mark, he heard shouts and screams.

"Bad guys at about one hundred yards in front of my position," he said to his men, as he popped off another half-dozen grenade rounds. Then he ran to join the rest of the team. He radioed headquarters, gave his team's position, and called for air support.

Another round of mortars rained down on where David had been a minute ago. Ross's body was probably obliterated. When the mortars stopped, all David heard was his own breathing. A minute passed. Then another. And another. Five minutes in all. Then a phalanx of armed men rose from crevices in the side of the mountain and moved toward the Americans. Like pop-up targets in an arcade shooting gallery, the tribesmen appeared, then disappeared, appeared, then disappeared again, shooting all the while. They moved toward both ends of the trench.

David had been in fire fights before and had learned how the enemy operated, what sort of tactics they used. He had to prevent the Taliban force from executing a pincer maneuver. His throat constricted as the reality of the situation hit home. With the enemy so close to them, it was too late for the Americans to retreat en masse to high ground, especially with some sunlight still present.

They'd be easy targets. They were out-numbered, pinned down in a depression, and low on ammunition. And the enemy controlled the high ground. The only hope they had was to pull back in small groups while the rest of the platoon provided cover fire. If they could reach high ground and hold off the Taliban until air support arrived, they might make it.

David ordered Sergeant Pritchard and three other men to find cover in the boulders above and behind them. Stooped over, Pritchard and his three men ran toward the boulders while David and the rest of the unit fired at any Taliban fighter who showed himself. The four men serpentined around rock formations and then raced up a goat path toward the elevated position, when a heavy automatic weapon suddenly opened up. David recognized the drumbeat of an NSV Utyos 108 mm machinegun, probably captured years ago by the *mujaheddin* from the Soviets. He looked back at Pritchard's team and saw one of the men lying on the goat path. Pritchard and two of the men had made it to the shelter of the boulders.

"Pritchard, what's your status?" David said over his headset.

"Johnson was cut to pieces. Fuckin' heavy machinegun."

"You all okay?"

"Yeah. Nothing serious."

"Stay low," David told Pritchard. "I'll touch base in a second."

When the sun dropped completely below the horizon, mortar rounds again fell from the sky.

"Check with air support," David told his radioman.

"FAC, this is Blue Team Six, where's that air support?" the radioman shouted into his radio.

"Thirty minutes out," the Forward Air Controller shouted back.

Thirty minutes! David thought. We'll be dead in thirty minutes.

Based on previous experience, David suspected what the Taliban leader might do. He'd drop mortar rounds on the trench for five or ten minutes until he'd done as much damage as possible and then he'd have the heavy machinegun rake the trench from one side, while the rest of his men attacked the survivors in the trench from the other side.

David flipped down his night vision device and scanned the

hillside in front of him. He caught brief glimpses of enemy fighters and huge greenish blooms that came off the mortar rounds as they exited their firing tubes. Mortar rounds impacted just in front of their position. The Taliban had zeroed in on them. They didn't need sunlight anymore. They knew exactly where David and his men were. The next rounds would wipe out his team.

To make matters worse, the heavy machinegun opened up again. The machine gunner fired a ferocious one-minute burst and then went inactive. Probably to reload, David thought. The hot lead from the weapon had bloomed on David's goggles.

"We've got to get out of here now," David told his men. "Fall back to that rock formation at the bottom of the goat path. Take weapons, ammo, and night vision goggles only."

David counted fourteen men leave the trench. He followed them to a large rock outcropping and slipped behind it.

The machinegun opened up two minutes later while mortar rounds destroyed the trench the Americans had just vacated. Then the machinegun went quiet and the Taliban stopped firing their rifles. They'll attack now, David thought. And once they found the trench unoccupied, they'd figure out the Americans had retreated up the back side of the hill.

"Fall back to Pritchard's position," David ordered.

His men left the rock outcropping and ran up the goat path toward high ground. David looked back at them and watched as they scaled the path. Without his night vision glasses, they would have been invisible. Then he looked back toward the trench.

David smelled the Taliban fighters before he heard or saw them. A mixture of goat, sweat, and tobacco. Then, through his goggles, he saw two men move noiselessly toward the right end of the trench and veer toward his position. They passed the edge of the rock formation he hid behind. David stepped out, covered the second man's mouth with his hand, and thrust his combat knife into the man's kidney. He slowly lowered the man to the ground and moved to follow the first man. He was three paces away, when the Taliban fighter turned and raised his rifle. David used his knife to deflect the muzzle of the rifle. But the weapon discharged and David felt a shock of hot pain hit his right thigh. His leg crumpled beneath him.

He shifted his weight to his left leg, pointed his knife hand at the man, and launched himself forward. His knife penetrated the man's chest and was nearly wrenched from his hand as the blade hit a rib.

The Taliban fighter dropped his weapon and grabbed David's wrist with both of his hands. David hopped forward and continued to press the knife against the man's chest. It took almost half-a-minute before he felt the man's grip weaken. Then the Taliban fighter sagged to the ground and went still.

David figured the jets were still about fifteen minutes out. He retreated behind the rock outcropping again. A minute passed and then he heard whispers. A group of half-a-dozen or so men passed him, stopped, and clustered around the two bodies of their comrades. He moved from the rocks and fired his assault rifle into the group until his magazine was empty. Then he again took cover, ejected the empty magazine, and inserted his last fresh one.

Voices echoed off the mountainside and mixed with the groans and cries of the men he'd just fired on.

Then he heard in his ear bud, "Sergeant Hood, where the hell are you?"

David ignored the voice and took a step forward when automatic weapons fire drove him back behind the rocks. Rounds struck and ricocheted off the rock wall behind him and propelled metal and rock shrapnel at and around him. Then something hot hit him in the back, knocked him to the ground, and drove the air from his lungs. He felt blood dribble down his back. Sharp shards of rock slashed his face and torso. Blood poured from a cut on his forehead and blinded him. He felt light-headed. Each breath he took felt as though someone twisted a knife in his lungs. On hands and knees, he sucked in minute quantities of air until his head cleared. He jerked the scarf from around his neck, wiped away blood from his eyes, and tied it around his head. He rose, stood on one leg, and lobbed two grenades in the direction of the trench. Then from above and behind him, his team rained a hailstorm of bullets down on the Taliban positions. The enemy fighters stopped shooting.

David took this opportunity to hobble up the goat path. He stumbled over the Taliban bodies that littered the trail. After a few seconds, the enemy fighters down by the trench opened up on him again. He dropped to the ground. Bullets slapped the rock wall behind him and kicked up dirt and rock from the path. His team again fired at the enemy. David tried to right himself, but his wounded leg wouldn't support him and his good leg cramped. Then his men stopped firing. They had to be out of ammunition. He looked down and saw tribesmen move in his direction. He rolled onto his back, aimed his rifle, and fired a burst. The first three men fell while the men behind them retreated.

Suddenly, a tribesman came out of nowhere, screamed "*Allah akbar!*" and charged. David shot him with his last bullet. He tried once again to stand; he didn't want to die on his back. But it was no good. He took his 9 mm pistol from his holster and vowed to kill at least one more of the enemy before they killed him. He had a brief thought about his brother before one of the Taliban fighters stepped onto the path and moved toward him.

David shot the man as he shouted, "Die, asshole!" He expected more of the enemy to appear when the sweet throaty sounds of jet engines roared overhead. Barely conscious, David saw two F/A-18 fighter jets scream past as they dropped incendiary bombs on top of the depression where David and his team had been a few minutes earlier. The planes circled around and fired their M61 Vulcan cannons into the side of the mountain. David could see Vulcan rounds impact the hillside twenty yards from where he lay.

David awoke at a field hospital. A man with Major's insignia on his white coat stood next to his bed. The man held a two-inch metal fragment.

"Nice to see you finally awake." He handed David the piece of metal. "That came out of your back. Thought you'd like a souvenir."

David couldn't have cared less about the metal shard the doctor had taken from him, but he said, "Thanks."

The doctor patted his shoulder.

"How are my men?"

"Two dead, including the lieutenant, and one wounded. The others all got back. Thanks to you."

"I didn't do a thing," David said.

The doctor shook his head. "I hear that shit all the time. Despite the fact you don't think you did anything, that firefight will probably get you a Silver Star, besides the two Purple Hearts for your wounds. And I hear you've been promoted to Master Sergeant. Not bad for being in the Army less than two years."

"When can I rejoin my unit?"

The doctor laughed. "That won't happen any time soon. It will be a couple months before your wounds heal and you're able to rehab your leg. You'll have a limp for a long time, if not forever." The man picked up a brown envelope off the bottom of David's bed and handed it to him. "Those are your new orders."

After the doctor left him, David opened the envelope and read the orders. He had been assigned to something called the Special Logistical Support Detachment at Headquarters, United States Forces-Afghanistan. His heart sank. They've assigned me to some bullshit desk job, he thought.

DECEMBER 22, 2002

CHAPTER 4

David reported in at Bagram Air Force Base for his new assignment. He cooled his heels for an hour in the air conditioned splendor of a camouflaged building the size of a Wal-Mart store before Marine Gunnery Sergeant Fred Laniewski came and led him out into one of the myriad corridors that crisscrossed the enclosure.

"Inside this place, you'd never know you were in the middle of a war zone," Laniewski said as he moved aside to avoid two Army generals.

David chuckled. "Sure isn't what I'm used to."

"I heard," Laniewski said. "You miss the boonies."

"Yeah, like a sharp stick in the eye."

"This place is the little sister of the Pentagon," Laniewski said. "We call it the Afghan Puzzle Palace. You can't walk around here without running into dozens of high-ranking officers. They all have one purpose in life—build up the enemy body count for the Pentagon so they can politic their way to a promotion."

David looked askance at Laniewski. "You're joking, right?" The grim, determined look on the Marine's face told David otherwise.

"So, what kind of unit is this? Grunts and Jarheads together?"

"Navy and Air Force, too," Laniewski said. "You'll see."

Laniewski led David through the halls and stopped at a metal-clad door in what appeared to be a vault planted in the middle of the building. The Marine picked up a telephone receiver from the wall and identified himself.

An Army lieutenant opened the door and frowned. "It's about time, Fred," he said, as he backed into the room.

David followed Laniewski through the doorway.

"The Colonel's having a conniption fit about the records you owe him," the lieutenant continued. "He owes CENTCOM a report." The lieutenant stared at David, as though he'd noticed him for the first time. "Is this the new meat?"

"Yes, sir. Sergeant David Hood, meet Lieutenant Eric Carbajal."

"Good to have you here," Carbajal said. Then he turned back to Laniewski. "Show Hood his desk, then take that information to Colonel Bishop."

Laniewski pointed at a gray metal desk in the second of three rows of identical ones. They were crammed into a forty-foot by forty-foot room. Most of the desks were occupied. "You've been assigned to the Special Logistical Support Detachment, a newly formed, top-secret unit," Laniewski said. "Our mission is code-named "Operation Harvest." The unit's commander is Army Colonel Rolf Bishop." Laniewski scowled and in a whisper said, "You sure as hell don't want to get on Bishop's bad side. He's the worst sonofabitch I've ever met. The guy's got steely-gray eyes that scare grown men and would give little children nightmares."

David thought Laniewski had exaggerated. Bishop would have to be a psychopath to be a worse sonofabitch than the men he'd fought against for the past few months . . . or men who worked for Gino Bartolucci back in South Philadelphia, for that matter.

"The War in Afghanistan is only in its second year," Laniewski said, "and it's already obvious the U.S. will smash the Taliban and their Al Qaeda buddies. The only questions are how long will we hang around, what kind of Afghan government and military will we leave behind, and how long will it take the Taliban to recover and replace the Afghan elected government? Some congressmen have already warned about Afghanistan becoming another Vietnam. There are threats in Congress to drastically cut funds targeted for Afghanistan, which is what happened in the early seventies in Vietnam."

"It's a bit early in this war to compare Afghanistan to Vietnam,"

David said. "In 1971, we'd already been in Vietnam for, what, eight or nine years."

"How do you know that? That's ancient history."

David shrugged. "I read a lot." After a beat, he asked, "So, what do we do here?"

"We bring weapons, ammunition, and all sorts of other equipment and materiel into Afghanistan that won't be needed here for years to come. The serial numbers of hundreds of critical items not even scheduled for production are inputted to Afghan government property books. As quickly as these goods are manufactured, they're shipped over here. The Pentagon's goal is to enable the Afghan military to continue to wage war against the Taliban, even after U.S. forces and U.S. financial support are eventually withdrawn.

"The Pentagon learned a big lesson in Vietnam. This time, in Afghanistan, it decided to find a solution in advance. It created the SLSD here, patterned after the Vietnam unit of the same name."

"Yeah, but what if we leave and the Taliban overthrows the government? They'd have access to all the equipment, materiel, and supplies we brought in."

"That's right," Laniewski said. "But it's a risk the higher-ups will take." He spread his arms as though he encouraged David to draw his own conclusion.

David's right leg suddenly ached so he stood to stretch it. "My God," he said, "if tons of stuff are shipped into Afghanistan, years before its needed, where's it all stored?"

"Great question. The SLSD is the ringmaster of this three-ring circus. It's a logistical nightmare. The unit's responsibility is to track the status, on a daily basis, of every shipment into Afghanistan. Every day, C-5 cargo planes unload massive quantities of equipment and supplies. The unit keeps records of these shipments: When they leave the States, where they are en route, when they're off-loaded, and where the goods are warehoused. The problem is that we have more stuff than we have warehouse space to store it."

David looked around the room and then back at Laniewski. "So, this unit was formed to hide the Pentagon's agenda from Congress. Could we go to prison if Congress discovers what the Pentagon is up to?" Fighting the Taliban in the mountains and valleys, wounds notwithstanding, might be preferable to this assignment, David thought.

Laniewski waggled his hand, but didn't give David a definitive answer or much comfort. He pulled a sheet of paper from under the telephone on David's desk and handed it to him. "This is a list of the members of our unit. Colonel Bishop has organized us into two teams of seven men each. The teams work twelve-hour shifts. Our team works 6 a.m. to 6 p.m."

He tapped the sheet of paper in David's hands. "Sergeant Campbell has been with Colonel Bishop at least eleven years. The other team members, all with combat experience, were pulled together from completely different units."

"What's my job?" David asked.

"Let me get my report to Peg Leg and then I'll explain your duties."

"Peg Leg?"

Laniewski looked around. He again whispered. "Bishop has an artificial leg. Got shot as an Infantry lieutenant on Grenada."

"The Army didn't muster him out?"

"The way I heard it, Bishop was a gung-ho West Point graduate who wanted to become Chief of Staff some day. Had visions of four stars on his shoulders. After he lost his leg, the Army offered him a medical discharge. He wouldn't take it. Fought like a wounded tiger to keep his commission. He finally won, but the Army transferred him from the Infantry to the Quartermaster Corps. No crippled Quartermaster officer will ever make General, let alone become Chief of Staff. He's been bitter ever since. Stay out of his way. He's a fuckin' asshole."

JANUARY 21, 2003

CHAPTER 5

Captain Andrew King removed his wire-rimmed glasses and mopped his face with an Army-green handkerchief. It was unusually hot in the SLSD vault and the air conditioning was on the fritz. He yelled across the room, "Hey, Hood, didn't that shipment of M16s, M-4s, and ammunition come in last week? Tuesday wasn't it?"

"Yes, sir." David glanced across the room at King. The officer looked like a subject of a Norman Rockwell painting: freckles, red hair, and a Midwestern, boy-next-door appearance. But like every other member of the SLSD, King had paid his dues in the field. For all his Opie of Mayberry looks, David knew the Infantry officer had proven himself under fire. Two Silver Stars, a Bronze Star, and two Purple Hearts said it all. "The ammo and rifles came in on a cargo plane. I met it at the airfield and had the shipment off-loaded onto trucks that were supposed to carry the stuff to the warehouse."

"That's what I thought, but I can't find the damned things anywhere on the computer. It's like they never existed. The Quartermaster Corps claims they have no record of the shipment and the cargo manifests have disappeared."

"I can run out to the airfield and track them down, Captain. I bet they're still on the trucks or stored on pallets, getting dirt and snow blown on them."

King grunted with disgust. "I wouldn't bet against you." He looked at his watch. "Nah. It's already past six o'clock. You've busted your ass enough hours today. Take off and get yourself a beer. I'll drive to the warehouse. I can't wait to hear the line of bullshit the warehouse guys give me about what they've done with ten thousand assault rifles and tons of ammunition."

King smiled when he walked out of the building into the cold Afghanistan air. Snow patches checker-boarded the landscape for as far as he could see. Glad for a break from computer reports and the heat in the vault, the cold and snow hardly bothered him. After he waited fifteen minutes for a Jeep from the motor pool, King drove out of the headquarters compound and headed toward the warehouse complex.

Despite the ravages of war and recent neglect, Kabul still showed some signs the English and Soviets had been in the country. The Brits had erected buildings to last and had designed a bit of style into them. The Soviets had destroyed more buildings than they'd built and the ones they'd constructed were ugly boxes that would crumble in a short period of time.

In a city that teemed with throngs of people and hundreds of thousands of cars, trucks, motorcycles, motor scooters, pedicabs, bicycles, donkeys, horses, and pedestrians, he had become accustomed to the way the locals ignored whatever traffic rules existed. Kabul traffic was anarchy in motion. The fatalistic philosophy of the drivers in this city was expressed in a word: *Inshallah*—God willing.

All in all, compared to his native California, it was a shitty country that hadn't been made any better by Allied bombs and Taliban explosives.

The clouds suddenly opened up and snow fell in a dense curtain of huge flakes that obscured the dirt road and the warehouse complex. The Jeep's windshield wipers helped a bit, but not enough to make a big difference. The vehicle's canvas removable doors flapped in the wind and let snow in through gaps between the Jeep's frame and the sides of the doors. King used the security lights on the fence around the warehouse complex to guide him to the entry gate. He showed his identification to the Afghan guard, who opened the gate. King drove one hundred yards to the parking lot, left the Jeep, and ran the twenty-five yards to the entrance.

Inside, he brushed snow off his uniform, removed his cap, and shook it a couple times. He stomped his feet on the concrete floor to knock the snow from his boots. For the millionth time since he'd arrived in Afghanistan, King cursed, "Fuckin' country."

It surprised him to find the warehouse entrance unguarded and the office vacant. He wandered around the enormous building. He called out, "Hello, anyone here?" In a land where anything not tied or nailed down would disappear, King knew there had to be at least two American guards on duty. Maybe they had come inside to get out of the snow. But King saw no one. He picked up a wall phone to call the military police, but put it down when he noticed the building's rear personnel door slightly ajar. He recalled this door opened onto a large vacant lot surrounded by a ten-foot-high fence, with a padlocked gate, and topped with razor-sharp concertina wire. King walked to the far end of the warehouse, opened the rear door, and peered into the snowstorm. The shadowy forms of three two-and-a-half-ton trucks stood twenty feet from the back of the building. Men moved quickly around the vehicles, but snow prevented King from seeing how many were there.

Then the snowfall suddenly abated. Eight turbaned tribesmen, under the supervision of Master Sergeant Robert Campbell, loaded shipping crates into the trucks. The crate markings, printed in large black letters, indicated the boxes contained M-16 assault rifles, M-4 Carbines, and 5.56mm ammunition.

King turned to look at the end of the line of trucks and noticed four heavily armed tribesmen in a ragtag mix of military and civilian clothing. They looked like bandits.

Campbell suddenly yelled at the tribesmen, "*Yullah! Yullah!* We gotta load these trucks and get them out of here."

King reached for the .45 pistol on his hip. Before he could clear the weapon from his holster, someone grabbed his arm and spun him around.

"What can I do for you, Captain?"

King jerked his arm free and drew his weapon before he realized he was about to draw down on his commander. He replaced the .45 in his holster.

"I . . . I came to track down the last shipment of rifles and ammo." He could hold Colonel Bishop's gaze—those implacable gray eyes; those damn scary eyes—for only a few seconds.

Bishop squinted at King and, in a gravelly voice said, "Go over there and wait for me, Captain." He pointed at a room behind King. "I'll be with you in a minute."

"I need to get back—"

"Did you hear me, Captain King?"

"Yes, sir."

Bishop walked to the rear door and went outside. King watched the door close behind the Colonel. He considered leaving the warehouse, disobeying Bishop's order. His knees shook and sweat drenched his body. He was convinced he'd just observed thievery on a large scale. And Bishop must be involved. What the hell could he do about it? Maybe his old Infantry division commander could help. Brigadier General Walter Parks was now assigned to the Afghanistan Puzzle Palace. He'd try to see him as soon as he returned to headquarters.

He entered the room Bishop had indicated. Metal coffins were stacked on racks three high. Tags hung off wires attached to the coffin handles. King slid a hand over the smooth, cold top of the closest coffin. He lifted the tag and saw the box was destined for Innocenti Mortuary in Queens, New York. He moved to the next box when the room door burst open.

King whipped around. Bishop and Sergeant Campbell entered. The Colonel sat on a table a couple feet from the door. Campbell walked behind King and leaned against one of the coffins.

"What do you think you saw out there, Captain?"

"A bunch of men loading crates on trucks."

Bishop lasered a look at King. "That's what you saw. I didn't ask you that. What do you *think* you saw?"

"Noth . . . nothing. I didn't see a thing, Colonel."

"Don't bullshit me. You saw American weapons and ammo being loaded on trucks by bandits."

Bishop paused as though he expected a response, but King just stood there and stared, and tried not to look scared.

"We're pouring billions of dollars of weapons, equipment, clothing, supplies, and all kinds of other shit into this country so the Afghans can wage war after we've deserted the place. None of the crap in this warehouse, except the coffins, is meant to be used by American soldiers. All this stuff is dedicated to the Afghans. You already know that, right?"

King nodded.

"So, what do you think will to happen to all this stuff after we leave Afghanistan?" Bishop waved a hand to indicate the entire building. "I'll tell you what will happen. The Afghan government will sell everything to the Taliban, or the mullahs in Iran, or some other rag head bandits who want to kill infidels."

King found his voice. "That's pure rationalization. You're stealing."

Bishop lowered his head and muttered, "Naïve asshole." He raised his head enough to look out from under bushy eyebrows at Campbell. He nodded once.

King noticed the Colonel's nod and turned his head toward Campbell. The sergeant held a 9 mm pistol pointed at his head. King only had enough time to think about his wife and the twenty-seven days left on his tour in Afghanistan. Campbell fired the pistol as King tried to say, "Oh, shit!"

Campbell knew his actions were necessary. Too much was at stake. Too much money. Too much risk. He and Bishop traded weapons and supplies to tribal bandits in exchange for heroin. They then sold the heroin to a mob connection back in the United States. Shipped the drugs in caskets of dead Americans to a mob-owned mortuary in New York. In only fourteen months, they'd earned an enormous amount of money from the sale of drugs.

He smiled and thought once again about Colonel Bishop's genius. Those caskets were vital. Maybe King's remains would be accompanied by a load of heroin. Campbell laughed at the irony. The introduction of Operation Harvest and the Colonel's assignment to head up the SLSD had made their side business easier and more lucrative. He recalled Bishop's words: "In the interest of ensuring that a new democratic Government of Afghanistan can defend itself, the U.S. has created opportunities for graft, thievery, smuggling, and myriad of other business activities."

CHAPTER 6

Back at the SLSD vault, in Bishop's office, Bishop asked Campbell, "Everything taken care of?"

Campbell nodded. "King won't be a problem. I dumped his body in an alley in central Kabul. He'll ultimately be found and turned over to us. We'll ship him out on a bed of heroin. I'll take care of the paperwork."

"Sit down, Bob," Bishop ordered. "We need to firm up plans."

Campbell sat and waited while Bishop, seated in an armchair behind his desk, propped his artificial leg on an open drawer. Bishop stared down at the leg; a sickly look momentarily crossed his face.

Then Bishop raised his head and smiled. "Just one-and-a-half years from retirement, Bob. We're set for life, with or without our Army pensions. I'd turn in my uniform right now if it wouldn't raise questions."

Campbell nodded.

"We rotate to the States on 14 February. I want you to meet with Zefferelli in Brooklyn on 16 February and coordinate delivery of the last shipment."

Campbell nodded again. "Gonna be a shame to have to shut down our operation."

Bishop shrugged. "I'll go to Zurich for final disposition of the money while you're in New York. When we're out of the Army, you can buy your ranch in Wyoming—hell, you can buy three or four ranches!"

"New Mexico, Colonel."

Bishop waved a dismissive hand. "Wherever."

"What do you plan to do, Colonel, after you get out?"

"I haven't decided yet. But whatever I decide, I'll be in touch with you. You and I have been together a long time and we've watched one another's backs in some tough situations. I want you by my side whatever I do."

FEBRUARY 15, 2003

CHAPTER 7

Frankie "The Pump" Zefferelli sat at a small, scarred wooden table in the Bayside Social Club in Howard Beach and looked across at his two capos, Bruno Giordano and Joey Cataldo. This was their normal place to meet, at the same table near the back of the twenty-five-foot-wide, seventy-five-foot-long room. Their table was ten feet away from the next closest table. Zefferelli turned up the volume on the boom box radio on a built-in shelf above the table. The sounds of the aria from *La Boheme* filled the room.

"Can't be too careful," he said to Giordano and Cataldo, as he waggled a finger at them like a teacher might lecture two schoolboys.

Zefferelli glared at the two men and saw appropriate respect in their eyes. He was the *Capo di tutti Capi* for the New York mob and, like a Roman Emperor, demanded respect from every man in his organization. He knew his hold over the Family and its control over a significant part of the import of narcotics into New York depended on it.

At a mere five feet, five inches tall and weighing 210 pounds, he appeared almost simian with most of his weight concentrated in his torso, short legs, and long arms. An enormous hooked nose and a Hitler-like mustache completed an almost comedic appearance. But no one dared laugh at Frankie the Pump. He had scary eyes. Dark, fathomless, shark eyes. And he was ruthless.

When Frank Zefferelli was coming up in the organization, he

was called Johnny Pump, the neighborhood name for a fire hydrant, which he resembled. As he made his bones, the nickname changed to Frankie Pump. When he became a made man, most referred to him as just "The Pump." Now that he headed up the family, people called him Mr. Zefferelli, or just Mr. Z by his closest associates.

Zefferelli liked to have men around who towered over him—men like Giordano and Cataldo, who each exuded a Mediterranean sensuality and powerful physical presence. He figured when people saw these two bruisers take orders from him, they would fear him even more.

Zefferelli glared at his men until each one looked away. "I arranged for a new supplier, now that our guy in Afghanistan is closing down." He paused. A habit he'd developed years ago. It was as though he felt his listeners needed breaks in order to process his words. "I need you guys to go down to Guadalajara with the *consigliere* to wrap up loose ends down there. But first, I got a job for you and I don't want no screw ups."

After a longer than usual fifteen-second pause, Zefferelli said, "You both know our Afghanistan supplier told us he could ship a minimum of two hundred keys of pure every month, on two conditions. One, we gotta agree to pay for the shipments with dollars put in a Swiss account. Two, we gotta set up a funeral parlor we can control. So he can deliver the "H" caskets."

Zefferelli paused again, shot his French cuffs, sipped a bit of espresso.

"I asked him why he brought this proposition to me. He says, 'Who else should I bring it to? You're the head of the mob in New York, aren't you?' " Zefferelli laughed. "Then I said, 'Maybe you read the damn newspapers too much.' He said, 'You want the dope or not?' "

He pointed a finger at his temple and said, "I ain't stupid. Fourteen months now, this guy does what he promised, and more. Over the past eight months, the shipments have come in at a faster rate—three, four hundred keys a week. Lots of bodies; lots of smack. I don't know what's changed, but I ain't complaining. What I think, even though I've never met our supplier, we've been dealing with some of Uncle Sam's finest. Hey, that's okay with me. These guys are over there getting their asses shot at, so let them put a little away for the future." He laughed again.

"You know this guy's name?" Joey Cataldo asked.

"Nah. He told me to call him "The Priest".' Zefferelli shrugged. "Maybe he's a chaplain over there.

"Anyway, bodies come in with a cushion of heroin underneath them. We take the junk out of the caskets and send the bodies on their way. As I said, lately the shipments have been huge. Hell, we got caskets coming in with no bodies. Just sandbags and 'H.'"

The *Capo* went silent again. Took another sip of espresso.

"The last shipment of caskets we'll get from these guys should arrive tomorrow. Eight caskets. I want the stuff stepped on and out on the street by next Thursday. Our friend over there is sending his man, a guy named Robert Campbell. He'll be here tomorrow. The brain behind this deal sends me a message yesterday. Gotta admire the guy. You know what he writes me?" Pause. "He says, 'As a token of my esteem, I'll discount the price of the last shipment by ten percent.' And next he says, 'It would be a big help to me if no one sees Robert Campbell again.' " Once again Zefferelli paused, a deadly serious cast to his eyes. "You think you guys can handle that?"

"Piece of cake, Boss," Giordano said.

"Be a pleasure," said Cataldo.

MAY 7, 2008

CHAPTER 8

In 2003, David's leg wound, which left him with chronic pain and a slight limp, earned him a medical discharge. Only three years after his discharge, he earned an undergraduate degree in business from Georgetown while he worked for a large security company that provided bodyguards for entertainers and corporate types.

After graduation, he partnered with Warren Masters, also an Army veteran with combat time in Afghanistan, to start their own company, Security Systems, Ltd. They provided personal security, but also entered the cyber and facility security consulting services arena. The company had grown rapidly after that, with offices in Bethesda, Los Angeles, and Zurich. It had armored Lincoln Towncars in all three locations, and had a long list of bank, oil and gas, and telecommunications clients.

On May 7, 2008, one of David's clients, World Technologies, called to schedule an appointment for one of their employees, Carmen Long. Long was assigned to liaise with David's company on the implementation of an IT security system to safeguard World Technologies' electronic databases.

Just before she was due to arrive for their appointment, David's assistant buzzed him.

"Mr. Hutchison with Explora Petroleum is on line two."

"Hey, Frank," David said into his receiver. "We still on for tomorrow?"

"Can we push it up to this evening? I've got to fly to Alaska tomorrow."

"I've got an appointment with another client in a few minutes. How about around six?"

"That will work. We need to prep for the testimony our people will give to the Senate Select Committee on Thursday."

"Warren's taking the lead on that anyway. I'll see if he can go over to your offices now and I'll join him as soon as I finish up here."

"Thanks, Dave. See you later."

Although Warren could more than handle the Explora project, David liked to keep on top of work the company did for its major clients. He decided to change the meeting with the woman from World Technologies. He buzzed his assistant to ask her to take care of it, but she told him Ms. Long had already arrived. David told his assistant to send her in; he'd give her ten minutes and turn her over to one of the other executives. But when the woman entered his office, she'd taken his breath away.

Tall and slim, Carmen Long had million dollar legs and an athletic figure. Her dark-brown hair flashed red in the office's lights. She had the glow of youth, complemented by sensuality.

Carmen had looked vaguely familiar to David, but he couldn't quite dredge up why. The ten minutes he planned to give her turned into an hour and then he asked if she was hungry.

At dinner in an Italian restaurant, Carmen asked the waiter if they served *mineste*.

"How do you know about *mineste*?" David asked her. "Not too many non-Italians have ever heard about the stew."

"Why do you think I'm not Italian?"

"Your name: Long."

"I changed it from Alongi, my mother's maiden name."

"I used to work for a man who made *mineste* once a week for all his employees. He'd start it early in the morning, pop in the pigs' feet around 2:00 p.m., and then we'd all feast on it after we closed down for the night." David laughed. "And he always complained he hadn't—"

"Added enough salt," Carmen said.

"How do you know that? That's exactly right."

"David, it's me, Carmela Bartolucci."

At a loss for words, David sat back in his chair and just stared.

"I hope you're not angry with me for not telling you earlier who I was."

He slid forward and shook his head in wonder. "The last time I saw you was—"

"2001."

"Why'd you change your name?"

"Too many skeletons associated with the Bartolucci name."

That dinner was the first of many, and six months later they married.

PART II

PRESENT DAY

MARCH 30

CHAPTER 1

"Not too bad for a couple of rednecks from Iowa, eh, Rolf? Two good ole boys shootin' the shit in the Oval Office."

"No, Mr. President. Not bad at all." Bishop smiled and thought what an understatement that was. He and the President could easily have wound up as stock boys in some giant warehouse back in bumfuck Iowa. Thank God for scholarships and government jobs. And for Swiss bankers. And for clever lawyers who knew how to launder huge quantities of cash.

The President dropped his country accent and adopted the lock-jawed speech pattern he'd picked up at Yale. "You're probably wondering why I asked you here." He didn't wait for an answer. He rose from his chair and crossed the room to the buffet table, poured himself a cup of coffee, returned to the sitting area, and took the chair across from Bishop.

"I've got a problem over at Langley. The Deputy Director for Intelligence bought a big block of stock in a computer company."

"Didn't know that was illegal, Mr. President."

"It sure as shit is when your agency signed a contract with that computer company. A contract that, when made public, will drive up the stock price."

"I see the problem," Bishop said. "What can I do to help?"

"You can say yes when I offer you the appointment to replace the crooked bastard." He showed a mouth full of capped teeth and smiled at his boyhood buddy.

Bishop's jaw dropped open. It wasn't often he was caught off balance.

"You look a bit surprised, Rolf."

"You're full of surprises, Mr. President. I turn sixty this year. Thought I'd retire and go fishing."

The President laughed. "Don't play that country boy routine with me." The President's brow knitted and the muscles in his cheeks twitched. "Yes or no, Rolf. I've got to make a move before the word gets out about this bastard's stock deal. I want the current deputy director to announce his retirement in time for the six o'clock news tonight. I'll let the media know of your nomination tomorrow morning."

"You sure about this?" Bishop asked.

"Rolf, you're a bonafide American hero. Combat tour in Grenada. Silver Star and a Purple Heart. Shit, you lost a leg there. One tour in Iraq. Two tours in Afghanistan. Three trips to Kabul as my Special Emissary since you retired. The only military decorations you don't have are the Legion of Merit and the Congressional Medal of Honor. Hell, you've even got a wooden leg. You've done more charitable work and raised more money for political campaigns than any ten men I know. Your record is squeaky-clean. The press loves you. When we release information about your nomination to fill the vacated position at CIA, it will become front-page news and be on all the television networks. I'll look like a genius."

Bishop tried to think of something momentous to say. He was hung up for a second on the President's comment about his squeaky-clean record. But he shook off his momentary reservation and said, "Yes!"

MARCH 31

CHAPTER 2

Eric Carbajal's neighbors in Belen, New Mexico looked up to him. He was a decorated former Army officer. He now ran his own construction company and always completed a job on time and within budget. He provided jobs for seven men from the community and paid his workers a fair wage.

As he did almost every night, before he drove home to Esmeralda and his five sons, Carbajal stopped at the *Cimarron Bar*. It was the last day of the month and he'd had to make payroll. He'd gone to the bank and borrowed against his line of credit. His loan officer had told him, with this advance, his line was tapped out. He'd had a sudden urge to puke.

How the hell had the money been taken down so quickly? A hundred thousand dollars! But he knew the answer. He'd used advances from the line of credit to play blackjack at the Indian-owned casino up the road. Why the hell did I ever start? He'd blown every dime the company had made over the last six months and gone into debt on top of it.

Carbajal drained his beer mug and turned on his bar stool, about to climb down. But he stopped, turned back to the bar, and stared up at the television mounted on the wall behind the bar. He thought he'd heard the news anchorman mention the name Rolf Bishop. Carbajal sat up straight and motioned to the bar tender. "Hey, Gillie," he said, "how about turning up the sound?"

Carbajal hung on the newscaster's every word. By the time the talking head finished and moved on to the next news item, a plan had already formed in Carbajal's mind. He got Gillie's attention, made a revolving motion with his finger, and mouthed the words, "One more." He never drank more than one beer before he went home to his family. But today was an exception. He just might have found a way out of his financial troubles.

Rolf Bishop sighed and pushed away from the desk in his home office. He stood up, stretched, and bent over to rub his leg above the prosthesis. The damned thing hurt all the time. He sat back down and looked around. This was his favorite room—bookcases stuffed with first editions he'd collected over the years, Oriental carpets he'd acquired while stationed in the Middle East, and other memorabilia of his military assignments. And of course, there was his *ego wall*, lined with framed citations, a glass-covered case with his medals and ribbons, and photographs taken in the company of great men.

He'd had his nose buried in the White House briefing books all day, ever since his nomination to the CIA position had been announced early that morning. His back and neck hurt, his eyes ached, and he felt as though he might be catching a cold. But he had committed to learn everything in the binders. He already had power and influence derived from having more money than he could ever spend. Now he would have real power and influence that came with position. He allowed himself a momentary feeling of giddiness, then reclaimed his seat and started in on the next section: *U.S. Policy: Turkish/Kurdish Relations.*

He'd just about absorbed the essence of this section when his desk telephone rang. I'll have to get an unlisted number, he thought. He lifted the receiver from the cradle. "Bishop!" he shouted.

"Colonel Bishop?"

"Who is this?"

The man on the other end of the line started to say something, but his voice cracked. Bishop heard him clear his throat and start again.

"Colonel, this is Eric Carbajal. Lieutenant Carbajal from

the Special Logistical Support Detachment in Afghanistan. You remember me? I was in your unit there in 2003, 2004."

Bishop remembered the name Carbajal. After all, the SLSD was a small unit, with only fourteen men assigned to it, besides himself. He couldn't recollect a face to go with the name, however. But he couldn't care less about some dumbshit former lieutenant. Why the hell was the idiot calling him?

"Yeah, Lieutenant, I remember you," Bishop lied, while his eyes remained fixed on a page in the briefing book. "What can I do for you?"

The man cleared his throat again and then his voice seemed to gain strength. "It's not what you can do for me, Colonel. It's what I can do for you."

The hairs on the back of Bishop's neck tingled. He sensed trouble and immediately concentrated on the call. He pushed the book away.

"I see you're about to go before the U.S. Senate for a confirmation hearing. From what I read, you're a shoo-in. Big hero, wonderful reputation."

Bishop continued to sit silently behind his desk. He instinctively suspected what was coming—he could hear it in the man's voice. But he hoped he was wrong. He'd thought no one knew about what he and Campbell had been up to. And Campbell was long dead, thanks to Frank Zefferelli. He squeezed the receiver as if to crush it and felt a headache coming on.

"You still there, Colonel?" Carbajal asked.

"Yeah."

"I wonder what would happen if my good friend, the Senator from New Mexico, found out about your side business in Afghanistan. Jeez, just imagine the scandal. You'd probably spend your golden years in a federal penitentiary."

"What are you . . .?"

"Let's not bullshit each other. Robert Campbell and I were good friends. Talked about buying a ranch together here in New Mexico. Robert was a good guy. I heard he got killed in New York. Bad break."

Bishop snapped, "What are you after?"

"Now, now, Colonel, be patient. I wasn't finished with my story."

The man was becoming cocky. Bishop was now both pissed off and shook up.

"Old Robert and I would shoot the shit over beers in Afghanistan. One night we had a few drinks. Then we went and found ourselves a couple nurses. Boy, that was the life. But you know Robert couldn't hold his liquor. Three, four beers or a couple scotches and he'd blab about his deepest secrets. That night, he told me all about your side business."

Sonofabitch! Bishop thought. Sweat now poured off his forehead. His sports shirt stuck to his back and chest. "What the fuck do you want?"

Carbajal's voice took on an ominous tone. "Let's keep this cordial, Colonel. You know, I always figured you were just another soldier with an angle; I never begrudged you the money you made. But I'm a little stretched right now and I just learned you're rolling in dough. What I want is two hundred thousand dollars. Cash. You deliver the money to me and I'll keep my mouth shut. I give you my word on that. If I don't have it in my hands by the end of business two days from now . . . ."

APRIL 1

CHAPTER 3

Belen, New Mexico had more than its share of DWIs, assaults, burglaries, drug deals, and even murders. But the typical crime victim tended to be someone involved with the criminal netherworld. Set between the Manzano Mountains and Interstate 25, cheek to jowl with the Rio Grande River, Belen is a sleepy little community. It probably wouldn't have had much criminal activity at all if it hadn't found itself a half-hour's drive south of Albuquerque, along the north-south arterial that started near the Mexican border and bisected the state—a natural conduit for drug trafficking. So, the town's residents often heard about drug busts and drug-related violence. But they could still be surprised when a respected member of the business community became a crime victim. When word got out that someone had shot Eric Carbajal in the head while he sat in his pickup truck, the shock felt by members of the community was palpable.

Rolf Bishop's cellphone rang at 7 p.m.

"It's done."

"Good. I've got more work for you," Bishop said.

"The same kind of work?"

"Correct."

"How much more work?"

"Seven."

"That's a lot of work. Very expensive work."

"I'll pay your usual fee."

"Better double it. More risky than usual. Too much exposure."

APRIL 12

CHAPTER 4

"David, you'd better be careful with that knife," Carmela Hood chided from the far side of the kitchen of her Bethesda, Maryland home. She moved behind her husband, pressed against his back, and wrapped her arms around his chest. "I don't want anything to spoil our anniversary dinner," she whispered.

David leaned back against her. "Nothing will spoil this evening." He put down the knife and the apple he'd been slicing, turned, put his arms around his wife.

Carmela purred. "You romantic devil." She ran her fingers through his long black hair. "You get more handsome every day."

"Yuckie," three-year-old Kyle announced in his megaphone voice, "Daddy's smooching Mommy again."

"Don't be a troublemaker," five-year-old Heather said.

David laughed, kissed Carmela on the neck, and moved to the kitchen table where Heather helped her forty-pound wrecking ball-of-a-brother with a puzzle.

Carmela watched David stare at their two children. He had that wide-eyed look of wonder on his face again. As though he couldn't believe his luck.

"Daddy, Daddy, can you help us?" Kyle pleaded.

"No, Kyle, we can do it ourselves," Heather said. "You'll see."

"O-o-o-kay," Kyle said.

So grown up, so confident, Carmela thought. Heather had

inherited David's seriousness and her Mediterranean passion. Carmela marveled at her daughter's quick mind and early maturity. She had naturally assumed responsibility for her younger brother. She always seemed to do the right thing, say the right thing. A "daddy's girl," she had already wrapped David tightly around her finger.

Kyle differed from his sister in just about every way. He resembled a linebacker as he fearlessly caromed around the house; a force of nature. He worried Carmela and she wondered with trepidation what the boy would be like when he grew to be a teenager. She shuddered at the thought.

Carmela came over to David and laid a hand on his shoulder. "My grandmother told me you can put the evil eye on a person when you stare at them like that." She kissed him on the cheek and said, "I love you."

David smiled. "I'm looking forward to tonight. Can you believe it's been six years since I met Carmen Long?"

She kissed him again and rubbed his back. "That woman's long gone."

"Nice pun."

Carmela groaned. "Don't give up your day job. You'd never make it as a stand-up comedian."

"I thought you liked my sense of humor."

"More like I humour your sense of humor." She laughed. "You'd better get ready; the sitter will be here in thirty minutes."

David nodded. He shucked the tie he'd worn to work, unbuttoned his shirt cuffs, and moved toward the hallway from the kitchen.

"Oh, I forgot," Carmela said. "Before you go upstairs, would you get a jar of carrots from the cellar for the children's dinner?"

"Sure." He reversed direction and headed for the cellar door.

"Can I go, Daddy?" Kyle yelled.

"Me, too," Heather said.

David knew the kids would slow him down. They'd want to explore the cellar, play hide and seek.

"No, you guys stay with Mom. I'll only be a minute."

David flipped the light switch just inside the cellar door and carefully walked down the wooden staircase that had been worn smooth and slippery with decades of use. For the thousandth time, he reminded himself he should put rubber treads on the steps. The cool, damp air assailed his nostrils. When he turned at the bottom of the stairs, he shook his head at the sight of the junk he'd let accumulate down here: an old bicycle; rusted lawn chairs, the webbing long since ripped; an old, leaky garden hose; an antique wooden icebox he'd threatened to repair and refinish. I've got to get rid of this stuff, he told himself. He walked across the concrete floor to the old fallout shelter added decades earlier by the previous owner, a Civil Defense contractor—Cold War paranoia. He and Carmela had converted it to a storage room for the vegetables Carmela grew and put up. A smile creased his face at the sounds of Heather and Kyle's voices that drifted down from the kitchen.

He yanked the door handle, opened the door, stepped up into the shelter, and pulled the chain on the ceiling light. The weighted shelter door closed behind him with a soft *whoosh*.

David selected a glass jar of carrots from a shelf, turned, and took a second to enjoy the quiet of the ten-by-ten shelter. The cellar's stone exterior walls, combined with the shelter's rebar-reinforced concrete, made the room a suburban fortress.

He reached for the door handle, but a huge *whump* startled him. The room swayed. The door handle was suddenly, inexplicably beyond his reach. Before his mind could process an explanation, he was thrown back against the wall opposite the door. Glass jars smashed, canned goods thudded on and around him. Wooden shelves cascaded on his head and shoulders. David brushed the debris off him and placed a hand on the floor to push himself up. "Damn," he shouted. A glass shard had impaled his palm. He pulled out the piece of glass and carefully stood.

Terror seized him. Even within the shelter's thick walls, he heard and felt the full roar and concussive force of a second explosion. The little room swayed from the concussion. The suppressed sound of the blast was all too familiar. He'd heard and felt enough of them in Afghanistan. He leaned against a side wall and struggled to keep his feet. This belonged to a time and place well in his past—

the bombers and fighter jets that unleashed their deadly loads; explosives detonated in Taliban caves and tunnels. He tried to deny what he knew—an enormous explosion had rocked his home.

With the exception of a muted bit of light that came through the Plexiglas window in the shelter door, the room had gone dark. The floor was now littered with wood shelves scattered amidst a syrupy mix of glass, fruit, and vegetables.

David screamed, "Carmela!" He took two steps and pushed the shelter door handle. It didn't budge. Through the small window he saw dim light stream into the cellar from where a solid wall should have been. Piles of plaster, brick, stone, and insulation were just visible in a dusty fog. His three-story Colonial home had fallen in on itself. More of the house continued to fall—pieces of furniture, wood beams, appliances, a tub. Flying dust thickly clouded the air outside the room and blocked David's view.

Once the death throes of the house subsided, funereal quiet returned, interspersed with intermittent groans as debris shifted. David felt his hands tremble. His heart beat against his ribs as though it wanted to escape the confines of his chest. "Carmela!" he screamed again. No answer. "Heather! Kyle!" The only answer he got were the sounds of his own voice as it reverberated off the shelter walls.

David again pushed on the door. It wouldn't move. He braced himself and slammed a foot against it, over and over again, but to no avail. Primordial shrieks echoed off the room walls while grief swept over him. He heard the shrieks, but couldn't seem to connect them to himself. Trapped inside the tiny shelter, he threw his body against the door until, bruised and battered, he had no more strength. As he collapsed in a corner, his mind filled with images of his wife and children and what the explosion might have done to them.

Time passed in slow motion. David could barely keep his eyes open. Sleep seduced him. He realized the lack of oxygen had begun to affect him. The shelter's filters must have been damaged in the blast.

With one last effort, he staggered to his feet and threw his body at the door. He bounced back, defeated, and dropped to the concrete floor behind the door. He stretched out and gasped for breath, as the warm blanket of unconsciousness crept over him.

CHAPTER 5

Bethesda Detectives Roger Cromwell and Jennifer Ramsey stood twenty feet from the edge of the crater and watched rescue workers pass debris from the hole to men above them, who loaded it into the scoop of a front-end loader. Ramsey turned away from the glare of floodlights on the front lawn and looked at the group of stunned neighbors behind yellow crime scene tape on the far side of the street. She turned back to the crater and shielded her eyes against the lights, which cast eerie shadows off the workers in the hole. Ramsey checked her wristwatch. It was just past 11 p.m. Almost five hours since the explosion.

"What's the name of the family?" she asked.

"Hood," Cromwell answered. "Married couple; two little kids. A neighbor said he's an Afghanistan combat vet."

"So there could be one more body," she said as she glanced at the broken bodies of the woman and two children in black plastic body bags near a rescue vehicle parked on the street.

"Your first dead bodies?" Cromwell asked in the condescending tone she had learned to hate and resent.

Ramsey forced a smile. She knew Cromwell really couldn't have cared less about her feelings. In fact, he'd probably love it if she puked her guts out. That would give the good old boys something to laugh about back at Homicide.

She turned and looked at Cromwell. Her eyes first went to his bulbous, vein-etched nose and quickly moved to his wet, beady eyes. "No, but thanks for your concern," she said in a mock-grateful tone.

She forced herself not to tell Cromwell to go to hell. She knew what went through the guy's mind: The fat creep had tried to undermine her since she'd been paired with him a couple weeks earlier. But she knew she had to kill him with kindness. To not let him bait her into doing or saying something stupid. She'd worked hard—two years as a street cop after college and the police academy, three more years in undercover, two years of graduate school—and had earned her promotion to detective. She wasn't about to throw it all away. She'd sandbag the sonofabitch until she established credibility as a homicide detective. That's what Pop had advised her to do. Her father had served with the New York Police Department for thirty-six years. The advice he'd given her had all been good so far.

Ramsey watched the workers burrow deeper into what had once been a basement. Then the sound suddenly stopped.

A man shouted and then another called out, "We found a body."

A man yelled, "There's a guy in a small room in the basement. We can see him through a little window in the door. I think he moved."

"Amazing," Ramsey muttered. Someone actually survived this horrific explosion. Then Cromwell grabbed her arm.

"Pay attention, Ramsey," his voice full of belligerence and condescension. "You might just learn something. I can feel it in my gut. How does only one member of a family survive when his house explodes? I got a gut feeling about this. I'll break this sonofabitch, you watch."

Ramsey shook off Cromwell's arm. Quite a speech, you fat, pompous pig, she thought. She heard Cromwell's heavy breathing and the sour smell that always seemed to hang over him like the dirt cloud around Linus in the Charley Brown cartoon. She watched the rescue workers swing into higher gear as they shoved aside colonial wreckage and opened the door of what appeared to be an old fallout shelter. They pulled out an unconscious man. Two men placed him on a stretcher and carried it out of the hole to an ambulance.

APRIL 13

CHAPTER 6

David woke to near-blackness and gasped for breath—the last physical sensation he'd had before he passed out in the shelter. The only light seeped around the sides of a dark window shade at the far right side of the room. At first nothing made sense. The bed, the chair, the shaded window all seemed out of synch. Then the odor of antiseptic hit him and a steady *beep, beep, beep* came from somewhere. His eyes slowly adjusted to the dark and he noticed the intravenous rack next to his bed. Then pain assaulted his head. The pain built and built until he thought his skull might explode.

He found the call button pinned to the bed sheet and pressed it. When a nurse responded and turned on a light over the head of the bed, he tried to speak, but his throat was parched and all that escaped his lips was a hoarse croak. The nurse guided a straw in a water glass to his lips.

"My family—my wife, my children?" he asked.

The nurse looked at him with mournful eyes and averted her gaze.

David turned his head toward the window. Tears rolled down his cheeks, slowly at first, and then in an anguished torrent. He roared; tried to smother his pain. He didn't resist the nurse when she injected something in his intravenous tube.

A voice penetrated his sedative-induced stupor. "Mr. Hood, can you hear me?"

David opened his eyes and squinted at the light in the room. The shade on the window to his right was now up and bright light streamed into the room. He slowly turned his head away from the window, toward the sound of the voice. A man and a woman stood next to the bed.

"This is Cromwell, Detective Roger Cromwell," the man said. He flipped open his wallet to show his badge and identification. "This is Detective Ramsey. We're with the Bethesda Police Department."

David eyed the man's badge and then looked up at his face. He had a first impression that unsettled him. The guy wore a sour look; there was nothing friendly about him.

"I assume you've been told what happened," Cromwell said.

"All I've been told is my family . . . is gone."

"You know there was an explosion."

David closed his eyes and ever so slightly dipped his head.

"You know what caused the explosion?"

"I assume it was gas."

Cromwell looked at Ramsey. The muscles in his cheeks twitched. When he turned back to David his piggy eyes were narrowed to slits. "Explosives, Mr. Hood."

"What the hell are you talking about?" David rasped.

"Plastique was used to blow up your house and kill your family, Mr. Hood. You know anything about plastique?"

David knew plenty about explosives. He'd been trained on all sorts of explosives at the Special Warfare School at Fort Bragg, North Carolina, and he'd placed explosives in Taliban tunnels in Afghanistan. He also knew enough to keep his mouth shut. Cromwell's accusatory tone told him he had nothing to gain from talking to the guy. But he'd learned something. Someone had planted explosives in his home. Which made absolutely no sense.

Cromwell sighed. He rubbed his face with both hands and then ran his hands through his short, gray hair. "As soon as you're out of here, we'll want to talk with you some more."

David stared at the detective as he felt his face grow hot.

"I got three murders here," Cromwell said, his voice now louder.

"I know you want to . . . help us solve this crime."

David averted his eyes for a moment and looked at the female detective. Her jaw was set, lips pressed together. There was something in her eyes that told him she was uncomfortable. Then he looked back at Cromwell. He saw the cop's mouth move, but his words washed over him, unheard. He caught the sounds, but couldn't distinguish one word from another. Then his world went gray, as though a filter had dropped over his eyes, and his chest felt heavy with despair. How could he go on with life without Carmela, Heather, and Kyle? What was the point?

"Mr. Hood, did you hear me?"

The cop's words seeped through David's fog, but he still didn't respond. He felt heat burn inside him, as though he'd stepped from a freezer into a blast furnace.

CHAPTER 7

Anger and the need for revenge had found a home in David's heart. But depression had become a stronger force. He needed to grieve—alone. And he needed to get away from the hospital because he guessed whoever blew up his house and killed his family must have targeted him, not them. Why would anyone want to kill Carmela, Heather, and Kyle? He was a sitting duck here in the hospital.

He'd thought a lot about who might want him dead. He considered his clients, but couldn't come up with a suspect. His company had identified hackers who had attacked some of his clients' computer systems, and had provided evidence that sent those hackers to prison. Perhaps there was a killer among that group of criminals.

He disconnected the intravenous tube from the IV stent in his arm. Dressed only in a hospital gown, he moved to the door and pulled up on the handle. The door wouldn't budge. He tried the handle again with the same result. Except this time, a uniformed cop opened the door and moved one step into the room. He held the door open with one hand and stared hard at David.

"You need something?" the cop asked.

Sonofabitch! David thought. That homicide cop, Cromwell, has me locked in. "Why's my door locked?"

"For your protection, Mr. Hood."

"Sure." David now knew he really had to get away from the

hospital. Cromwell had only one suspect in mind: David Hood. "How about finding a nurse for me? The call button's not working."

"Okay." The cop dropped his hand from the door, turned, and walked back into the hall.

David yanked the IV stent from his arm and stuck it between the door lock and the jamb. The door closed. He hoped the lock hadn't engaged. He took in a deep breath and let it out slowly. Then he tried the door handle. This time the door opened. The IV stent fell to the floor. He stuck his head out into the hall and looked for the cop. He spotted him twenty yards down on the right. He was bent slightly over the nurses' station counter, his back to David.

David slipped out of his room, quick-stepped down the hall to the left, and took the emergency stairs to the floor below. He searched for a room where he might find a change of clothes. He opened a door marked DOCTORS LOUNGE. There was no one in the lounge, so he moved to an inside door on the far side of the room with a sign that read LOCKERS. As soon as he walked into the locker room he heard the sound of running water. At the end of two rows of lockers on his right was a clothes bar, on which hung a sports jacket, shirt, and slacks. A pair of shoes and socks sat on top of a locker. David turned the corner at the end of the lockers and saw the closed curtain in one of the showers.

He turned back to the locker room and reached for the clothes on the rack—just as the door to the locker room opened and a man entered. He had a name badge pinned to his sports jacket: Frank Siler, MD. Had David worn anything but a hospital gown and had there not been large bandages on the back of his head and on his left hand, Doctor Siler might have ignored him.

"What are you doing?" the man demanded.

David took the hangers off the rack, draped the clothes over his left arm, grabbed for the shoes and socks on top of the lockers, and moved to leave the room. The doctor blocked his way. David lowered a shoulder, hit the man in the chest, and drove him sideways. The man tripped over a bench and fell to the floor. The guy appeared more stunned than hurt, as he looked at David with saucer-eyes.

"Sorry," David said to the now-cursing doctor as he exited the locker room.

He rushed through the lounge, out into the corridor, and then left to the emergency exit staircase. He ran down to the basement and turned into an equipment room. His head hurt and he felt dizzy. After he took a moment for his head to clear, he changed into the stolen clothes. In a pants pocket he found a wallet with four twenty-dollar bills and a few ones. He placed the wallet with all of the doctor's credit cards, family photos, and IDs on a desk, and left the hospital by a back door, climbed over a three-foot wall, walked two blocks, and hailed a taxi.

"I need a cheap but clean motel," he told the cabbie. Then he slouched in the seat and closed his eyes.

"Hey, Mack," the driver said ten minutes later, "do you think she'll like this one?"

David opened his eyes and saw across the street, in the middle of the block, a one-story, dumpy strip motel. "Who?" he asked the driver.

"Your hot date."

David ignored the driver's comment and stared across at the motel. A cluster of kids who wore backward baseball caps and Oakland Raider jackets stood on the corner down from the motel. Cars did "touch and goes" at the corner. Drivers handed money to the kids in return for little plastic bags. This was a neighborhood that had seen better days. Good, David thought. The cops probably won't look for me in a place like this. If the police don't care about drug deals in the neighborhood in broad daylight, they probably didn't even cruise the area. "Yeah," he told the cabbie. "This will do."

The cabbie drove across the oncoming lane and pulled up at the motel office. David paid the fare, stepped out of the cab, and went into the motel office.

The clerk was tall and thin, with a prominent Adam's apple, large Roman nose, and thin lips. His sandy hair looked like a rat's nest. He eyed David the moment he entered. The clothes he wore were good quality and fit him reasonably well. But he hadn't shaved since yesterday morning and he wore bandages.

The clerk gave David a bored look and asked, "You need a room for a couple hours?" The guy sounded like he asked that same question a hundred times a day.

"No, a few days."

"Cash or credit card?" the clerk asked, still looking bored, but a bit surprised. "Forty bucks a night."

"Cash. One night in advance." He passed two-twenties to the man. The clerk handed him the key to Room 113.

"I need to use your phone to make a local call."

The guy eyed him suspiciously, but lifted a telephone console from under the counter and removed a cordless phone from the cradle. "One dollar," the guy said. When David gave him a dollar, the clerk handed him the phone.

David stared at the clerk until the man averted his gaze, then moved to the far side of the lobby and dialed the number for Warren Masters, the Chief Financial Officer at their company, Security Systems, Ltd.

"Warren," David said, as soon as the man answered, "I need you to bring me a few things."

"Dave, where are you? We're all worried sick. I'm so sorry about what happened to—"

"I know, Warren, and I appreciate it. But I can't talk right now."

"The police called here a minute ago. Some guy named Cromwell. Claimed you're wanted for questioning about the explosion at your home. Said you ran away from the hospital."

David paused a beat. "The guy's an idiot. I'll call him when I get settled."

"Okay, Dave. What do you need?"

"I want you to come by the Corona Motel on Sixty-Third Street. Room 113. I need a couple changes of clothes, a throw-away cellphone, some cash, and a fully-equipped car."

"Fully-equipped? You mean one of the armored vehicles? What's going on, Dave?"

"Trust me, Warren."

"How much cash?" Warren asked.

"Say a number," David answered.

"Five thousand."

"Double it," David said.

After Warren Masters dropped off the things he'd asked for, David hung a plastic DO NOT DISTURB sign on the door handle. He slept some and cried a lot and whatever he ate came from a vending machine twenty yards from his room, or from a pizza delivery service. Most of the time he thought about where he came from and how life led him to Carmela and gave him his children—and how someone stole them from him.

Time passed in the unlighted, drape-shuttered room.

David saw visions of his children. He remembered how they played together, the way his heart filled at the sounds of their innocent laughter, their hugs, how he inhaled the fresh scent of their skin and hair. He'd loved to read stories to them while they nestled in his arms. And he recalled how they fell asleep, confident of their safety. And he cried inconsolably at the thought he had failed them and that he would never see them again.

Then, there were the memories of Carmela, the life they had made together, how much she had meant to him. How was he to move forward without his beloved wife and children?

But the worst of his memories and nightmares came on him in an insidious way. He never saw them coming. They were there when his mind turned an unexpected corner. He could have allowed Heather and Kyle to go to the shelter with him, as they'd wanted. They died because he had told them to stay in the kitchen with their mother.

APRIL 14

CHAPTER 8

At 10 a.m., the day after he checked into the motel, David telephoned Bethesda Police Headquarters and asked for Detective Roger Cromwell, who picked up a minute later.

"Cromwell."

"It's David Hood. What have you done to find the people who murdered my wife and children?"

"Where the hell are you?" Cromwell shouted.

David could tell from the bowling alley-like echo from the telephone line that Cromwell had him on a speakerphone. He said, "I'm sick of the insinuation I hear in your voice. If you have any reason to suspect me, besides some BS-cop intuition, then charge me. If not, get off your ass and do something constructive."

"Listen to me, you sonofa—"

"Why'd you leave the hospital?" a female voice said. "That wasn't smart, Mr. Hood." She sounded as though she wanted to defuse the tension between the two men.

"How much life insurance did you have on your wife?" Cromwell interjected.

"You have a piece of paper and a pencil handy, Detective?" David said. He forced calm into his voice.

"Yeah, why?" Cromwell said.

"Write this down!" David gave an address and phone number to the detective. "My lawyer's name is Glen Truax, Gilchrist &

Truax. Any other stupid questions you have for me can be directed through him."

"Sonofabitch!" Cromwell exploded. "The guilty always hide behind their lawyers."

David slammed down the receiver. He checked out of the motel and drove his company's armored Lincoln Towncar out of Bethesda. On a Maryland country lane, he pulled onto the shoulder and stared out through the windshield at the arrow-straight road. The ribbon of pavement seemed to stretch forever, to the horizon, and beyond. The road was like his quest, seemingly endless, with who knows what at the end.

"Carmela. Heather. Kyle. I'll find them and I'll make them pay."

CHAPTER 9

Montrose Toney leaned against the closed Washington, D.C. motel room door and shivered under Rolf Bishop's undisguised look of disgust. He knew the meeting here in this fleabag motel room was not what Bishop was used to. With its sway-backed mattress, stained bed spread, and soiled carpet, the room was more commonly used by whores and their johns, not by CIA bigwigs or world-class wealthy megalomaniacs. He also knew Bishop's coming here, risking recognition, meant Bishop was beyond pissed off. And that the stakes, whatever they were, had to be very high. Toney decided to keep his mouth shut and wait for Bishop to speak.

Bishop suddenly leaped from his chair, pointed his hand—gun-like—at Toney and shouted, "You fucked up!"

Toney watched Bishop's neck stiffen and face redden. He felt fear bubble in his gut. Taller than six feet, white-haired, erect, trim, and well dressed, sixty-year-old Bishop was still intimidating. Toney knew the man could not abide failure. And he had definitely failed. He wished Bishop would move his devil-eyes off him.

Toney stood six feet, three inches tall and weighed 250 pounds. He'd spent his thirty-four years of life split between Washington D.C.'s meanest ghettos and various penal institutions. He was not easily intimidated. But Bishop had the disposition of a wounded tiger and he'd been a great meal ticket for the last few years. Toney didn't want to lose that meal ticket.

"What do you think I pay you for?" Bishop hissed. "All you accomplished was to murder a woman and two kids." He walked to the window, pulled back the curtain a couple inches, and stared outside. He whipped around and shot eye-daggers at Toney.

"Who's that by your car?" Bishop said.

"My . . . partner, Jim Francis."

Bishop looked disgusted. "He looks like a derelict waiting for a methadone fix."

"He's a former Marine demolitions expert. He knows—"

"He doesn't know shit," Bishop screamed. "*You* don't know shit! Let me recount the harm you've done. Everyone's investigating the explosion in Bethesda: the FBI, the ATF&E, and the local cops. Even insurance people are involved because of claims filed by neighbors for broken glass, surface, and foundation cracks in buildings, destroyed cars, and damaged personal property. And you failed to eliminate the target, a man you could have dispensed with in a simple car accident or a mugging. Instead, you blew up a whole fucking neighborhood!"

Toney hadn't thought Bishop's face could turn any redder, but he was wrong. He wouldn't tell Bishop he'd let his imbecile partner, Jim Francis, handle the job alone, while he screwed a U.S. Senator's daughter. He should have known better. Toney didn't know why Bishop wanted David Hood dead, nor did he care. He vowed to never again let anything in a skirt distract him from business. After all, what other alumnus of the Federal Corrections System had such a good deal? He'd done jobs for Bishop for years. And if this tight-assed, power-hungry, megalomaniacal white man wanted him to eliminate the whole NAACP hierarchy next, that would be okay with him.

"Mr. Bishop," Toney quietly said, "I let you down and I'm sorry. I promised you I'd take care of this matter and I'll do just that. No more screwups. I give you my word."

Bishop's features eased; the crimson faded from his face. He lowered himself back into a chair and said in a tone that matched Toney's, "I'll hold you to it. Of that you can be certain. Now get the hell out of here and finish the job!"

Toney opened the motel room door and turned to look back

at Bishop, to give him a reassuring smile. Bishop pointed a finger at Toney, who shut the door.

"Get rid of that useless piece of shit," Bishop said. "Now!"

"I don't think—"

"You don't think I know you were with Senator Swift's daughter, Amanda, while your partner blew the shit out of the Hood house. That idiot is dangerous. He has a flair for the dramatic and no sense. That's a bad combination. Get rid of him!"

Toney nodded and left the room. He realized he now had two problems: Get rid of Jim Francis; finish the Hood job.

Bishop seemed anchored to the motel room chair, overwhelmed with anger laced with fear. He thought about how far he'd come and how far he could fall if his past became known. Hood was the last of the men who served in his Afghanistan unit—the only man alive who might know about what he and Robert Campbell had done. As far as he was concerned, Hood was a pissant. A small businessman who had neither the skills nor the resources to go up against a powerful man. If Toney performed, Hood would be an insignificant casualty no one would miss. In the general scheme of things, a thousand Hoods would always be sacrificed so leaders could prosper. That was the natural order of the universe.

"This has been one stressful morning," Toney said after he and Jim Francis climbed into Toney's white, supercharged Acura. "I could use a hit."

"Ooh, that sounds just right, my man. You always know just what Jimbo needs. Let's go down to that bar out by National, find your pimp friend. What's his name . . . Speedo? Yeah, that's it, Speedo. He always got the best shit."

Toney had watched Francis become a stone-cold drug addict with a narcotics consumption rate that grew while his tolerance for the stuff increased. The wiry, leather-skinned thirty-year-old who looked fifty due to his insatiable appetite for drugs, booze, and junk food was now a liability Toney couldn't afford. He drove to a bar near National Airport, went inside, bought a bag of pure heroin, returned to his car, and gave the drugs to Francis. While Toney drove to a nearby park and stopped near a giant oak tree, Francis prepared his drug cocktail and injected the hot shot into the inside of his forearm.

Toney knew Francis trusted him, that it would never cross the man's mind his friend would give him a lethal dose of pure heroin— not even when he turned feverish and the tremors started. By the time Francis started to convulse, Toney realized the end was near. He stepped out of the car, walked around to the passenger side, easily lifted Francis's wiry, emaciated body from the front seat, and placed him on a park bench. Fascinated with death, he watched while the convulsions continued and Francis vomited. Then he saw a quarter mile down the path a city parks department garbage truck collect trash from a receptacle. He returned to his car and pulled away. In his rear view mirror he saw Francis's body topple sideways on the bench. "One down and one to go," he murmured, while he turned up the radio volume and listened to Dinah Washington sing the last few lines of *As We Say Goodbye*.

APRIL 15

CHAPTER 10

Clouds over the cemetery on Bethesda's north side were so thick and dark it seemed like the middle of the night instead of 11 a.m. The dreary day matched David's mood. He'd wanted the funeral to take place as quickly as possible, with only family members in attendance. With his Carmela, Heather, and Kyle buried, he would then focus on what he needed more than anything: A deep, "old country" brand of retribution. His father, Peter, understood and so did Gino Bartolucci. The two warhorses lent him silent support as they stood on either side of him at the burial service.

His father had essentially tolerated him since his brother Tommy was killed. The old man never said so, but David always felt his father blamed him for Tommy's death. That presumed blame had weighed on David for over twenty years. It wasn't until he had married and Heather and Kyle were born that he and his father had reconciled—sort of.

At sixty, Peter Hood stood ramrod-straight, lean as an athlete. A lifetime in construction had hardened his body and toughened an already steely temperament. He was a silent, reassuring presence. Something icy in his dark eyes discouraged any of Carmela's family members from even attempting conversation. He spoke only to his son.

After the service, he put his hands on David's shoulders and said, "I'm with you." While he continued to stare at David with tear-filled eyes, he added, "We need to find out who took my babies."

David had seen his father so emotionally distraught twice before: when Tommy died and when David's mother died. But now there was anger in his father's voice and David needed his father's anger more than any other emotion.

Gino Bartolucci and his wife, Rosa, hugged David after the service and then Gino pulled Peter aside.

"Peter, I know you never liked it when David worked for me. And you were upset about him marrying into my family. But I love your son like my own. He'll need both of us now. You think maybe we can put our differences aside and work together to help him?"

"Gino, I've always believed in doing things the right way, the law-abiding way. When you took the mob route, we became strangers to one another. But I never had a problem with David marrying Carmela. I loved her like she was my own child. And I've always appreciated your affection for David." He paused. "But maybe you were right and I was wrong. What has a lifetime of respect for law and order brought me? A son murdered years ago by street punks, and now the loss of a daughter-in-law I truly loved and the grandchildren who owned my heart." Peter put a hand on the shorter man's shoulder and nodded. "Call me when you're ready."

The Bartoluccis left the cemetery in a limousine with two bodyguards. Gino had not spoken one word to anyone other than Peter and David at or after the service. While Rosa quietly wept and fingered her rosary, Gino stared at the monotonous scenery they sped through without seeing a thing. He focused on one thought: Had one of his enemies killed Carmela, Heather, and Kyle? Payback against him for something he'd done in the past? He couldn't get the thought out of his mind. Had he been responsible for the bombing?

David drove with Peter from the cemetery in the armored black Lincoln Towncar Warren Masters had delivered to him at the

Corona Motel. The vehicle was equipped with bulletproof glass, body armor, and mechanical systems upgraded for rapid evasion maneuvers. It had a small metal locker installed on the floor within easy reach for the driver. The locker held three fully loaded and licensed weapons: an Uzi machine gun, a Sig Sauer 9mm pistol, and a Colt .45 pistol.

Montrose Toney had polished off a 32-ounce Big Gulp while he watched David Hood bury his family. He had a perfect view from the front seat of the stolen Camaro, parked on a hill that overlooked the cemetery. He noticed when Hood and an older man left the cemetery in a black sedan. He started the Chevy, smiled, and said, "Come to Papa, baby. Come to Papa."

From three vehicles back, Toney watched the Lincoln as it wound its way through city streets. He had no idea where Hood was headed, but he was a patient man and knew his opportunity would present itself sooner or later. The Lincoln pulled onto the I-95 on-ramp. Toney liked that. Drivers on the freeway were more likely to concentrate on traffic in general than on any specific vehicle. Besides, his target was a businessman, not a killer. The guy didn't have a chance. He chuckled when it began to rain. The rain offered cover of a sort. Things are workin' out, he thought.

"What will you do now?" Peter asked.

David shot a glance at his father. "I'll find the bastard who killed my family. And then I'll kill him."

Peter sighed. "That's a slippery slope, son. It always is when someone takes the law into their own hands."

"You might be right, Dad. But that changes nothing."

David saw his father slide down in his seat and stretch his legs. He knew the old man was right. But it made no difference. Tommy's killer had never been brought to justice. That would not happen with the man who had murdered Carmela, Heather, and Kyle.

The droning hum of the car tires filled the Lincoln. David drove as he always did—on the alert. Because he assumed he had been the target of the attack that killed his family, he was now especially alert. Because of the rain, the sparse traffic moved more slowly than usual. Spray flew from the vehicles in front of the Lincoln and splattered against its windshield. David cranked up the windshield wiper speed. He looked in the rear view mirror and tapped his brakes a couple times to signal the asshole in the Camaro directly behind him to back off.

"Sonofabitch!" David said.

"What's wrong?" Peter said.

"There's a red Camaro on my ass."

David flipped on his turn signal and moved to the lane on the right. The Camaro mirrored his maneuver. The lane opened up in front of the Lincoln.

"Why don't we check it out, Dad?" He accelerated from fifty-five to seventy-five miles per hour and looked in his mirror. The red Camaro was now about three car lengths back.

David felt a surge of adrenaline. He rapped his knuckles on the weapons locker and told his father, "Take out a pistol. I need to find an exit."

Based on a sign on the side of the highway, the nearest exit was seven miles north. He abruptly increased his speed to ninety miles an hour, shifted back to the middle lane, and aimed the Lincoln straight ahead. The Camaro followed.

The two cars hurtled down the road. They jockeyed from one lane to the next. David couldn't put any distance between them and the Chevy. Soon their pursuer moved to the far left lane, abreast of the Lincoln. Both vehicles blasted down the freeway and sprayed torrents of water from the rain-drenched roadway in their slipstreams. David laid heavily on the Lincoln's horn to sweep slower-moving vehicles out of the way.

Peter shouted, "Brake now! Now!"

David hit the brakes. The Lincoln skidded on the rain-slick pavement and fishtailed right, then left, and right again. The Camaro rocketed past. Car horns blared and tires screeched all around them. David hit the gas, straightened the car, and accelerated after the Camaro.

Toney, now two hundred yards farther down the highway, frantically looked for Hood in his rear view mirror. He saw the Lincoln skid and fishtail in the middle of the wet road. Then it picked up speed and closed the distance between them.

Peter lowered his window and switched the 9mm pistol off safe. David kept the Lincoln just feet off the Camaro's bumper. "I've got a clear shot," Peter shouted.

Suddenly, the Camaro switched lanes, sideswiped another vehicle, and raced ahead again until it vanished in the heavy rain.

David took the next exit and drove east to US 1, and then north. In Dorsey, Maryland, he stopped outside a diner and took a minute to calm down. His head hurt and his hands shook as he came off the adrenaline high. His stomach ached as though an acid tap had been turned on there.

"What the hell have you gotten yourself into?" Peter said.

"What are you talking about?"

"I thought maybe the explosion was a mistake. I mean, maybe someone got the wrong house. But that sonofabitch in the Camaro was after you. You must have done something bad to someone."

"It's always my fault. Right, Dad? Tommy's death. Mom losing it. All my fault."

"Ancient history, David. Just because you feel guilty, don't blame me."

"You made me feel like I was nothing from the time I was twelve years old. If it hadn't been for Gino Bartolucci, I wouldn't have had anyone to talk to."

Peter's mouth dropped open and his eyes misted. "I didn't blame you for Tommy's death. I blamed myself. A father's supposed to be able to protect his children."

David glared at his father. "How the hell do you think I feel?"

"I know exactly how you feel. I didn't know how to get past Tommy's murder. I never blamed you; you've got to believe me. I know I didn't give you the support you needed. And I resented Gino for being there for you." He paused a couple seconds. "I've always been proud of you, son. And I've always loved you. Perhaps I can't make up for the past, but I'll do my best to try."

"Let's go inside," David said.

David didn't think he could eat, but he followed his father into the diner. He watched Peter eat a hamburger while he sipped at a cup of bad coffee, which only aggravated his already-sour stomach. When the waitress cleared their plates, David looked at his father. "What you said in the car, about doing something awful to someone that would make him want to kill me. I can't think of a damn thing I've ever done that would drive someone to want to commit murder. Even guys my company caught breaking cyber laws, and who went to prison, wouldn't retaliate by committing murder. I've thought a lot about it. The whole thing makes no sense."

Peter appeared to think about that for a while. "Maybe the explosion and that maniac in the Camaro were payback for something Gino did."

David shook his head. "Then why not go after Gino? He's not that well protected."

Peter rubbed his forehead and closed his eyes.

"Are you okay, Dad?"

"My body can't do most of the things it could do years ago, but my mind's intact, and I can still shoot a pistol or rifle. The Army taught me well."

"That was a long time ago," David said.

"It's like riding a bicycle. You never forget." Peter sighed. "Whatever you've gotten yourself into, I'm here for you. I'll watch your back. Don't treat me like some decrepit old codger. And don't ever question my love."

David's voice broke when he said, "Dad, I won't rest until I find out who killed my family." He then coughed to clear his throat. "I can come up with all sorts of reasons why you should stay out of this, but I know you won't listen. So, I accept your help. And your love. But on one condition. I have final say on all decisions."

By the time Toney arrived at his D.C. apartment, his headache had become intense. He placed a call to Rolf Bishop as soon as he had the chance to grab a beer and sit down. He hoped Bishop wouldn't answer, but after the third ring Bishop's distinctive, commanding voice came over the line.

"What?"

Toney wasn't about to tell Bishop he'd blown another chance to eliminate Hood. "I followed him from the cemetery to I-95. He and an older man seemed to be headed toward Pennsylvania. I lost them near the Pennsylvania border. Maybe you can get me information on whether Hood has family there." Toney heard Bishop exhale.

"I'll call you back," Bishop said, and hung up.

APRIL 16

CHAPTER 11

Out of the blue, Chicago Detective Dennis Aloysius O'Neil succumbed to the nostalgia bug. One day, nine years after he left the Marine Corps, he wondered about the members of the Marine unit he'd served with in Afghanistan. He'd periodically thought about his old comrades, about getting together with them, but this time he was motivated to do something about it. He'd heard and read about Marine Corps reunions. He decided to try to organize one.

O'Neil called the Marine Personnel Office in the Naval Department at the Pentagon and was connected to a Gunnery Sergeant Sam Collins.

"Gunney, my name is Dennis O'Neil. I'm a Chicago detective and served in the Marines. I'd like to organize a reunion of my old unit from Afghanistan. The unit was there from 2003 to 2005. But I don't have names and addresses."

"I get a lot of that," Collins said. "Lot of guys want to get back together. I'd be happy to help. Give me your Marine ID number, your old unit designation number, and contact information. I'll pull up a list of all the men who served in your unit."

"How long will it take?"

"About a minute. Computers are amazing. I'm going to put you on hold."

Collins came back on the line a little over a minute later.

"There were a total of three hundred fifty-seven names on the list. Of that number, forty-six left Afghanistan in coffins and another twenty-five died in Veterans Hospitals from wounds suffered in combat, or from illnesses. Another twelve died from other causes— car wrecks, suicides, one drowning, etc. The addresses I have for most of the men were those recorded in their files as of their dates of separation from the Marine Corps."

"Thanks, Gunney."

O'Neil sent invitations to the members of his unit and within five days received a few responses. He heard from men thrilled about the reunion. Some invitations came back "No Longer at This Address," "Address Unknown," or "No Forwarding Address." Three letters arrived from widows in Anaheim, California; Belen, New Mexico; and Wildwood, New Jersey. Each expressed sorrow that her husband would be unable to join his old friends because he had been killed within the past month.

Thirty-four-year-old Dennis O'Neil had become a cop, then a detective with the Chicago Police Department after he left the Marines. He was a good cop for a variety of reasons. He was honest, had a tremendous work ethic, and cared about what he did. He had excellent instincts. And he didn't believe in coincidences.

"Damn, that makes three."

"What makes three?" Detective Joji Kimura asked.

"Sorry, Joji. I didn't realize I said it out loud. You know I've been working on this reunion for my old Marine unit. Well, three of the guys who were in the unit were all murdered in the last few weeks."

"Sounds like a coincidence to me. And I know how much you believe in coincidences."

O'Neil laid the three widows' letters side-by-side on the table in front of him and re-read them. The women had said their husbands were *killed*. Not that they had died. They'd been *killed*. Three murders of former Marines from the same unit in a 30-day period seemed too much coincidence for a career cop with a sixth sense.

CHAPTER 12

Bethesda Detective Jennifer Ramsey had heeded her father's advice since she'd joined the Bethesda Police Department. She'd kept her mouth shut, even when confronted with the worst sort of misogyny and outright malice. But she couldn't anymore. She knew Roger Cromwell was an experienced homicide detective, but there was no question in her mind he was way off base about David Hood. There was no way Hood would murder his own family. And there was no evidence he had. She fidgeted in her chair as Cromwell laid out his theory on the Hood case for Mickey Croken, the Chief of Detectives.

". . . and it's too much of a coincidence. Hood's down in the bomb shelter when the explosion happens. Give me a break!"

Croken glanced at Ramsey and knitted his brows. "What the hell's your problem, detective. You got ants in your pants?"

"No, sir. Well, yes, sir. I mean—"

"What are you trying to say?" Cromwell interrupted.

Croken gave Cromwell a stern look and turned back to Ramsey.

Ramsey took a deep breath and let it out slowly. She glanced at Cromwell. "With all due respect to my partner," she said, "I don't think there's any way in hell Hood would murder his wife and kids. The more we focus on him, the less attention we put on finding the real killer."

Cromwell laughed. "What do you base that on, female intuition?"

Jennifer had had enough of Cromwell's bullshit. "That's a better basis for Hood's innocence than the trumped up nonsense you're spewing."

Cromwell's eyes looked as though they'd pop out of their sockets. His already florid face reddened to the shade of a ripe tomato.

"There was no insurance on the wife or the kids," Jennifer continued. "Hood's business is so successful he can't spend what he makes, and every person we talked to told us the guy was the best father and husband they'd ever seen. Straight arrow all the way. Two Purple Hearts and a Silver Star earned in Afghanistan. We got nothing that points at Hood as the killer. He's a victim, not a criminal."

Jennifer felt as though she'd just finished a marathon. She was exhausted from tension. But she felt good at the same time. She looked at Cromwell, who glared back at her. When she shifted her gaze to Croken, she was rewarded with a smile.

"Roger, I tend to agree with Jennifer," Croken said. "I want you to focus on other angles, other suspects."

Cromwell looked stunned. His face was still crimson and his mouth hung open as though he'd been poleaxed. "Hood is another one of those maniacs being manufactured by the military. The Army trains these guys to be stone-cold killers and then turns them loose on America's streets. Mark my words, that sonofabitch murdered his wife and kids."

Croken looked from Cromwell to Ramsey and said, "I've made my decision. You're excused. I expect some progress on this case, or I'll have to assign other detectives to it."

Cromwell shot to his feet and stormed from the office. Ramsey stood and turned to leave the office.

"Detective," Croken said.

Ramsey turned back to her boss. "Yes, sir?"

"I know Cromwell's a Neanderthal and a royal pain in the ass. But you might want to slip him a little slack. His teenage daughter was murdered by a vet with PTSD who went on a shooting rampage. He's got a blind spot when it comes to military vets."

"I'll keep that in mind, Chief."

Ramsey felt even more uncomfortable about Cromwell after

what Croken had just told her. The guy could be a loose cannon out on the streets. But she decided to try to mend things with her partner, anyway. She walked over to where he stood a few yards away from Croken's office.

Cromwell growled, "I want to talk to you." He walked past his and Ramsey's desks and entered an empty interrogation room. He kicked a metal folding chair against a wall, slammed the door behind Ramsey, and drilled her with the most hateful look she'd ever seen. He stepped to within inches of her and jabbed the center of her chest with one of his sausage-sized fingers.

"You made me look bad in there, Ramsey," Cromwell hissed. "You'll pay for that. I promise you."

Ramsey slapped the man's hand away and, her voice laden with venom, said, "Don't you ever touch me again."

"Or what?" Cromwell laughed. "The only thing you women are good for is sex." He then shot out one of his enormous hands and jabbed one of her breasts.

Mickey Croken breathed an enormous sigh. For the first time all day no one knocked on his door and his telephone didn't ring. He reached over toward his inbox to work on the files accumulated there, when the sound of breaking glass propelled him from his chair and out of his office. Detectives had already assembled outside the door to one of the interrogation rooms. Shards of mirrored glass littered the floor outside the room. Croken pushed his way through the crowd and stopped at the open doorway. His first instinct was to laugh, but quickly suppressed it.

Jennifer Ramsey stood over a prone Roger Cromwell, flat on his belly on the floor. Ramsey had his left arm twisted behind his back in a hold Croken guessed was quite painful.

"What's going on?" Croken demanded.

"Uh," Ramsey said, "Roger asked me to show him a judo hold. I guess I just got carried away."

"Is that right, Cromwell?" Croken asked.

By this time, Ramsey had released Cromwell. He turned over and slowly got up, rubbed his shoulder. Cromwell glared at the half-dozen faces around him.

"Yeah," Cromwell said. "I guess I wasn't paying attention."

One of the cops standing around said, "Yeah, right!"

"What the hell happened to the window?" Croken demanded.

Ramsey shrugged. Cromwell just stood there and looked stupid.

"All right, everybody," Croken ordered. "Let's get back to work."

While the crowd dispersed, Ramsey whispered to Cromwell, "I've put up with your crap long enough. You don't want me as your partner. Fine. Request reassignment. But you step out of line with me just once and I'll have you up on sexual harassment charges so fast you won't be able to get a job as a rent-a-cop."

Cromwell babbled something unintelligible, then spat, "Fuck you!" and left the room.

CHAPTER 13

When his cellphone rang, Toney was parked on an unlighted dirt lane a half-mile from an exit off I-95. Already a little spooked by the lack of visibility due to the darkness and rain, his ringing telephone made him jump. When he answered, his voice was higher than normal.

"Well, what have you done today to earn your pay? Maybe I should guess. I suspect nothing! Absolutely nothing."

Toney couldn't come up with a response, nor did he trust his voice.

Bishop then said, "David Hood's father, Peter, lives in Philadelphia. Write down this address."

Bishop read off the address. "I'm losing patience," Bishop said. "I don't think you want to disappoint me."

Bishop hung up before Toney could clear the lump in his throat.

Seated in his Georgetown home office, Bishop reflected on how efficiently he'd eliminated the other members of his Afghanistan unit. The job had turned out to be smaller than he'd anticipated. Three of the fourteen men had been killed in Afghanistan after serving with the SLSD, two had died in car accidents years ago, and of course, Campbell had been killed in New York in 2004. One call to the assassin who went by the code name Paladin was all it took. He'd needed a real pro; a killer of unparalleled talent. Over the past month, the man had murdered seven of the eight remaining members of the Special Logistical Support Detachment. The seven were spread out all over the United States, mostly in the Mid-West and West. Bishop had assigned Montrose Toney to kill David Hood because Toney lived in D.C. and Hood lived in nearby Bethesda. He'd had a long-standing arrangement with Toney. He'd used the man for muscle jobs—to remove or scare off political opponents of men he supported, rough up business competitors, a couple arson jobs.

Bishop had no idea if any of the men, other than that prick Carbajal in New Mexico, ever had even an inkling of what he and Campbell had really been up to in Afghanistan, and he really didn't care. To him, the men were merely loose ends to be eliminated. He knew the FBI had initiated extensive background checks on him the minute the President tapped him to fill in at the CIA. If he had any hope of Senate confirmation for the Deputy Director position, his record would have to come up clean. He also knew there was only a slim chance any member of his old unit would be interviewed. But he couldn't take the chance even one of them would raise any doubts about his past. What if one of them, in addition to Carbajal, had known he and Campbell had swapped stolen U.S. weapons and ammunition to tribal groups for narcotics? Or that they had shipped drugs to the States in caskets.

All it would take was one man being asked, "Do you know anything in Rolf Bishop's past that might make him ineligible to be in a sensitive government position?", and the man answering, "Well-l-l, I once heard someone say . . . ."

With the removal of Hood, Bishop would have only one other man to dispose of: Montrose Toney. He would be the last person alive who could tie him to any of the murders. Paladin wasn't a problem—he'd been hired at arm's length. The assassin had no idea who had employed him. Besides, the man was a professional who did "wet work" for whoever could pay his price.

CHAPTER 14

David always marveled at how little his old Philadelphia neighborhood had changed over the years. Sure the houses showed signs of age, as did the people he recognized while they drove down Rosemont Street. But, all in all, the neighborhood looked pretty much as it had years ago. Brick, garage-less, row houses with window flower boxes, three-step stoops, and shallow porches lined the street.

David helped his father carry their bags into the Hood home and then moved the Lincoln. He didn't want the company car announcing their location. He found a place to park it two blocks away and walked back to the house with the 9mm in one pants pocket, the .45 in the other pocket, and the Uzi under his suit coat.

Gino Bartolucci was a robust, vibrant sixty-year-old. Although he still owned Bartolucci's Market and had an office there, he'd long ago passed on the reins of his illegitimate enterprises to much younger men, and no longer had any overt mob involvement. Gino had outlasted the expected career life span of a Philadelphia Mafia Don. Those who didn't die at the hands of a rival usually wound up in a federal penitentiary on a racketeering or murder conviction. Gino had been a survivor because he was smart, careful, had surrounded himself with blood relatives, and had been damn lucky.

On the drive from Bethesda to Philadelphia, Gino called and left a message on a private cellphone that belonged to Louis Burkett, a bookish-looking clerk at the Federal Bureau of Investigation's Philadelphia office.

As his driver pulled off Broad Street, ten minutes from Gino's South Philadelphia home, Gino's cellphone rang.

"Yeah?" he answered.

"It's Louis."

"So, whatcha got?"

Burkett was the prototypical records clerk and always surprised people when they inquired about his job and learned he worked with the Bureau. Because he read everything that crossed his desk and had a photographic memory, he could converse in detail about some of the most sensational FBI Investigations. People assumed Burkett was a Special Agent rather than a clerk, and he saw no reason to disabuse them of their assumptions. But Louis Burkett was damned good at his job, and his computer-like memory made him a fabulous resource for Gino Bartolucci.

Ten years earlier, Gino had picked up gambling markers Burkett had run up with an Atlantic City bookmaker. He allowed the man to work off the balance of his debts by providing information. But Burkett had a problem: He continued to gamble and lose. And Gino continued to bail him out of trouble—for a price. Burkett told Gino everything he knew about the Feds' RICO investigations in Philadelphia. Gino then sold that information to his "friends."

"I haven't found much about the bombing in Bethesda," Burkett said. "No evidence points to a specific individual or group. Part of the detonator and traces of the explosive survived the blast, but were too fragmented to tell us anything. The killer used plastic explosive, that's certain. And it's obvious he went for overkill. But there's no way to trace the stuff to a supplier."

"That's not much."

"There is one thing, though. The detective assigned to the case, guy named Cromwell, thinks your son-in-law was responsible."

"That's how much the cops know."

"The bottom line is nobody knows anything."

"That's not quite correct," Gino replied. "There's at least one guy who knows something. The killer."

After his driver dropped them off in front of their South Philadelphia home, and his bodyguard walked them to the front door, Rosa passed through the entry and made her way to the kitchen. Gino went down a set of steps and into the basement. He entered a one hundred fifty-foot long corridor that spanned the width of five row houses, all owned by Gino under corporate entity names. This underground passageway had allowed Gino, his family, and his men to elude the police and thugs on several occasions. Near the western end of the corridor, Gino stepped into a room equipped with office furniture, sound equipment, and a telephone listed in the name of Angela Tartaglia, an eighty-four-year-old widow who lived rent-free on the first floor of the house above. He made four calls and gave each of the persons who answered the same cryptic, coded message: "Your order will be ready for pick-up at eight tomorrow morning."

CHAPTER 15

In a matter of hours, Chicago Police Detective Dennis O'Neil gathered quite a bit of information about the murders of the three former Marines. Cops in the three cities where the men lived faxed him copies of the homicide reports. Each man was killed by a single gunshot to the head, just behind the left ear—assassination-style. A different .22-caliber silenced pistol had been used in all three murders. The weapons had fired jacketed hollow-point magnum rounds. The killer had removed the suppressor and dropped the murder weapon next to each victim's body. No witnesses.

O'Neil knew the murdered men were neither victims of random crime nor targets of a thief. Thieves and common criminals didn't use suppressors. And didn't leave behind their victims' wallets or their weapons. The men lived in three different regions of the country. If he hadn't started to put the reunion together, none of these murders would have been connected.

Although the three murders were really none of his business— at least on a professional basis, O'Neil couldn't help himself. The victims were Marines, some of whom he'd served with. He just couldn't drop it. There had to be some common denominator. He called Gunnery Sergeant Sam Collins on the Marine Corps Personnel Desk, at The Department of the Navy.

"Gunney, this is Dennis O'Neil from Chicago. How's things at the Puzzle Palace?"

"Hey! Dennis, howya doin'?" Collins responded. "You gettin' your reunion organized?"

"You bet, Gunney. You were a big help. I couldn't have done it without you. But listen, I've got another request. I need some more information on three names. Could you fax me copies of their personnel files?"

"You know I can't do that."

"Even if the files are for men who were all murdered in the last month?"

"You gotta be shittin' me."

"Nope! Something's fishy. Three former marines from my combat unit in Afghanistan were murdered in the last thirty days. I really need your help."

Collins didn't immediately respond. O'Neil waited.

"You gotta keep this to yourself. You didn't get these files from me, you understand?"

"I understand."

"Okay! Give me their names. I'll get back to you as fast as I can."

Collins pulled up the names of the three murdered Marines on the Marine Corps' computerized personnel system. In less than thirty minutes, he'd retrieved the three personnel files of Lieutenant Eric Carbajal of Belen, New Mexico; Gunnery Sergeant Zachary Perkins of Anaheim, California; and Gunnery Sergeant Fred Laniewski of Wildwood, New Jersey. He attached the files to an email addressed to Dennis O'Neil, sanitized them by removing any classified data, and sent the email.

O'Neil reviewed the three files; searched for commonalties. He found the men had three things in common: Each had been assigned to O'Neil's old Marine company in Afghanistan; each had been wounded and then furloughed to something called the Special Logistical Support Detachment-Afghanistan; and each had been murdered in the last thirty days.

CHAPTER 16

Montrose Toney dumped the stolen red Camaro and retrieved his white Acura. He drove to Philadelphia and found Peter Hood's street at 11 p.m. He drove past the house and looked for the Lincoln Towncar he'd chased back in Maryland, but it was nowhere in sight. He continued down the street, made a right turn, and circled back toward the house.

Carmine Santori had worked for the Bartolucci Family since he emigrated from Sicily at the age of sixteen—forty-four years earlier. First for Gino's father and then for Gino after the old man died. He was one of the four men Gino had called to meet with him at the market at eight that morning. The meeting had lasted only ten minutes. All Gino needed to say to the four men was, "My son-in-law is in danger—maybe from the same people who killed my Carmela and my grandchildren. I want you to keep an eye on Peter Hood's house on Rosemont."

Carmine kept watch over the Hood home from a second-story bedroom in the front of Johnny Galante's house, across the street from the Hoods. Johnny Galante was happy to do a favor for Don Bartolucci.

"Hey, boss," Carmine said into his cellphone. "I don't know if I got something, but some guy cruised the street here two times in the last five minutes." He gave Gino the description of the car and the plate number.

"Sit tight and watch," Gino said. "You don't do nothin' that's gonna warn him off. You got that?"

"Sure, boss."

Armed with Carmine's information, Gino called Philadelphia Police Sergeant Sean Rafferty who had long ago decided to milk his police job for all he could get and then retire to the Jersey Shore before some strung out lowlife decided his chest looked like a bull's-eye. It hadn't taken him long to come to the attention of the Bartolucci family. Rafferty recognized Gino's voice.

"What's up?" he asked.

"I need a quick ID on a D.C. plate."

"It's nearly midnight."

"And that's a problem because . . . ."

"No problem. Give me the plate number."

Rafferty used his home computer to access the D.C. Department of Motor Vehicles. He inputted his access ID and password and printed out the motor vehicle records of a Montrose Toney. He then accessed the FBI's National Crime Data Network and downloaded and copied Toney's criminal records. He walked to a pay phone near police headquarters and called Gino.

"I got what you wanted."

APRIL 17

CHAPTER 17

David mindlessly channel-surfed on Peter's television. When he hit C-SPAN, he saw a name from his long ago past crawl across the bottom of the screen: U.S. Senate Confirmation Hearing for Rolf Bishop, Deputy Director of Central Intelligence. This was the first time since he left Afghanistan that he'd heard or seen his old commander's name. Curious, he watched the hearing, which seemed to proceed well for Bishop, who'd been a loyal member of the President's political party. Bishop's military record proved he was a bona fide American hero. The opposition party members of the Senate apparently could find no substantive reason to oppose Bishop's nomination to the position of Deputy Director of the CIA.

David had to admit the man looked good. He had to be close to sixty years old, but he looked younger. Distinguished and trim, he presented a wonderful image on the tube. He remembered what an insensitive bastard Bishop had been and thought the former Army colonel would probably be the perfect choice for the CIA position.

Then David noticed a slight, almost imperceptible look of surprise register on Bishop's face when a crusty old senator from South Carolina asked him a question:

"Ah read yo Army 201 file, Colonel Bishop, and ah'm mighty impressed. But one thang confuses me. What was this Special Lo-gistical Support Dee-tachment you headed up in Afghanistan? Ah cain't find any reference to any sech unit in any of the military's

Tables of Organization. Ah'm jest kinda curious."

"Mr. Chairman, Senator Birdsong, the Special Logistical Support Detachment's mission was to match up field units' needs with supplies, equipment, and materiel that was shipped to Afghanistan. It was our job to ensure no unnecessary delays occurred in putting much-needed equipment, food, ammunition, etc., into the hands of our men and women in the field. I commanded the unit for about a year-and-a-half. It was standard Quartermaster Corps procedure."

"What a bunch of crap!" David said.

"What's that, son?" Peter asked as he entered the room.

"Oh, nothing, Dad," David replied. "Just reacting to the crap that flows from Washington, D.C. This guy on the hot seat commanded the last unit I served with in Afghanistan. He's up for one of the top CIA jobs. He just lied to the Senate Intelligence Committee."

Peter sat on the couch and looked at the television screen while the camera moved in for a close up shot of Bishop. "I wouldn't trust that guy as far as I could throw him," he said. "Look at his eyes. They're dead—like shark eyes."

It was a relatively slow day for Dennis O'Neil. He needed to be in court to testify in a homicide trial in two hours, so he'd decided to stay in the squad room to review his case notes. He took a break for a moment and stretched his sore back muscles. He looked down, took his spare tire-of-a-belly in both hands, shook it, and grunted. He'd have to go on a crash diet before the Marine reunion. He didn't want his old buddies to see him like this. There wasn't much he could do about his gray hair and white mustache, short of hair dye, and that wasn't his style. At six feet, three inches, he knew he still made a good first impression—except he had to do something about the extra twenty pounds he carried.

Detective Joji Kimura sat across the room and watched the small color TV set on the middle of an empty desk.

"What the hell are you watching?" O'Neil asked.

"The confirmation hearing on the new CIA Deputy Director, Rolf Bishop."

O'Neil laughed. Kimura, the squad's resident conspiracy

theorist, always fixated on anything to do with the CIA. Dennis paid no attention to the TV and returned to his notes about the trial, until he heard someone mention "Special Logistical Support Detachment."

The odd feeling in his gut that occurred when coincidences happened suddenly returned. He scribbled in his notebook a reminder to call his Pentagon contact, Sam Collins. Then he wrote: "What is or was the SLSD?" and "Get names of all persons ever assigned to SLSD, and names of all men who served with three dead Marines."

O'Neil left his chair and walked over to where Kimura sat transfixed by the television screen. While he watched, O'Neil zeroed in on Bishop's face. He thought, at first, he recognized the man. But, after a moment, he realized it wasn't Bishop's face he found familiar. It was the look in the man's eyes, the set of his mouth, and the overall impression he left. O'Neil had seen other men with the same sort of "look." Some had been well dressed, some were criminals, some were cops. But they all had one thing in common: an inhuman, sociopathic coldness in their eyes.

When the hearing ended, O'Neil watched Bishop move to the raised platform where the senators sat and chatted them up. O'Neil noted that the retired Army officer had some of the most influential and powerful men in the country eating out of his hands.

"That dude is smooth," he said.

"What was that, Dennis?" Kimura asked.

"Nothing, Joji. Just thinking out loud."

While O'Neil drove cross-town to the courthouse, he pushed all thoughts of his testimony in the homicide trial to the back of his mind, and focused on his new mystery. Three former Marines had been killed in the previous few weeks. All apparent executions. Then he'd learned from Pentagon records each of the three murdered men served in Afghanistan in a unit called the Special Logistical Support Detachment. And he'd just found out the next CIA Deputy Director had commanded the Special Logistical Support Detachment. O'Neil briefly considered the possibility all of this might be pure coincidence. But he quickly discarded the thought.

Montrose Toney had cased the Hoods' street several times and come to the conclusion that an attack on his target here was not his best alternative. He ticked off the problems in his mind: too restrictive a physical environment, limited parking close to the house, and being on foot in this neighborhood could be suicidal. He felt like an Albanian Muslim in a Christian Serb neighborhood. But he knew this street like it was his own. He'd grown up in an all-black neighborhood that looked just like it. The row houses served as bleachers for the residents, with the street as their arena. Toney knew he fell into the category of "troublemaker" as far as these people were concerned. He knew the residents had probably already spotted him.

He could tell someone was at home at the Hoods'. He'd seen movement through the sheer front window drapes. But he had no idea if David Hood was in there. He pondered the problem for a few minutes and then remembered the name of the detective in charge of the Hood murder investigation: Roger Cromwell. He'd read all the accounts in the Baltimore and D.C. papers about the case. He called 4-1-1 on his cellphone and got the number for Peter Hood on Rosemont Street in South Philadelphia. He called and when a man answered, Toney said, "This is Detective Cromwell with the Bethesda Police Department. Is Mr. David Hood there? I need to speak with him."

"He's out right now," a man said. "Can I help you? I'm his father. Can I have him call you back?"

"That's all right, I'll call later," Toney replied, and hung up.

After Toney's most recent swing down Rosemont Street, Carmine Santori again called Gino, who immediately telephoned Bobby Galupo, the man he'd picked years ago to take over the Philadelphia organization. Galupo, in turn, called one of his men, Rocco Fortunato, stationed in a car at the end of the Hoods' block, and told him to follow the white Acura and report back every fifteen minutes.

Rocco Fortunato, a beefy young hoodlum in his twenties, tailed Toney. He followed him from South Philadelphia all the way past the Philadelphia sports complex, out past the oil refineries on the south side of the city, and finally to a motel near the Philadelphia International Airport. After he watched Toney take a small suitcase from the trunk of the Acura and enter room 157, Fortunato called Bobby Galupo.

Toney had been on the move for nearly sixteen hours, most of it in the driver's seats of the stolen Camaro and his own Acura. He was exhausted and needed sleep before he went after Hood. He had to come up with a way to hit the man and get away clean, and he knew he'd be able to think more clearly after he'd had some rest.

Jennifer Ramsey rapped on the side of the doorjamb of Lieutenant Croken's office. "You wanted to see me, Lieutenant?"

"Yeah, take a seat."

She sat down in one of the two chairs in front of Croken's desk.

Croken picked up a piece of paper from his blotter and waved it at Jennifer. "This is Detective Cromwell's request for reassignment."

Jennifer said nothing. She was thrilled that she might be rid of Cromwell, but she was surprised the man had requested the personnel action. Things had to be pretty bad between partners for one to ask for a reassignment. Her relationship with Cromwell obviously qualified. A request for reassignment by one partner, however, could leave a black mark on the other partner's record. She wondered what reason for reassignment Cromwell had put in the official request.

As though he read her mind, Croken said, "Detective Cromwell claims you were insubordinate, didn't back him up in a dangerous situation, and"—here Croken paused—"that you have a substance abuse problem."

Jennifer knew these charges made by an experienced detective with years of service with the Bethesda Police Department could ruin her career. Even if she rebutted the charges and won in a hearing, she would be tainted forever within the good old boy network. "I . . . that's all nonsense. You can't believe I—"

Croken raised a hand to stop her. "You're right, Ramsey. I don't believe a word of it. I'll make this paperwork disappear. But I'll give Cromwell another partner. He's off the Hood investigation. I want you to take it over. I'll assign you another partner as soon as I can. But for now, you're on your own. You're doing a great job. Don't let assholes like Cromwell affect your attitude about a career in law enforcement." Croken gave her a brief smile and added, "Now get out there and find the killer."

Jennifer said, "Thanks, Lieutenant," and backed out the door. Croken's nose was already buried in some report.

APRIL 18

CHAPTER 18

The shrill ring of his cellphone brought Toney out of an erotic dream. Not quite sure where he was and still half asleep, he rubbed his eyes and glanced at the bedside clock: 6:17 a.m. He picked up the phone and said, "Hello," in a voice thick with fatigue.

"You'd better have something good to report," Rolf Bishop said.

The man had a way about him that caused Toney to produce massive quantities of adrenaline and stomach acid every time he spoke to him—or whenever he just thought about him.

Toney took a deep breath. "I got everything under control," he said.

"When you've completed your assignment, then I'll know everything's under control," Bishop snapped. "Until that happens, nothing's under control, and your assurances are nothing but bullshit. I'm sick and tired of excuses. If you don't solve the problem by noon today, I'll have it solved some other way. Understand?"

Toney was wide-awake now, and frightened. Bishop had just told him he was about to be fired. The thought of losing his meal ticket panicked him.

Elderly female shoppers know that if they don't get to the market early, all the best fresh produce and choicest cuts of meat will already be sold. So, early most mornings a gang of old, gray-haired women, many of them widows dressed in black, marched into Bartolucci's Market. While they shopped, they caught up on gossip—complained about lazy daughters-in-law who spent their beloved sons' hard-earned money; or how no good sons-in-law treated their innocent, kind-hearted, virginal daughters. And of course, they boasted of their beautiful, brilliant, and athletic grandchildren who loved their grandmothers more than anyone else.

David Hood entered that stage at 7 a.m.

"*Ciao,*" Gino said from his office doorway.

David walked over to Gino and they hugged. Gino turned and led the way into his office. David sat down. Gino closed the door and moved to his desk chair.

"They were killed because of me," David blurted. "I've got to find out why."

"You don't know that," Gino said. "It could have been something else." He thought, Maybe it was retaliation for something I did. Although he didn't believe it.

"I've got to destroy the people who did this."

Gino was worried. The last thing he wanted David to do was sacrifice his own life in pursuit of revenge. "You let me handle this, David!" Gino said. "Your hands never have to get dirty."

"I *want* to get my hands dirty."

Gino needed to keep David out of the revenge business. It was only a matter of time before he got his hands on the *mulanyan* who had cruised past Peter's home. This Montrose Toney character. Peter had told him about the guy in the Camaro who'd chased them. Gino guessed that guy was Toney, or someone associated with him. When he got his hands on the bastard, he'd find out what was going on.

Gino opened his mouth to tell David it would be foolhardy for him to get involved, but stopped himself when he saw the cold, determined look in his son-in-law's eyes. He knew at that instant there was nothing he could say to dissuade him. And it was better that he brought David in with him than have David running around on his own. "All right, David, we'll work together," Gino agreed. "But you gotta stay calm and professional. No cowboy tactics, you understand?"

"I understand, Gino. This is business."

"*Bene!*" Gino exclaimed. But he didn't believe a word of it.

David told Gino everything he knew about the explosion, which unfortunately wasn't much. He then answered questions Gino threw at him. These questions took him back to the military, through the birth and growth of his company, who his friends, associates, and competitors were. Gino asked if he had any enemies, not just competitors, but David couldn't think of any—except for whoever was behind the wheel of the red Camaro that had chased him and his father after the funeral.

Gino's desk telephone rang. He glanced at the screen on the phone, recognized the number, and said, "I need to take this."

Gino snatched up the receiver and said, "*Ciao, Roberto.*"

"The *mulanyan* from D.C. is on the move," Bobby Galupo said. "He left the motel and drove out to the area around 45th and Spruce. You know, out past the Penn campus. He stopped at the drive-in at a Mickey Ds. Now he's kinda driving around, like he can't make up his friggin' mind what he wants to do next. But I can tell you one thing . . . he's heading to South Philly."

"*Bene, Roberto, grazie,*" Gino said. "I think we both know where he's headed." "My boys are ready to go," Galupo said. "Everything's set up."

"Thanks. But tell your boys we sure as hell want this done real quiet. And I want the guy alive."

"*Capisco.*"

As soon as Gino put down the telephone receiver, David demanded in a strained voice, "What's going on?"

"Whoa, calm down," Gino said. "Remember, no emotion. This is business. I've had guys watching your father's place since yesterday. We spotted a white Acura cruise the street. If someone goes to the trouble to blow up an entire house and kill people, and if they're after you, as you think they are, then they ain't gonna quit. We've been on this *mulanyan* in the Acura since last night and it looks like he's on his way back to your dad's place."

"Maybe the same guy that was in the red Camaro."

"Maybe."

"So, what are we going to do?"

Gino stared at David. "We're going to wait here until we hear from my friends." He thought again about what Peter had told him about the man in a red Camaro. He was now convinced the explosion had nothing to do with anything he'd done. This was about David. Suddenly the love and affection he held for David grew thin. If his son-in-law had done something wrong, committed a crime that got his family murdered, he would make him pay.

Montrose Toney wasn't an educated man; but he wasn't stupid. He'd never taken action without proper planning. But he was about to put himself at great risk with no planning at all. He had a choice. He could point the car in any direction that would take him as far away as possible from Philadelphia, D.C., and Bishop. Or he could take a chance and go after Hood. But he was no more able to walk away from Bishop than a junkie would be able to walk away from a free fix. He'd become accustomed to the good life made possible by Bishop's money. Besides, if he ran, how the hell would he ever be able to hide from a top guy at the CIA?

Toney parked the Acura in the block south of Rosemont Street. He walked casually, as though he belonged in the neighborhood, and approached the Hood house. There was no one out on the street. He assumed that by this hour of the morning, 9:15, the working stiffs had gone off to their jobs and the local kids were in school. But it surprised him there were no women pushing baby strollers, or old men and women ambling along the sidewalk. Especially on a warm, sunny morning.

He climbed to the top of the Hood stoop and walked the two paces across the shallow porch to the front door. A sixty-something man sat next to the front window, newspaper in hand. It was the man who'd been with Hood at the cemetery in Bethesda. He'd have to do him, too.

Toney rang the bell. The man inside dropped his newspaper and got out of the chair.

The door opened and the man said, "Come in; I've been expecting you. My son isn't here right now, Mr. Toney. Why don't you sit down and relax? He should be back soon."

Toney developed an instant pain in his chest while he mechanically followed the man into a small living room. "What the . . . how do you know my name?" he asked as he reached for his pistol.

"Please excuse my rudeness. I haven't told you my name. It's Peter Hood." The man smiled and added, "I'm not the only one who knows your name, Mr. Toney. Actually, for someone who's been in Philadelphia for just one day, you're quite well known. Why don't I introduce you to some of my friends?"

Toney backed away as though Hood had a contagious disease. He'd fucked up. He backed toward the front door, but before he could reach it, three men stepped into the living room—one with a large pistol in hand and two with shotguns. All their weapons pointed directly at his chest.

The man with the pistol shouted, "You got one second to drop that pistol or we're gonna blow your ass all over the wallpaper."

When Toney's pistol hit the carpet, the older man kicked it out of the way, and the man with the pistol took three steps toward Toney and cold-cocked him.

Toney felt like he had the mother of all hangovers. Even before he opened his eyes, he remembered he'd messed up in a big way. For a moment, he considered not opening his eyes, hoping blindness would protect him from reality.

He drew a huge breath and slowly opened his eyes. He was in an unfinished basement with one small boarded-up window. A light bulb hung from the ceiling on an electric cord. He couldn't see the entire room because he was tied at the wrists and ankles to a metal chair and his head was strapped to the high back of the chair with tape. He could only look straight ahead and a bit to the left and right. He shuddered when he realized he was naked and the chair had been placed inside a shallow metal tub with a couple inches of water in the bottom.

Gino watched through a one-way window and saw Toney had a "deer in the headlights" look. Now that the man was conscious, he would let him sweat it out in the basement. An hour passed before he sent in two of Galupo's enforcers. Gino watched Marco Siracusa approach the killer and take his head in both of his hands.

Marco bent over, almost nose-to-nose with Toney, and said, "Monty . . . you don't mind if I call you Monty, do you?"

Toney seemed confused, as though he wasn't sure if the man expected an answer, but was too scared to say anything anyway. He just stared back at him.

Marco stepped back from the chair, looked at his sidekick, Vinnie Rosario, and said, "Vinnie, I don't think Monty likes me."

Vinnie stepped on a floor switch next to the metal tub, which delivered an electric current into the water at the bottom of the tub. The electric charge shocked Toney and caused his body to spasm. Gino knew from previous such sessions with traitors and enemies, the pain that shot through the man's body was horrific and would cause his body to go rigid, his jaws to clench. After a few seconds, Vinnie released the switch. Toney's gasps for breath sounded like a bull moose in rut.

He seemed to gather his senses and screamed, "Monty's good! Call me Monty!"

Marco looked at Vinnie. "See, sometimes you just gotta remind them that good manners are important."

Vinnie grunted.

"Now that we got your attention, Monty, I want you to know how bad you screwed up this time. When you messed with the Hood family, you made some of their closest friends very angry. You understand?"

There was no hesitation this time. Toney quickly tried to nod his head. When that didn't work, he yelled, "Yes."

"Good," Marco said. "Now, I'm gonna to ask you some very easy questions. You gonna answer each question and you gonna tell me exactly what I want to hear. You hesitate or give me an answer I don't like, Vinnie here hits the juice."

Toney answered one question after another. Gino didn't believe he held anything back.

When David returned to his father's home, Peter told him about a guy named Montrose Toney who'd showed up there and wanted to see him.

"What happened?" David asked.

"A few of Gino's friends were here. They took the guy away."

"Where to?"

Peter shrugged.

"When did all this go down?"

"While you were with Gino at the market."

"You were here when this happened?"

Peter shrugged again.

"Sonofabitch!"

David called Gino's cellphone.

"Yeah, David," Gino answered.

"What's going on?"

"Maybe you should come by my house."

One of Gino's bodyguards met David at the front door of Gino's row house and escorted him to a basement office. He sat down for a minute, but became too antsy and paced.

The bodyguard stood in a corner and stared.

"I don't suppose you'll tell me anything," David said to the man.

"I'll tell you one thing. Your old man's got bigger balls than an elephant. I hear he looked that killer in the eye and never blinked once. Guy coulda plugged him and he just stood there like he was a visiting neighbor."

"What the hell are you talking about?" David demanded.

The bodyguard smiled and said, "You better ask the Don."

An hour later, Peter was escorted into the room.

"What's been going on?" David said.

"Gino and I played a little game and—"

"I thought we agreed I'd call the shots," David shouted. He then turned on the bodyguard and said, "Where's Gino? I want to talk to him. Now!"

Peter didn't let David continue. "Son," he said, "I appreciate your concern, but I'm a grown man. I can make my own decisions."

"What did you do?" David asked.

Peter explained in detail what had happened back at the house. "We caught the guy who chased us from the cemetery."

It took David a moment to come up with a response, but finally he quietly said, "I love you, Dad, but sometimes you really piss me off."

"Yeah, I know," Peter replied. "That's my job."

Then Gino entered the basement room. The old Mafioso smiled as though he didn't have a care in the world.

But his smile disappeared when David said, "That was one stupid stunt you pulled."

Gino ignored David's insult and said, "I want you to listen to this." He took a DVD from his suit coat pocket and inserted it into a player built into the wall. He fast forwarded the disk. Then a man screamed.

"That's the guy in the Camaro," Gino said.

David heard a man set down the rules for Toney, and then:

Man: "You come to our neighborhood with a gun, and you gonna kill two of our friends, the Hoods. Why?"

Toney: "I got orders to kill the son. If the father is in the way, I gotta kill him, too."

Man: "Who hired you?"

Toney: (Hesitation. Screams. Thirty second pause, then gasps.) "Rolf Bishop."

David stiffened. That makes no sense at all, he thought.

Man: "Who's this Bishop?"

Toney: "A former Army officer. The guy who's been picked by the President for a top job at the CIA."

Man: "You shittin' me?"

Toney: "No, it's the truth."

Man: "Vinnie, find out if this guy's blowin' smoke up my ass."

Toney's screams of agony were so intense this time David was about to tell Gino to stop the torture, forgetting for a moment this was a recording.

Man: "Jesus, Vinnie; what you tryin' to do, fry the son-of-a-bitch so he can't tell us squat? Get your damn foot off that switch."

"Right here the tape machine was shut off for fifteen minutes," Gino said. "Until Toney could talk again."

Toney: (Weakly) "I'm telling you the truth, I swear. I'm not lying. Please don't hurt me anymore."

Man: "Okay! You still saying this CIA guy told you to kill David Hood?"

Toney: (Gasping) "I swear, I swear. He told me to do it."

Man: "Why?"

Toney: "Please don't hurt me again. I give you my word, I don't know why. He just said, 'Go kill Hood.'"

Man: "Did you bomb Hood's house in Maryland?"

Toney: "I didn't do that. It was a guy named Francis, Jim Francis. He was a crackhead. He planted the explosives. Fucked up the job real good."

Man: "How do you know this Francis guy blew up the house and killed the woman and her two kids?"

Toney: "Cause I was the one supposed to kill Hood, but I let

Francis do it instead. All he had to do was shoot him or run him off the road into a telephone pole. Whatever. The stupid bastard wasn't supposed to use explosives."

Man: "You got any idea why Bishop wants Hood killed?"

Toney: "No!"

Man: "So where do we find Francis?"

Toney: "Probably in the D.C. morgue. He died of an overdose."

Man: "Well, Monty-baby, you did pretty good. Anything else we should know?"

Toney: "No, except Bishop ain't gonna quit 'til Hood's dead."

(Brief pause)

"We gotta assume," Gino said, "that this *moulie*, Toney, has been missed by now and that Bishop is unhappy and worried about it. I know what I would do if I was in Bishop's shoes and wanted someone dead badly enough—send out a hit team with a lot of firepower."

"We can't just sit here and wait for someone to get lucky and kill David," Peter said.

"You got that right," Gino responded. "First of all, neither of you can stay at your house." Gino paused for a moment. "I figure Bishop thinks he's going after a business executive and his elderly father. He probably knows nothing of my involvement. That's to our advantage. I think you both should stay here today. Tomorrow morning we'll all move out to my place in Chestnut Hill."

Then Gino looked directly at David and said, "Why would Bishop want you dead?" The question was asked in an even voice that broached no equivocation, no holding back.

David heard Gino, but he absentmindedly shook his head as though he was overwhelmed with what he'd heard on the tape.

"What's on your mind?" Peter asked. "You look like you're off in Never-Never Land."

"It makes no sense. I don't have a clue why Bishop would want me dead. The last time I saw the guy was in early 2004, when I was assigned to his unit."

"Okay," Gino said. "We'll find out about this guy Bishop. And then I'll kill the son-of-a-bitch."

APRIL 19

CHAPTER 19

Marine Gunnery Sergeant Sam Collins was usually glad to help a fellow Marine, whether he was on active duty or a veteran. But Chicago Lieutenant Dennis O'Neil had tried his patience. Collins thought it was great O'Neil wanted to organize a Marine reunion, but his job in the Marine Corps Personnel Office was a full-time affair. So, when O'Neil called again, at 7:30 a.m. sharp this time, Collins snapped, "Look, I'm pretty busy right now. Maybe you could call back later."

"I know you're busy, Sam. But I wouldn't call you if it wasn't really import—"

"You're going to get my ass in trouble if anyone discovers I sent you copies of those three files," Collins whispered.

"Sam, I badly need your help. Look, I'll catch the first flight out of Chicago for D.C. I need to see you tonight. I'll call you at your office when I get there."

Before Collins could respond, O'Neil broke the connection.

Dennis O'Neil called his boss and told him he needed a couple "personal days." Then he booked a seat on a flight that would put him into Ronald Reagan National Airport in the middle of the afternoon. He had a couple hours to burn before he had to drive to O'Hare and used the time to make a few more calls.

131

Elizabeth Perkins, in Anaheim, answered the phone on the seventh ring. Her voice was tremulous, almost frightened-little-girlish.

"Mrs. Perkins, this is Dennis O'Neil from Chicago. Your husband and I served together in Afghanistan."

"Oh, yes, Mr. O'Neil, I remember. You're putting the reunion together." She paused a moment and said, "Zach would have loved so much to get together with all of you. What a shame that . . . . "

She began to cry. Dennis waited.

"I'm sorry about that, Mr. O'Neil. I can't seem to do anything but cry about Zach."

"That's understandable, Mrs. Perkins. I really am sorry to bother you, but I have a few questions, if you don't mind."

"Questions? What kind of questions?" she asked, suspicion suddenly in her voice.

"First of all, I need to inform you that I'm a detective with the Chicago Police Department. When I read your note about Zachary's murder, I looked into the circumstances of his death. There are a couple things that concern me. I should also tell you I have absolutely no authority to investigate a crime in Anaheim, so if you hang up on me now I'll understand."

"Mr. O'Neil," she said with sudden strength in her voice, "if you can help find whoever killed my Zach, I'll talk with you until hell freezes over."

"Thanks, Mrs. Perkins. Were you and Zachary married when he was in Afghanistan?" Dennis asked.

"First, please call me Beth," she said. Then she expelled a quick laugh and said, "Well, I should hope so, Lieutenant. We already had two kids and I was three months pregnant with Amy when Zach shipped out. But what does that have to do with anything?"

"Do you recall if he ever mentioned a unit in Afghanistan called the Special Logistical Support Detachment?"

"No, I'm sorry. My husband never told me anything like that. He would never really talk about any of his assignments, especially if they were classified. In fact, the only thing he ever talked about was how much waste he saw over there."

"I can relate, Beth. I saw a lot of young men get wounded or

132

killed in Afghanistan."

"Oh, I'm sure that must have been awful. But that wasn't what I meant when I referred to waste. You see, Zach was transferred to a unit in Afghanistan after he got wounded. He spent the last four months of his tour with that unit. I can't tell you how happy and relieved I was when he wrote that he wouldn't be in the field anymore and would be in an air-conditioned office. The waste Zach referred to concerned things he saw after he was wounded and transferred. I don't know what he did. I was just glad he wasn't getting shot at anymore."

"Thanks for your help, Beth. I promise I'll try to find out who killed your husband."

O'Neil made two more calls, to Eric Carbajal's widow in Belen, New Mexico, and to Fred Laniewski's widow in Wildwood, New Jersey. Neither could shed any more light on her husband's murder or his involvement with the SLSD. But there were common strands in their stories. Each of their husbands had been transferred to an office job near Kabul after being wounded in the field, to a unit that had something to do with logistics. They remembered their husbands had written about their new assignments and, after they returned to the States, reminisced about the tons of stuff that came into Afghanistan. One widow mentioned that her husband had thought someone at the Pentagon had lost his mind.

The late spring heat and humidity enveloped O'Neil when he stepped out of the terminal at Reagan National Airport. His dress shirt went limp by the time he reached the taxi queue. He felt as though he'd walked into a steam bath. And the taxi he was assigned had no air conditioning. The taxi driver was a Nigerian who spoke quite elegant British English, referred to O'Neil as "My good man," and used the word "bloody" to describe everything about Washington D.C.—"bloody weather," "bloody politicians," "bloody traffic . . . ." By the time the driver dropped him off at his hotel, across the street from the Watergate Complex, O'Neil was in a nasty mood.

After he checked into the hotel and found his room, O'Neil

called Sam Collins.

"Hey, Sam," O'Neil said. "I'm here in D.C. Can you meet me?"

"You really flew all the way from Chicago? And didn't know for sure I would actually see you?"

"Dead Marines, Sam! Murdered Marines! All I want from you is an hour of your time."

"All right. Meet me at McNally's Tavern on 9th Street in two hours."

"I'll be there."

O'Neil got to McNally's Tavern at 6:30 p.m., fifteen minutes before Collins was due to arrive, and after he ordered a beer, looked around the bar. The place had the appearance of a blue-collar bar converted to a yuppie club. It was half-filled with men and women in business suits. The bar, fronted by stools and a gleaming brass foot rail, extended from the front window all the way to the back wall. There was a narrow circulation area between the bar and tables along the wall opposite the bar. A man and a woman occupied a table close to O'Neil's. He caught snatches of their conversation—something about a two hundred million dollar IPO for a social media company. O'Neil sighed. He'd never cracked the sixty-five thousand dollar salary level. He quickly pushed the envy out of his mind. If he had to do it all over again, he'd still be a cop.

He considered his approach to Collins. The man could make his search for information easy. But if he refused to cooperate, getting information from the Pentagon would be tortuous and time-consuming, at best. And maybe impossible.

A fortyish man with buzz cut blond hair, dressed in a Marine khaki summer uniform, walked up to the table. "Detective O'Neil?" he asked.

O'Neil nodded his head, stood up, stuck out his hand. He read the nametag pinned over the Marine's left blouse pocket: COLLINS. "Nice to finally meet you, Sam. Please call me Dennis."

Collins grunted something and took O'Neil's hand.

O'Neil could tell from the Marine's frown he wasn't happy about this meeting. He pointed at the chair on the opposite side of the table. "Please sit down, Sam. I appreciate you meeting me."

Collins dropped into the chair and looked around the bar, as though he was reconnoitering the place for enemies. O'Neil quickly looked him over. Collins looked lean and hard, with that square-jawed look seen in Corps recruitment posters.

"How'd you know to pick me out in this place?" O'Neil asked.

Collins smiled. "Look around."

Dennis laughed when he realized he was the only man over forty in the place, and the only one, besides Collins, with a Marine buzz cut.

They ordered two draft beers from a harried waitress and then Collins said, "So, tell me what you need."

"I told you before that three Marines who served in my unit in Afghanistan have been murdered in the last few weeks. Assassination style. Gunshots to the head. The murders have to be connected. There's only one thing I can find that all three men had in common, besides being dead and serving in the same Marine unit. After each of them was wounded, he was transferred from the Marine unit to something called the Special Logistical Support Detachment."

O'Neil paused when the waitress returned with their beers. "Then I heard on TV this morning that the President just nominated a former Army colonel named Rolf Bishop to a top spot at the CIA."

Collins's eyes snapped wide open.

O'Neil leaned forward across the table and lowered his voice. "In Bishop's Senate confirmation committee hearing, it came out that he was the commander of this Special Logistical Support Detachment."

"Let me get this straight," Collins said. "You really do think the murders of three former Marines are connected in some way. You think the murders may be tied to this SLSD unit. And you think the new CIA Deputy Director may be tied to this—"

"No! No!" O'Neil interrupted. He leaned even closer to Collins. "I didn't suggest Bishop had anything to do with the murders. I just know he commanded the dead men's unit."

"I hope to God Bishop isn't involved. In this town, that guy's got more juice than Ocean Spray."

"I hear you, Sam."

"Okay, so what do you want?"

"I want to know the names, addresses, and phone numbers of every person who served with the Special Logistical Support Detachment."

"Jeez, what if there are hundreds of them?"

"God, I hope not," O'Neil said.

Collins sighed. "Okay, I'll do my best. Where can I reach you?"

O'Neil gave Collins his cell number and then picked up the tab for the beers. They walked from the bar together. O'Neil turned down Collins's offer of a ride back to his hotel.

"I need the exercise."

After Collins pulled out of the parking lot, O'Neil walked toward his hotel. It was now dark but it was unseasonably warm—a good evening for a walk. While he waited for the traffic light to turn green at the first corner, he noticed the headline on the front page of a newspaper in a newspaper box. It read, "Bishop Confirmed to CIA Post."

Rolf Bishop relaxed in the plush back seat of his CIA limousine. It was after 11 p.m. and had been a very long day. But he was full of the feeling that life was good. The U.S. Senate had confirmed him in his new CIA post. The President had then introduced him to the White House press corps and to the nation at a press conference in the Rose Garden. Afterward, Bishop had been driven out to Langley where he presided over a CIA staff meeting of his senior department heads. A dinner in his honor at the White House had capped everything off. The dinner was really nothing but an excuse to raise a million dollars or so for the party, but he still relished the attention and deference paid to him. This was heady stuff for a poor kid from Iowa, and he ate up every bit of it.

Bishop thought about the David Hood matter and felt a slight tremor of doubt that eroded his euphoria. He hadn't heard from Montrose Toney. He thought the guy had probably run off. He'd have to track him down and eliminate him.

The first order he'd issued as Deputy Director of the CIA was for an intelligence trace to be put on any inquiries about the Special

Logistical Support Detachment or Operation Harvest that hit the computer files of any government agency or department. Even though he assumed once Hood was taken care of, there would be no one left alive who would ever be interested in tying him to the SLSD, he wanted to know if that question asked by the senator in the confirmation hearing had put any reporters on the trail of the SLSD and Operation Harvest. Even if the subject of drugs never came up, he realized the activities of the unit could prove embarrassing, considering the tremendous fraud perpetrated by Operation Harvest on Congress and the American people. He realized he was acting paranoid, but he believed in taking every precaution. Although the Pentagon had buried Operation Harvest so deep it would probably never be unearthed, all it would take was one asshole reporter having a drink with some pissed off Pentagon clerk with a long memory.

He rested his head against the leather headrest and closed his eyes. That bastard Toney! He'd fix his ass for good. In the meantime, he hoped his backup plan would work.

APRIL 20

CHAPTER 20

Gunnery Sergeant Sam Collins's throat was dry and his stomach ached. He rang Dennis O'Neil's cellphone from a pay phone a few minutes before noon. He nervously looked through the phone booth's windows.

"Hello," O'Neil answered.

"Meet me in an hour where we had a couple of beers yesterday."

When Collins showed up at McNally's Tavern, a half-hour late, O'Neil noticed the Marine was jittery. His hands shook and he frequently looked over O'Neil's shoulder at the tavern door. O'Neil ordered shots of Jack Daniels for both of them.

"What's up, Sam?" O'Neil asked. "You act like you just robbed a bank."

"I wish it was that simple," Collins replied in a nervous, subdued voice. He pulled a folded sheet of paper from his blouse pocket, placed it on the table in front of him, and covered it with his hand. "You have no idea what you've stuck your nose into." He took a sip of the whiskey, then looked at his glass and downed the whole thing.

O'Neil signaled the waitress for another round of drinks. "Listen, Sam, why don't you start at the beginning?"

Collins breathed deeply and slowly let the air out of his lungs. "Okay. I got into work a little early today so I could dig up the information you wanted. I logged into Big Bertha—that's our mainframe system—and I queried the computer to cross-reference all personnel who ever had anything to do with the Special Logistical Support Detachment. I got a readout that said, 'NEED TO KNOW BASIS ONLY - ACCESS RESTRICTED. TOP SECRET.' I've got a Top Secret/Crypto clearance, so it was no big deal to access the data file. But it's against the law for me to tell you what I learned."

"Jeez, Sam, what the hell! I—"

Collins pumped a hand at O'Neil. "I've got a very bad feeling about this. I think someone is fucking with the system. I'm going to tell what I learned, but you never heard it from me."

"Okay. I got it. But what did you mean when you said, '. . . someone's fucking with the system'?"

"The SLSD file was unclassified until yesterday. It got classified at someone's request. I don't know why or by whom."

O'Neil squinted at Collins. "I'm totally confused, Sam."

"Okay, here's the deal. I got into the program and it spilled out the names of every Defense Department analyst who planned or worked on the creation of the unit, every officer and enlisted man ever assigned to it, and every individual who ever touched it in any way. I concentrated on the names of those who'd been assigned to the unit in Afghanistan in its eighteen-month existence. A total of fifteen men. The unit managed a mission called Operation Harvest. The files didn't go into any detail about what that was.

"So, I had a list of fifteen names, some of which I immediately recognized." Collins uncovered the piece of paper and unfolded it. He read from the paper. "Bishop, the new CIA Deputy Director, was the commander of the SLSD, and we know he's still alive. Then there's your three dead Marines: Carbajal, Perkins, and Laniewski. I pulled up the files on the other eleven names, and this is where things got weird."

The waitress brought another round and Collins snatched up his glass and downed half its contents.

"Oh, before I forget, I learned your three dead Marines were the only Marines assigned to SLSD. The other men came from the other combat services. One of them—an Army captain named Andrew King—died in Afghanistan. Another man—Roland Wilson—

died in a car accident a few years ago. Emile Jackson—died from cancer in 2011. And an Army Master Sergeant, Robert Campbell, was murdered while on leave in New York City in 2004. Can you imagine? The guy spends a career in the Army without getting a scratch on him; then he visits the Big Apple and gets killed. Go figure.

"Anyway, I eliminated Bishop, the three Marines, and the four men I just mentioned. That left seven names. All of them got out of the service either immediately or shortly after they left Afghanistan. I figured the addresses on file were probably worthless. Then I got a brain flash and checked Veterans Administration records. You know, maybe some of these men got VA loans, or took courses under the GI Bill, or accessed the VA medical system. In any case, I thought I might find more current addresses there." Collins paused. "You may want to down that drink before I continue."

"I'm okay," O'Neil said.

Collins shrugged and finished his own drink. "So, I inputted a name in the VA database—guy named Jeffrey Schmitt. The most recent entry in his file—just two weeks ago—was a request for Veterans Burial Benefits. I typed in the next name—Lawrence Goldstein—and I got the same damned thing. Request for burial benefits a week ago. I thought that was a little strange. I mean, what are the odds? Then I input Robert Zimmerman's name. Nothing. The same with a guy named David Hood. After that, I entered Ralph Connors, Ernest Butler, and Clay Elmer's names. All three had burial benefits requests on record. You gotta figure that's a high ratio of former servicemen from one unit dying so young, in their twenties and thirties. But get this! Connors, Butler, and Elmer also died within the last few weeks. That's eight men from the SLSD, including your three Marines, who died over the past thirty days. And they didn't just die. All of them were murdered. Nine of the fifteen men assigned to the SLSC, including Robert Campbell who was killed in 2004, have been murdered."

"That leaves Bishop, Zimmerman, and Hood still alive," O'Neil said.

Collins stared at O'Neil. "The look on your face would be comical under most any other circumstances. You look as shocked as I am."

"Is that it?"

"Oh, no. I gotta tell you, Dennis, I was sweating bullets, freaked out. But I was hooked; so I tried something else. I had two names unaccounted for on my list—Zimmerman and Hood. I called the telephone numbers from their files. The number for Zimmerman was still good; a lady answered. Julie Zimmerman, Robert Zimmerman's mother. She cried when I asked to speak to her son. You want to guess what she tells me?"

O'Neil shook his head. "Don't tell me. Her son was killed in the last few weeks."

"You got it! Somebody put a bullet in his head. Zimmerman didn't show up in VA records because his mother had yet to claim burial benefits. That's nine guys murdered in less than thirty days. I can't believe any of this, but it's true and it scares the shit out of me. I tried the same thing with the telephone number in the Hood file, but I got a recording with no name mentioned. I've got no idea if the number's any good or if it's been reassigned to someone else. Hood got VA benefits to go to school, but the number in the VA database wasn't any good either."

Collins passed the piece of paper to O'Neil. "Here's all the information I was able to pull up. Names, dates of death, addresses, phone numbers." Collins paused to pull his chair even closer to the table and lowered his voice to barely a whisper. "You're on your own from now on," he said. "I don't know what's happening, but I'm not ashamed to admit I'm scared. Including Robert Campbell, we've got ten men murdered out of fifteen who served together ten years ago. Nine of them killed in the last thirty days. There are only two alive—Hood and Bishop—out of the fifteen, as far as I know. Hood could be dead. Bishop might be on a target list, too."

Collins abruptly stood up. He pushed his chair under the table and leaned over the chair back. "Don't tell anyone where you got this information. Remember it's classified." He pointed a finger at O'Neil and added, "Don't call me anymore."

O'Neil didn't have time to thank Collins before the Marine walked out of the bar.

Detective Jennifer Ramsey had pulled together all the information available on David Hood. She wanted desperately to sit down and talk with the man, but he'd dropped off the face of the earth. No one at his company headquarters seemed to know where he was—or wasn't talking, and every time she called his father's number in Philadelphia, the answering machine told her to leave a message. She'd left three, so far. She needed to go to Philadelphia and try to find Hood.

Chief of Detectives Croken typed at his computer keyboard when Ramsey knocked on his door jamb.

"Chief, you got a second?"

Croken held up a finger signaling her to wait. When he finished typing, he looked up and pointed at a chair in front of his desk.

"I haven't had any success finding David Hood in Bethesda. There's a good chance he's with his father in Philadelphia."

"So, you want to go there?"

"Right."

"I'll authorize one week of travel expenses. Take your unmarked. And I'll call the Philadelphia P.D. to let them know you'll be in their jurisdiction and that you'll be armed."

"Thanks, Chief."

"Try not to shoot anyone while you're there."

In his "Read" file, Bishop found a one-page report from an assistant. The Subject line read: "Apr 20, 0710 hours. Computer Inquiry, Special Logistical Support Detachment." Sweat formed on his brow and his face got hot. He really hadn't expected any inquiry into the SLSD. While he scanned the report, his concern rose. A Gunnery Sergeant Samuel Collins from the Marine Personnel Office had initiated an inquiry. Collins now had the names of every man in the old unit. Bishop knew that thirteen of the fourteen men who'd served under him in the SLSD were dead. He was confident his hired assassins would soon take care of Hood. But dead men might tell tales, especially if Collins kept snooping.

Bishop buzzed for his assistant and told him to bring any other copies of the report into his office. When the man entered with the one copy he had made and handed it over, Bishop instructed him to purge his computer of any record of the report. Bishop then ran the original and copy through a paper shredder.

Bishop sat in his office and stared at the ceiling. As far as he knew, David Hood was still alive. And now he had another problem: Gunnery Sergeant Samuel Collins. He took out his cellphone and dialed a number.

"Yeah?"

"Paladin?"

"Who is this?"

"Talon," Bishop said, using the code name Paladin knew.

"What can I do for you?"

"I want to place another order."

"How big an order?"

"One."

"Name, please."

"Gunnery Sergeant Samuel Collins. I'll wire work and home addresses to you shortly."

"What's the timing?"

"A-S-A-P."

"Wire the fee."

APRIL 21

CHAPTER 21

Jennifer Ramsey had tossed and turned most of the night in the queen-sized bed in her Philadelphia hotel room. She'd counted every flower in the wallpaper accent trim at the top of the walls three times. She'd tried to watch a late movie, but couldn't concentrate. She could normally drop off as soon as her head hit the pillow, even in a strange bed. But her mind had been in a whirl since she plugged in her laptop the night before and, on a lark, inputted the name *David Hood* in Google. An article about the bombing in Bethesda popped up. She knew more than anyone else about that—except for the bomber himself—and was about to erase the article, when something caught her eye. The article mentioned Carmela Hood's maiden name: Bartolucci. Carmela Bartolucci-Hood was the daughter of a former Mafia chieftain. Could there be a mob connection to the deaths of Hood's wife and children?

At 5 a.m., Jennifer abandoned hope of sleeping and got out of bed. After a thirty minute jog on downtown streets, she showered, dressed, and ordered breakfast from room service. She'd wait until a reasonable hour and drive to the Hood residence in South Philadelphia.

Rodney Strong and Zeke McCoy arrived in Philadelphia on a Delta flight from Atlanta at 7 a.m. They'd worked together on several occasions and had a long and successful history as hired killers. Their client, code-named Talon, had used them twice before to remove business opponents.

Strong and McCoy were native Georgians who grew up around guns and took their weapons skills into the U.S. Army and became Army Rangers, where they honed and complemented their skills with a variety of other talents: survival and hand-to-hand combat training; explosives fabrication; sniper training. They were the products of a very efficient military training program funded by the taxpayers. Now they employed their skills exclusively against some of those same taxpayers. Neither of the men had ever gone to war on behalf of their nation and had never killed an enemy of their country. But they'd killed several dozen citizens who'd in some way alienated the wrong people.

The Georgians made enough money to dress well, eat at the best restaurants, and fly first-class, but they still talked like the under-educated hicks they were. However, they usually didn't say much. They appeared to be two well-dressed businessmen on their way to a meeting. They were businessmen of a sort . . . they performed a service for a fee.

Their target in Philly was a business executive named David Hood. They had the target's photograph and address. They didn't know if the man was married or single, was a father, went to church on Sunday, coached little league, or supported the United Way. They couldn't have cared less. They planned to take care of business this morning, in time to catch the early afternoon return flight to Atlanta.

It took them an hour to pick up a Ford Explorer from Hertz, to drive to a black market weapons dealer they knew, then to drive to Rosemont Street, and to reconnoiter the target's father's residence—where they'd been told Hood might be holed up. They circled the block and found a restaurant parking lot where Strong, in the rear seat of the Explorer, changed from his suit to a USPS mail carrier's uniform—a disguise he'd used before. McCoy then drove back to the Hood's block on Rosemont. Halfway down the block, he noticed a black Lincoln Towncar double-parked in front of the Hood residence. The Lincoln's trunk lid and two rear doors were open. McCoy pulled into a parking place on the street, eight car lengths from the Lincoln. He stayed in the car while Strong got out and approached the house.

From his vantage point in a rocker by a second story window in the Galante house across from the Hood residence, another one of Gino's geriatric "watchers" saw the Explorer slow down as it passed in front of him. He didn't do anything about it until, a few minutes later, the Explorer returned and parked up the street. He immediately put down his coffee cup and a chocolate biscotti and phoned Gino's command center. He told Gino a car drove past the house, then came back, and had now parked. One guy stayed with the car while a second man, dressed like a mailman, was on foot.

Gino hung up and called Frankie Siracusa on his cellphone. "Frankie, my lookout tells me a brown Ford Explorer just parked on Rosemont. One guy behind the wheel and a second guy dressed like a mailman. How about you send a guy by there to check things out."

"Boss," Frankie replied, "Paulie and I are still on Rosemont. At the Hood's. We got stuck on Broad Street because of an accident. We just got to their house ten minutes ago. Remember you told me to bring them here so they could pick up some clothes. David and Peter are just now leaving the house. Hey, I see the mailman."

Rodney Strong was confident. People always opened their doors for a mailman, especially if they thought he might be delivering a special package. But instead of "special packages," Strong carried a MAC-10 in his mailbag. His eyes moved from the Hood residence to the Lincoln. Two men sat in the front seat. Then movement to his left drew his eyes back to the front porch of the residence. He immediately recognized his target, swung the mailbag from his side to his chest, and reached for the weapon.

"Goddammit, Frankie, get the hell out of there," Gino shouted. "That ain't no mailman! They don't deliver this early."

David followed Peter down from the porch, tossed their bags into the open car trunk, and slammed the trunk lid shut. Peter walked around to the open rear right side door and got in. David turned to the other side of the car, when he heard footsteps behind him. He looked over his shoulder just when Frankie screamed, "David, get in the car, quick!" Fifty feet away, David saw a man pull a weapon from a leather bag. The man went from a fast walk to a run.

A hand grabbed his arm, pulled him along the side of the vehicle, and pushed him into the rear seat of the Lincoln. David heard automatic gunfire erupt and the thump of bullets against the Lincoln's reinforced steel shell. Then the answering sounds of a fired pistol. David righted himself on the seat and looked out the still-open door. Frankie was returning fire. Then Frankie groaned and fell to the pavement.

Detective Ramsey saw the double-parked black Lincoln forty yards ahead on the one-way street, just as she heard the unmistakable sounds of gunfire. She slammed the brakes of her Crown Victoria and screeched to a stop. As she snatched her .38 Special from her purse on the seat next to her, she opened the driver side door and jumped from the car.

David leaped out of the Lincoln and crouched next to Frankie. The sound of the automatic weapon had been replaced by the *pop-pop-pop* of a pistol. He couldn't see who fired it, but he saw a mailman sprint back up the street. David grabbed the pistol from Frankie's hand and fired at the man. He tossed the weapon through the open car door to Peter and dragged Frankie into the back seat.

Paulie Rizzo, Gino's driver and second bodyguard, floored the accelerator and the powerful engine leaped forward. The open door David had jumped through slammed shut. David looked back through the rear window and saw the mailman get into a brown Ford Explorer. Then he saw the oddest thing in the middle of all the hell that was busting loose—a woman ran in a combat crouch along the sidewalk, just ten yards from the Explorer. She used parked cars for cover. The pistol in her hand appeared to buck several times.

"What the hell did I just walk into?" Strong yelled. "I thought this hit was supposed to be easy. And who the hell was that broad?"

"Did you get Hood?" McCoy said.

"Hell, I don't know. I did more ducking than shooting. I think I hit one guy."

Ramsey's heart raced, her pulse pounded in her throat as she ran back to her car. She thought she'd recognized Hood, but wasn't certain. She'd driven right into the middle of a gun battle that had all the telltale signs of a professional hit. She threw the Crown Vic's shifter into DRIVE and raced after the Explorer, but had to brake when a garbage truck pulled out of an alley and blocked her.

While the Lincoln's engine roared and catapulted the vehicle down the narrow street, Paulie remembered the call from Gino. He picked up the phone from the front seat and tossed it back to Peter. "See if Gino's still on the line."

"Gino, you there?" Peter said.

"Where do you think I am?"

"Some guy shot at us! Frankie got hit in the arm. Everyone else's okay. But we got a tail. A brown Ford Explorer."

"Which way are you headed?" Gino demanded.

"East on Rosemont."

"All right," Gino said, "here's what you do. Head south to Roosevelt Park. I'll call Bobby Galupo to send some guys there. You got it?"

"I got it," Peter replied. "We should be there in fifteen minutes." Peter then relayed Gino's instructions to Paulie.

Paulie was able to put a little distance between them and the Explorer, but not enough to lose it. While David bandaged Frankie's arm with strips of cloth he tore from his shirt, Peter leaned over the front seat and took the two pistols and the Uzi from the car's weapons box.

Paulie zigzagged through South Philadelphia streets. He tried to avoid sideswiping parked cars—with limited success—as he careened around the corners of the narrow streets. When he finally entered Roosevelt Park, he punched the car's accelerator to the floor and slalomed around the serpentine lanes inside the park.

Peter suddenly yelled, "Look out!"

A city crew trimming tree branches that overhung the road had parked their bucket boom truck in the middle of the road. Three men stood around the truck; one man was in a bucket at the end of a thirty-foot boom. There was no room to pass the truck, and the curbs on either side were too high for the Lincoln to drive over. Paulie hit the brakes. The car swerved sideways and came to a stop with the driver's side facing the oncoming Explorer.

Zeke McCoy saw the other car slide to a stop, its tires smoking, and stopped the Ford Explorer about seventy feet away. He and Strong got out and walked toward the Lincoln. Still forty feet away, they raised their weapons. The four tree trimming guys gawked at them, and then the three on the ground raced away, leaving their co-worker stranded in the bucket. McCoy and Strong fired their weapons. The MAC-10s chattered; bullets thudded and clanged against the Lincoln's skin. They didn't notice their rounds hadn't penetrated the Lincoln's body or windows until they'd emptied their magazines.

David was the only one in the Lincoln who fully understood the vehicle's qualities. While Peter, Frankie, and Paulie dived to the floor and covered their heads with their hands, David kept an eye on the two men outside. As soon as he saw they'd emptied their magazines, he opened the right rear door and jumped out, raised the Uzi over the top of the roof, and shouted, "Drop your weapons."

Zeke McCoy was a wise country boy with loads of common sense. It took him only a split second to realize his predicament and to drop his weapon. But it was his bad luck that his partner had just inserted a fresh magazine into his weapon.

McCoy shouted, "Don't!" as Strong raised his weapon. The man on the far side of the Lincoln immediately opened fire.

McCoy groaned, "Shit!" as rounds struck his body. He fell to the pavement and tried to scream. But no words came out. His body shook and he suddenly couldn't breathe. And then he felt nothing.

Frankie Siracusa stepped from the Lincoln as four of Bobby Galupo's men in a black Escalade stormed onto the scene. Frankie yelled, "Paulie, check on David and Peter. Get them into one of the other cars." Then he whipped out his cellphone, called Galupo, and briefed him.

"Is the Lincoln drivable?"

Frankie checked and then told Gino: "Lots of dents and pitted glass. The tires are "run flats," so we can get it outta here. The vehicle the gunmen were in looks fine, too."

"Good!" Galupo said. "Put the bodies of the two killers inside their car. Take it over to the moving company. I'll call with instructions."

CHAPTER 22

Dennis O'Neil's flight landed at O'Hare International Airport at 11:15 a.m. Although he hadn't slept in over twenty-four hours, he was too worked up to go home. He drove to his office, where he again reviewed the information Sam Collins had given him. There was no question in his mind his next step was to locate the unaccounted-for man on Sam's list: David Hood. Information on Hood was readily available on Google. He pulled up an article about a bombing at Hood's home in Bethesda, Maryland in which Hood's wife and kids were killed. "Holy shit!" he muttered. Had Hood also been targeted for death? But the cop in O'Neil bubbled to the front of his mind. Had Hood arranged the deaths of his family members? Could Hood also be behind the deaths of the men who served in the SLSD?

He learned from Google that Hood was the principal shareholder of a company named Security Systems, Ltd. He found a telephone number online for the company's headquarters, called it, and was routed to a man named Warren Masters.

"Mr. Hood is out of the office," Masters told him. "What may I ask is the nature of your business with Mr. Hood?"

"It's a personal matter," O'Neil said. He gave Masters his cellphone number.

O'Neil went back to Sam Collins's list of names. Hood had entered the Army from Philadelphia. His father's name was Peter

J. Hood. He called 4-1-1 for Philadelphia and discovered there was one Peter J. Hood listed on Rosemont Street, at the same address that David Hood had listed as his residence when he entered the service. He asked the operator to connect him.

"Hello."

"My name is Dennis O'Neil. I'm a detective with the Chicago Police Department. May I please speak with Mr. Hood? David Hood."

"Mr. Hood ain't home."

"Can you tell me when he's expected?"

"Not in the near future," the man responded. "Leave your number and I'll see if I can get a message to him."

O'Neil terminated the call. He closed his eyes and rubbed the middle of his forehead. *What now? I wonder if the Bethesda P.D. knows anything.* Dennis pulled up the Bethesda Police Department on Google, found its telephone number, and called. He was routed through the police switchboard to the Detective Bureau. The officer who he talked to told O'Neil no one had been able to locate Hood since the funeral. The detective now in charge of the investigation was a Jennifer Ramsey and she was out of town. O'Neil left a message.

As soon as Rudy Anderson, a rookie Bethesda cop who manned the phones in the Detective Bureau, replaced the receiver after he took down a message from a Chicago detective named O'Neil, Detective Roger Cromwell landed on him like a buzzard on carrion. "Did I hear you say Ramsey was out of town?"

"Yeah, Detective. Philadelphia. She called in a coupla' hours ago. Said she's trying to find David Hood."

"Who was that you just talked to?" Cromwell asked.

"Some Chicago cop."

"You hear anything else from this Chicago cop, or from Ramsey, for that matter, I want to know."

The cop gave Cromwell a sour look and said, "I thought you were off the Hood case."

Cromwell bent at the waist and stuck his nose in the rookie's face. "You fuckin' with me, Anderson?"

"No . . . no, sir."

"I didn't think so," Cromwell said and walked away.

Dennis O'Neil answered his phone.

"Did you just call a number in Philadelphia?" a man asked.

"Who is this?"

"That's of absolutely no importance. Answer my question or I'll hang up."

"Okay! Okay!" Dennis said. "Yeah, I called a number in Philadelphia a few minutes ago."

"What number did you call?"

Dennis recited the Hood number.

"All right, Detective. I'm a friend of David Hood's. You won't be able to contact him unless you've got a damn good reason."

"Look, Mister, maybe I'll tell you why I called if you tell me why you're screening his calls."

After a pause, the man said, "Because assassins have tried to kill him three times in the past week."

The full import of the man's words struck Dennis like a lightning bolt. Hood could now be moved from the "Suspect" column to the "Potential Victim" column. O'Neil had a momentary sinking feeling. That left him without a suspect in the murders of eight men. Except, perhaps, Rolf Bishop, which made no sense. He circled Bishop's name on the list and drew in question marks next to it. But why would a top CIA guy murder a bunch of average citizens? Bishop could be a target, as well. But the guy probably had bodyguards around him. He wouldn't be an easy target.

O'Neil said, "There have been eight murders around the country in the last few weeks. I believe there may be a connection between those murders and the murders of David Hood's wife and kids. I need to talk with him as soon as possible. He may be able to help me establish a motive for these killings."

"Okay, Detective O'Neil," the man said. "Here's how you're gonna get to talk to Mr. Hood."

O'Neil put down the phone and stared at it. This was getting more complicated by the minute. He thought about trying to contact Rolf Bishop. As far as he knew, Bishop was still alive. But he wasn't ashamed to admit that a confrontation with a CIA senior official about several murders was not his idea of a good time. He'd never been a conspiracy buff and didn't think of himself as being paranoid, but that didn't mean there weren't boogey men around the corner. "Oh shit, what have I got—?" The ringing telephone interrupted him.

"Hello!" he said, louder than he'd really intended. "Dennis O'Neil."

"This is Detective Jennifer Ramsey of the Bethesda Police Department. I got a page you called me."

O'Neil moderated his tone. "Thanks for returning my call, Detective Ramsey. I'm a detective with the Chicago Police Department. I wondered if you could provide some information about a case you're working."

"Which case?"

"Last name's Hood. I understand his wife and kids were killed in an explosion. Can you tell me anything about it?"

"How about you give me your badge number and I'll call Chicago and verify you are who you say you are."

O'Neil recited his badge number, spelled his full name, and said, "Please call me right back. It's important."

O'Neil wondered if Detective Ramsey would call back. Fifteen minutes later, his telephone rang. He breathed a sigh of relief when he saw it was from the Bethesda area code.

"O'Neil."

"Jennifer Ramsey, Detective."

"Thanks for calling back."

"I'm intrigued that a Chicago cop is interested in David Hood."

"It's a long story. For now, I hope it'll suffice to tell you it has to do with eight murders around the country."

Ramsey remained silent for a few seconds and then said, "What I can tell you is that someone wants David Hood dead. Three hours ago, a hit team tried to take him out in front of his father's house in Philadelphia."

"How did you learn about it?" he asked.

"Because I was right in the middle of it."

"What happened?"

"I was trying to track down David Hood when bullets started flying. I fired at the men who shot at Hood. Unfortunately, when I tried to follow them, I got blocked by a garbage truck. I don't know what happened after that."

"Was Hood hit?" O'Neil asked.

"I don't think so," Ramsey said. "But I can't be sure. He had armed men with him who fired at the attackers. They sped away from the scene, followed by the hit men."

"What armed men?"

Ramsey paused again. "I don't know for sure, but I'd guess they were Bartolucci's men."

"Bartolucci?"

"Gino Bartolucci. Former Don of the Philadelphia mob. David Hood's father-in-law."

O'Neil's mind whirled with all he'd just heard. Maybe there was more to this than just the Special Logistics Support Command. He felt a knot grow in his gut.

"We need to meet, Detective," O'Neil said. "As soon as possible. Maybe we can help one another."

APRIL 22

CHAPTER 23

An unmarked moving van left Philadelphia just after midnight and followed the Interstate to Washington D.C. The driver drove at the speed limit, used his turn signals whenever necessary, and carefully observed traffic signals and stop signs. He wasn't about to be stopped by a cop.

At a few minutes past 4 a.m., the driver pulled the van into a parking lot near the Georgetown University campus. He and his passenger—both Galupo Family soldiers—left the cab and walked to the back of the van, opened the lock, and jerked out the pins that held the back doors in place. They secured the doors to each side of the van and pulled out two metal ramps. The passenger walked up one of the ramps, took an old Army-issue gas mask from a hook in the cargo bay, and put it over his head. He got behind the wheel of a brown Ford Explorer and started the vehicle. After he carefully backed out the SUV, he parked it, and left the engine running. The two men replaced the metal ramps and closed and secured the van doors. The passenger returned to the SUV and, still wearing the gas mask, drove it to a residential street in Georgetown seven blocks from the campus.

He parked in a space a block up from the address he'd been given, left the vehicle, removed the gas mask, and walked sixty yards uphill to a cross street, where the van waited. He stuffed the gas mask under a thick, low-growing juniper bush, climbed into the van's cab, and told the driver, "Let's go home."

According to her daily schedule, at exactly 6:15 a.m., Dorothy White-Simpson took her two Pekinese for their morning constitutionals. The dogs decided to pee on a very large maple tree next to a brown Explorer. Precious and Tinkerbell watered the maple, while Mrs. White-Simpson warily looked around the street. After all, one could never be too careful—even in gentrified Georgetown. She scrunched her nose and looked down at Precious and Tinkerbell and wondered if one of them might be sick. The stench that assailed her nostrils was overpowering. Then her gaze fell on the brown vehicle by the curb. At first, Dorothy thought her eyes deceived her. She stepped closer, and the stench got stronger. She dragged the dogs with her, held her nose, and peered through the vehicle's rear passenger window.

A woman's screams alerted Rolf Bishop's two bodyguards seated in a black Suburban parked in front of Bishop's townhouse. They jumped from their vehicle. One man ran up the street toward a screeching woman, while the other moved up the stairs to Bishop's house and pounded on the door. Bishop opened it almost immediately.

"What happened?" Bishop demanded. "Who's screaming?"

"Not sure," the guard said. "Stay inside; keep the door locked." Then he ran back down to the street and raced uphill to join his partner. He found him attempting to calm a woman tangled in a couple leashes attached to two yapping dogs.

"What's wrong, ma'am?" one of the agents asked.

The woman babbled and pointed a shaky hand at the Explorer. Apparently, the sight of dead bodies and pistols was too much for her. She collapsed into the arms of one of the agents, who unceremoniously dumped her on the pavement.

The agents looked inside the vehicle, saw two bullet-riddled, bloody bodies there, and immediately drew their sidearms.

Normally, the CIA would immediately call the local authorities if one of its employees found dead bodies in a vehicle. But because these bodies were located just a short distance from the front door of a CIA Deputy Director, one of the agents called in a damage control team from Langley. Before that team could arrive, Bishop's bodyguards opened the SUV's back doors and were immediately overcome by the stink of decomposing flesh and body wastes. One man vomited; the other gagged. They slammed shut the doors and backed away from the vehicle. One of them, however, had glimpsed an envelope pinned to the jacket on one of the bodies. He reholstered his pistol, put a handkerchief over his nose and mouth, held his breath, reopened one of the car doors, leaned into the back seat, and pulled the envelope free. After he reclosed the door and backed away from the car, he read the words typed on the front of the envelope: "For Rolf Bishop's Eyes Only."

The agent held the envelope by its edges, between thumb and forefinger, raced to Bishop's door, and knocked. When Bishop opened the door, the agent quickly briefed him about the bodies and the call he'd made to headquarters, then held out the envelope. Bishop glanced at it, grunted at the agent, snatched the envelope, and closed the door in his face.

With no regard for forensic evidence, Bishop tore open the envelope and pulled out a single sheet of paper on which was typed: "Three up and three down. Now it's my turn at bat."

Rolf Bishop was confused. He leaned against the front door, note in hand. 'Three up, three down.' What did it mean? He pushed off the door, spun around, and opened the front door. One of his CIA guards ran over to him as he reached the sidewalk.

"You shouldn't be out here, sir," the man said.

Bishop ignored him and strode up the slate sidewalk to where the other guard stood. He walked over to the Explorer and bent over. There were two corpses in the back seat. Bishop didn't recognize the faces, but he had a gut feeling he was staring at Rodney Strong and Zeke McCoy. He hadn't heard from the killers and there had been no news about David Hood. Bishop straightened and backed away from the car.

"You recognize these guys?" one of his bodyguards asked.

"How the hell would I know who these people are?" Bishop responded. He pulled the lapels of his silk robe across his chest and tightened the sash. Then, with as much control as he could muster, he marched back to his home.

"What the fuck!" he shouted after he slammed the front door and collapsed into an armchair in the entryway. 'Three up, three down.' Then it hit him. He'd sent one hardened criminal, Montrose Toney, and two professional assassins, Rodney Strong and Zeke McCoy, after one businessman, David Hood. He hadn't heard a word from Toney; and now Strong and McCoy, both dead, had been dumped at the threshold of his house. Three up, three down.

How in God's name could David Hood have made all this happen? He remembered Hood as a quiet, almost reclusive young non-com, who did as he was told and never caused trouble. He knew Hood had extensive training as an Army Ranger, and had been decorated for bravery in action, but Jesus, that was a decade ago.

CHAPTER 24

Dennis O'Neil carried a large, hard-sided briefcase and a soft-sided overnight bag from the airplane and walked the length of the Jetway into the Philadelphia International Airport terminal. In the baggage area, he looked at people's faces. Detective Ramsey had told him she'd meet him here. He spied a woman in her thirties who stood off to the side and held a piece of paper with "O'Neil" hand-printed on it. He walked over to her and asked, "Detective Ramsey?"

Ramsey stuck out her hand and smiled. "Yes," she said. "I'm Jennifer Ramsey. Nice to meet you."

O'Neil placed his briefcase on the floor and took her hand in his. He quickly looked her up and down and thought, nice package: five-eight, swimsuit model legs, drop-dead figure, blonde hair, and classically beautiful. O'Neil thought how nice it would be to be thirty again. He met Ramsey's gaze and noticed the hard set of her hazel-colored eyes. All business.

"Call me Dennis," he said and released her hand.

"Welcome to Philadelphia, Dennis."

"City of Brotherly Love," O'Neil said. "Seen any of that brotherly love since you got here?"

Ramsey laughed. "A little," she said. "I left my car out by the curb. Found a friendly cop who offered a little professional courtesy."

"See," O'Neil said, "brotherly love."

They took the escalator down one level and walked outside

to a Crown Victoria parked by the curb. He tossed his overnight bag in the back seat, got in the front passenger seat, and placed his briefcase between them.

While she drove away from the terminal, O'Neil reached inside his suit jacket pocket and extracted a folded sheet of paper. "I got instructions here I'm supposed to follow." He told Ramsey to take the highway to the downtown exit, then to follow Market Street across Broad Street to the Reading Terminal Market.

"I want you to let me out on the south side of the market, then circle the block. I was told to go through the market to the north side. There's supposed to be a Cadillac waiting for me there. Follow that car."

"What then?" she asked.

O'Neil raised his hands as if to say, who knows? He'd agreed to work with Ramsey because she'd been able to provide information about Hood he couldn't come up with himself. Especially Hood's relationship with Gino Bartolucci. The organized crime connection had intrigued O'Neil. First the CIA, now the mob. Besides, it was always better to have a partner to watch your back. He turned to look at Ramsey's profile and said, "Just make sure you hang back. I don't want whoever picks me up to know they're being followed."

When she stopped at the market's south entrance, O'Neil got out, briefcase in hand, and entered the building. He walked through the sprawling complex to the north door, exited the building, and saw a silver-colored Cadillac with heavily tinted windows parked at the curb. He walked over to the right rear car door and placed his ID up against the window, just as he'd been told to do. The door opened and a man in the back told O'Neil to get in. The man slid across the seat, making room for O'Neil. Only a driver was up front. The man in the back seat took the briefcase from O'Neil, lifted it over the front seat, and placed it next to the driver.

He gave O'Neil a squint-eyed look and said, "No luggage?"

Damn! O'Neil thought. I left my bag in Ramsey's car. "Uh," he said, "I left it in a locker at the airport."

The guy just nodded, faced forward, and told the driver to take off. Then he turned back toward O'Neil and said, "I'm going to frisk you, then I'll blindfold you."

O'Neil cooperated. Then he asked several questions, but got the same response each time: "Mr. Hood will explain everything to you."

O'Neil tried to count left and right turns, but after five minutes lost track of them. He guessed the car was soundproofed because he couldn't hear anything outside the vehicle.

Just past a sign that read Chestnut Hill Cricket Club, Jennifer Ramsey watched the Cadillac make a left turn onto a residential street, slowly pass two gated entrances, and then pull into a driveway blocked by an imposing wrought-iron gate anchored on both sides by seven-foot-high stone walls that appeared to front a very large estate. She continued up the tree-shaded street past the entrance, turned left at the first corner, parked on the street, and waited.

Cornelius Capital Resources owned the three-and-a-half-acre estate the Cadillac turned into. CCR operated several hundred consumer loan offices in twenty-seven states and Washington, D.C. The company was, in turn, owned by *Credit d'Or-Belgique*, headquartered in Brussels. *Credit d'Or-Belgique* was a wholly owned subsidiary of *Societa Financiaria*, a Milan-based investment firm. Gino Bartolucci owned *Societa Financiaria*—lock, stock, and barrel.

Located in one of Philadelphia's oldest and most exclusive suburbs, the Chestnut Hill estate was spectacular. If the founder of the merchant banking firm who built the mansion on fifteen acres in the latter part of the nineteenth century could have known his dissolute great-grandson had forfeited the property to a notorious Italian gangster, he would have risen from the grave for revenge. The crack-addicted great-grandson had borrowed massively from Gino's loan-sharking operation. But the deed to the mansion had squared all debts between the two men.

Jennifer heard the Cadillac's driver honk his car horn and saw him open his window. A guard, an enormous man with muscles that threatened to bust the seams of his sharkskin suit, stepped out of a shack on the other side of the gate. He eyeballed the car and driver, returned to the guardhouse, and opened the electric-powered gate. The driver steered through the gateway and it closed as soon as the Cadillac's rear bumper cleared the gate.

The man in the Cadillac's back seat removed O'Neil's blindfold. O'Neil turned his face away from the glare coming through his window. When his eyes adjusted to the light, he saw they were slowly moving up a long, curved driveway bordered by dense trees and shrubs. The car stopped in a circular courtyard with an enormous fountain at its center.

The driver took O'Neil's briefcase inside the house, while the second man ran around the car and opened O'Neil's door.

O'Neil looked up at a three-story stone mansion. Several dormers with large windows punctuated its steeply-pitched gray slate roof. Expansive, perfectly-manicured lawns extended from the house to a narrow strip of trees that separated the grass from the exterior walls. Flower gardens bordered the walls of the house. A man came out of the mansion's big front door and walked down the steps.

He extended his hand and said, "Detective O'Neil, my name is David Hood. I understand you want to talk with me."

"Do I ever, Mr. Hood."

Hood led O'Neil into the mansion and took him to a small but lavishly furnished drawing room, with carved crown moldings, floor-to-ceiling built-in book cases, and plush leather furniture. Hood pointed to a stuffed chair. After O'Neil sat down, Hood sat across from him on a sofa. Almost immediately, a maid carried in a tray laden with a pitcher of lemonade, a bowl of ice, ice tongs, and two large glasses. She filled the glasses halfway to the top with ice, and poured the lemonade. She left without a word.

"My friend tells me you are investigating several murders that could be connected to the death of my family. Is that true?"

"Is your friend the man who called me in Chicago?" O'Neil asked.

"That's right."

"Well, your friend has a strange way of doing things. But what he told you is correct. Except the word 'several' is an understatement. As best as I can make out, eight men have been murdered in the past month or so. Their deaths look like the work of a professional killer or killers, and each and every one of the victims served with you in Afghanistan."

Hood's mouth dropped open.

"I won't go into how I originally stumbled on this whole business, but I *will* tell you that of the fifteen men assigned to the Special Logistical Support Detachment, including the unit commander, only two are alive today. You and Rolf Bishop, the new CIA Deputy Director."

"You know all this for a fact?"

"Yeah."

"So, what are you doing here?"

"I started out wanting to find out why three Marines were murdered. But it's gotten much bigger than that. About half of the men you served with in the SLSD have been murdered. Mob style."

O'Neil watched Hood's reaction, alert for a "tell." Hood's eyes narrowed and his jaw tightened.

Hood said, "If you're suggesting Gino Bartolucci had anything to do with these murders, you've got your head up your ass." Surprise suddenly showed on Hood's face and his mouth formed an "O." "You think I might be involved."

"I'm a good detective, Mr. Hood. I always consider every possibility. But unlike some of my colleagues, I never pre-judge a suspect. I work on the facts. Even you have to admit that your name should be on any list of suspects."

"I'll give you that, Detective. But if you're here to undermine my efforts to find the man who killed my wife and children, I'll have your ass thrown off this property."

"I'm not here to undermine anything. Just being here has put my job and pension in jeopardy. But I'm not going to stop trying to discover who murdered those men. It's become personal to me."

"Have you shared your information with the Feds?"

"Not yet."

"Why not?"

O'Neil hesitated a beat. "I probably should have, but my instincts told me to hold off. Candidly, I don't know who to trust. On the off chance Rolf Bishop is involved in these murders, reporting this to the Feds would have brought the power of the CIA down on me. But even if Bishop is involved, I can't come up with a motive."

David had heard the tape of Montrose Toney's "interrogation" and knew Bishop was behind the attempts on his life. But why would Bishop have put into motion a killing machine responsible for the deaths of so many people? And what had he or the other men he'd served with done to cause Bishop to come after them? "Even with the facts laid out in front of me, I find this whole thing unbelievable, Detective," David said.

"I find it all pretty fantastic myself—and believe me I've seen and heard some mighty grotesque things since I became a cop. I came here because I hope you might shed a little light on this assignment you had in Afghanistan. The Special Logistical Support Detachment. The only thing every one of the murdered men had in common, as far as I've been able to determine, was they served in that unit. What in the name of God did you guys do over there that would make someone try to wipe you all out? And why wait ten years to do it?"

"You got me, Detective."

It took an hour for O'Neil to brief David on all he'd learned about the murdered men. They shot questions at one another for another thirty minutes. The problem for both men was that the only tie between the dead men and Rolf Bishop was the SLSD. David swore there was nothing the unit had done, as far as he knew, that would be reason to commit murder.

"Sure," David said, "the unit's mission was Top Secret, and we stretched the logistical and budget rules, but not to the point someone would want us dead. At least, I don't think so."

They sat in silence for a minute. Then David went to a DVD player and inserted the Montrose Toney interrogation disk. "I think you'll change your thinking after you watch this."

O'Neil sat through the recording without saying a word. When the disk ended, he stared at David Hood and slowly shook his head. "Who the hell produced that disk?"

"None of your business."

"I guess I already knew the answer."

"Let's take a break and eat something," David said to O'Neil. He used his foot to depress a buzzer under the carpet beneath the coffee table. The woman who'd served the lemonade returned to the room.

"What can I do for the *signori*?"

"Rosa, could you bring us something to eat? And perhaps now would be a good time for Mr. Bartolucci and my father to join us."

"*Si, signore*, I will have food for you soon in the dining room. And I will call *i signori Bartolucci e Hood prontamente*."

"*Grazie*, Rosa," David said.

After Rosa left the room, O'Neil asked, "Is this guy Bartolucci the one who called me and gave me instructions?"

"One of his men called you. Gino Bartolucci has probably saved my life twice in the last week. He's also my father-in-law and our host in this palace he calls home. Why don't we go to the dining room? Gino and my father, Peter, will meet us there."

When David introduced Gino and Peter, O'Neil recognized the old Don from news footage he'd seen years earlier. He tried to keep the emotions he felt from showing. Bartolucci had been a bad guy who had ruined a lot of lives. And here he was, a cop who hated everything about the Mob, the guest of a *Mafioso*.

After they were all seated at the table, Rosa brought in *antipasti*. While she walked a giant platter to each person around the table, Gino described each of the items on the platter. He went into a great deal of detail about the correct names and origins of each of the *peperonata, salsiccia, formaggio,* and *vegetale*. The *antipasti* were followed by a pasta dish—penne with sundried tomatoes and calamari. Then plates of veal piccata. Each course was served with an Italian wine.

While Rosa served steaming espresso to the men, a young man

cleared the dinner dishes. The four men sat around the table for hours and rehashed what they knew about the murders and Rolf Bishop.

The meeting finally broke up a few minutes past midnight. "Come on, Detective O'Neil," Gino said, "I'll show you to your room."

O'Neil followed Gino to the bottom of the staircase that led to the floors above. He'd raised a foot to climb the stairs when all hell broke loose. The front door to the mansion flew open and two burly men came through the entryway, struggling to hold onto a writhing, kicking female bundle of fury.

"Get your hands off me, you bastards," the woman yelled. She struck out with a foot, connecting with the shin of one of the men.

Out of breath, the other man said, "We caught her on the wall. She claimed she's with Detective O'Neil."

Gino turned and looked at O'Neil. "You want to explain this?"

O'Neil's face reddened. He looked up and swallowed. "Gentlemen," he said, "I'd like to introduce you to my new partner, Detective Jennifer Ramsey." O'Neil then looked at Ramsey and pointed at Gino. "Jennifer, say hello to Mr. Gino Bartolucci."

Ramsey's eyes widened. Apparently, all she could think to say was, "Oh shit!"

APRIL 23

CHAPTER 25

Dennis O'Neil woke in a dark room at 5:30 a.m. It took him a moment to remember where he was. He hadn't slept very well and his eyes burned. He flipped on a lamp on the nightstand and shielded his eyes against the sudden light. He stretched his arms, worked the kinks out of his shoulders as he admired the richness of his surroundings: hand carved crown moldings at the tops of twelve-foot-high walls, original oil paintings on the walls, antique furniture, and velvet drapes that covered eight-foot-high French doors that opened onto balconies. O'Neil wondered who the asshole was that said crime doesn't pay.

He noticed his soft-sided bag on the floor near the room door. Someone had been kind enough to retrieve it from Ramsey's car. At least he wouldn't have to wear the same clothes he'd had on yesterday. After he showered, shaved, and dressed in jeans and a white dress shirt, he left the room and tiptoed down the hall to the staircase. He'd descended only a few steps when a very large man in a shiny suit appeared at the bottom.

In a hoarse whisper, the man asked, "You need somethin', sir?"

"Thank you," O'Neil said. "I thought I might be able to get a cup of coffee."

They walked to a sunroom where the man told O'Neil to take a seat at a small table and left him there. A second man soon appeared with a silver tray. On the tray were a folded copy of the *Philadelphia*

172

Inquirer, a silver coffee service, a small bowl of fruit, and a plate of pastries. Alone again in the quiet of the room, with the morning sun peeking through the windows, O'Neil opened the newspaper and flipped through the pages. A small article on page 11 caught his eye: "Marine Found Dead."

The article said that Gunnery Sergeant Samuel Collins, a personnel specialist at the Pentagon, had been murdered in his automobile outside his home, killed by one shot to his head. O'Neil's breath caught in his chest. The police stated there had been no witnesses. No suspects. No motive. The article noted that a wife and five children survived Sergeant Collins.

O'Neil felt sick, as low as he'd ever felt. One shot to the head. The same MO as in the slayings of Richard Sykes, Eric Carbajal, Fred Laniewski, and five others. Dennis dropped the newspaper on the table and covered his face with his hands. He didn't just feel sick; he felt heartsick. He recalled how shook up Collins had been when he saw him last. Now that it was too late, he realized Collins's instincts had been better than his own. He thought about calling the D.C. police to tell them what he knew, but abandoned the thought. As he'd told David Hood, he didn't know who to trust anymore.

Ramsey felt rested when she woke at 8 a.m. She looked around the room and shook her head. Wonder what Lieutenant Croken would say about this. She thought she'd better check in with her office as she'd been out of contact for over twenty-four hours. Croken would, at the very least, be worried by now. She suspected he'd be pissed off, too. He didn't like it when his people dropped off his radar screen.

She reached for her purse to get her cellphone and remembered one of Bartolucci's men had confiscated her phone. She dressed and went downstairs. One of the guards stood at the front door.

"I need to use the telephone. I haven't checked in with my office for over twenty-four hours."

The man pointed at a small table in the entrance foyer. "There's a phone in the drawer. Don't tell anyone where you're at."

"Detective Bureau, Rudy Anderson."

"Anderson, it's Jennifer Ramsey. Is Lieutenant Croken in?"

"No, not yet. Can I take a message?"

"That's okay," Ramsey said. "Put me into his voicemail."

When Detective Roger Cromwell entered the Bethesda Detective Bureau offices at ten that morning, he made a beeline to the reception desk. "Anything from Ramsey?" he asked Rudy Anderson.

"Yeah, she called in about two hours ago. Left a message for the lieutenant. But he isn't in yet."

Cromwell crossed the room to the break room and poured himself a cup of coffee. He knew exactly what he would do by the time he reached his desk.

The voicemail system in the Detective Bureau was simple. A caller could leave a message on an individual extension. The owner of the extension could pick up his messages by dialing a common seven-digit number, waiting for a recorded message, and punching in his four-digit extension number. Then he had to enter a security code. Most of the detectives just used their extension number as their security code. It was easier to remember. Cromwell accessed the voicemail system, punched in Croken's four-digit extension, and then held his breath as he tapped in Croken's extension again. He let out his breath when the code worked. He scanned through Croken's messages—eight of them—until he came to Ramsey's message. He was surprised to learn she was in Philadelphia and had connected with David Hood. She went on to say she was convinced of Hood's innocence, mentioned the murders of men who had served with Hood in Afghanistan, and that two more attempts on his life had occurred.

"Sonofabitch," Cromwell said. It appeared that Hood might be innocent, after all, which made Ramsey look good and him look bad.

"That bitch!" he muttered.

What really surprised Cromwell was Ramsey's comment about possible CIA involvement. She mentioned a name: Rolf Bishop.

Cromwell licked his lips. He needed to do something. He had

to find out Ramsey's location.

Cromwell called a contact at the telephone company and told the guy he needed a favor.

At 11:30 a.m., Dennis O'Neil, Peter and David Hood, Gino Bartolucci, and Jennifer Ramsey met around Bartolucci's large mahogany dining table.

O'Neil rolled his shoulders and stretched his neck. He stared at the sheet of paper with the names of the SLSD personnel Sam Collins had given him. He'd briefed the others about everything he'd learned about the SLSD and the deaths of the men who'd served in that unit. He also told the group about his connection to Collins and the Marine's murder.

Gino provided information his men had acquired from Montrose Toney, which implicated Rolf Bishop. But no one had been able to come up with a motive.

"You know, we've talked a lot about the murdered men," Gino said. "But, weren't there others in the unit? I seem to recall there were four more besides David and Bishop."

"That's right," O'Neil said. "But remember they were all accounted for, at least in the sense they all died years ago—according to their military records in two cases, and police and VA records in the other two cases."

"Okay, so humor me," Gino said. "Let's talk about the other four who died years ago."

It took a few minutes for David to talk about Roland Wilson, the man killed in an automobile accident, and Emile Jackson, the one who had died of cancer.

O'Neil added what he'd learned from Collins about the men's deaths. "There was nothing suspicious about those two men's deaths," O'Neil said.

"Who's next on the list?" David asked.

"Andrew King," O'Neil answered.

"God, I can remember my conversation with Captain King as though it happened yesterday," David said. "He went out to the U.S. Army Warehouse Complex in Kabul to try to locate a recent shipment of M-16 and M-4 rifles and ammunition. I volunteered to go, but King told me he'd take care of it. It could have been me who died that day." He told the others in the room how King's body had been found in a Kabul alley. He'd been shot.

They all agreed there was no way they could tie King's death to Bishop.

The last name was Sergeant Robert Campbell's. O'Neil related the story he'd gotten from Sam Collins. "Two kids were necking in a car near a marshy area outside New York City in 2004. Apparently, it was a warm night and the kids had their windows down. They smelled something awful outside the car and the boy stepped out to investigate and found the body."

"You mean the body was just *there* by the side of the road?" Ramsey asked.

"No," O'Neil said. "It had been stuffed into a fifty-five-gallon drum. The top had come off the drum. It had contaminated waste markings on it. The cops in New York assumed it had been an organized crime hit because of the drum and the location where it was discovered. Apparently, it was a popular way and location to dispose of bodies. But when they identified the body, they were surprised. The victim was a soldier, not a New York Family member."

Gino's body fairly vibrated with tension. Dennis O'Neil's tale about Robert Campbell's death, the discovery of the man's body in a fifty-five-gallon drum, and the markings on the drum set off his internal radar. He left the others and placed a call to a private cellphone number in New York City. A man answered.

"This is an old friend from Philadelphia. I need to talk to the boss."

"Would this old friend have a name?" the man asked.

"Tell him it's Gino."

A second later, Gino heard Joey Cataldo's rich baritone voice. "*Come va?*"

"*Bene,*" Gino said. "How would you feel about a visit from an old friend?"

"I am always open to visits from old friends. Especially distinguished old friends. On what day would that visit occur?"

"Tomorrow for dinner at the same place we met on my last visit."

CHAPTER 26

It took Rolf Bishop almost a full day to calm down enough to think rationally. The two dead bodies and the note found inside the Explorer had driven him to fruitless speculation about who could have orchestrated the stunt. It had to be David Hood, he thought. But how could Hood, a small businessman, have tied him to Strong and McCoy?

On Thursday, in his office, and in a much less emotional state, he wrote a list of action items:

1. Declare Hood a clear & present danger to national security.

2. Identify all Hood associates, friends, & family.

3. Get Hood's credit card account numbers. Try to track his movements through purchases.

4. Have the NSA trace calls to and from Hood's phone.

5. Get police to put out APB on Hood's vehicles.

6. Key employees at Hood's company. Any aware of his location?

He reviewed the list and got a sinking feeling. The list was no better than some kid's Christmas gift wish list. Action on any or all of the items on the list would raise red flags that could bring attention to him.

Bishop called in Winfred Kingston, his personal assistant, and told him he needed his help. Kingston was an earnest young man who had been at the Agency for fourteen months.

"I need you to run down some information for me," Bishop said, "and you need to keep this confidential. It's personal, but I think you'll understand after you hear the whole story. Do you recall that explosion in Bethesda about two weeks ago?"

"Yes, sir," Kingston replied. "The one that killed an entire family. They ever catch the people who did it?"

"No," Bishop said. "The local cops have no real suspects. But you're not quite correct. One person survived the blast. His name is David Hood. He served in one of my units in Afghanistan. He was a fine soldier . . . Army Ranger, highly decorated, tremendous potential for advancement. But he left the service after he was badly wounded. Went on to college. Anyway, Hood has vanished since his family was buried. I want you to find him. He may need my help.

"Not only must we find Hood," Bishop continued, "but we must also try to find out who killed his family."

Kingston looked as though he was in orgasmic ecstasy. His face was red and his eyes were wide open. He licked his lips and said, "I would be thrilled to assist, sir."

Bishop handed the list of action items to Kingston. "I promise you, Winfred," he said, "I won't forget your help in this matter."

After he left Bishop's office, Kingston went directly to his desk and used his computer to search the database for every byte of information he could pull up on David Hood. He was a man on a mission. There was no way he would let Bishop down. For the next four hours, he captured all the mundane facts about Hood: date and place of birth; parents; Hood's father's stint with the Army; the deaths of Hood's brother and mother; schools he attended; military service; jobs; Security Systems, Ltd.; foreign travel; date of marriage; children's names and birth dates; tax returns; etc. He pulled up Peter Hood's military file. All for nothing. Then he looked into Carmela Maria Hood's background. He learned her maiden name. He typed "Bartolucci" into the computer.

The computer spewed data—page upon page about Gino Bartolucci. While he scrolled through the information, Winfred Kingston became very excited. Did the Director know Carmela Maria Hood was the daughter of Gino Bartolucci, a Mafia Don?

He reached for his telephone.

"I just bet you could tell me all sorts of little secrets," the thirty-eight-year-old wife of the Secretary of Defense whispered in his ear. Her Texas accent dripped with promise of things to come. When he tilted his head slightly in her direction, Bishop got a full shot of her ample freckled bosom and of the fortune in diamonds and emeralds strategically placed to accent her cleavage. The woman once again squeezed his thigh under the table.

He smiled at her; his white teeth flashed, predator-like. "But Madam, if I told you secrets, then I would have to kill you."

The cabinet secretary's wife tittered, glanced across the table at her much older husband deep in conversation with some senator's wife, again placed a hand on Bishop's leg, and whispered, "Why, Mr. Bishop, you do say the most exciting things."

Once again amazed at the seductive nature of power and position, he was about to slip her his personal card with his private phone number, when another guest, Walter Preston, asked, "Director Bishop, do you think the Russian government will ever be able to break the stranglehold the Mafia has on their country's economy?"

Bishop knew Preston had invested hundreds of millions of dollars in Siberian gas exploration. He understood the man's question wasn't casual. He also knew Preston's partners in the gas deal were top players in the Russian Mafia, the *Bratva*. Preston was fishing for information, perhaps to find out if the CIA knew about his business arrangements and what the CIA might be up to in Russia.

"It would be my suggestion to anyone who wants to do business in the Russian Republic that they attempt to coexist with all centers of influence," Bishop said.

Preston smiled, apparently pleased with the response. He looked as though he was about to say something more when Bishop's cellphone vibrated. Bishop rose from his seat at the dining table, excused himself, walked to the hallway outside the dining room, and took the call.

"What is it, Kingston?" he demanded, irritated at the interruption.

"Mr. Bishop, I have information that could be of interest to you."

Bishop waited for Kingston to continue.

"David Hood's wife's maiden name was Bartolucci. She was the daughter of Gino Bartolucci, the Philadelphia Mafia Don."

Bishop's heartbeat accelerated. Suddenly, a lot of things made sense. If Hood had allied with Bartolucci, then the resources available to Hood were indeed significant. "Good job, Kingston," Bishop said. "Fax the information to my home machine."

He returned to the dining room and apologized to his host and hostess. "Business," he said. "I'm sure you understand."

On the ride to his Georgetown townhome, Bishop considered his next steps. One thing was certain. He would have to eliminate Kingston. The kid could be a liability.

APRIL 24

CHAPTER 27

New York City *Capo*, Joey Cataldo, had been happy to hear from Gino Bartolucci. He'd always liked and respected the old Don. But the call had intrigued him, too. He sipped his Amaretto and thought again that Bartolucci wasn't the type to socialize without some ulterior motive. To Cataldo, and to just about every *Mafioso* in the country, Don Bartolucci was a legend. The man had never been indicted or convicted of any crime, had amassed a fortune, and now lived off the earnings of a score of legitimate enterprises. He was a model for the modern-day *capo*. But while he sat in a private dining room at *Il Stazione* Restaurant in Manhattan and waited for the old Don to show up, he wondered again why, after so many years, Bartolucci had called him.

Cataldo was a phenomenon in his own right. He'd survived while the rest of the leaders of the old Zefferelli Family had either been killed or put away for the rest of their lives. When the Feds brought RICO indictments against the Zefferelli hierarchy, all they could pin on Cataldo was a racketeering conviction for bookmaking. This was such an inconsequential crime, as far as the trial judge was concerned, that Cataldo spent only thirteen months in a Federal Penitentiary. Frankie Zefferelli and several of his lieutenants received life without possibility of parole for murder, drug trafficking, prostitution, gambling, and myriad other crimes. A total of thirteen senior members of the Family were sent away.

After Joey Cataldo got out of prison, he took over the organization. And in a brilliant political maneuver only one week after his release from prison, he invited the Dons from all the crime families to a summit conference in Guadalajara, Mexico.

Cataldo established himself as a visionary leader when he announced to the group he would allow each of the other families to buy into the Zefferelli Family's Caribbean casinos—"to dip their beaks." The acceptance of the offer by the other Dons sent a message to the entire underworld that Joey Cataldo had been accepted and anyone who challenged his authority would challenge the judgment of all of the Families. Of course, what choice did the other Capos have? Cataldo had a huge amount of information about their involvement in narcotics trafficking and had let them know how that information would remain "in a safe place" as long as they supported him.

Il Stazione Ristorante was one of Cataldo's "legitimate" businesses. It was now one of Manhattan's "in" places: dark and intimate, white tablecloths, Deruta ceramics on high shelves, tuxedoed waiters, one of the best wine cellars in the city. Cataldo and one of his bodyguards sat at a corner table in the back, set ten feet away from the next closest table. He swept his hands through his thick, salt-and-pepper mane of hair. He was vain about his looks and his wavy hair had always been a part of that vanity. He knew he was a handsome man—the women had let him know that even before he had power. Even as a teenage street thug, Cataldo attracted the girls. He was tall—six feet four—and still powerfully built.

When Cataldo saw Bartolucci enter the front door, preceded by a powerfully-built man who Cataldo knew was the old man's bodyguard, he stood, buttoned his suit jacket, and waited respectfully. Other than the mass of the older man's belly—which was bigger by at least two belt sizes since Cataldo had seen him last—Bartolucci still exuded authority. While Bartolucci walked toward him, Cataldo did what most people did—he stared at the old man's hands. They were the biggest hands Cataldo had ever seen on a man Bartolucci's size. He thought those hands could snap a man's neck with ease.

They exchanged greetings in Italian and embraced. After the

further formality of introducing their bodyguards to one another, the two Dons took their seats at the table. The bodyguards sat at a table by the front door.

Cataldo and Bartolucci spoke cordially, even affectionately, in whispered tones. Cataldo expressed condolences about Carmela's death and the deaths of Gino's grandchildren. They talked about old times and joked about characters they both had known. Not a word of business was spoken during their two-hour, five-course dinner.

After the waiter brought espresso, Gino said, "Joey, I know you would do anything you could to help me find the *seppia* who killed my angels."

"Of course, Don Bartolucci. You know I'd personally rip the bastard's heart out. But naturally, I would leave that honor to you."

"Well, maybe you *can* help me. I believe the man who killed Carmela and my two grandchildren was really after my son-in-law. I also think the same man killed many other people who were in Afghanistan around the time my son-in-law served there. And I believe I know who that man is. But there is one thing I can't figure out—the reason for the murders. It's important because I need to know if I take revenge against this guy my son-in-law will then be safe. I figure this man has something big to hide. I want to know what that is. And I want to make sure there aren't other people working with this guy." Gino paused. "I've come across some information that maybe someone here in New York can explain. I figure you can probably find out who that might be."

"Don Bartolucci, you know I'll do all in my power to assist you. What is this information you have?"

"It's about a murder, Don Cataldo. I'm hopeful you can ask around, see if anyone knows something about it. You see, one of the men who served with my son-in-law in Afghanistan was killed here in New York back in 2004, just two days after the guy left Afghanistan."

Cataldo was confused. "Don Bartolucci. You have got to know there are a lot of murders in New York. And 2004 was a long time ago." After a beat, Cataldo added, "What would I know about such a murder?"

Bartolucci nodded. "Sure, I understand all that. I'm not saying you know anything about it."

"Of course, Don Bartolucci. What can you tell me about this . . . incident?"

"The police never found the killer. The guy's body was found in a fifty-five-gallon drum."

Cataldo nodded. "Doesn't sound like a random mugging."

"Right!" Bartolucci said. "Even more interesting, the drum the guy was found in had a label that sounded awfully familiar: AWD. I racked my brain and tried to remember why I knew that name. And then it hits me. That was one of Frankie Zefferelli's companies. Atlantic Waste Disposal."

Cataldo knew there were dozens of bodies packed away in drums all over the eastern seaboard. The body Bartolucci referred to could have been dumped by any one of hundreds of wiseguys connected with any one of dozens of criminal organizations. Hell, Cataldo had disposed of three guys in the same way himself, including one around 2004.

"What is it you want me to find out?" Cataldo asked. "You know nobody's about to step forward and admit they killed this guy."

"All I want to know is why this guy was hit. I don't care who killed him."

Cataldo asked, "What was the guy's name?"

"Robert Campbell," Gino replied. "Master Sergeant Robert Campbell."

Cataldo felt a sharp pain in his stomach. He hoped his expression hadn't changed. He couldn't believe Campbell's name had resurfaced after so many years. Cataldo excused himself and walked into the men's room at the back of the restaurant. He paced the floor. He could promise Bartolucci he would try to help him and then do nothing. But he knew the old man was no dummy. If Bartolucci found out he'd been lied to, he would be a dangerously unhappy man.

Cataldo wet a paper towel and pressed it to his eyes. He took a deep breath and returned to the table.

"Don Bartolucci, I gotta tell you I'm uncomfortable about this . . . matter. I don't need to check around about this Robert Campbell."

"Why's that, Don Cataldo?"

"You see, I know who killed Campbell."

"You gotta be shittin' me."

"Bruno Giordano and I were with Frankie Zefferelli. He told us all about this drug connection he had in Afghanistan and how it's about to be shut down. He told us our only contact with the supplier had been this Robert Campbell and he'd suspected all along Campbell was just a messenger boy for the real brains behind the operation. Campbell thought he'd been sent to New York to pick up payment for some dope. But he was there to get whacked."

"Did Zefferelli ever say who the guy was who sent the wire?"

"No, he never said and I don't think he ever knew. He referred to him as "The Priest." But I'll tell you one thing. Whoever that guy was, he was one mean son of a bitch. I mean, he wants a guy taken out who I assume has been his partner. Whatever, Campbell gets whacked and stuffed in a drum."

Cataldo paused to sip his coffee. "Galupo and I picked up Campbell at The Plaza Hotel. The guy just left the asshole end of the universe and comes to New York and checks in at the friggin' Plaza." He shrugged. "I guess I'd do the same thing if I was in his place.

"Anyway, Campbell's like a kid at Christmas. He's pumped about being back in the States and he can hardly wait to get his hands on the dough. The whole time in the car he kept talkin' about buying a ranch somewhere out west . . . Arizona, New Mexico, I don't know. We took him out to the truck yard. It's after 6 p.m., so there ain't no workers around. Coupla of our guys put a few rounds in him and stuffed the body into one of the fifty-five-gallon drums they got there."

"So, this is at Zeff's AWD?"

"Yeah, we used it a lot back then. You could set off a bomb in that joint and no one would be around to hear it. It's ten miles way the fuck out on the island. Anyway, they put the barrel on the back of a semi-truck already loaded with dozens of other drums filled with toxic waste.

"That night, all the drums were put on a barge and dropped in the East River. The toxic waste drums got weights in them so they sink right to the bottom. Except for the drum with the body. Our guys forgot to put rocks in the drum. Coupla' weeks later, the drum pops to the surface, floats down the river, and gets washed up in some marshy lowlands. One night, some kids out messin' around in a car found the drum and called the cops. There was a lot of heat on Atlantic Waste Disposal because of its name being on the drum. Can you believe it? Our guys put the body in a marked drum. Frankie's attorney finally convinced the cops somebody must have stolen one of the company's drums. Eventually, the pressure went away. But the guys who packed the body were on the shit list for a long time."

Gino smiled at Joey. "Thanks."

"Anything else I can do for you?"

"Can you tell me how the heroin came in?"

Cataldo smirked. "This had to be the sweetest deal you've ever heard of. In fuckin' coffins! Every gram of the stuff came in under the bodies of boys killed in Afghanistan. It was pure genius, this guy who thought it up."

"Not so brilliant; the guy just copied what had been done back in Vietnam. The operation over there did about the same thing, except the "H" was packed inside the corpses to make it more difficult for dogs to sniff the stuff. Caskets got shipped to family funeral homes with government contracts."

"Yeah, sonofabitch, almost the same thing here. After we unloaded the smack, we sent the caskets to the soldiers' hometowns."

"And you have no idea who that guy was?"

"Not a clue. But whether he copped the idea or not, he must have had juice, brains, and balls to pull it off today, with all the computers and shit they got today."

"Thanks," Bartolucci said again. "You've been a big help." He stood, and Cataldo rose with him. The two men embraced.

"Joey," Bartolucci whispered.

"Yeah?"

"Take my advice. Next time, put some bowling balls in the drum before you dump it in the river."

Bishop's driver pulled the car into the garage at the back of the townhouse. Bishop entered the house and hurried up the stairs to his second-floor office, flipped on the lights, and removed several sheets of paper from the fax-machine tray. The message read: *David Hood's wife was born Carmela Bartolucci. Her father, Gino Bartolucci, was one of ten crime bosses in the U.S. until his "retirement" several years ago. Supposedly, his only business activities today are legitimate. I have included a list of all of Bartolucci's known businesses, as well as all of his known addresses.*

Kingston had already told him about David Hood's connection to Gino Bartolucci, but the information about Bartolucci's businesses might prove valuable. Then it hit Bishop that someone must have talked to Bartolucci and told him about his involvement with the attempts on Hood's life. Either Zeke McCoy, Rodney Strong, or Montrose Toney.

Bishop felt a sudden chill. Why had there been no attempt on *his* life? Although he was not an easy target, he was not an impossible one.

APRIL 25

CHAPTER 28

Bishop called Kingston at 2 a.m. His assistant was still at his CIA office.

"What else have you come up with?" Bishop asked.

"Piles of stuff on Bartolucci. You want me to fax it, sir?"

"No, bring it by my house." Bishop gave Kingston his address and told him to drive as fast as he could. His assistant dropped the package off one hour later.

Kingston hadn't exaggerated when he said he had piles of stuff. His package contained hundreds of pages about Bartolucci and his businesses, past and present, legitimate and illegitimate, that the FBI, Interpol, and various state and local police organizations had gathered over many years. Through the complicated web of interlocking directorates, corporations, and subsidiaries, Bartolucci had tried to hide the real ownership of his various business interests. Bishop was impressed with the extent of the man's holdings, including an estate in Chestnut Hill.

Before he'd finished his first read of the documents, Bishop dispatched a three-man private reconnaissance team to Philadelphia. He'd used the men before because they were loyal and competent. And they owed him. They were all former Special Ops who had been thrown out of the Army after they were caught trying to smuggle some of Saddam Hussein's gold out of Iraq. Bishop bankrolled them into their own private operation and had hired them on numerous occasions.

One man would watch the Bartolucci home in South Philadelphia. The second man would park outside Bartolucci's Market. The third was sent to the Chestnut Hill estate. Their assignment: Locate Gino Bartolucci and follow him. Bishop was hopeful that sooner or later Bartolucci would lead him to Hood. Then Bishop could give the order that would finally resolve his problem. And this time he would see to it there were no mistakes.

Gino didn't even try to sleep in the back seat of the Cadillac on the trip back from New York City. He was too worked up about what he'd learned from Joey Cataldo. He opted to go to his South Philadelphia home instead of the Chestnut Hill estate. His wife would be worried about him and he always slept better when they were together. He arrived home at 3 a.m. and dozed off an hour later.

Bishop's man outside Gino's house saw him arrive and reported to his team leader outside Bartolucci's market. The team leader called Bishop.

"Sit on him," Bishop ordered. "Tell me if he goes anywhere."

Gino woke at 7:00 a.m. and felt exhausted, with a pain in his chest that felt like heartburn. By the time he'd showered, shaved, and eaten a light breakfast, it was 8:30. He was anxious to tell his guests out in Chestnut Hill what he'd learned from Cataldo.

When Gino walked out of his home, the watcher there spotted him get into a black Cadillac, joined by two other men. He radioed his two partners. The team leader in a car outside Bartolucci's Market instructed the third member of the team to sit tight at the mansion in Chestnut Hill. Then he called Bishop on his cellphone.

"When you determine where Bartolucci's headed, I want you to call me ASAP," Bishop said. "Got it?"

"Yes, sir," the team leader said. "But can you tell me what we're dealing with here? We're following a former Mafia chief who's with a driver and another passenger. All three might be armed. I don't want to walk into something blind."

Bishop generated his calmest and coldest tone of voice. "As long as you continue in a surveillance mode, you and your men have nothing to worry about. I need you to tell me where that mobster goes and who he meets with. Do you think you can do that without questioning my instructions?"

"I'm sorry, sir. I meant no—" Bishop disconnected the man in mid-sentence.

When it became apparent the Cadillac was headed for the Bartolucci mansion, the agent dropped even farther back. He radioed a warning to the man posted outside the mansion, who slouched in his seat when he saw the Cadillac approach. After the Cadillac had gone through the gate and disappeared up the driveway, the third agent called his two teammates with a status report and waited for further instructions.

David and Peter had just finished a walk around the grounds of the Bartolucci property and saw Gino's car roll up to the mansion. They picked up their pace to meet the car when it stopped.

"What's up, Gino? Where've you been?" David asked.

Gino smiled. "Ah, the impatience of youth," he said to Peter. "Hold your water, David. I have some interesting news. Let's go inside and find Dennis and his long-legged partner so I only have to tell my story once."

Gino, trailed by David and Peter, entered the dining room where Dennis O'Neil and Jennifer Ramsey were seated and asked, "You two come up with anything new?"

"Nah!" O'Neil said. "How about you?"

Gino smiled. "Well, I might have come up with a thing or two."

David knew Gino well enough to know he loved drama. He could tell from Gino's smile the old man knew something important. "What is it?" he asked.

Gino held up both hands. "Okay, okay. Sit back and pay

attention. Because you won't believe this."

Gino told his story after he made it clear his source could never be identified.

David shook his head as though he wanted to deny the truth of Gino's story. But the whole thing at last made sense.

"Colonel Rolf Bishop was not just in charge of the SLSD. He was a Quartermaster Corps officer whose MOS—military occupational specialty—was logistics. But the Quartermaster Corps does not limit its activities to supplies and materiel. It's also responsible for handling the bodies of dead Army personnel. It's the Army's mortician, so to speak. This branch of the Army touched every dead American serviceman who had to be shipped back to the States. Bishop was the senior Quartermaster officer in Afghanistan. That bastard had access to every coffin. And he and Robert Campbell had worked together for years." David shook his head. "Bishop had to be the brains behind the drug scheme."

"But why murder the other men?" Ramsey asked.

David thought about the question for a while. "Maybe Bishop's afraid one of us knew or suspected what he was up to. He's cleaning house just to be safe."

"Nine men, including Campbell, murdered in case one of them *might* have known something?" O'Neil said.

"And my wife and children," David said, his voice rough with anger.

"The sonofabitch . . . the rotten sonofabitch!" Peter growled.

"Why wait until now to kill these men?" O'Neil asked.

"Again, we can't be sure," Gino said. "But it could be because he had no real public exposure until the President nominated him to the CIA position. Maybe he just got paranoid. Who knows?"

"What do we do with this information?" O'Neil asked. "We have no evidence, no proof we can use to get him arrested. Toney's confession was tortured out of him. Besides, Toney's criminal record would raise questions about his credibility. Mr. Bartolucci, I take it your informant in New York is not about to testify he committed murder as part of a narcotics smuggling ring. And David, the connection you made between the drugs and the responsibility Bishop had for coffin shipments is nothing but circumstantial. We could try to use the news media to ruin Bishop's reputation through hearsay and innuendo. But that wouldn't be enough even if the media would play along, which I doubt."

No one spoke for a long while.

"Gino, one thing is missing from the information you got in New York," David said. "Your informant told you he bought drugs from someone in Afghanistan and how the drugs were shipped into the United States. Did he tell you how they paid for those drugs?"

Gino stared quizzically at David. "With cash, of course. Checks and credit cards aren't usually accepted in the drug business."

"No, no, Gino. I mean how were payments made? Was cash transferred to some bank account in the seller's name, or maybe to a numbered account in some foreign bank? Is the cash buried in some vault somewhere?"

"Of course," Jennifer said. "If we could track the money we might be able to discover who the seller was."

"Excuse me for a moment," Gino said. "I need to make a phone call."

From another room in the house, Gino used a cellphone to dial Joey Cataldo's number.

When Cataldo got on, Gino said, "That was a great dinner we had last night. We need to do that more often."

Cataldo replied, "I would enjoy that."

"Do you think I could impose on you just one more time with a question I failed to ask last night?"

"Ask and if I have the answer it's yours."

"*Grazie*, Joey. When you paid for those . . . boxes from Asia years ago, how did you deliver the money to the manufacturer?"

"I understand, my friend. How much do you want to know?"

"Everything you can tell me. The name of the bank or banks where money was sent. The account numbers. Dates of money transfers. And whatever else you got."

"That's a lot to ask, *mi amico*."

"Yeah, I understand."

After a ten-second pause, Cataldo said, "I think maybe we

should have a nice dinner again, in two days. Same place, nine o'clock."

"Fine," Gino agreed. "I'll see you then. And thanks."

"I ain't promisin' nothin'," Cataldo said. "See you Thursday."

Bishop forced himself to remain calm. He didn't know what was happening to him. He'd never lost his cool before, no matter what the pressure. But there had been too many screw-ups lately. A plan had formed in his mind and he knew he had to put the pieces together carefully. He couldn't afford any more mistakes. The buzz of the intercom broke into his thoughts.

He pressed the send button. "Yes?"

"Mr. Bishop," Kingston said, "I've got a Detective Roger Cromwell on the line. Claims to have information for you. Something about David Hood. Should I take a mess—?"

Bishop broke in and said, "No, no, put him through."

"This is Bishop. How may I help you?"

"This is Detective Roger Cromwell. I'm with the Bethesda Police Department. I've got a homicide case that involves the deaths of a woman and two children. Family by the name of Hood."

"Yes?" Bishop said.

"I . . . I thought you might have an interest."

Bishop heard Cromwell's voice quaver. The man wasn't confident of whatever information he had.

"Why don't you continue, Detective Cromwell? You never can tell what I might find interesting."

The man's voice firmed up a little when he said, "There's a Bethesda detective by the name of Jennifer Ramsey who's holed up with David Hood; Hood's father, Peter; and a mobster named Gino Bartolucci on Bartolucci's estate somewhere in the Philadelphia area."

"And why do you think this information would be of interest to me?"

"Detective Ramsey left a message here. In that message she said something about several murders."

"And you've called me because . . . ."

"Ramsey mentioned your name."

Bishop forced himself to maintain control. He let out the air in his lungs very slowly, quietly. "And what do you think, Detective?" he asked.

"I think it's just more of Detective Ramsey's bullshit."

"I'll consider this information, Detective Cromwell. We can't have people use other people's names in vain, can we?"

"That's exactly what I thought."

"And what's your interest in all of this?" Bishop asked.

"I like to see the good guys win."

"Can I infer you don't include Detective Ramsey in that same group of good guys?"

"You could come to that conclusion, Mr. Bishop."

"Should I look into this matter, Detective, as if you and I never talked?" Bishop asked.

"I think that would be the wise thing to do."

CHAPTER 29

At 10:15 a.m., the leader of the three-man surveillance team was parked outside Bartolucci's estate when Deputy Director Bishop called him and gave him a list of instructions. While he listened to the Director, he thought maybe it was time he got into another line of work. This operation had acquired a bad smell.

Rolf Bishop stared across his home office desk at Tim Morton, Special Operations Director, Drug Enforcement Administration (DEA). Bishop understood the power of a CIA Deputy Director was theoretically limited by the laws of the land and by Congressional oversight, but, in actuality, that power was mitigated only by the Deputy Director's moral constraints and the size of his testicles. Bishop knew that a man with no ethical parameters owns power without bounds.

"Nice saying," Morton said. He pointed at a wall plaque behind Bishop.

Bishop turned and looked at the plaque inscribed with Lord Acton's saying: *Power tends to corrupt and absolute power corrupts absolutely*. He turned back to stare at Morton. The man had put on a huge amount of weight since Bishop had last seen him a couple years earlier. He had to be carrying 230 pounds on a five-foot, eight-inch frame. His face was florid with broken blood vessels. His bloated nose looked like a road map of little red veins that spider-webbed onto his cheeks. "Yeah, nice saying," Bishop said.

"What can I do for you?"

"How much would it take for you to risk your job, your pension, and your marriage?"

Morton's expression barely budged. He met Bishop's gaze, seemed to reflect on the question, and answered, "One dollar for the marriage; two million dollars in a numbered account for the rest."

"Done," Bishop said.

Morton smiled. "We've done a lot of business together over the years. You've paid me well and I know you've got me by the balls. But you've never offered me that kind of money. What's up?"

Bishop ignored Morton's question. He looked at his wrist watch: 10:55 a.m. Late afternoon in Zurich. He picked up his cellphone and dialed a private number in Switzerland. When the call went through, he was prompted to enter his code number and then his password. Thirty seconds later a man came on the line.

"Bergstrom!"

"Hello, Bergstrom. I want you to execute a transaction for me."

"Yes, of course. Please proceed with your instructions."

"Transfer two million dollars from my account into a new account in the name of Timothy Morton. Mr. Morton will call you later to set up a code and password."

After he terminated the call, Bishop fished a one dollar bill from a pocket, smiled, and handed it to Morton.

CHAPTER 30

Tim Morton left Rolf Bishop's office at Langley, drove to his DEA office, typed up a letter of resignation, and submitted the retirement papers he'd had in his desk for the past sixteen months. April 26 would be his last day at the agency. He finally had all the money he needed. He called the mayor of Philadelphia and requested an emergency meeting with him at two that afternoon. Morton was confident a call from the DEA special operations director was a rare enough occurrence that the mayor would clear his schedule to meet with him. Then he requisitioned a helicopter and flew from D.C. to Philadelphia.

Morton slugged back a swig of coffee. He placed the cup on the table and stared at the three men across from him—Mayor Katz, Police Commissioner Clarence Sullivan, and S.W.A.T. Commander Abraham Lincoln Brand. Katz and Sullivan had the self-satisfied looks of well-fed bureaucrats. Brand appeared to be the antithesis of a bureaucrat. The guy was tall, muscular, and wore a skeptical look complemented by piercing, intelligent, coal-black eyes.

"Gentlemen," Morton said, "I am about to provide you with highly classified and extremely sensitive information. This is a matter of national security with diplomatic implications, so I must have your agreement that anything you hear today will be kept secret." Morton could sense excitement radiating off the mayor.

The mayor spoke for the three of them. "There's no harm in hearing you out, Mr. Morton. If we don't like what you're selling, then you have our promise not a word of what you tell us will ever leave this room."

The other two nodded.

"All right, gentlemen, let's proceed. On the outskirts of this city is an estate listed on your city's property tax rolls in the name of Cornelius Capital Resources. I won't bore you with the details of how this company is related to a series of other companies, some of which are foreign. I *will* tell you, however, that if you strip away the legal camouflage you will find the true owner of the estate is none other than Gino Bartolucci, the former head of *La Cosa Nostra* in Philadelphia."

The Philadelphia contingent did not seem particularly surprised. "No disrespect intended, but that's not a startling revelation," Police Commissioner Sullivan said. "We've got neighborhoods in this city where half the buildings and businesses are owned by someone other than the person named on the title and tax records."

"I understand," Morton replied, "but let me finish and then you'll see the whole picture. On the grounds of that estate are several men who are behind a massive drug smuggling operation. Their product comes from one of the largest and most ruthless poppy growing syndicates in the world, based in Kampuchea, formerly known as Cambodia, and run by former high-level military leaders of the Khymer Rouge. Their goal is to gain control of a significant slice of the world narcotics business. They make the tactics of the Colombian and the Mexican cartels, for example, seem like child's play. The DEA, FBI, and CIA have gathered intelligence on this syndicate for several years, but it was not until recently we discovered the connection to Bartolucci. It is our theory that Bartolucci abdicated leadership of the local mob to create a smoke screen. He effectively cleared his table of other criminal enterprises to concentrate on the development of this Cambodian partnership.

"We developed a tactical plan to expose Bartolucci. The exposure was to have coincided with a drone strike on the processing plant in Kampuchea. That's where diplomatic considerations come into play.

Unfortunately, we learned early today one of our undercover agents who is inside Bartolucci's estate may have been compromised. We believe Bartolucci knows he has a spy in his camp and he suspects it's our agent. He has called a summit conference of all of his partners for tomorrow morning at the estate and we're afraid he plans to expose our agent at that meeting. You can imagine what they'll do to him. This has forced us to move on Bartolucci earlier than we had planned. We've got to get our man out of there in one piece . . . tonight. I have agents in the area, but not enough to get this done. That's where your S.W.A.T. team comes in. Besides, there would be a lot of noise involved with an assault on the compound. We couldn't very well go in there without coordinating with local authorities."

"Just a minute, Mr. Morton," Captain Brand said. "We don't engage S.W.A.T. until we have carefully and completely analyzed a situation. We have to know the physical layout; the number of personnel in the compound, including innocent bystanders; how well-armed our adversaries are; et cetera. You want us to enter unknown territory in the dead of night. That's how cops and innocent people get killed."

Morton eyed the S.W.A.T. Commander. He pulled from his briefcase the files Rolf Bishop had given him, including doctored aerial photos, and spread papers on the mayor's conference table. "This first diagram shows the grounds of the Bartolucci estate. These next drawings are floor plans for each level of the house. These aerial photos were taken by a drone earlier today. They show a total of eight heavily armed guards, each carrying a large caliber pistol in a shoulder holster and a MAC-10. The grounds and the house are wired with motion and pressure sensors. But all electronic security systems are primarily dependent upon power from your local utility. If the juice is cut to the estate, the detection systems switch to generators which automatically kick in—but only after a one minute delay.

"One more thing. There's a heroin stash on the estate. My agent reports there is enough heroin on the estate to fill a panel truck. This could be a very big drug bust. And, gentlemen, that bust will be yours. The DEA will take no credit for any part in the seizure. If I had the time to gather an assault team, I wouldn't ask for your help. I would only have called you after my people assaulted the estate."

"That's about the most candor I've ever heard from a Fed," Sullivan said.

Morton laughed. "I hate to admit it, gentlemen, but I need your assistance. There's a very brave man inside that estate I want to rescue and a lot of heroin that would make my career. There's about to be a bunch of Mafia gonzos in there I would love to arrest. But I don't have time. My undercover guy will experience a horrible death if we don't take immediate action."

"Why don't you just tell your man to take a walk and get out of there?" Brand asked.

"We haven't been able to communicate with him for twenty-four hours."

The mayor looked at his two police officials before he responded. "Mr. Morton, why don't you give the three of us a couple of minutes to discuss your request among ourselves."

After Morton stepped out, Mayor Katz looked at the other two men and asked, "Well, what do you think, boys?"

Katz had run Philadelphia for almost eight years and had done a great deal to make the city's streets safer than they had been for decades. He was a popular mayor. His ever-smiling face made him seem like everybody's favorite uncle. But his appearance and demeanor disguised a merciless political nature grounded in a winner-take-all mentality. He loved the opportunity Morton had laid out for them. A huge drug bust on a *Mafioso's* property would make Katz a hero. Today mayor, tomorrow governor.

"What do you think, Linc?" Sullivan asked his S.W.A.T. team commander.

Katz noted Captain Brand's scowl. "Linc, you're the guy who will have to lead an assault," the mayor said. "What's your opinion?"

"I got alarm bells ringing in my head. Since when does any federal agency ask for help from locals? And I gotta tell ya, I don't buy Morton's story about Gino Bartolucci running a drug operation. He got out of the rackets because he didn't want to deal drugs. He's been as clean as a whistle ever since, as far as we can tell. Something just isn't right."

Mayor Katz asked Commissioner Sullivan to weigh in.

"Mr. Mayor, I think Captain Brand has raised good questions. However, I feel he has, in the interest of prudence, ignored the fact that a senior DEA man came all the way from Washington. I can't believe he would have done that unless this was very important. His presence here raises his story's credibility. I think it's admirable he cares more about his undercover agent than he does about getting credit for the arrest of a bunch of mobsters and confiscation of a huge narcotics haul. I understand Linc's point about the Feds usually not coordinating with local authorities, and just because Bartolucci has been clean for years, doesn't mean he's clean now. Once a mobster, always a mobster. I recommend we do this."

For the mayor, Sullivan's support more than cancelled the S.W.A.T. Captain's reservations. "All right, gentlemen," he said. "I want you to work with Mr. Morton."

"Then I've got to lay out some rules before we agree to this," Brand said.

After Brand explained what he wanted, Katz left the room and brought Morton back in. He shook the DEA man's hand. "Mr. Morton, it's a go. Captain Brand will command the operation. He will have ultimate authority over the entire mission. Do you agree?"

"Agreed, Mr. Mayor."

Morton reached into his briefcase and pulled out a large photograph. He handed it to Mayor Katz. "That's the undercover guy inside Bartolucci's estate. My sincere thanks to all of you."

Morton shook hands with each of the men, turned to leave, but stopped at the door. He raised a hand and said, "Oh, I nearly forgot. There's a crooked Maryland cop who's in league with Bartolucci. She's fed him intelligence information. Her name's Jennifer Ramsey. She may be on Bartolucci's estate. Be careful. She has every reason in the world not to be taken prisoner."

When Morton left Philadelphia's City Hall, he called Bishop's cellphone number. "It's a go," he told Bishop.

"Did you give them the photos I provided?"

"Yeah. Who's that undercover guy?" Morton asked.

Bishop laughed. "Don't have a clue. I copied it off some guy's Facebook page."

Morton laughed. "Does Bartolucci really have eight heavily armed guards on his estate?"

"He has two or three guards armed with pistols," Bishop said. "It's amazing what you can do with Photoshop."

"I wish I could hang around and watch what happens."

Bishop said. "Where will you be?"

"Where I can't be found. Some place far away, where the back blast from this operation can't blow shit all over me. I put in my retirement papers this afternoon. Thanks for the retirement fund. It's been great working with you."

Bishop stared at his cellphone. He'd thought about eliminating Morton. Another possible loose end. But maybe it was best the man just took off and disappeared. In any case, he'd think about what to do with Morton, if anything, at a later date, after he'd finally taken care of David Hood.

An hour later, Morton rendezvoused with a CIA team parked in a van in a closed shopping center lot. He sat in the front passenger seat and turned to the four men in the rear of the vehicle. They all had the chiseled looks and the eyes of stone-cold killers. He guessed they were former members of Special Ops. Special Ops types who did off-the-books wet work. Fuckin' Bishop was pulling out all stops on this one.

"The mission is a go," he said. "A police S.W.A.T. unit will mount an assault tonight. While they neutralize the guards, you'll go in and erase the traitor and anyone near him. That includes a rogue cop named Ramsey. Jennifer Ramsey. She's feeding information to the traitor. This man,"—he passed a photograph of David Hood to them—"has betrayed dozens of our undercover agents. I don't want him to have the luxury of a trial. Anyone inside that estate is an enemy of the United States."

CHAPTER 31

At 7 p.m., Rolf Bishop called the private surveillance team leader, now stationed outside the Bartolucci estate. "You and your men can stand down. Payment has been wired to your account."

"Thank you, Mr.—"

Bishop had already hung up.

S.W.A.T. team commander Linc Brand pored over the architectural plans and aerial photographs Tim Morton had provided. A seven-foot stone wall surrounded the property. There appeared to be wide-open fields of fire north and east of the house. The mansion had been built close to the south and west walls. The south wall bordered the Chestnut Hill Cricket Club's golf course and the west wall separated the Bartolucci grounds from an adjacent estate. The north and east walls fronted on city streets. Brand sent one of his men out to reconnoiter the area. He reported back that the neighbors on the west were in the British Isles and their home was empty, other than for a caretaker in a carriage house behind the main house.

The city's best S.W.A.T. team reported to police headquarters at 8 p.m. and took seats in a briefing room. When Brand entered the room, he sensed his men's excitement and nervousness. He briefed them on the operation and then answered questions. Afterward,

Brand ordered his men to prepare their equipment and weapons.

Rolf Bishop, now in the back of a limousine on his way from D.C. to New York City, congratulated himself on the mastery of his plan and the sale of his fairy tale. The CIA Black Ops unit believed David Hood was a long-time mole for the Russians. He had fabricated a file on Hood that made him appear to be the personification of the anti-Christ. There was mention to them about a DEA undercover agent. The members of the assassination team had put aside their usual cool detachment. This had become an emotional issue for them. If Hood was on the Bartolucci estate, Bishop was confident the team would take him out, if the cops had not already done so in the orchestrated confusion of the raid.

And it sounded as though Morton had done a great snow job on the Philadelphia mayor and the police. All in all, Bishop was hopeful, despite the problems he'd had in eliminating David Hood.

At 11:30 p.m., Police Commissioner Sullivan established a perimeter around the area, which extended for two blocks in three directions from the Bartolucci property. Four street cops had been stationed on the golf course behind the estate's twelve-foot-high back wall, the highest wall on the property. At 11:35 p.m., Brand and his S.W.A.T. team assembled on an open field across from Wissahickon Park, near Chestnut Hill Academy. The black S.W.A.T. van was parked on the street next to the field. Brand checked the equipment and weapons of all twelve of his men. He again went over the tactical plan.

"Okay, people, listen up. We've reinforced our team with four snipers with infrared scopes. I want you guys over the wall and in place before the rest of the team goes in. Position yourselves at the edge of the tree line and try to pick off anyone who's a threat. The electric company will cut power at exactly 00:15. When the streetlights go off, it will take one minute for the estate's generators to kick in. That should be enough time for you snipers to get into position and for the rest of the team to get over the wall. When all the lights around the estate go back on, you'll be vulnerable, so the snipers will immediately shoot out the security lights.

"Once the security lights have been shot out, Atkins and Villanucci will crash the front gate and subdue the guard there. Doherty will run across the lawn with the cable cutters and disable the generator. Lovett, you'll go with Doherty and cover his back. When the generators are disabled and the house goes dark, that's the signal for the rest of you to move across the lawn. This is where it will get tricky. More than likely, some of the guards will be inside, along with household staff, the DEA undercover agent, the Bethesda cop, and who knows who else. Let's hope that most of the occupants are asleep.

"Remember, guys," he concluded. "There's an undercover DEA agent in that house. You've seen head shots of the man, so let's bring him out alive. Let's not get trigger happy." Brand looked at his watch. "All right, I've got 23:57. Let's load up and get this show on the road."

Tim Morton, with Rolf Bishop's black ops team, was now parked midway along the service road beside the third fairway of the golf course, half-a-mile behind the Bartolucci estate. They had already subdued the four police officers at the back wall, chloroforming them, tying, and gagging them. The team leader opened the sliding door and the team piled out. The driver and Morton stayed in the vehicle and drove away. A helicopter then landed where the van had been and the four men climbed aboard.

"You men have the opportunity to right a lot of wrongs tonight," the leader told the others. "I want everyone in that house dead, but I especially want that traitor Hood killed."

APRIL 26

CHAPTER 32

Ever since Gino had moved David and Peter to his estate, he'd assigned three guards to rove the estate's grounds. Each was armed with a 9mm pistol and a shotgun the Sicilians called *Il Lupo*. Each man also carried a radio transmitter/receiver to stay in touch with the house, where David currently manned the command center. The third guard was also armed with two additional weapons—a pair of one hundred-fifty-pound Anatolian Shepherd guard dogs. Alert, intelligent, and naturally protective, these animals had been imported from Turkey, where they traditionally protect livestock from wolves and other predators. Dark-gray colored, they were almost invisible at night, despite the fact each stood thirty-two inches at the shoulder.

At precisely 12:15 a.m., an electric-company supervisor tripped a switch on a junction box that served a four-square-block area around and including the Bartolucci property. All of the security lights on the estate went off, along with every other light and electric appliance in the four-square-block area.

The two guard dogs had shown signs of agitation for several minutes before the lights went out. They now whined and tugged at their leashes. Their handler had taken his cue from the dogs and become especially watchful. When the lights went out, the dog handler used his radio to warn the other guards he was about to release the dogs. He gave the two other guards thirty seconds to retreat to the front of the house, then released the animals, which raced into the tree line. From the way the animals zeroed-in on one particular spot, the handler knew something or someone had penetrated the grounds. The dog handler radioed the house.

When the call came in from the dog handler, David was with two of Gino's men in the small room off the kitchen that served as a communications center. The two men rushed to the front entry.

S.W.A.T. Officer Guy Allen sensed movement to his left. As he reacted and turned, a snarling mass of fury hit him in the chest and drove the air from his lungs. All Allen could do was roll into a fetal position, protect his face and throat with his hands and arms, and try to catch his breath. The animal bit Allen's arm, shook it for a couple seconds, and then ran off.

Officers Warren Doherty and John Lovett sprinted across a wide expanse of lawn toward the generator when a dog ran Lovett down from behind. When he fell, his forehead struck the butt of his assault rifle, knocking him out.

The two dogs—silent, dark specters that caused havoc among the S.W.A.T. team members—raced back into the trees. Even those snipers who *thought* they saw one of the dogs couldn't fire their weapons for fear they'd hit one of their comrades. Two of the snipers climbed into trees, while a third scaled the wall back out to the street. Suddenly, the generators kicked in and the entire estate lit up like a football stadium. The snipers were no longer in position to shoot out the pole- and building-mounted security lights. One of the cops saw the dog handler run toward the tree line, shotgun in hand. He fired at the man who dropped as though he'd been poleaxed. The man screamed like it, too.

Two of Bartolucci's guards who had retreated behind a ten-foot stone pillar at the mansion's front entrance opened fire in the direction of the flash from the cop's weapon. This forced the S.W.A.T. team members to shoot back while hunkered down in the trees. But with the dogs creating confusion in the police ranks, their aim was less than true. The situation was bad enough when the lights were on, but when Officer Doherty belatedly cut the cables to the generators, all hell broke loose in the sudden darkness lit only by gunfire.

One of the dogs attacked another cop, who raised his automatic weapon, fired, and wounded the animal. But several rounds from his rifle went over the hurtling beast and hit one of the S.W.A.T. team members square in the chest. His bulletproof vest saved his life, but the force of the bullet knocked him unconscious.

The second dog went for the throat of another police officer when a nearby teammate ran over and tasered the animal.

Gino's two guards who'd been in the communications center with David had run out the front door and fired pistols at weapons flashes that came from the far side of the yard. They were out of range of the intruders and only succeeded in creating more confusion. The rate of gunfire accelerated dramatically. Shotgun blasts echoed like thunder off the walls of the estate. The police officers' silenced rounds added to the mayhem as they ricocheted off concrete and stone surfaces, sounding like high-pitched fireworks.

"Cease fire!" Captain Brand shouted. It took almost thirty seconds to get them to stop shooting. Bartolucci's men also stopped firing.

Brand had had enough of the circus this operation had turned into. He knew his team had suffered casualties and he was not about to have any more of his men wounded if he could help it. He called to his radioman, who knelt on the ground about four feet behind him in the trees inside the walls. Brand removed a bullhorn attached to a small pack on the man's back. He hit the power switch and announced, "This is the Philadelphia Police. Throw down your weapons, walk out on the lawn, and lie down on the grass. If you don't do as I say, I'll order my men to fire again."

One of Bartolucci's guards yelled back into the darkness, "What kind of cops are you assholes? What gives you the right to come chargin' in here?"

"You heard what I said. Either show yourselves or we open fire."

"How do we know you're really cops?"

Good question, Brand reflected. "I'm going to walk over to you with my arms over my head and without a weapon. I'll come no closer than twenty yards and then I'll toss my badge to you. If a single shot is fired from your side, my men will blow you and the house to pieces. Do we have an understanding?"

"Yeah," the guard yelled.

As Brand unstrapped his equipment belt and dropped it, along with his weapon, his radioman looked at him and said, "No disrespect intended, Captain, but are you out of your friggin' mind?"

"Maybe, but I don't think so. This whole thing has seemed screwed up from the start. That guy over there sounds to me like he wants this over with as badly as I do."

Brand walked into the open and approached the house.

"Over here," a man shouted.

Brand walked toward the man's voice and stopped twenty yards from a stone staircase. He tossed his badge case toward the steps. A man rushed out, picked it up, and ran back beside the staircase.

After only a few seconds, a man shouted, "It's the cops, alright. Put down your weapons and come out."

Four men showed themselves, placed their weapons on the pavement in front of the steps and assumed the prone position on the edge of the lawn. Brand then ordered his men forward.

David Hood had sprinted from the commo center to the stairs that led to the bedrooms on the second floor. Between the gunfire, shouts, and screams, it sounded as though a full-scale assault was in progress. The first room at the head of the staircase was Gino's. He found Gino had already dressed. The two of them gathered up Dennis, Peter, and Jennifer, who were already out of bed and in the process of dressing.

"There's no time to finish dressing," David said. "We have to get out of here."

"Who's out there?" Peter asked.

"I don't know," David answered. "But I'll bet Rolf Bishop had something to do with it."

They all ran downstairs and quickly moved toward the rear of the house.

The gunfire out front had stopped, but then David heard the thrumming sound of a helicopter and the sounds of breaking glass from somewhere upstairs.

"Is there another way out of here?" David asked Gino.

"Yeah. Give me a second," Gino said as he walked to a small desk in an alcove off the kitchen, took out paper and pencil, and quickly scribbled something. He put the paper in an envelope, sealed it, and pulled a piece of tape from a dispenser. He moved to the basement door and taped the envelope to the door.

"Come with me," Gino said, as calmly as though he had suggested they all go out for a leisurely walk. He led them into the basement. In the wine cellar he pushed aside a wine bottle-laden rack that stood on hidden rollers and revealed the entrance to a tunnel. He urged them into the tunnel and followed, after he pulled the wine rack snug behind them.

The tunnel took them under the wall that separated the Bartolucci property from the adjoining estate and led to a door flush with the ground. Gino opened a latch on the door and said, "David, you need to put your back against it."

David climbed three steps up to the door, turned around, stooped over, and heaved up against the door. At first, it wouldn't budge. But a second effort did the trick. He pushed the door open, heard dirt slide off its surface, and then got a dirt shower for his efforts. He stepped out in the darkness and reached down to assist the others out of the tunnel. They were just on the other side of the wall, in a dense grouping of bushes and trees. Gino closed the door and kicked dirt back over it.

"Glad the neighbors never found this little secret exit of mine," Gino said. "I had it dug one summer when they were out of the country."

The leader of Bishop's black ops team had heard shouts outside the house and then someone blared away on a bullhorn and ordered the inhabitants of the house to come outside. "Where the hell are they?" the team leader asked.

"They're gone," one of his men said. "I even checked the basement. Nothing."

The team leader looked at his watch. "I got five minutes until the chopper lifts off," he said. "Let's at least get part of this right." He led his men into the dining room. Each man had entered the house with fifty pounds of heroin in a backpack. They placed the packs on the dining room table.

CHAPTER 33

David moved to the back of the neighbor's property and pulled himself up to get a look into the yard at the back of the Bartolucci house. He had a clear view of the second-floor windows—or where the windows used to be—on part of the back of the house. The window frames and glass of the room where Peter had slept just minutes earlier had been destroyed. He was about to drop back to the ground when something on his right moved. A man dressed in black sprinted from the back of the house, climbed a rope to the top of the wall, and dropped out of sight. Then a second, and a third, and finally a fourth man followed the first man over the wall. David dropped to the ground and turned to join the others, when he heard the distinctive sound of a helicopter's rotors. He assumed the four men were part of the Philadelphia police force.

Linc Brand sent one of his men to talk to a small group of bathrobe-clad neighbors gathered across the street from the Bartolucci estate. He instructed his officer to apologize for the noise and to inform the neighbors that one of the owner's grandsons had acquired a huge quantity of illegal fireworks and a bullhorn and decided to scare the hell out of everyone. The officer assured the neighbors there would be no more such pranks in the future.

"What about the electricity?" a woman asked.

"Must be a power blackout. It had nothing to do with the fireworks. I'm sure it will be back on momentarily."

This, and the news the boy had earned a spanking, seemed to satisfy the neighbors. They straggled back to their homes.

The S.W.A.T. team spread out through the Bartolucci home and searched for Gino, a DEA undercover agent, and a huge cache of illegal drugs. They were disappointed on all counts. They did find four backpacks with stacks of plastic-wrapped heroin inside, but it was a lot less than what they had been led to expect by Tim Morton of the DEA.

One of the S.W.A.T. team's members found a note taped to the basement door and turned it over to his commander. Printed in pencil on the envelope: "For Rolf Bishop's Eyes Only!"

"Who the hell is Rolf Bishop?" the man asked.

"A CIA bigwig."

"What the hell does he have to do with this?"

Brand just slowly wagged his head.

CHAPTER 34

David and Gino were the only ones of the five who'd fled the house who were fully dressed. Dennis wore pajama bottoms, a T-shirt, and black lace-up shoes, without socks. Peter wore a pajama top, dress pants, and slippers. Jennifer Ramsey had apparently had the presence of mind to put on a pair of running shoes to go with a t-shirt and dark-blue sweat pants. The temperature had dropped enough that David felt chilled. He suspected the others must feel the cold even more. "Gino," David said, "there must be someone who can pick us up."

"Sure!" Gino responded. "We could call Bobby Galupo. But I don't have my cellphone. It's back in my bedroom. Anybody got a telephone?"

No one had brought a phone.

"I'll go over the wall and try to find a pay phone," David said.

"I'll go with you," Jennifer announced.

David was inclined to argue with her, but decided he didn't have time to waste. He just nodded and jogged away from the group. He crossed the neighbor's estate until he came to another high, ivy-covered stone wall. He thought for a moment about helping Ramsey over the wall, but decided she'd have to make it on her own; he didn't need her along if she couldn't hold up her end. He gripped vines that covered the wall and pulled himself up. After he made certain no one was on the other side, he dropped onto a sidewalk. Ramsey landed next to him a second later.

David could see the reflections of police lights bounce off walls and trees, but the police vehicles were not visible, parked around a curve in the street. He crouched low, ran across the street, and headed into another street perpendicular to Gino's street. Ramsey trailed close behind. After only one block, he had to slow to a fast walk. Years behind a desk had taken their toll. He noticed Ramsey's breathing was shallow, unlabored.

David saw the lighted sign of a Southeast Pennsylvania Transportation Authority commuter train station two blocks ahead. He hoped there would be a public telephone there. The houses along the street were closer together than they'd been on Gino's block, each situated on lots that appeared to be about a fourth of an acre. But just as he was about to sprint to the station, a police cruiser pulled up and stopped in the middle of the street, right in front of the steps down to the station. With emergency lights flashing, two police officers got out of the cruiser and stood in the street.

Ramsey laid a hand on David's arm and said, "Give me three minutes." She raced down the sidewalk on the opposite side of the street.

David caught glimpses of Ramsey as she ran toward the cruiser. She was dressed like your everyday jogger, but it was a bit late at night for a recreational run. She was about a half-block from the police vehicle when David noticed the two officers move away from their car.

One of the cops shouted, "Hey, stop."

Ramsey stopped for a couple seconds, reversed direction, and ran back the way she had just come. While David knelt behind a parked car, he heard her run by. A half-minute later a cop passed him. The gear on his utility belt made all kinds of racket. His breathing was loud and labored. Then the other cop came by in the cruiser, lights flashing and siren howling.

David stood up and jogged toward the station as soon as the cops passed him. He looked down at the tracks, sixty feet below street level, and spotted a pay phone. He descended three flights of stairs to the concrete platform and walked briskly toward the phone, which was set in the midst of giant trees that formed a wall between the train platform and a steep grassy bank leading to a paved parking lot. David picked up his pace, quickly reached the phone, deposited coins, and dialed Bobby Galupo's number, which Gino had given him. While he waited for someone to answer, he noticed the train schedule posted in large block letters and numerals in front and to the left of him on the station wall. The last train of the night was due at 12:55 a.m. The wall clock above the train schedule showed 12:49 a.m.

David heard a sound behind him. His breath caught as he jerked his head around just as he felt something hard press into his back. At the same time, a hand grabbed his left shoulder and a voice rasped, "Drop that phone or I'll put a cap in your ass." David heard a man's voice on the telephone just before he replaced the receiver in its cradle.

The man behind him said, "Give me your wallet and whatever you got in your pockets. Put 'em up on that phone shelf. Also your watch and ring."

David really didn't care about his wallet, money, or watch, but there was no way he would willingly hand over the ring Carmela had given him. He tensed, then tried to relax. He took his wallet from a rear pants pocket and laid it carefully on the phone shelf. He removed his watch and put that on top of the wallet. With his left hand he reached into a pants pocket and pulled out change. He was about to drop the coins onto the shelf when a loud "Hey!" punctuated the night.

The shout seemed to distract the robber. He momentarily lessened the pressure of the pistol, but then pushed it even harder against David's back. The sound of footsteps hammered on the wooden steps. The robber cursed: "What the fu . . . ."

David felt the pistol shift slightly to the right. He pivoted to his left, came face-to-face with the gunman, their chests almost touching. He used his left hand to grab the man's right wrist, immobilizing his gun hand. He drove his right hand into the man's throat with all the force he could muster. Despite being slightly off-balance and seriously out of practice, David did enough damage with the blow that the gunman dropped his weapon, grabbed his throat, fell to his knees, and croaked like a seal. David felt momentary satisfaction from the man's pain. He picked up the pistol and slammed it against the man's temple. The mugger fell sideways, unconscious or dead. David got down on one knee next to the man and searched his pockets. In the left pocket of his hooded sweatshirt he found a key ring with the distinctive keys of a Chrysler product.

Ramsey ran up while David gathered his things from the telephone shelf. "Are you all right?" she asked.

"Goddamn punk!" David exclaimed.

"What do we do now?"

A bright light suddenly appeared in a tunnel about five hundred yards up the tracks.

"We'd better get out of here," David said. They sprinted away and were halfway up the stairs by the time the train stopped at the station. At the street, David noticed a single dark sedan parked in the lot behind the train station.

"Come on," he said to Ramsey. He ran down the sidewalk, turned into the parking lot, and ran to the car—an ancient, rusted-out Dodge Dart. He tried the driver's side door and found it unlocked. He got behind the wheel and tried the car key he'd taken off the mugger. When the engine came to life, Ramsey slid into the passenger seat. David tore out of the lot and drove down Highland Avenue back to Gino's street.

"We've got to get off the streets around here," Ramsey said. "There are probably police checkpoints all around the area."

"I don't know," David said. "I don't see the emergency flashers anymore. We'll have to pull onto the property where we left the others. Neither Gino nor my father would be able to scale the wall."

David cut off the Dodge's headlights and drove into the driveway. Twenty yards off the street, the driveway curved slightly to the right and was blocked by a huge wrought iron gate. On the driver's side was a speaker box. David pushed the button on the box. The sound of a ringing telephone came through the speaker. Then a man's groggy voice.

"Jeez, who is it? It's the middle of the night."

"Philadelphia Police," David said. "We're after a prowler who might have scaled the wall from next door onto your property. Who am I speaking to?"

"Is that what all the noise is about?"

"Yes, sir. What's your name?"

"Arthur Ellison; I'm the caretaker here."

"Would you open the gate so we can search the grounds?"

"I'll be right there," the man said.

"No, sir," David said. "You stay inside and lock your doors. I don't want you hurt. The man we're after is armed and dangerous. Can you open the gate remotely?"

"Sure. I'll do that."

The speaker box squawked and then went silent. David looked over at Ramsey and hunched his shoulders. She smiled at him. "You know impersonating a police officer is a crime?"

"I suspect that would be the least of my worries."

The gate retracted to the left. He drove onto the property and, in the rear view mirror, watched the gate automatically close behind them. He drove along the brick driveway until he had a clear view of the front of the house. The spot where they'd left the others was across a wide stretch of lawn, twenty yards to the left. He tapped the gas pedal just enough to roll across the lawn. A couple yards from Gino's secret tunnel, David stopped the car and said to Ramsey, "Get behind the wheel. I'll find the others. You need to be ready to drive this heap out of here as soon as we're all aboard." He got out and walked into the bushes, and whispered, "Dad, Gino."

Gino, Peter, and O'Neil moved out of the bushes.

"Anything happen since I left?" he asked.

"Nothing, except the cops patrolled the grounds next door until a few minutes ago," Peter answered.

"They're not still there?"

"I don't think so. It's like they wanted to get away as fast as they could."

"Well, let's get out of here before someone thinks to check on this side of the wall," David said.

When they were all in the car, David told Gino, "As long as we're in Philly we'll be targets of every cop in town. You're supposed to meet with your friend in New York tomorrow evening, anyway. So maybe now's a good time for all of us to make the trip there."

"Good idea," Gino replied. "Where did you get the car?"

"Stole it!" David said.

"Couldn't find anything better?" Gino said.

Jennifer Ramsey drove back across the lawn to the driveway and then down to the gate, which opened automatically. She pulled away from the estate and drove out of Chestnut Hill.

Thirty minutes into the drive toward New York City, Gino was asleep in the front passenger seat, as was Peter in the back seat. O'Neil, in the back between David and Peter, was awake, as was David. Ramsey adjusted the rear view mirror so she could better see David's face. She thought about the way he'd handled himself at the train station and at the neighbor's estate. The man knew how to take command under pressure. She admired that in a man. Sure he was handsome, but it was more than that, more than physical attraction. Jennifer bit her lower lip and reminded herself that Hood had just lost his wife. Don't waste your time on this one, she told herself.

CHAPTER 35

Two hours after the raid, Captain Lincoln Brand met with Police Commissioner Sullivan and Mayor Katz at the mayor's house.

"Let me get this straight, Brand," the mayor said. "You have five wounded officers, two with dog bites. You wounded one of Bartolucci's guards, found no trace of an undercover DEA agent, or Gino Bartolucci, or anyone else, for that matter. You wounded two dogs. And you woke up the neighborhood. Is that about right?"

Brand could see where the blame for this fiasco was about to be placed. "Well, that's about right, Mayor. Except"—and here his tone was thick with sarcasm—"don't forget we found a stash of heroin." His voice rose. "But it sure as hell wasn't enough to fill a panel truck, as the DEA guy told us."

The mayor gave him a squint-eyed look and said, "How the fuck will I explain all this to the press? And wait 'til the animal rights people find out my S.W.A.T. team hurt a couple puppy dogs."

In a perverted, vindictive sort of way, Brand enjoyed every bit of the mayor's discomfort. Although Commissioner Sullivan had yet to say anything, Brand could tell from the anguished look on his boss's face and his continual shifting in his chair that Sullivan was in agony.

The mayor's mood suddenly changed. "Hey, we can tell the media we had intelligence about a stash of drugs at Bartolucci's place. No one says a thing about the dogs. The story will be that

Bartolucci's gangsters fired on our men first and wounded several brave police officers."

Sullivan gave Brand a pained look and finally said to the mayor, "I don't think any of that will pass muster."

Brand felt he had no choice but to further ruin the mayor's brief moment of optimism. He held up a hand, fingers spread, and ticked off the points he felt needed to be made. "First, about the drugs," he said. "We had no probable cause for the raid. You'll remember it was the DEA that put us up to this. But my guess is the DEA will pull a Sergeant Schultz. They won't know nothing. They'll never admit to having anything to do with any of it. So, a defense attorney right out of law school could get a case against Bartolucci tossed out of court—if it even got past the DA's office. Second, why would a wily old Mafia Don who's been around forever have a couple hundred pounds of heroin on a dining room table? Why would he take that kind of risk? Third, what about the DEA undercover agent we were told was on the property? There was no one there. Bartolucci's people had no clue about a DEA agent when we questioned them. Fourth, when I confronted Bartolucci's men and told them to lay down their guns, they were honestly surprised we were cops. Now, why would a bunch of supposed drug runners be surprised that the cops raided their place? They seemed to expect trouble, but not from the police. Right now, Bartolucci has a potential lawsuit against the City of Philadelphia. If you go to the press with some story that smears his name, he could own the City. Fifth"—he wiggled the little finger on his raised hand—"we found a bank of busted windows on the south side of the house. We never went near that side of the house. Something really stinks. Oh, and by the way, we found this envelope taped to the basement door when we searched the house."

Brand pulled an envelope from an inside pocket of his tactical vest and waved it at the mayor. "It's addressed to Rolf Bishop, the recently confirmed CIA Deputy Director."

"Why in God's name would anyone in that house leave an envelope for a top CIA guy?" Sullivan asked.

The mayor's face sagged. He had an expression as though he finally realized he'd been scammed. "What's in the envelope?"

Brand pulled the note from the envelope and handed it to Katz. The mayor read it aloud: "When you play ball with the wrong people, you get the bat shoved up your ass. Bend over, Rolfie Baby, your time has come." The mayor read the message aloud a second time.

Brand could barely contain his laughter.

The mayor refolded the note and returned it to Brand, who put it back in the envelope. "Captain Brand," Katz said. "I think the commissioner and I will figure out how to deal with this mess. While we do that, why don't you go out to my living room and try to get CIA Headquarters on the phone. Tell them we need to immediately talk with Deputy Director Bishop. When you reach him, tell him we found a letter addressed to him. Don't tell him we've looked in the envelope."

"Yes, sir, Mr. Mayor, I'll get right on it."

"Oh, one other thing," Katz said. "Why don't you call that asshole DEA guy, Morton, and see what he has to say?"

"I already tried. The DEA night duty officer checked his computer for me and discovered Timothy Morton retired from the agency. No forwarding address."

It took Brand fifteen minutes to connect to the Langley duty officer. She told him to leave a recorded message for Deputy Director Bishop. Brand waited for the beep and then spoke into the phone: "This is Captain Abraham Lincoln Brand of the Philadelphia Police Department. We found a letter addressed to you. If we do not hear from you soon, we will open the letter." He added his telephone number and hung up.

Brand rejoined the mayor and the police commissioner who had brandy snifters in hand.

Katz fixed his gaze on Brand, pointed at a chair.

"Linc, Clarence and I have decided we have only one course of action. We'll call a press conference for ten this morning. We'll announce that the Philadelphia S.W.A.T. unit executed a surprise raid on an estate in Chestnut Hill that is secretly owned by the former head of organized crime in Philadelphia. We'll say we had information that a significant amount of illegal drugs was hidden on the estate and we will display the drugs your team captured. We'll say Bartolucci's guards opened fire on the S.W.A.T. officers. We will also say the guards at the estate were heavily armed. We will announce that each of the men who took part in the raid will receive the Medal of Merit."

The mayor turned to his police commissioner. "Did I cover everything, Clarence?"

"Sounds like you got it all, Mr. Mayor."

The mayor returned his attention to Brand. "You have any suggestions?"

Brand first looked at his boss and then at the mayor. "No disrespect intended, gentlemen," he said, "but you've got to be kidding. You go out and tell that crock of shit to the press and it will come back and bite us all on the ass. You tell that story and you'll have to bring charges against Bartolucci and every one of his men. Their lawyers will rip those charges to shreds. I believe Gino Bartolucci was as much a dupe in this scam as we were. I think the agenda of that DEA son-of-a-bitch, Tim Morton, had nothing to do with the story he gave us. There are way too many unexplained things about this whole operation. And what about that busted bank of windows I mentioned earlier? And what about that note addressed to Rolf Bishop? Until I saw that note, I thought the DEA had orchestrated this clusterfuck. Now, I'm not so sure. Maybe the CIA used Morton to play us. This whole thing stinks."

"Maybe stray bullets knocked out the windows," the mayor said, although without much conviction.

"I don't think so, Mayor. Those windows were on the far side of the house, away from the action. Another thing that puzzles me is the amount of debris we found beyond the south wall of the property. Leaves and small branches were scattered on the golf course a couple hundred yards from the back of Bartolucci's property. I thought I heard a helicopter in the area after Bartolucci's men surrendered, but I didn't think anything of it. I knew we didn't have any aircraft deployed on the mission. With all that debris beyond the wall, I suspect a chopper landed there and picked up men who were not part of my team. The same men who drugged and tied up four Philadelphia policemen who were assigned to guard the back wall of Bartolucci's place."

"What!" Katz shouted.

"Yeah, we found them trussed up, unconscious on the edge of the golf course. They couldn't tell us a thing. None of them saw who attacked them. That sounds like a Special Ops team to me. And another thing, what happened to Bartolucci and the undercover DEA agent? When we questioned the guards, they said they had no idea where Bartolucci might be, but that he'd been asleep in an upstairs bedroom. They were as confused about his whereabouts as we were. And one of the guards told us there had been three other men and a woman in the house. And get this: One of the men and the woman were cops."

"Cops!" Katz shouted. "Were they ours?"

"No, I don't think so. One of Bartolucci's men told us they were from someplace out of state."

Brand waited to see if Katz had any more questions, and then continued. "The other two men were Bartolucci's son-in-law, David Hood, and Hood's father, Peter. All four people were Gino Bartolucci's guests."

Brand paused to allow the other two men to fully process all he'd said. Then he added, "I checked on David Hood and learned he has a sterling reputation. He heads up a highly respected international security firm. And Hood's wife and two children were killed in a bomb blast at their home in Bethesda on April 12.

"Mr. Mayor, Commissioner, I don't think we gain a thing from a press conference and we potentially lose a lot. There are only a couple of small groups of people who know about this operation. There are my men, who won't say a word about it. They're not about to blab about a raid that turned into such a mess. Bartolucci's men could spill the beans, but I really don't see that happening. Who would believe them anyway? The neighbors think all the noise they heard was from fireworks, so there's no worry on that front. We maintained strict radio silence on our side, so no one could have monitored the raid on a scanner. I'll come up with a reasonable story for the wounded officers to tell their families. And one other thing. Your story won't stand up to press scrutiny. If your media friends discover you lied to them, they'll turn on you like rabid dogs."

"Aw jeez," the mayor groaned. After a few seconds, Katz added, "We need to find Gino Bartolucci. And the minute you hear from this guy Rolf Bishop, call me. I want to know what he might have had to do with this fiasco."

"If I was Gino Bartolucci," Brand said, "I would get away from Philly as quickly as possible."

"Shit! Shit! Shit!" Katz shouted.

Not up to the mayor's usual eloquence, Brand thought.

CHAPTER 36

Bishop slouched in his government Towncar and tried to sleep on the trip up to New York from D.C. But the gears in his brain spun at a thousand miles an hour. Sleep just wouldn't come. When his cellphone *brrred*, he sat up straight, breathed in a great quantity of air, exhaled slowly, and hoped for good news. He pushed the TALK button on the phone.

"Mr. Bishop?"

Bishop recognized the voice of the leader of the CIA black ops team he'd sent to the Bartolucci estate. "How did it go?"

The man recited what had happened. The news was not good. The team had basically accomplished nothing.

Bishop cut the connection; he was wide awake now. He wanted to scream. Nothing was going well. And now he had to get to New York to meet with the President for the G-8 meeting that would include a series of briefings scheduled for the leaders of some of the world's most powerful economies. Bishop's assignment was to personally update the heads of state and their intelligence agency directors on information the CIA had gathered on several hot spots around the globe: Syria, Iran, Egypt, Iraq, and Afghanistan. CIA analysts, specialists on each of the subject areas, had prepared his script. Bishop estimated his driver would get him to The Plaza by 3 a.m. He could then, hopefully, catch four or five hours sleep before he had to take part in a 10 a.m. practice briefing session. Lunch with the President and the other G-8 leaders would follow, and then his part of the briefing, set for 2:30 p.m. After that he would have the rest of the day free to decide what he should do about Hood.

Bishop cursed the black ops team and thought about his options. Then the car phone beeped. He picked up the receiver.

A woman said. "Copley here; verify ID, please."

Bishop punched in his seven-digit identification code on the telephone receiver.

"Sir, I have message traffic for you. Hold while I play it back."

A series of beeps and tones played in Bishop's ear. He heard a voice say he was Captain Brand of the Philadelphia Police Department and had found a letter addressed to him.

"Now what?" he muttered.

Bishop cut the connection and dialed the number Brand had left.

"Sergeant Moynihan. How may I help you?"

For some reason, the sergeant's crisp tone aggravated Bishop and put him in a worse mood than he was in already.

"What you can do for me, Sergeant, is get Captain Brand on the line immediately."

Moynihan hated the graveyard shift while the rest of the world was home in bed. Now he had an asshole on the line giving him a ration of shit. "Why don't you give me your name and a little less attitude, mister, and maybe I'll see if I can track down Captain Brand for you in the next week or so."

"You listen to me, *mister*. This is CIA Deputy Director Rolf Bishop. You get Brand on the line or I'll have your ass demoted to some friggin' backwater precinct where the natives are always restless."

Moynihan knew how to handle crank callers. "Hey, I think maybe you should go back to whatever cage you escaped from. Or maybe just haul your butt down to the closest police station. I'm sure your friendly neighborhood cop would just love to talk with a CIA Deputy Director."

Moynihan laughed boisterously and hung up.

Bishop took the phone away from his ear and stared at it open-mouthed. He took a couple of deep breaths until he'd regained his composure, and hit the TALK button again. The phone automatically re-dialed Philadelphia Police Headquarters. This time, a female cop answered.

"This is Officer Wilson of the Philadelphia Police Department, how may I be of assistance?"

Bishop tried charm this time. "Officer Wilson, my name is Rolf Bishop. I received a message that Captain Brand needed to talk to me A-S-A-P. Do you think you could connect us, or perhaps take a message for him to call me back?" He gave the officer his cellphone number.

"Mr. Bishop, give me a moment to see if I can reach Captain Brand." After a moment, the woman came back on the line. "Mr. Bishop, I have Captain Brand. Please hang on while I patch you into his car."

There were a few seconds of dead air and then, "Mr. Bishop, it's Captain Brand. Thanks for calling me back at such an ungodly hour."

"That's okay, Captain. What's up?"

"I've got an envelope addressed to you."

"Yeah, I got that from your message. Who's it from?"

"Can't be sure about that. But we found it taped to a door in Gino Bartolucci's house in Chestnut Hill."

Bishop wanted to scream.

"Mr. Bishop, Mayor Katz wants to meet with you immediately. You don't happen to be in Philadelphia?"

Cute, Bishop thought. Brand just tried to put me in Philadelphia. Maybe to tie me to the raid on Bartolucci's home. "Not only am I not in Philadelphia," Bishop said, "but I haven't been there in months. Why do you ask?"

"I guess I was confused, Mr. Bishop."

"I'm on my way to New York City. Tell me what the mayor wants to talk with me about."

"I have no idea what Mayor Katz wants except he mentioned he plans to call a press conference about a raid on the Gino Bartolucci estate. He wanted to talk with you before he made any statements about possible CIA involvement in that raid."

"You have me confused," Bishop said. "Who is Gino Bartolucci and why would the Philadelphia mayor be so misguided as to connect the Central Intelligence Agency to a raid on some gangster's place. Do me a favor, Captain. Kindly tell Mayor Katz I'll be tied up in New York for a couple days. I'll call him when I return to Langley."

"Yes, sir. But the mayor won't be pleased."

Finally, after a long pause, Bishop said, "Tell me about the envelope."

"Oh yeah," Brand said, as though he'd forgotten about it. "As I said, we found it taped to a door."

"Why don't you tell me what's in it?"

"Mr. Bishop, I have no idea what's in the envelope. Do I understand you want me to open it?"

Bishop guessed the envelope had already been opened. But he couldn't help admire how well the man handled deception. Brand would be a real asset to the CIA. "Of course, Captain Brand," he said. "Please open the envelope and tell me what's inside."

"All right, sir," Brand replied. "Huh," he said, after several seconds had passed. "I don't understand the note, but here goes. It reads: 'When you play ball with the wrong people, you get the bat shoved up your ass. Bend over, Rolfie Baby, your time has come.' Do you know what that means, Mr. Bishop?"

"I have no idea. But I'll think about it."

"Thank you, Mr. Bishop," Brand said. "I'll be sure to pass your message on to the mayor."

"You do that."

Brand chuckled. Bishop had claimed he didn't know who Gino Bartolucci was, but then he'd referred to Bartolucci as a 'gangster.' The man had lied.

CHAPTER 37

David had spelled Jennifer Ramsey behind the wheel of the Dodge after they crossed into New Jersey. It was now 3:15 a.m. While he drove the stolen car north, Gino slept beside him and Peter and O'Neil slept in the back seat, with Jennifer Ramsey sandwiched between them. David stifled a laugh when he looked at her in the rear view mirror and saw her bemused expression.

The scene in the back seat made David want to laugh. His father snored loudly; O'Neil's head rested on Ramsey's shoulder. Drool leaked from the corner of his mouth. The clothes they wore, which they'd acquired at a Wal-Mart outside Philadelphia, only made the scene more humorous. Peter, O'Neil, and Ramsey were dressed in an assortment of Wal-Mart athletic shoes, sweatshirts, and jeans that David had hurriedly bought. O'Neil wore a sweatshirt adorned with the cartoon character, Foghorn Leghorn Rooster. Peter's sweatshirt was emblazoned with the Washington Redskins' logo. Ramsey's was free of logos and writing, but it was a god-awful pink with glitter in the shape of a star on the front.

They'd been on the road for over two hours when David pulled off the New Jersey Turnpike into a rest stop. The others awoke when he stopped in front of a Roy Rogers restaurant. They were an hour's drive from New York City.

"I'll take the car around to the gas pumps," David said. "Why don't you all make a pit stop, get some food? I'll meet you back

234

here in fifteen minutes. Oh, Dennis, why don't you see if they have prepaid cellphones for sale inside?"

Jennifer used the pay phone in the women's room and put in a collect call to Lt. Croken's cell.

"Jeez!" Croken shouted. "This better be a matter of life or death. Do you know what time it is?"

"Lieutenant, it's Detective Ramsey. Sorry about the time."

"What the hell are you up to? You left me a goddamn cryptic message that you'd found Mr. Hood, the guy Cromwell believes murdered his family."

"I also left the message that I am convinced Hood had nothing to do with the explosion at his home."

"Yeah, I got that, too."

"Lieutenant, Cromwell's an idiot. I know for a fact Hood's innocent. Gino Bartolucci is helping Hood try to find out who killed his family. He's protecting him at the same time."

"Gino Bartolucci, as in Don Gino Bartolucci, the Mafia Capo?"

Ramsey swallowed hard. "Yes, that Bartolucci."

"I got a call from the Philly P.D. They claimed there was a gun battle on the street where Hood's father lives. They also claim some woman was involved. You wouldn't know anything about that, would you?"

"Uh-h-h, sort of."

"You were *sort of* involved in a gun battle?"

"I went by Hood's father's house to try to track down his son. I just happened to be in the wrong place at the wrong time."

"Jeez! Any other surprises, Ramsey?"

"The Philadelphia P.D. staged a raid on Bartolucci's place a few hours ago."

"What!"

"Listen, Chief, I gotta go. The others will wonder where I am. I'll call you later."

"Don't you hang up on me, Ramsey," Croken screamed. "Don't you fuckin'—"

They all stood outside the restaurant when David returned. Their clothes and their obvious self-consciousness about them made David smile.

"Ah say, ah say, boy, what's so damn funny?" O'Neil asked in an imitation of Foghorn Leghorn Chicken's voice, and the others cracked up.

After they piled into the car, David pulled onto the highway, drove for about an hour, and then exited again after Rahway, New Jersey.

Gino got out and called Joey Cataldo on the prepaid cellphone O'Neil bought at the truck stop. It took ten rings before someone answered. It took another couple minutes before Cataldo came to the phone.

"Gino, it's 4:30 in the morning; I assume this is important."

"You know me how many . . . maybe thirty years? You think I'd call you if it wasn't important?" Gino said

"Right. What can I do for you?"

"I got a stolen car I need to make disappear and I need another car to replace it. I need a place to hole up for maybe a couple days, along with four friends. And we all need changes of clothes. Lastly, that matter we planned to discuss over dinner tomorrow night, you think you'd be ready to meet tonight instead?"

"Yeah, no problem," Cataldo said. "I found out what you wanted to know. As for the other stuff, where are you now?"

"Off the Jersey Turnpike, just south of the city."

"Okay, here's what you do. Take the exit for the Lincoln Tunnel. When you go through the tunnel, look for the turnoff to the Meadowlands . . . you know where the sports stadium is?"

"Sure."

"Pull into the stadium lot. You'll see a blue Ford van parked near the east ticket window with two men in it. Give your car keys to one of them. One of the guys in the van will be my nephew. He'll take care of you. Clothes and stuff we'll take care of later. You need anything else?"

"No, Joey. Thank you. I'll see you tonight. Where do you want to meet?"

"My nephew will fill you in."

It took a bit over a half-hour to locate the right exit and another ten minutes to reach the stadium. Gino spotted a solitary vehicle in the lot.

"That's our guy. Blue van."

David stopped ten yards from the van. Gino got out and walked the few steps to the vehicle. The two men there got out and one of them said, "Don Bartolucci, my name is Sal Fanelli. It's an honor to be of service to you. Jimmy here will take care of your car."

Gino waved back at the Dodge. The others got out and approached the van. Fanelli opened the van's sliding door and waited for them to climb aboard. Gino got into the front passenger seat. When they were all seated, he asked, "So, where you taking us, Sal?"

Fanelli stared at Gino, surprised. "Didn't Uncle Joey tell you, Don Bartolucci? I was told to bring you all out to his place on Long Island. You'll be his guests."

Rolf Bishop woke at 8 a.m. He'd slept fitfully and felt just as exhausted as when he went to bed a few hours earlier. The stump of his leg hurt more than usual. He attached the prosthesis to the stump and staggered to the bathroom. He had to get ready for the day's events. He'd always been up to any task, but the pressure of the last few weeks had begun to take a toll. He actually felt sorry for himself—a first for him. He rose from bed, went into the bathroom, and stared at the tired face in the mirror. Bishop yelled at the image in the glass, "Suck it up, man." He then asked the question he'd asked countless times before, "What would an extraordinary person do in this situation?"

At Joey Cataldo's Long Island estate, Sal Fanelli dropped his exhausted passengers in front of a two-story stone guesthouse. A butler with an English accent greeted them as they left the van. "Welcome to *Casa Sogna*. My name is Cyril. If you will follow me."

David glanced around at his companions. They all looked as though they'd been rescued from a ship wreck. Each was in need of a shower. Their clothes were not only wrinkled, but were spotted with catsup, mustard, and coffee. To Cyril's credit, he didn't react to their appearance.

Cyril was about as proper as an Englishman can get. He was tall and erect and his clothes would have passed the most detailed inspection at any Marine boot camp. His blond hair was slicked back in the continental fashion and his eyes, magnified by a thick pair of spectacles, looked particularly blue. His mustache was thin, straight, and perfectly trimmed. He showed them to their rooms, pointed out where they would each find towels, pajamas, robes, and slippers, and asked them to fill out a card on the dresser in each of their rooms with their clothing sizes. He explained he'd return for the completed cards in thirty minutes.

Cyril took Gino to an especially extravagant suite at the end of a hall. "Please feel free to get cleaned up and rest," he said. "At 10 a.m., a man from a haberdashery will be here to fit you for new clothes. Don Cataldo told me to inform you his business in the city will occupy him through the morning and most of the afternoon, but he promised to be here early this evening to formally welcome you to his home."

At 10 sharp, Cyril ushered a short, nattily dressed, sixty-something man into Gino's room. "Antonio Persico," Cyril announced, "the best tailor in New York."

The little man accepted the compliment gravely. He bowed deeply to Gino and said in an accent heavy with the strains of southern Italy, "It is a great honor to be of service to a friend of Don Cataldo's." He walked over to the bed and carefully—almost lovingly—laid out several garment bags he'd carried in draped over both arms. He removed a suit, a sports jacket, a pair of slacks, and several shirts from the garment bags. Cyril had a large shopping bag in each hand and deposited them on the floor next to Gino. From the bags, Antonio the Tailor took underwear, socks, shoes, ties, belts, and toiletries, and laid them on the bed, too.

The tailor asked Gino to put on the articles of outerwear so he could be sure the sizes were appropriate. After Gino had done so, the man sighed with pleasure and said, "Maybe a little change here, a little change there."

"*Si*," Gino responded. "*Molto bene. Grazie.*"

At noon, Cyril tapped gently at each of their bedroom doors and suggested they "repair to the veranda for lunch." They looked like patients in a hospital, in their pajamas, bathrobes, and slippers. Cyril treated them to a meal: Several types of cold cuts and garnishes, salads, freshly baked Italian breads, imported Italian soft drinks, coffee, and a variety of pastries. After they'd finished and the dishes were cleared, Cyril informed them their host would arrive around 5 p.m. Then he left the veranda.

"I need to tell you all something," Gino announced. "This place belongs to the head of the New York . . . organization. And he's not retired. I need each of you to give me your word anything I tell you or anything you hear around here will remain completely confidential. I need to know that none of you will ever do anything to make me regret bringing you into this."

David and Peter nodded. Gino spoke directly to the Bethesda policewoman. "Are *you* in agreement, Detective Ramsey?"

Jennifer was no starry-eyed idealist or self-righteous ideologue, but "hanging out" with two Mafia Dons was well beyond her definition of appropriate behavior for a career law enforcement officer. She realized Gino wanted her to plead the Fifth or outright lie if she should be questioned or forced to testify about any of her activities with these men. The ethical and professional quandary she found herself in seemed to have anesthetized her vocal chords, until David gave her a painful look that seemed to beseech her to go along for the ride.

Before she knew what she was doing, she nodded and said, "I give you my word."

Gino grunted his approval, and looked at O'Neil.

"I've thought a lot about how all of this will play back in Chicago," O'Neil said. "I've also gone over in my mind on numerous occasions why we are knee-deep in the shit Bishop has generated. Some of us are here for very personal reasons. Gino, David, Peter, you've all lost family members and that pain is the worst pain a man can endure. But I, too, feel a pain I will never get over. That CIA son-of-a-bitch not only killed your family members, but he had a lot of brave men murdered—men who fought for our country. I'm also certain he had Gunnery Sergeant Sam Collins killed. I'll always suspect if I hadn't asked Sam to help me, he would still be alive. I assure you, Gino, I'm in this thing 'til the end. And yes, I will never use anything I see or hear against you or anyone else who helps us take down Bishop." Then O'Neil smiled and said, "As long as you give me your word you won't tell anyone how I spent my East Coast vacation."

Gino laughed, held up his right hand, fingers extended. "Scout's honor."

Peter slowly got out of his chair and stretched in a futile effort to work the kinks out of his sore back. "My friends," he said, "it's about time I put these old bones back to bed. Woe to the sorry, insensitive son of a gun who cuts my nap short by even one minute."

David watched his father slowly ascend the stairs from the veranda to the guesthouse's back entrance. Peter looked tired and old. He remembered the little Maryland diner where he'd agreed to let his father join him in his hunt for the murderer of Carmela, Heather, and Kyle. And once again, the thought crossed his mind he might live to regret that decision.

After Peter disappeared into the house, the others also stood and moved in that direction. They'd almost reached the door when Peter came back out with a copy of *The New York Times*. He waved the paper in the air to get their attention and yelled, "Well, lady and gentlemen, guess who made the front page of the *Times*." Before anyone had a chance to venture a guess, Peter said, "It's our buddy Rolf Bishop. And this time he's with the President."

David moved next to his father to get a look at the front page. There was Bishop, handsome and dignified, in a photograph, just under the paper's banner. The caption read, "CIA Deputy Director, Rolf Bishop, will brief heads of state at this week's G-8 summit conference in New York (see story on page 5)."

"Turn to page 5," David said.

Peter turned the pages and read aloud:

CIA Deputy Director of Intelligence, Rolf Bishop, will provide the keynote briefing at today's G-8 meeting at the United Nations Building in New York City. The United States hosts the summit, which is the third in a series held over the last fourteen months. The previous two conferences concentrated on financial and economic matters. This conference focuses on issues of global security. Deputy Director Bishop's briefing—for the heads of the G-8 nations, as well as for their security chiefs and other key international security personnel—will cover strategic security matters, including an analysis of trouble spots in the Middle East.

Premier Armand d'Espy of France told the Times *he looked forward with great anticipation to Deputy Director Bishop's remarks.*

Bishop will also participate in several other meetings associated with the summit conference and will attend a State Dinner at the end of the conference, hosted by the President at The Plaza Hotel.

This will be the first opportunity the President has had to present his new CIA Deputy Director to other world leaders.

Bishop retired from the U.S. Army in 2004 with the rank of Colonel. He holds a number of decorations.

Since he retired from the military, Bishop has served in numerous volunteer positions and on the boards of directors of a number of national and international corporations.

Chief of Detectives Mickey Croken was having a hissy fit. He'd been in a terrible mood ever since Detective Ramsey woke him in the middle of the night and then hung up on him. Now in Police Headquarters, he stormed around the detective bureau. This was his day for case briefings and the word had gotten out among the detectives the boss was in a rage about something.

The entire detective squad had assembled in the briefing room. Team by team, they shared whatever progress they'd made on their cases: new suspects, solved cases, status of trials, etc. Croken's comments to the detective teams were even more caustic than usual. There wasn't a cop in the room who couldn't wait for the meeting to end.

When the last team completed its briefing, Croken sent them all on their way with, "Get out there and try to accomplish something for a change."

Roger Cromwell hung back and let the other detectives vacate the room. He followed Croken to his office. "Hear anything from Ramsey, Lieutenant?" Cromwell asked from the office doorway.

Croken plopped down into his chair and stared back at Cromwell while he unwrapped a piece of nicotine gum. He popped the gum in his mouth and rolled the wrapper between his fingers. He put his feet up on the corner of his desk and said, "Yeah, I heard from Ramsey. What do you care?"

"Just curious. I haven't seen her around for a few days."

"She found David Hood in Philadelphia. Apparently, the police there raided Hood's father-in-law's place for some reason. That's about all I know."

"Ramsey wasn't hurt in the raid on the Bartolucci place?"

"Not as far as I know."

"That's good," Cromwell said and left the office.

Croken squinted. The gum tasted like shit. Then he stared at his empty office doorway and thought, How the hell did Cromwell know Bartolucci was David Hood's father-in-law?

CHAPTER 38

Manny Segal started out as an attorney in New York City. After years of legal grunt work, he got the chance to defend a mid-level member of the Colombo crime family in court. The man had been indicted for the murder of a drug dealer who'd encroached on Colombo territory. Manny knew the man was guilty. He also knew the DA had an open and shut case against his client. So Manny did what any attorney with no moral compass would do: He bribed a juror.

But a month after Segal's client was acquitted, a traffic cop in Queens stopped the bribed juror because of a broken brake light. The man appeared to be unusually nervous, so the cop asked him if he could search the car. The juror gave his permission. What he hadn't noticed was that the cop had a four-legged partner that waited patiently in the back of the patrol car. It took Rex the Wonder Dog less than ten seconds to sniff out a kilo of heroin packed inside the spare tire. So the juror was arrested for possession of narcotics with intent to distribute. He was in a cell awaiting trial when he realized he might be able to get a suspended sentence in return for giving up evidence about Manny Segal's jury tampering.

The New York State Bar Association disbarred Manny and a District Court judge sentenced him to five years in the state penitentiary. While in prison, he decided what he would do when he got out of prison.

With the assistance of his old mob client, Manny developed

a whole new sort of practice after his release. Manny the lawyer became Manny—code name: Paladin—the hired killer. And a damn good killer at that. Manny never knew who his clients were and frankly didn't care. If they had his telephone number, they had to be powerful men who required anonymity.

Rolf Bishop decided the David Hood problem had reached the crisis point. He needed to turn the problem over to the highest level professional he knew—Paladin. The assassin had eliminated seven of the men who served under Bishop in the SLSD, as well as Gunnery Sergeant Samuel Collins. Paladin had done his job well. A sharp pain hit Bishop's stomach. Why the hell didn't I have Paladin take out all the men in the unit? he thought. He'd assigned Toney to the job because of proximity, and Toney had blown it. Then he'd hired the two Georgia men because he thought two killers would be better than one. They'd also screwed up. Now everything he'd worked for was threatened because of their failures.

The risks to Bishop had grown exponentially. The bodies in the SUV on his street in Georgetown and the note found at the Bartolucci estate represented something well beyond reputational or legal risk. David Hood and his supporters now hunted him. Hood and his father had to be taken out without delay! Bartolucci and that Bethesda detective had to be eliminated, as well.

But Bishop knew how Paladin worked. He didn't act precipitously; he researched his targets and never took unnecessary risks. That type of caution took time. Time Bishop couldn't afford.

He dialed Paladin's unlisted number.

"This is Talon. We need to talk." He left his cellphone number. The assassin called back in less than a minute.

"You've interrupted the *Allegro Molto* of *Rachmaninoff's Symphony Number 2*," a man's high-pitched voice complained.

"I require your services."

Bishop heard the man put down the receiver. Music played in the background. The music suddenly went silent and Paladin returned to the phone. "Are you familiar with Rachmaninoff's work, Talon?" he asked in a superior tone.

"Yes, I am quite taken with Rachmaninoff," Bishop said. "In fact, that piece you had on is one of my favorites. However, I must tell you I find the *Allegro Molto* movement a little frivolous and fanciful. Now the *Adagio* is the one I truly love. It has nuances of passion and romance that approach the spiritual." He paused a moment and then said, "My apologies for the interruption."

Bishop realized he'd laid it on a little thick, but he hoped the total silence at the other end of the line indicated Paladin was surprised and impressed. He needed to be in Paladin's good graces.

"I had no idea, Talon, that we had a mutual admiration for classical music. Suddenly, I regret my business arrangements require arms length relationships."

"I have an assignment for you that will require your immediate attention. This matter is so urgent it will not accommodate the usual lead time."

"Explain."

"I need the assignment concluded within twenty-four hours."

"Where is the man located?"

Bishop paused. "I'm not sure. And it's three *men* and one *woman*, not one *man*. But I believe if you find one of them, you will find all of them."

"This is impossible," Paladin said.

"I have found nothing is impossible if enough money is thrown at the problem."

"Please define *enough*."

"My need is critical and time is of the essence. I am prepared to pay $200,000."

"As much as I would like to accommodate you, Talon," Paladin said, "that is not my definition of *enough*."

Bishop said, "I'll pay you two hundred thousand dollars up front, and another two hundred thousand dollars upon successful completion of the assignment. The down payment will be wired to your account tonight. The balance will be put into escrow for transfer the instant you accomplish the mission."

There was a long pause at the other end of the line. Then Paladin said, "Talon, I look forward to assisting you in this matter. What are your instructions?"

CHAPTER 39

Cyril politely knocked on Gino's door. "Mr. Bartolucci," he said, just loud enough to be heard. When Gino opened the door, Cyril said, "Mr. Cataldo has arrived and would be pleased to meet with you."

"I'll be right with you," Gino said.

"I'll wait downstairs."

Gino threw off the tasseled cashmere throw he had around his shoulders and dropped it on a chair. Come on you old bastard, he told himself, let's move. He felt . . . he couldn't come up with the right word. Heavy, sloggy. Too much excitement; too little sleep, he thought. He went to the bathroom, splashed water on his face, and toweled off. He put on a shirt and tie, slacks, and a sport coat, and went downstairs and outside, where Cyril sat behind the wheel of a golf cart.

Cyril drove Gino one hundred yards to the main house. Joey Cataldo waited by the front door. When Gino stepped out onto the pavement, Cataldo hugged him and then led him into the house.

"Welcome to my home," Cataldo said. "I hope you've been comfortable. I apologize I couldn't welcome you when you arrived."

"You've gone out of your way to accommodate my friends and me. I am again in your debt. I apologize for the intrusion."

"On the contrary. You bring great honor to my home."

Cataldo guided Gino to a room decorated in the style of a 19th century baron's library. The furniture was done in deep maroon-colored leather and the pictures on the walls showed hunt scenes full of horses, dogs, and well-dressed gentry.

After they sat in plush chairs, Cyril escorted a young olive-skinned woman who carried a tray into the room. She wore a maid's uniform that highlighted her figure. Cyril pointed at a low table between the two men. She placed the tray there.

Then Cyril said, "*Endoxie!*" and she left the room. "Tea or coffee?" Cyril asked.

They each selected coffee. Cyril poured and left the room.

"What's with the doll?" Gino asked. "I thought maybe she was Italian, but now I'm not so sure. What did your man say to her?"

Cataldo laughed. "I don't like to have hired help around the main house who might overhear something they shouldn't. So I only use immigrants here. That little girl is right off a boat from Greece. She works hard and keeps her mouth shut, and Cyril can somehow communicate with her." He smiled. "And she's damn good to look at."

"What about the English guy?"

Cataldo smiled. "When I found Cyril he was in the country illegally . . . his work permit had long expired. I fixed that and then brought his whole family over. I wish some of our own people were as loyal as he is."

Gino raised his coffee cup by way of compliment. Cataldo returned the gesture.

"Don Bartolucci, you asked for certain information that might help you find your daughter's killer. If this were not about Carmela's death, I would never agree to furnish this information to you."

Cataldo pulled an envelope from an inner suit coat pocket and slid it across the table. When Gino reached to pick it up, Cataldo lightly touched the back of his hand and waited until Gino looked up. "There's nothing in that envelope that can be tied to me. But still, it goes against my instincts to divulge that information."

"I hope the information in this envelope will erase any doubt in my mind as to who was responsible for my daughter's murder."

Cataldo stood, hunched his shoulders, and spread his arms out, palms up. "If that takes care of business, let's take a stroll around the house before we eat. I want to show you my garden. I'll have Cyril ask your friends to join us for dinner in an hour. I look forward to meeting them."

"You need to know something before we go any further in this matter," Gino said. "There are four people with me. My son-in-law, David Hood, and his father, Peter. I trust both of them." Gino paused. He had to tell Cataldo about O'Neil and Ramsey. But how to do so without losing Cataldo's support.

But Cataldo broke into Gino's thoughts and said, "You gonna tell me about the two cops?"

Gino coughed in surprise. "I was about to, but how'd you know?"

Cataldo shrugged. "You don't think my men can recognize heat. I hear the woman's a real knockout, but she walks like she wore a gun belt her whole life." Cataldo laughed and imitated the walk all beat cops seem to acquire from wearing a heavy leather utility belt laden with weapon and equipment.

Gino laughed along with Cataldo. He raised a hand as though he held a wineglass. "*Salute.* My compliments, Don Cataldo."

"Shall we take that tour now?"

Gino nodded. He followed Cataldo through the house to a set of French doors that led out to an English garden. Hedges and flowerbeds covered an area of nearly two acres. The garden of *Casa Sogna* was a tribute to taste, beauty, and someone's attention to minute detail. Under any other circumstance Gino would have enjoyed the gardens. But he couldn't get his mind off the envelope in his jacket. He forced himself to pay attention while Cataldo described this plant or that shrub.

Then one of Cataldo's men approached at a fast walk. He carried a wireless telephone. "Mr. Cataldo, you got a call."

Cataldo took the phone. "My apologies, Don Bartolucci," he said with a shrug, and walked twenty yards away.

Gino took advantage of the moment and sat on a stone bench. He removed the envelope from his jacket and opened it. Inside was a single sheet of paper. On it was the name of a bank and what appeared to be an account number at the top. Below that were two columns, one with dates and the other with dollar-denominated amounts. At the bottom of the page was a single sentence: *On the dates shown above, the corresponding dollar amounts were deposited in the account number shown.* Joey Cataldo had handed over a record of every payment the Zefferelli Family had made for drug shipments from Afghanistan a decade earlier. If the account noted on the paper belonged to Rolf Bishop, Gino knew he would be able to prove Rolf Bishop had betrayed his country, had violated his oath as a military officer, had broken U.S. and international laws, and had motive for murder. That evidence would be dramatically more compelling than the video of Montrose Toney, an ex-con, spilling the beans about Bishop while under torture. He replaced the list in the envelope and slipped it back into his pocket.

He thought about what Bishop had done to his daughter and grandchildren and thought once again that he could kill the man based on the information he already had. But he understood men like Bishop. Death was an easy way out. For men like Bishop, there were more painful things than death. Gino would kill the man's reputation before he took his life.

Cataldo returned. "Nice spot for deep thoughts, wouldn't you say, Don Bartolucci?"

"None better, Don Cataldo, none better. It's a perfect place to think about friends and enemies . . . how to thank and reward one's friends, and how to punish one's enemies."

Cataldo looked intently into Gino's eyes. Finally, he smiled. "I count myself fortunate I'm a friend and not an enemy of Don Bartolucci."

"Don Cataldo, you are much more than a friend. You are a creditor." He patted his chest. "This envelope puts me in your debt for the rest of my life."

"*Grazie*, Don Bartolucci, *mille grazie*."

Gino looked at his watch. He suddenly felt weary and mildly nauseous. "I see we have a little time before dinner. Would you mind if I returned to my room to wash up?"

"I think that's a good idea. I need to do the same. Let me call Cyril so he can drive you to the guesthouse."

"No, no, the walk will do me good."

"Whatever you say. I'll see you and your friends in the dining room in thirty minutes."

Gino was anxious to put Cataldo's list into David's hands. He knew his son-in-law had international bank clients. Perhaps one of those clients might be able to fill in the one piece of information that wasn't on the sheet of paper Cataldo had given him: the name of the owner of the bank account. Gino ignored the rapid beat of his heart and his shortness of breath and forced himself to continue to the guesthouse. By the time he arrived there he gasped for air, his body awash in sweat. A sudden pain struck his chest. He realized he was in real trouble when he felt pain shoot down his left arm from the shoulder. He staggered through the front door and bumped into Peter.

One look at Gino's face was enough for Peter. He put his arms around his old friend and helped him to a sofa. He quickly removed Gino's shoes and loosened his belt and tie. After he elevated Gino's legs on pillows, Peter ran to the telephone and pressed a button labeled Main House. Cyril answered.

"We need an ambulance here," Peter said. "Now! Gino's having a heart attack."

Within twenty minutes, an ambulance and a team of paramedics arrived. The paramedics did everything they could do to stabilize Gino and then loaded him into the ambulance. David rode along. Gino was conscious but weak. He reached out for David's hand and squeezed it. David bent toward Gino, who hoarsely whispered, "Jacket. Find my jacket?"

"Don't worry about your jacket."

At that moment the ambulance jerked to a stop at the hospital, its rear doors were flung open, and Gino was taken away. David found Gino's jacket stuffed under the gurney. He snatched it up and ran to follow the paramedics.

Reporter Beth Crombie stood outside St. Joseph's Hospital's emergency room. She held a microphone and looked into a television camera. She told her cameraman to stop the film when an ambulance sped behind her. Then she rotated her hand and signaled her cameraman to start the camera again.

"And so, Officer Patrick Elliott will survive," she resumed. "The man who shot him, believed by authorities to be a Russian mob member, died on the sidewalk in front of Sovereignty State Bank from two shots fired by Officer Elliott. Once again, we see that crime doesn't pay. This is Beth Crombie. Action News."

At a signal from her cameraman, she lowered the microphone and said, "Let's go inside, Freddie. See if we can find a member of the cop's family we can interview."

A name scrawled in grease pencil on an acetate board in the emergency room caught Crombie's eye: "Bartolucci, Gino." She had recently won an award for her investigative reports on organized crime. She knew the names of many of the East Coast *Mafiosi*. Past and present. But New York was packed with Italians. This could be just a coincidence. She decided to play a hunch.

She stopped a nurse and asked about Gino Bartolucci. The harried nurse gave Crombie an impatient look and waved in the direction of a curtained-off examination area. With the arrogance of an Action News television star, Crombie parted the curtains and stood behind an orderly who bent over an elderly man on a gurney. Despite the patient's pallor and the oxygen mask that covered the lower part of his face, Beth knew immediately it was the Gino Bartolucci who'd once headed up the Philadelphia mob.

"What's the matter with him?" she asked.

The orderly said, "Heart attack." Then he looked over his shoulder at her and asked, "Who the hell are you?"

Before the orderly could throw her out, several people in white smocks rushed into the room. Crombie wheeled around, left the exam room, and rushed over to her cameraman.

"Get that damn thing on; we got ourselves another story."

"Where?"

"Just follow me. This one's for the network," she said.

When she saw Freddie was all set, she said, "This is Beth Crombie with an exclusive story from KBIW in New York City. You may recall a little over a year ago, this reporter did a special investigative series on organized crime. One of the segments in that series covered the voluntary retirement several years earlier of one of the East Coast's most successful—and notorious—Mafia figures, Gino Bartolucci. Bartolucci allegedly used a grocery market he owned as a cover for his illegitimate activities. He was also alleged to own or control numerous other legitimate businesses— all acquired with the ill-gotten gains of criminal activity. But those allegations were never proved. While I covered the story of a brave police officer shot in a bank robbery this afternoon, this reporter discovered that Gino Bartolucci had been admitted to St. Joseph's Hospital. Mr. Bartolucci apparently suffered a heart attack. Doctors are with him at this moment. We do not have a condition report. We do not know why the former Mafia chief is in New York. We will update this story when more information becomes available. This is Beth Crombie, Action News."

CHAPTER 40

Manny Segal walked into an alley and found the file exactly where Talon said it would be. He carried the file to a cafe on 47th street, bought a cup of tea, and sat in a back booth. As usual, Talon had been thorough. The file had background information about his target; the man's family members, friends, and business associates; addresses, and the man's possible locations. He was not pleased to read that the target was originally from Philadelphia and now lived in Bethesda. How the hell am I going to find this guy in twenty-four hours?

Segal was intrigued by the target's connection to a mobster. Maybe I should have demanded a bigger price for this job, he thought.

He considered his options and thought about his first step. He'd go to Philadelphia. His gut told him Hood would go to Bartolucci for support. About to leave the café, his cellphone rang.

"Yeah?" he answered.

"It's Talon. It looks like I overpaid you."

"How so?"

"I think I know where the . . . assignment might be. I just saw on the news that our man's father-in-law just had a heart attack and was admitted to St. Joseph's Hospital on Long Island. You want to bet that he's in New York with his father-in-law?"

While the doctors worked on Gino, David paced the emergency room floor. He'd dropped Gino's jacket on a plastic chair in the treatment room and suddenly remembered how insistent Gino had been about him finding it. He picked up the jacket and checked the pockets. In an inside pocket he found an envelope with a single sheet of paper inside. On the paper, under the name of a Swiss Bank he knew quite well, were columns of dates and amounts. The dates on the paper were from 2003 and 2004, the same period of time he'd served in Afghanistan. David did a quick calculation in his head and guessed the dollar amount to be a staggering twenty-two to twenty-three million dollars.

Gino had already told him about Cataldo's information about drug smuggling from Afghanistan. But they had yet to prove Bishop was involved in such a scheme. All they had was information provided by a gangster. Perhaps the paper David now held in his hand would make that connection. Could it be his Rosetta Stone, the key to the mystery that had turned his life upside down? He looked at his watch. Zurich was eight hours ahead. It was barely 7 a.m. there. After he put the document and envelope into his jacket pocket, David went in search of someone who could give him a status report on his father-in-law.

APRIL 27

CHAPTER 41

David couldn't get any specific information on Gino's condition until after midnight, when the cardiologist who'd performed an angioplasty told him Gino would recover, but needed to stay in the hospital for observation for at least forty-eight hours. He said Gino could not have visitors until the morning, when he would be moved from intensive care to a private room.

From a courtesy phone, David called the Cataldo estate and told Cyril of events at the hospital. He asked to have a car and driver sent to take him back to the estate.

"Don Bartolucci's driver, Paulie Rizzo, just arrived here from Philadelphia. He should be outside the emergency room entrance in a dark gray Infiniti QX80."

"Thank you, Cyril."

Paulie Rizzo was parked in one of the slots reserved for "Ambulances Only."

David walked over to the vehicle. "You think you could drive me back to the Cataldo estate?"

"How's Don Bartolucci?" Rizzo asked.

"They fixed a clogged blood vessel. He's fine. But they won't let anyone see him until later."

Rizzo stared at David as though he wondered if he'd been told the truth. Finally, he asked, "You're sure the Don's fine?"

"I don't know if he's fine, but the doctor told me the operation went well." He watched worry drain from Rizzo's face. Rizzo crossed himself and his lips moved ever so slightly.

"Okay, get in the car," Rizzo said.

David sat in the front seat. He was wired from stress and worry. In an effort to burn off some of his tension, he tried to make conversation with Rizzo.

"I saw you parked in an ambulance slot. You have any problems with hospital security?"

"No, not really," Rizzo answered. "A couple times the hospital rent-a-cop came by and eyeballed me. The third time, he told me I wasn't allowed to park there."

When it became obvious Rizzo wouldn't volunteer any more information, David asked, "So what did you tell him?"

Rizzo looked over at David and, with a straight face, said, "I showed him Detective O'Neil's police shield."

David gaped at Rizzo. "Why would O'Neil give you his shield?"

Rizzo grinned. "He didn't *give* me his shield."

Manny "Paladin" Segal parked outside St. Joseph's Hospital and waited to see if David Hood would show up. After an hour, he saw Hood leave the hospital and get into the front seat of an Infiniti SUV. He trailed the luxury SUV from the hospital to an estate on Long Island and cruised by a gate the vehicle entered. Segal tapped the steering wheel of his rental car to the beat of Ravel's *Bolero* playing on the radio. He thought this would be the easiest money he'd ever earned.

David answered questions about Gino's condition thrown at him by Cataldo, Ramsey, O'Neil, and his father. When he ran out of answers, Cataldo said, "Let's eat."

None of them had eaten anything substantial since the meal they'd shared on the guesthouse patio. They walked into the dining room behind their host. The room seemed dominated by a huge lead-crystal chandelier that hung from a fourteen-foot-high ceiling. A table that seated twelve had been set formally with china and silver.

A tense silence overhung the room. Joey Cataldo, after all, was a stranger to his guests, and they were more than strangers to him. They represented danger. One slip of the tongue could undo him. No one seemed able to initiate comfortable conversation. It was left to Cyril to enter the room and get them talking again. Unfortunately, what he said only raised the level of anxiety in the room.

While one of the members of the house staff served soup, Cyril asked Cataldo, "Sir, did you happen to catch the late news tonight?"

"No," Cataldo responded. "I try to avoid the brain damage those bastards cause."

"Well, sir," Cyril answered, "some woman reporter did a story on Don Bartolucci's admission to St. Joseph's Hospital."

"Oh shit," Cataldo groaned. "Every damn punk in town with a ten-year-old grudge against Gino now knows where he is. We got no guards on him! Whatsamatta with me?"

Cataldo pointed at Paulie Rizzo. "Paulie, you and three of my men go to the hospital. You carrying?"

"Yes, Don Cataldo."

"Paulie, I want you inside the Don's room. One of my guys will stay in the corridor; another will be in the lobby. The fourth guy will be outside. You'll all stay with the Don until I send in another team."

"David and I can take a shift," Peter said.

Cataldo looked at Peter and smiled. "I appreciate your offer to help out, but I got men who are better equipped to do this kind of work. Why don't you stay here and get some rest."

Peter glared at Cataldo. "I know I am a guest in your home and I assure you I mean no disrespect when I say, 'Kiss my ass.' "

Cyril said, under his breath, "Oh my goodness!"

No one else dared say a word.

Cataldo directed a dead-calm stare at Peter.

David started to say something to diffuse the tension in the room, but Peter waved him into silence.

"You don't know me," Peter said. "So you have no way to know what I'm capable of. No one, even one of your best men, could have a stronger motivation than I do to protect my friend Gino. Don't write me off just because I'm old enough to be your father."

Cataldo glowered at Peter. Everyone in the room waited tensely for his reaction.

Finally, he cracked a terse smile. "All right, Mr. Hood. You want to help, that's okay by me. You and your son and two of my men can take the second shift. That's better, I think, than me kissing your ass."

Cyril laughed, seemingly out of pure relief.

CHAPTER 42

Manny Segal viewed his chosen profession in the same way another man might view his job as a banker or a merchant. It was just another way to make a living. A way to pay his expenses. Of course, the difference between Manny and most others was that his expenses were quite high.

At 2 a.m., Segal blackened his face and left his car parked on a quiet residential street one block from the estate David Hood had entered earlier. He was dressed in all black: knit cap, pullover, a pair of pants gathered at the cuff, a fanny pack, and a pair of rubber-soled shoes. He crept along the stone walls that fronted the unlighted road. He stopped at a nine-foot-high wall, about thirty yards right of the estate's entrance gate. He stayed away from the security camera that pointed at the gated entrance. About to launch a plastic grappling hook attached to a rope over the wall, a sudden noise alerted him to movement down at the gate. He dropped to the ground and pressed against the base of the wall. After a few seconds, he heard the gate open. Security lights mounted on stone pillars illuminated a vehicle that slowly pulled out to the end of the driveway. Manny recognized David Hood at the steering wheel. There was another person—an older man—in the front seat. Maybe Hood's father, another of his targets.

A voice from inside the gate shouted, "Say hello to Mr. Bartolucci for me, will ya?"

The car sped off. After the gate had closed and the security lights switched off, Segal ran back to his own car. He knew the hospital surely wouldn't be as well protected as was this estate. David and Peter Hood, and Gino Bartolucci in the same place at the same time—it would be like shooting fish in a barrel. Maybe Jennifer Ramsey would be there, as well. He reached into the back seat for a towel and rubbed the black grease from his face and neck. He removed the knit cap from his head and smoothed his hair.

Segal used his cellphone to call St. Joseph's Hospital.

"Mr. Bartolucci's room number please," he said to the hospital's switchboard operator.

"Room 532, sir."

Manny snapped his fingers. Nothing to it, he thought.

He reached the hospital at 3:10 a.m. There was an SUV with a man behind the wheel parked near the front entrance. The man eyeballed him as he drove past. Segal figured the man for one of Bartolucci's men. He drove around to the rear of the building where he spied a loading dock. After he parked in the employees' lot, he walked to the dock, climbed a set of stairs, and attempted to open the double doors there. Locked. He moved to an adjacent personnel door and saw it was card key-activated. Segal took a tool from his fanny pack and worked on the lock until it popped open.

Inside, a dozen large, wheeled canvas baskets were piled high with laundry. Manny extracted a white smock from one of the baskets and put it on. The smock reached to his knees, partially hiding the sinister appearance of his black outfit.

Dennis O'Neil was well beyond having gone stir crazy. He suspected Jennifer Ramsey was as stressed as he was, but was better at not showing it. They sat in the guest house den and shared ideas about how to take down Bishop. After an hour, they were both frustrated.

"I've got to do something. I feel as useless as a screen door in a submarine."

"Let's drive out to the hospital," Ramsey said.

"In what? We don't have a car, and it's the middle of the night. You want to call Cataldo and wake him up? Ask him to have one of his guys drive us?"

Ramsey shrugged. "We could *borrow* one of his vehicles."

"You want to steal a car from a mobster?"

"It wouldn't be stealing. I said '*borrow*.'"

"And how will you get the car past the gate guard?"

Ramsey groaned. "Good point. Maybe Cyril could help."

O'Neil frowned at Ramsey. "He won't be happy about you waking him up either."

She shrugged.

O'Neil picked up the phone and called Cyril's room. He answered after only one ring.

"You think Ramsey and I could borrow a car?" he asked.

"I'll arrange it," he said. "Do you know how to find the hospital?"

"How did you know we were going to the hospital?"

"That's where I would go, sir, if I were in your situation."

"Amazing," O'Neil said under his breath. He thought that as long as he was asking for favors, he might as well ask for a really big one. "What's the possibility of borrowing a couple handguns?"

"Detective Ramsey's service pistol will be in the glove compartment of the car that will be in front of the guest house in ten minutes. There'll be one there for you, too."

O'Neil hung up the phone and turned to Ramsey. "If that guy was a woman, I'd marry her."

The bell of a nearby church tolled once at half-past-three when O'Neil and Ramsey arrived at St. Joseph's Hospital. O'Neil spotted a man in a large SUV outside the hospital entrance. Maybe one of Cataldo's crew; maybe not. As they exited their vehicle—a black Lincoln Towncar—and walked toward the smoked-glass hospital entrance door, the guy in the SUV watched them like a hawk zeroes in on a mouse.

John Spellina, a Cataldo crew member, watched the man and woman leave their vehicle and walk to the hospital entrance. He didn't recognize them and immediately used his radio to call his partner, Tiny Santori, who was stationed in the hospital lobby. Twice, he tried to contact Tiny, with no success. "Dammit!" he cursed, tossed the radio on the passenger seat, and got out of the SUV.

As he followed Ramsey through the hospital's automatic entry doors, O'Neil saw out of the corner of his eye, the courtesy light illuminate in the SUV.

There was no one at the reception counter, which was on the far left side of the empty lobby. A printed sign on the counter instructed visitors to proceed to the emergency room entrance on the south side of the building. A bank of elevators was behind the counter.

"Get down behind the reception counter," O'Neil told Ramsey. "We got company."

As Ramsey hustled to hide, O'Neil moved to the elevators, pressed the "UP" button, ran back to the reception counter, and crouched behind it with Ramsey. He heard the lobby doors open and sounds of footsteps on the marble floor. Then, around the side of the counter, he saw a stocky man in a black suit walk toward the elevators when a chime sounded there. The man reached inside his suit coat.

O'Neil held up a hand and showed Ramsey three fingers on his left hand. He folded one finger at a time into the palm of his hand while he pulled out his pistol with his other hand. He and Ramsey stood and raced across the lobby.

"Police!" O'Neil shouted. "Freeze!"

The guy raised his hands over his head. O'Neil snatched a pistol from his right hand.

"Turn around," O'Neil ordered. "Who the hell are you?"

The guy turned. "You got a badge?" he said.

"Yeah, I got a badge. You'll see it after you tell me your name and why you're here."

The man glared at O'Neil for a few seconds, but finally broke it off and said, "My name's John Spellina. My partner and I are here to keep an eye out for a patient here."

"That patient have a name?"

"Yeah! Let's see that badge first."

O'Neil pulled out his ID wallet and flashed his badge at the guy. Spellina hesitated, but finally said, "Gino Bartolucci."

"You work for Mr. Cataldo?"

Again the guy hesitated, but then said, "Yeah; how'd you know?"

"We're staying at the Cataldo estate. Where's your partner?"

Spellina's eyes widened. "Somewhere around here. He's supposed to be watching the lobby and the first floor exits."

O'Neil had a clear view past Spellina of the now-open elevator. "Is that your partner in the elevator?"

Spellina turned and exclaimed, "Shit!" He moved into the elevator car while Ramsey stuck her foot against the door. "Someone's cut Tiny's throat."

"Someone's after Bartolucci," Ramsey said. "We've got to get to his room. What floor's he on?"

"Five!" Spellina said.

"Maybe you should cover the lobby," O'Neil told Ramsey. He saw she didn't like it, but she nodded her agreement. Someone needed to watch the hospital entrance.

O'Neil stepped into the elevator, punched the "5" button, and watched the door slide shut. He handed Spellina's pistol to him. "You might need this. I want you to guard the fifth floor elevator lobby. Stay there and call 9-1-1. Anyone who comes through the lobby, stop him."

O'Neil left Spellina outside the elevator on the fifth floor. He looked left and right and spotted a nursing station to the right and ran there.

The nurse behind the desk appeared to be in her mid-50s. She looked tired, harassed, but competent. She reminded him of the Marine drill sergeant he'd had in boot camp.

"Ma'am," O'Neil said, "I'm looking for Gino Bartolucci's room. It's a matter of life and death."

"I've heard every form of BS over the last thirty years, but that one takes the cake. It's past visiting hours, so you need to get out of here and let our patients rest."

O'Neil flashed his badge. "This isn't bullshit. There's a dead guy in the elevator. Someone slashed his throat. I want to know Mr.

Bartolucci's room number NOW!"

She pointed back to the right and squeaked, "Room 532."

O'Neil reached the end of the corridor. A sign on a corner of the wall showed rooms 500-550 were to the right.

Manny Segal marched toward an elderly man seated in a chair outside a closed door. The man looked up at him as he approached. Segal saw the room number behind the old man: 532.

"So," Segal said, "how's Mr. Bartolucci?"

The man rose from his chair. "He's still asleep, Doctor."

"Well, I'll try not to disturb him," Segal said, as he stuck his hands into the pockets of his smock and wrapped his fingers around the handle of the knife in the right pocket.

O'Neil reached the end of the second corridor. A sign on the far wall of the cross corridor had an arrow that pointed to the right with the numbers 526-550. He turned the corner and saw a little guy in a white smock standing a couple feet away from Peter Hood. The little guy pulled something from a pocket.

O'Neil raised his pistol from where he held it beside his right leg and shouted, "Hey!" just as he spotted a knife in the little guy's hand.

The man with the knife spun around. O'Neil crouched, raised his pistol, and shouted, "Drop it!"

At that moment, David Hood opened the door to the room behind the two men and stepped into the hall.

O'Neil shouted, "Get out of there! Now!" But David charged the guy, grabbed his knife-arm with both hands, and smashed it down against his own raised right thigh. The knife clattered to the floor. The little guy twisted his arm free and squared off with David. He stepped forward, just as Peter kicked him in the back of his knee. Then David landed several punches to the man's face and midsection, kicked him in the balls, and smashed a fist into the side of his head.

O'Neil ran forward to help, but all that was left for him to do was pick up the knife and search the unconscious man. He frisked the guy and found a garrote in a smock pocket and a Glock 9mm pistol in a shoulder rig.

O'Neil eyed David and Peter. "Good job. How's Gino?"

David said, "Sleeping. He seems to—"

Just then a nurse came around the corner. "What are you people doing here?" she rasped. Before anyone could answer her, she apparently noticed the knife and gun O'Neil held and the unconscious man on the floor. She gasped, "Oh my Lord!" She wheeled around and ran back down the hall, just as John Spellina turned into the corridor.

David looked at Spellina. "John, where's Tiny?"

He pointed at the unconscious man in the white smock. "I think that guy killed Tiny. Cut his throat. He's back in the elevator."

"We have to get this guy out of here," David said. He turned to O'Neil. "Have you got a car?"

"Yeah."

"Okay! Help John carry this guy out to your car. Take him out to the Cataldo place."

David took a roll of surgical tape from a medical cart in the hall and tossed it to Spellina who taped the assassin's hands, feet, and mouth, and then hoisted the man onto his shoulder.

Just as Spellina walked away, O'Neil heard the wail of sirens. "When the police get here, don't tell them a thing about Tiny or the little guy. Just say you chased off some guy who you saw in the hall. Tell them you have no idea what the nurse saw."

"Why?" David asked.

"You tell the police an assassin murdered Tiny and tried to kill Gino, and you'll be tied up for days in interrogation and the police will invade the Cataldo estate."

CHAPTER 43

After two of Cataldo's men replaced David and Peter at the hospital, the Hoods returned to the estate. They found their host in the library in conference with Detectives O'Neil and Ramsey, Paulie Rizzo, and two other men, introduced only as Vince and Sylvio.

Cataldo shook David and Peter's hands. "You guys did good," he said. He smiled at Peter as though he remembered Peter's earlier comment. "Paulie's got something to tell you." Cataldo nodded at Paulie.

Paulie tapped a side pocket in his jacket and said, "I've got Don Bartolucci's cellphone. He got a call from a Philly cop who's on his payroll. Said the S.W.A.T. team that attacked the Chestnut Hill estate found a note addressed to Rolf Bishop taped to a door there."

"I saw Gino tape something to the basement door," David said, "but I didn't see what was on it."

"I'll get to that in a minute," Paulie said. "But get this. A DEA guy named Morton came to Philadelphia and met with the mayor, the police commissioner, and the S.W.A.T. commander. Morton claimed one of their undercover agents had infiltrated Bartolucci's organization, had been compromised, and was Bartolucci's captive. Morton also said there was an enormous amount of heroin on the estate. It was the dope that got the mayor and the police commissioner excited. They had visions of juicy, vote-getting headlines."

"That old man in the cardiac wing at St. Joseph's has never gone near the drug business," Cataldo said, disgusted. "That's one of the reasons he walked away from the . . . his position. He wanted nothing to do with drugs and he realized there was too much money in narcotics for the business to be ignored." Cataldo stood and waved at Vince and Sylvio. "I'll be back in a minute."

"The police did find heroin stacked on a table in Bartolucci's house," Paulie said, after Cataldo and his two men left the room. "But they didn't find any DEA undercover agent."

"You said this DEA guy told the police there was an 'enormous amount' of dope at the Bartolucci estate," Dennis O'Neil said to Paulie. "Did he say how much?"

"He said 'enough to fill a panel truck.' That would mean about six, seven thousand kilos. Maybe 15,000 pounds."

"And how much did they find?" O'Neil asked.

"Hell, a lot less than that," Paulie answered. "About 200 pounds."

"We ran right through the dining room on our way to the basement," O'Neil said. "There wasn't a damn thing on that table."

"Anyone check on this DEA guy. Morton?" Ramsey asked.

"Yeah," Paulie said. "Our guy on the Philly police said the S.W.A.T. commander called Morton at DEA headquarters and was told he'd retired. Left instructions where he wanted his retirement checks deposited, but left no forwarding address or contact information."

Peter said, "What was in the note the police found?"

Paulie smiled. "The note read 'When you play ball with the wrong people, you get the bat shoved up your ass. Bend over, Rolfie Baby, your time has come.' "

For a few seconds, no one said a word. Then Jennifer Ramsey laughed. In a few seconds, they all joined in. They had just begun to quiet down when Peter said, "That Gino! That old man's got rhinoceros balls."

Ramsey asked, "What the hell is going on? Why a DEA connection?"

"I don't think there's a DEA connection," David said. "I'd bet anything Morton was a rogue agent on Bishop's payroll."

Ten minutes later, Cataldo came back into the room. "Well, people," he said, "we just had a conversation with the little guy from the hospital. He became really quite cooperative after Vinny had a talk with him. His name is Manny Segal. But his professional name is Paladin. He's an artist at what he does—he kills people. I've heard about this guy for years but I never met him before. Actually, no one I know has ever met him before. And get this, Rolf Bishop agreed to pay the bastard two hundred thousand dollars up front, with a promise of another two hundred thousand when he killed Gino, David, Peter, and Detective Ramsey."

"Hell," O'Neil said, "there are at least ten million people in this country alone who'd kill someone for way less than that." He laughed, but no one joined in.

David paced and said, "Why would Detective Ramsey be on Bishop's hit list. How would Bishop even know she was here?"

After a long silence, Ramsey said, "There's only two ways I can think of how Bishop learned I was here. One, someone in this room talked. Two, someone with the Bethesda Police Department talked. If it was someone in Bethesda, I would put my money on a guy named Cromwell."

"The cop who was your partner?" David said.

Ramsey nodded.

"So, what do we do now?" David asked.

"I got a couple ideas," Cataldo said. "We're gonna make the message in Gino's note to Bishop come true. Especially the part about the bat and his ass."

CHAPTER 44

One of the benefits of the Cataldo Family's relationship with the Hospitality Workers of America Union was the ability to get jobs for the Family's sons and daughters, nephews and nieces. Some of the beneficiaries of the Family's influence got paid even if they didn't show up for work. Others, however, worked diligently and advanced up the hotel organization charts. Lois Carbone, the niece of Tomasino Portello, the *caporegime* of the Cataldo Family, had graduated from New York University with a Hotel Management degree, and had received a number of attractive offers from some of the better hotels in the city. But she wanted to work at the most famous of all the hotels in the country—The Plaza. Lois wanted to get her foot in the door there. Given the opportunity, she was determined to make the most of it. So, Lois spoke to her Uncle Tomasino, who then talked to the head of the union. Lois started at The Plaza Hotel two days later.

She'd worked first as a night clerk, then moved to the Catering Department. After only three years with the hotel, she became Director of Special Events, in which role she was now the hotel's liaison with the White House to make certain the President of the United States's dinner was a success. Her normal duties were aggravated by the involvement of the security people and White House staffers. But she'd been through that before. It was now all fairly routine to her. She was on her way to a staff meeting when her cellphone rang.

"Hi, Lois," Tomasino Portello said. "You doin' okay?"

"Sure, Uncle Tommy," she replied. Why is he calling me at work? she wondered. This was a first. She sighed as she thought about all she had to do. She didn't have time for personal matters.

"Sweetheart, I need to sit down with you . . . as soon as possible. You think you could find time for your favorite uncle this morning?"

Oh shit, Lois thought to herself. Any day but today. She wanted to say, I'm awfully busy, Uncle Tommy. But instead, she agreed to meet him. After all, she owed her uncle.

"Let's see. I got eight now. How about we meet in that little coffee shop down the street from the hotel in about fifteen minutes?"

Lois made a couple quick phone calls, doled out assignments to underlings, postponed her staff meeting, and then hurried from her mezzanine level office, down the stairs to the hotel lobby, and out the front door. She was at the coffee shop when her Uncle Tomasino strolled in. She stood and they hugged affectionately. Lois truly loved her uncle and she knew he thought the world of her. He once told her, "You got bigger balls and more brains than most of the boys in the family."

After their coffees were served, Tomasino looked intently at Lois. "I need to know something," he said. "This is very important or I wouldn't ask. You understand?"

"Sure, Uncle Tommy."

"You workin' on this big dinner tomorrow night with all the hotshots from England, Germany, France . . . whatever?"

Lois smiled. "That's right. I'm in charge of the whole thing."

"Tell me what the program will be at this *stravaganza*."

Lois hesitated.

Tomasino reached across the table and put his hand on her cheek. He looked into her eyes and said, "Don't you worry about a thing, *mio bambola piccola*. You got nothing to worry about."

Lois took a big breath. "Well, you know, there will be a lot of boring speeches and all of the bigwigs will be introduced. A small orchestra will play at the dinner. And at the end of the dinner there will be a presentation."

"That's when the video will be shown?" Tomasino asked.

"How do you know about the video?" Lois tensed.

"Sometimes I hear things, *Bambina*. Tell me about this video."

She hesitated a beat and then said, "The President has declared this the Year of the Child. So the White House put together a bunch of clips of some of the heads of state and senior members of the administration that show those people today and also back when they were kids. I think it will be fun to see what the most powerful men and women in the world looked like when they were small."

"What do they got, some guy from the White House to show the video?"

"No, Uncle Tommy," Lois responded. "The tape's been given to Hal Norris, the head of the hotel's Audio/Visual office. He's the one who will set up all the equipment and play the tape. Why?"

"It's better you don't know why. And don't tell anyone we met this morning. Before I go, I gotta ask you one more question. Where does this Hal keep the video and when could someone maybe take a peek at it?"

CHAPTER 45

Scott Dundee had always had a look of authority about him. His six-foot, three-inch, two hundred-pound frame and military bearing had served him well for his seventeen years with the New York Police Department.

He might have made it to the top floor of One Police Plaza if a drunk driver hadn't plowed into his car one night. The collision left him with a chronic back problem which was still bad enough that he spent half-a-dozen days a month in bed. Surgery might fix the problem, but Dundee had a pathological fear of the operating table.

After he took early retirement, Dundee opened his own private-detective agency. The business had barely survived until a night when he was in a bar in lower Manhattan. It had been kind of a slow night so Leo Brill, the bar's owner, took the stool next to Dundee's and struck up a conversation.

Just before midnight, two cokeheads entered the bar. The taller one aimed a pistol at the kid behind the bar and ordered him to empty the cash register. The kid froze. The other cokehead waved his pistol at Dundee and Brill.

"Take it easy, guys," Leo Brill said. "You can have the money. Just don't do anything stupid."

The shorter cokehead screamed, "Who you calling stupid, asshole?" and hit Brill on the side of the head with his pistol.

The blow opened a gash from above Brill's hairline down to his cheekbone, and knocked him to the floor. The guy pointed his pistol at Brill and, purple with rage, seemed about to shoot the dazed and bloodied bar owner. With both the robbers' attentions now on Brill, Dundee pulled a .45 caliber pistol from a shoulder holster under his jacket and blew a hole in the center of the shorter robber's forehead. The impact of the bullet sprayed blood and brain matter all over the other cokehead, who shrieked as though he'd been shot and dropped to the floor. The guy screamed and begged for mercy.

Dundee walked over to the man and calmly took the pistol out of his hand. Then he kicked him under the chin, which broke his jaw and most of his teeth, and knocked him out.

Brill, a "made man" in the Cataldo Family, saw to it from then on that the one-man Dundee Detective Agency had as much business as Dundee could handle. The latest in the family's long string of jobs was for Dundee to "borrow" a flash drive from The Plaza Hotel's Audio/Visual Department Manager's desk.

Dressed in a dark suit, Dundee arrived at the hotel at 9 a.m. The lobby was packed with employees, guests, and a large number of men and women with Secret Service pins on their lapels and radio buds in their ears. Dundee crossed the lobby as though he belonged there and went to a bank of house phones. He looked like a Secret Service agent, even down to the radio bud stuck in his ear and the fake pin on his lapel. Besides, he carried himself with unquestionable authority, albeit with a slight limp.

He used one of the house phones and asked the hotel operator to connect him to Hal Norris in the Audio/Visual Department. When Norris came on the line, Dundee introduced himself as Lyle Mason, a member of the Secret Service detail.

"Can you and your assistant attend a security briefing for hotel staff in ten minutes? In the grand ballroom?"

"Of course," Norris said. "How long will it last?"

"Ten, fifteen minutes."

After he hung up the phone, Dundee walked across the lobby and entered one of the elevators. He got off at the mezzanine level and walked along a row of offices until he found a door marked Audio/Visual Department. Hal Norris's name was painted on the door. He waited twenty yards down the hall until a man and a woman walked out of the office, hustled down the hallway, and took the stairs to the lobby. Dundee moved to the Audio/Visual Department door. He knocked. No answer. He tried the doorknob. Locked. He pulled a shim from an inside jacket pocket, slid the tool between the doorjamb and the lock, and popped the lock. Then he cautiously opened the door and peeked inside to make certain the office was vacant. He quickly moved past a desk to an inner office. Hal Norris's nameplate was on the desk there. Dundee opened the center drawer, but found nothing of interest. He tried the top side drawer, then the second drawer. Still nothing. In the third drawer he found a black flash drive in a Ziploc bag labeled "State Dinner-April 28." He removed the flash drive from the bag and slipped it into a side pocket of his jacket. Then he took a handful of blank flash drives from a pocket, found one that best matched the one he'd removed, placed it inside the bag, and put the bag back in the desk drawer.

Dundee closed the drawer and moved to the office door. He pushed the locking button in the inside door knob, shut the door, and left. Instead of exiting through the lobby, he walked to the end of the hall, went through the emergency exit door, and descended the stairs to the street.

Outside, in a Jeep Cherokee double-parked sixty feet from the hotel entrance, Dundee's friend and client, Leo Brill, waited with Sol Lesser, an audio/visual and computer expert. Dundee walked down the sidewalk, slipped between two parked limousines, and moved to the passenger side of the vehicle. He tossed the flash drive into Brill's lap through the open window. Then Dundee passed by the nose of the Jeep and hailed a cab. He ordered the cabbie to take him to the parking garage where he'd left his own car. His back hurt. He would go home, chase a Percocet with a glass of scotch, and try to sleep.

CHAPTER 46

"*Guten Morgen, Banque Securite Swisse,*" a woman said. "*Kann ich ihnen helfen?*"

"*Kann ich Herr Muther sprechen?*" David asked. "*Hier ist* David Hood.*"

"*Ein moment, bitte.*"

"David, where are you," Willy Muther asked with enthusiasm a moment later. "Are you here in Zurich?"

"No, Willy. I'm in New York. How are Inge and the children?"

"Great! Great! Everyone's fine! How's your family?"

"Everyone's fine here, Willy," David lied. "I need your help and need you to trust me."

"David, we've done a lot of business together. When your company uncovered the embezzlement at my bank, you probably saved us tens of millions of *francs.* Besides, we've been friends for years. What can I do for you?"

"Willy, I've got a list in front of me with dates and amounts of large deposits made to an account in your bank back in 2003 and 2004. What I don't have is the account owner's name."

Willy coughed. "Listen, David. Our banking laws are strict for a reason. We don't give out that kind of information to a private citizen—even if he is a friend. You wouldn't want me to get into trouble for breaking the law?"

"No, Willy, I wouldn't," David said. "But if what I suspect is true, every dollar in that account is drug money. If that's the case, your bank could be in real trouble."

Willy groaned. "*Gott in Himmel!*"

David waited.

"Give me the account number and a telephone number where I can reach you. I won't promise to give you the name on the account, but I promise I'll call you back before the end of the day."

"It's Joey calling from New York."

It took Bobby Galupo a couple seconds to figure out which "Joey from New York" might be calling him. When he suspected it was Joey Cataldo, he said, "Hey, Joey, *come va?*"

"*Bene, e tu?*"

"*Bene!* Listen, I got to ask a big favor. You know that old friend of ours who's got the market down your way?"

Gino! Bobby Galupo had heard the news on television about Gino's heart attack. "Yeah, of course. How's our friend?"

"Pretty damn good," Cataldo answered. "It looks like he'll recover. But our friend needs your help. You think you could send a car up here with a couple of your boys. Our friend's driver tells me you got a guest down there who I need to meet. Maybe you could have your boys escort this guest of yours to my place."

CHAPTER 47

Leo Brill and Sol Lesser drove to the Cataldo estate. They unloaded a heap of gear from Leo's Jeep Cherokee and carried it to the mansion's media room, a thirty-foot by forty-foot windowless enclosure equipped with multiple computers, two large screen televisions, a movie screen and projector, DVD players, and various stereo equipment.

Cataldo ordered Cyril to find David and Peter and their three cop friends and bring them to the media room. Then he picked up his desk phone and called his man Vince and told him, "You and Sylvio bring Manny Segal to the media room. I'll meet you there." Cataldo stood up, adjusted his tie, and walked down the hall.

Vince and Sylvio, with Segal in tow, arrived at the room as Cataldo got there. The others were already seated in plush theater seats. A chair sat in the middle of the stage, with a movie screen behind it.

"Put Segal in that chair," Cataldo ordered.

Vince and Sylvio dragged Segal onto the stage and pushed him into the chair. The assassin appeared to have lost all of his poise, all of his arrogance. One of his eyes was badly swollen. He could barely sit straight in the chair. And he looked scared to death.

Cataldo walked onto the stage and put his hand on Segal's shoulder. "Hey, all you gotta do is tell the truth. You do that and you can walk outta here. You can go enjoy all the money you got put away."

Cataldo's touch, his words, seemed to have a magical effect on Segal. He asked for a glass of water and, after he took a couple of swallows, said, "Okay, guys, let's get this over with."

The Manny Segal Show was exactly what Cataldo wanted. The little killer's words were chilling—made even worse by Segal's penchant for detail and almost gleeful delivery. When added with David Hood and Dennis O'Neil's earlier recorded comments, Manny Segal's testimony became a part of a plan to ruin Rolf Bishop.

Cataldo whispered to Vince, who left the room. Everyone in the room seemed exhausted. Segal had literally taken their breath away. All eyes were on Cataldo, the director of this film extravaganza, who just sat in his chair and ignored the others, one hand stuck in his pants pocket, a cigar in his other hand. He didn't move until the theater door opened and Vince returned. He nodded at Cataldo and took a seat behind his boss.

The sounds of footsteps came from the hallway. Then three men entered. Peter recognized two of the men: They were part of the armed Galupo crew that hid in his home and captured the guy who came to kill David. Then he muttered, "Oh my God!" when he realized the third man with the two Galupo soldiers was that same assassin. His face was badly bruised and his eyes swollen nearly shut. The big man glanced around furtively. He appeared spiritless and scared witless.

Cataldo announced, "I'd like you all to meet Montrose Toney, the next star of our production." Cataldo chuckled.

By the time videographer Sol Lesser's work was finished with Montrose Toney, it was nearly 6 p.m. He'd been at it for almost eight hours and had been rewarded with eyestrain and a killer headache. He handed Joey Cataldo six flash drives, including the original taken from The Plaza Hotel.

"When will the others be ready?" Cataldo asked Lesser.

"By noon tomorrow."

Cataldo handed him a stuffed zippered leather folio. "Don't spend it all in one place." He clapped him on the back.

Cataldo gathered David, Peter, the two cops, Paulie Rizzo, and Leo Brill again in the media room. "Not a bad day's work," he said. "I don't need to tell you what we got here. The video on this drive will raise holy hell. Leo, you take the original flash drive and have your private-eye friend put it back in the hotel office." Brill immediately left the room with the original flash drive.

Cataldo gave copies of the drive to O'Neil and Ramsey. "If I'm right about what will happen," Cataldo said, "these drives could be very helpful for you in court—if it comes to that. Remember, you agreed you wouldn't tell anyone about my involvement in this. If you are asked where you got that flash drive, you'll say, 'Someone sent it to me anonymously.' " He handed another flash drive to David. "I don't know if you really want a copy. It's full of sadness and bad memories." He shrugged and then turned to Paulie Rizzo. "Paulie, this copy is for Don Bartolucci. Twenty-four hours from now this will all be over as far as I'm concerned. I had nothing to do with any of this and I expect each and every one of you to honor that. Nothing personal, but I don't expect or want to ever see any of you guys again. I took risks here that could ruin me. I did it out of respect for Don Bartolucci. If I'm ever drawn into the aftermath of this, I will have the person responsible hunted down. Do you understand?"

They all nodded.

"Good," he said. "It's been fun. Oh, one other thing. You don't show those videos to anyone for twenty-four hours." With that, Cataldo walked out of the room, a smile on his face.

APRIL 28

CHAPTER 48

At a few minutes past 1:00 a.m., Leo Brill met Scott Dundee on the fourth level of a parking garage on Lexington Avenue. Dundee got out of his car and into Brill's Jeep Cherokee.

"Hey, Scott," Brill said, "sorry about being so late."

"I understand," Dundee replied. "It wouldn't have been a big deal if my damned back didn't hurt so bad."

Brill could tell from the strained look and sweat on Dundee's face the man was in terrible pain. "Didn't you take your medicine?" he asked.

"Shit, yes, I took my medicine. If I take any more of those pills I'll be a zombie. They just don't ease the pain much anymore."

"You gonna be able to finish this job?"

"I ain't ever walked away from an assignment before, and I ain't about to begin now. Give me that flash drive."

Despite the late hour, there was still plenty of activity outside The Plaza. Several couples in evening attire climbed into limousines, and dozens more were queued up. Horse-drawn carriages discharged late-night revelers.

A dozen solid-black Suburbans with heavily tinted windows were parked along the curb near the hotel entrance.

"See all those SUV's?" Dundee said. "They're Secret Service. With the President and all those foreign guys here, the place is probably infested with Feds. Getting in there is gonna to be trickier than it was earlier, when all the big shots were down at the UN. We gotta tweak the plan a little bit. The offices on the Mezzanine should be closed down. But the lobby will be packed."

Brill glanced over at Dundee. "What are you thinking, Scottie? I don't want this thing screwed up. You know what Cataldo will do to me if we mess up."

"I know, Leo, I know. Drive around the block. Let me think about it."

Brill found a parking space on 60th Street, about three blocks from The Plaza. He and Dundee walked back to the hotel. The walk took a toll on Dundee. The pain in his back had escalated and now radiated down his left leg. He couldn't fully extend either of his legs, and his normal stride had devolved into little more than a shuffle. It took them twenty minutes to reach the hotel and by the time they climbed the stairs into the lobby, Dundee sweated as though he'd just run the New York Marathon. He grabbed Brill's arm and guided him toward the bar off the lobby. Dundee chose a table in the darkest part of the room and waved for the cocktail waitress after he slowly eased into a chair.

The waitress came over. Before they could place an order, she said, "This is last call, gentlemen. By all rights the bar should have closed an hour ago, but these government guys do like their toddies." She looked at Dundee more carefully and added, "You look like you could really use a drink."

"You got that right, ma'am," Dundee said. "Bring us a couple double bourbons."

While the waitress walked away, Dundee looked around the lounge and out into the lobby. The place was packed with Feds—dark suits, military haircuts, ear buds, and lapel pin transmitters. "There must be two dozen agents in this place, Leo."

"What the hell are we doing in here then?" Brill whispered. His eyes darted around like he was a rabbit surrounded by coyotes.

Dundee laughed and downed half his drink. "I'll be right back."

It took considerable effort for Dundee to get up from his chair. He whispered to Brill, who nervously drummed his fingers on the table, "Try to relax. You look worse than I feel."

Dundee shuffled out of the bar and over to the front desk on the opposite side of the lobby. There was one clerk on duty, a fussy, thirty-something guy with light-brown hair highlighted with blond streaks. He ignored Dundee for several seconds while he typed at a keyboard. When he raised his head to acknowledge Dundee, the clerk wore an officious look he had no doubt perfected on the job at The Plaza. Dundee pulled out his old New York Detective's gold shield and stuck it under the clerk's nose.

"I'm with the security detail covering the G-8 conference," he told the clerk. "I've just been instructed to check out a possible security breach. We just received a report someone entered the emergency stairwell on the fourth floor and may have gone down to the Mezzanine level."

Dundee noticed the desk clerk now at least paid attention. "We know the guy didn't go up," he continued, "because there's a guard stationed in the stairwell on the fifth floor. Whoever he is, the guy is either still between four and the mezzanine, or he walked all the way down the stairs and out of the hotel. Probably nothing to worry about, but we can't be too careful."

"So what do you need from me, officer?" the clerk asked.

"I need someone with a pass key to go up to the Mezzanine with me. I want to look into each of the offices up there. Or you can just loan me the key. I'll bring it right back."

Dundee hoped the clerk wouldn't call an in-house security guy to accompany him. The security staff at The Plaza was more than likely loaded with retired New York City cops, including some who might recognize him.

The clerk looked at Dundee as though he were an insect. "I hope you didn't just suggest I accompany you. I cannot leave the desk uncovered."

"Listen, mister," Dundee told the man, "you got the President of the United States upstairs. For all we know, there's a kook with a bomb in his pocket running around this building. Do you think the best use of my time is to stand here having a conversation with you?"

The desk clerk shot Dundee a worried look and exhaled loudly. "Okay, okay. Here, take my passkey. But make sure you bring it back."

"You got it, little buddy." Dundee turned toward the elevators.

Several members of the Secret Service Detachment were assigned to cover the hotel lobby. Each wore communication devices that allowed him or her to stay in touch with all the others at all times. One of the agents, Elise Finch, had watched Dundee shuffle across the lobby from the bar to the front desk. She had watched a couple of hundred other people do the same thing that evening and, in every case, had determined the people were basically harmless and posed no threat to the President. Finch came to the same conclusion about the man with the limp. When she saw the desk clerk hand something to the man, she assumed it was just his room key or a message. Out of habit, Finch made a mental note of the limping man's clothing, his height, weight, and hair color. While the man approached the elevators, Finch was about to erase all she'd noticed about him from her memory bank. Another agent would take over the observation of this man when he got off the elevator, on whatever floor. But something made her look back at the guy as he limped into an empty. After the door closed, she looked up at the floor indicator above the elevator door and was surprised when it stopped on the Mezzanine level. This was not what she'd anticipated. The offices on the Mezzanine had been vacated hours earlier.

The Secret Service trains its agents to notice—and act on—anything out of the ordinary, no matter how inconsequential. Finch spoke into her lapel mic as she moved quickly toward the front desk. "I have a possible situation. Everyone hold position while I check this out."

The desk clerk had gone through a door behind the counter area. Finch pounded the bell on the counter. This brought the clerk back out.

"You don't need to break the bell, ma'am. I was only a few feet away."

Finch flashed her identification. "That man who just left here. You handed him something. What was it? Who was he?"

"First of all," the clerk said disdainfully, "I gave him a passkey. And second, I should not have to tell you who the man is since he's a member of your own security team."

Finch felt the hair rise on the back of her neck. She reached over the counter, grabbed the clerk by the front of his jacket, and jerked him close. "Listen to me; I've got no time for your bullshit. Tell me what that man told you. Now!"

The clerk talked so fast Finch had to slow him down.

Pass key. Security. Intruder in the stairwell. Offices. Finch had heard enough. She raced across the lobby toward the Mezzanine stairs. At the same time, she spoke into her mic: "Possible intruder on the Mezzanine level." She heard other agents running after her as she took the stairs two at a time.

Finch reached the Mezzanine and turned right into the hallway. The man she'd seen had just come out of one of the offices.

"Hold it right there, mister," Finch ordered.

The man stopped, slowly turned around, and faced Finch, who approached with her pistol down by her right thigh.

Finch sized up the intruder and instinctively knew he was no ordinary second-story man. While she walked to within five feet of the guy, she heard her backup crew reach the top of the stairs behind him. She focused all of her attention on the intruder. "U.S. Secret Service," she said. "What are you doing here?"

"Look, I can try to blow smoke at you, but that would only waste your time and piss you off. So I'll give it to you straight. I'm a private detective." He slowly took his ID out of his shirt pocket and handed it to the agent.

"Scott Dundee," Finch read aloud.

"Yeah, that's right. I got this client who suspects his wife has been messing around. He gave me a couple of names of guys who might be playing hide-the-salami with the wife. One of the names is this guy Hal Norris." Dundee jabbed a thumb in the direction of the office door. "I figured if I could get into his office and check his appointment book, his desk drawers, maybe I could find something incriminating."

"Assume the position," Finch ordered.

When Dundee put his hands against the wall, Finch kicked his feet apart.

Dundee blurted a noise somewhere between a grunt and a

scream. When Finch found a flash drive in Dundee's pocket she stuck it under Dundee's nose. "What the hell is this?"

"It's blank. It's nothing."

Finch turned the drive over and looked at each of the edges. There was no label on it.

After she scrutinized the man's ID again, Finch slipped it and the flash drive into her jacket pocket and asked, "Why'd you tell the desk clerk you're with the security detail here at the hotel? Impersonating a federal officer is a crime."

"I know that was kind of lame," Dundee responded, "but I got this bad back and I got to use every shortcut I can find to get the job done. I'm sorry if I upset you. I sure didn't mean to."

Finch waved at two backup agents, then faced Dundee again. "Okay, Mr. Dundee, here's what we'll do. I'll have two of our agents drive you home. They'll search your place and then you'll go with them to your office. I assume you'll agree to a search of both locations without the need for a search warrant?"

Dundee nodded.

"If they find anything that makes them the least bit suspicious, they'll haul your ass downtown and will, I assure you, make your life a nightmare. Do you understand?"

"Yes, ma'am."

Finch beckoned one of the agents over and handed him Dundee's ID and the flash drive. "Check out Jim Rockford here. Go to his home and office. You find anything that bothers you, lock him up and interrogate him hard. If everything looks all right, give him back his stuff and turn him loose."

Dundee and the two Secret Service agents reached the bottom of the stairs and crossed the lobby toward the hotel doors just as Leo Brill walked out of the lounge. Brill gave no sign of recognition. He let them reach the doors and descend the steps to the sidewalk and then followed. Through the doors, he saw Dundee loaded into the back seat of one of the black Suburbans.

What in hell do I do now? Brill thought.

A wave of nausea hit Brill while he watched the big black vehicle pull away from the curb. If Dundee had switched the flash drives, Brill would be in good shape. He knew Dundee wouldn't tell the Feds a thing, so Cataldo's plan would go off without a hitch. But if the flash drives had not been switched, the plan would be dead in the water. Like Brill.

CHAPTER 49

With the heads-of-state tied up in conference meetings all day, Bishop had squired several of his intelligence agency counterparts on a tour of the Statue of Liberty.

The tour terminated at 3:45 p.m., after which Bishop returned to his room at The Plaza. Although he didn't believe there was a God, he hedged his bets and prayed that David Hood was already dead. With Paladin on his trail, the man doesn't have a prayer, he thought. He spent an hour-and-a-half on the telephone on CIA business and then thought about contingency plans for taking care of Hood. Afterward, he watched television news. At 6:30, he showered, shaved, and dressed for the State dinner. He admired himself in the room's full-length mirror. Even at his age, he believed, he could still turn an eye or two.

"Rolf Bishop," he said to his image, "you've come a long way."

But then a bubble of bile hit the back of his throat. Fucking David Hood, he thought.

David once again reminded himself he had to control his emotions to be effective. Pent-up sorrow and anxiety, excitement, and anger had combined to make him a nervous wreck. It was the waiting that was so difficult. He now knew without a doubt Rolf Bishop was responsible for Carmela's, Heather's, and Kyle's murders, and he was confident he understood the motive: Bishop's drug sales to the New York Mafia had earned the man tens of millions of dollars. That money had allowed him to buy political influence. But he couldn't take the chance one of the men in the Special Logistical Support Detachment had been aware of his smuggling operation. So the bastard had killed all of the survivors except David.

David's greatest source of anxiety was the pending plan Joey Cataldo had shared with him. But there was nothing he could do about it until later this evening, after the State Dinner. So he sat for a couple of minutes, paced for a couple of minutes, sat again, paced again.

As David had told Cataldo, if Manny Segal could track them down at *Casa Sogna*, then they had no idea who else might know their location. Cataldo had spirited them out of his estate in the wee hours of the morning in the back of a van. Now David, Peter, Jennifer, and Dennis, were cooped up in an apartment above one of Cataldo's restaurants near 3rd Avenue and 42nd Street.

Out of sheer desperation for something to do, David suggested they review the plan for that evening, and the others readily agreed.

"Anything to get you to sit down and stay down," Ramsey said.

They once again went over the plan, step-by-step. He knew they would need luck for it to succeed, but he was convinced, if all went well, Rolf Bishop's reputation would be finished forever.

At 7:30 p.m. sharp, a liveried waiter on The Plaza Hotel's staff walked through the corridor outside the ballrooms and lightly struck a small three-plate xylophone, the signal for the start of the cocktail hour.

Bishop felt ecstatic. His presentation yesterday had been extremely well-received. He'd interacted well with the chiefs of some of the world's most sophisticated intelligence agencies. He noted there was a general feeling of accomplishment over the work completed at the conference and everyone seemed to be in a jovial mood. He basked in the glow of his own importance. People he met wanted to talk about him, about his career, his new position, his priorities. He couldn't help but feel bloated with self-importance, surrounded as he was by the world's elite who complimented him at every turn.

The guests entered the Grand Ballroom at 8:15. Bishop guessed the decorations and table settings impressed even the most jaded attendee. The centerpieces on the tables were three-foot-tall fluted vases that spilled cascades of dendrobium orchids. Massive, multi-tiered crystal chandeliers sparkled like starships. The room's lights were adjusted to display the guests to best advantage—not so bright as to accentuate physical flaws but bright enough to allow the women to display their hairdos, jewels, and gowns.

He turned his attention to the dais when the New York City mayor welcomed the audience and then introduced the President of the United States. The President toasted his foreign counterparts. Each of the heads of state on the dais then toasted the President and one another. While the dinner was served, with a different wine for each course, the cordiality grew almost frantic and the noise of conversation in the ballroom escalated.

The President rose after dinner. The audience immediately quieted. The President announced, "We accomplished much this week. We dealt with the key elements of international security, including intelligence, economic, and strategic issues. And we are all committed to do our best to build a safer, healthier, and more prosperous world for every child on the planet. There is no future without our children and there is no future unless the children are prepared to provide leadership in their turn. It is for this reason I have declared this year to be the Year of the Child in the United States of America."

Bishop nodded. His head bounced like a bobble-headed dog in a car rear window. He caught himself and stopped. Don't be an idiot, he told himself.

"All of us in this room are privileged," the President continued. "We have the best life can offer. But if you are like me, you may sometimes forget you too were once a small child, weak and vulnerable. So I thought we all might enjoy a trip back in time to when we were, each and every one of us, a long way from our present positions of power."

The President offered his most charismatic smile and waited

while the lights slowly dimmed until the room was almost completely dark. The soundtrack on the video started while four large screens dropped from ceiling booms. Soft music wafted over the room like a light breeze, then built in volume, and finally subsided when an image of the President in the Oval Office was projected on the screens and the President's recorded voice filled the ballroom. It was apparent the audience appreciated the effect, as "oohs" and "ahs" were heard from every corner of the room. The President spoke of power and privilege. Then the picture suddenly changed to a photograph of the President as a small child dressed in tattered, dirty overalls, in front of a ramshackle house. It was an image the White House spinmeisters loved. It conjured up an echo of Lincoln. The President spoke of how many children around the planet lived in poverty and lacked any opportunity to escape from it. Other photos showed the President as he grew from a young boy to a teenager to a young adult. "It is opportunity that makes the difference in a young person's life, and it is the realization of that opportunity which makes our world a better place," the President's voice said.

The next image on the screens was of the French President. His round, smiling face stayed on the screens for a few seconds and was then replaced with photos of him at various ages. The voice of the U.S. President on the soundtrack spoke of the French leader's life as a poor farmer's son sent on scholarship to military school miles away from his home. The photographs and the background music had been matched beautifully and created an empathetic atmosphere in the room.

Each head of state, in turn, was featured. Their images as children seemed to delight the guests. A couple of women at Bishop's table actually had tears in their eyes. After all eight leaders were highlighted, the video showed the images of several other persons in attendance, including the Chief Justice of the U.S. Supreme Court and the Secretary-General of the United Nations. Each had been included because he or she came from a poor background and pulled themselves up by the bootstraps. The point of the program was to show that children from other-than-privileged situations could grow up to make significant contributions to their countries and to the world—if given the opportunity.

Bishop felt perspiration on his brow. He knew what would happen next. The President had briefed him. He looked at the screen nearest his table and forced a neutral expression on his face. Even when his photograph showed on the screen he didn't react. But inside, he was full of electric excitement.

The President's voice boomed from the speakers. "The next person I want to introduce is a good friend who comes from my home state and who grew up in conditions of poverty and hunger. He attended The United States Military Academy at West Point, served in Grenada, Iraq, and Afghanistan, is a military hero, and a true American patriot. He has served his nation and the free world at great personal risk and sacrifice, in conditions of hardship and deprivation, and always without complaint. He lost a leg in combat. And he has done much for his country and in the interest of peace. I am proud to include in tonight's program my life-long friend, Rolf Bishop."

The picture segued to a photo of a small boy dressed in torn clothes, fishing rod in one hand and the hand of a smaller boy in the other. The photo drew a loud murmur of approval. Bishop felt his face redden as numerous attendees glanced over at him. This was truly his moment in the sun.

The mood in the room was now almost euphoric. The evening had been a tremendous success. Suddenly, the background music stopped. A different voice came from the speakers. Then a photograph of a man, woman, and two children showed on the screens.

"Good evening, my name is David Hood," the voice said. "The photograph you see was taken of my family four months ago. Some of you know me. I provide security services to many of you and your organizations. I want to say a few words about the great American hero, Rolf Bishop."

Bishop had an almost uncontrollable urge to scream. He felt as though his mind was out of balance. How was this possible? He looked around. Although the flow of the video presentation had been broken, most of the people he saw reacted as though Hood's appearance was part of the program.

"Rolf Bishop is known throughout the United States as a hero," Hood's voice continued. The voice paused for a second and then said, "Let me tell you the truth. Rolf Bishop is a thief, a traitor, a drug smuggler, and a murderer. He hired the assassin who murdered my wife, Carmela, and my two children, Heather and Kyle."

The image on the screens changed. More photographs of the once happy and alive Hood family came up. Then the image changed to a picture of the bombed out Hood home. "The rest of this video includes proof of Rolf Bishop's perfidy and betrayal," Hood said, in voice-over mode. "Eyewitness proof! I ask you to watch and listen carefully, because, as unbelievable as what you will see and hear might seem, it is true in every detail and the proof is incon—" At this point, someone cut the power to the projectors.

The President called for quiet. The room was in an uproar. Some people stood and craned their necks to get a look at Bishop. The President raised his arms. It took a while for the commotion to subside. When it did, the President shouted, "It looks as though someone has played a practical joke. We have had a wonderful evening. I thank you for your attention and ask you to focus on my message about the world's children. Please go forth and make a difference."

The President wheeled to his right, left the podium, and rushed out of the room. His Secret Service detail had to hustle to catch up with him. By the time they reached him, the President had buttonholed his chief of staff and squeezed the man's arm so hard that anyone could see he was inflicting pain. The President pulled the man close.

"I want to know what happened here tonight! I want to know who fucked with that video. And I want to know if there's a shred of truth about what that guy said about Bishop! And I want to know now!"

"Yes, sir, Mr. President," the Chief of Staff answered. "I'll get right on it."

"You do that," the President said. "And destroy that fucking recording before the press gets hold of it."

"Anything else, sir?"

"Yeah. I want to see Bishop in my room. After I've talked to him, I want the helicopter to take me back to Washington. I've been in the goddamned Big Apple long enough."

Every word the President had spoken about the Year of the Children turned out to be a complete waste of time and effort. The only thing anyone remembered from the evening was David Hood's aborted speech. The guests murmured among themselves as they filed toward the exits. The room fairly reeked with the odor of scandal.

As the guests filed through the ballroom exits, men dressed as waiters—members of Tomasino Portello's crew—thanked the guests for their attendance and handed each a gift-wrapped package.

A woman looked at the package thrust into her hands and asked, "What's this?"

"A token of appreciation from The Plaza Hotel."

Portello's men handed out five hundred copies of the flash drives Sol Lesser had made.

CHAPTER 50

"What the fuck was that fiasco downstairs," the President growled.

"I don't have a clue, Mr. President," Bishop lied.

"I hear someone handed out flash drives to our guests tonight. Copies of what we saw tonight?"

"I don't know," Bishop said.

"Here's one of the flash drives confiscated by the Secret Service. Why don't you watch it? Maybe then you'll be able to tell me something other than *I don't know*."

The President suddenly switched from outright rage to simmering anger. "Rolf," he said, "if I find out you've done anything to jeopardize my administration, I'll have your balls. I'll ruin you."

Irving Gold rushed from his table toward the closest door out of The Plaza Hotel ballroom. When a man handed him a small wrapped box, he continued through the ballroom exit and ripped the wrapping off the box. Inside, he found a flash drive. He stuck the memory device in his pants pocket and scurried toward the street. Short, fat, and out of shape, Gold ran as fast as his three-pack-a-day lungs would permit and beat most of the other guests to the row of limousines out front. He ran up to the first one in line and screamed at the driver, "I got five hundred dollars that's yours if you can get me to *The New York Times* fast."

The driver, who Gold guessed had been hired to take one of the dinner guests home, hesitated only a couple seconds. "Okay, Buddy, let's go. But I want the money now."

Gold reached into his pocket, pulled out five bills, tossed them on the front seat of the limo, and settled into the back seat. He hoped his wife would be able to catch a cab home . . . and wouldn't be totally pissed at him.

Five minutes after he arrived at his office, Gold and a senior editor named Mickey Gallagher viewed the video on the flash drive. Gold knew a couple of dozen other members of the news media had been in that ballroom. Television and radio would certainly broadcast the story within the hour. But he planned to have the best possible print coverage of the "Rolf Bishop Story" in tomorrow's paper. He and Gallagher watched the disk twice from the point where David Hood appeared on the screen. Neither said a single word through either viewing.

CHAPTER 51

In his room at The Plaza Hotel, Bishop inserted the flash drive the President had given him into his computer. While he packed a bag, he watched his career and reputation dissolve. He knew it would not take the media long to verify the accusations on the drive. As badly as he wanted Hood dead, the man's death now would do him no good whatsoever. It was too late. The damage had been done. He had to put his contingency plan into motion.

Bishop left the hotel by the rear delivery entrance and walked to the end of the alley. He'd instructed his driver to park there. He got into the car. "Let's take a ride in Central Park. I need to think."

They'd only gone a short way into the park when Bishop told his driver to pull over. "I want to get some air. I don't feel so well all of a sudden."

His driver immediately pulled over to the curb, got out, and ran around the rear of the car to open Bishop's door. He reached in and helped his boss out of the back seat. As Bishop stood in the street and leaned into the driver, he stabbed him with a seven-inch, razor-sharp knife. The knife penetrated the man's lower torso, sliced deep into his upper intestines, his stomach, and his liver. Bishop held on to him as he twisted the blade and continued to lean on the knife. Then he pushed the man backward toward the cover of some trees, where he released his hold. The young man sank to his knees on the damp earth. Bishop stared into his eyes until life drained out of them.

Now covered in his driver's blood from the middle of his chest to his shoes, Bishop removed his jacket and tossed it into the car trunk. He took his topcoat from the backseat and put it on over his soiled shirt and dark pants, and used his handkerchief to clean off the top of his shoes as best he could. Then he tossed the blood-stained handkerchief at his driver's body. Bishop got in the front seat and grabbed the wheel. His bloody hands stuck to it. He removed his hands from the wheel, took a water bottle out of the cup holder, and washed off as much of the blood as he could. Then he drove the car to a street four blocks from the apartment he'd secretly owned under a fictitious name for years. He abandoned the vehicle, removed his suitcase from the trunk, and walked to the apartment.

Bishop guessed the government would freeze all of his accounts it could unearth, but he would be able to access his foreign accounts. He needed to get out of the United States. With the aggressive policies of the NSA and the IRS, he wasn't confident he could access those accounts remotely. He would have to fly somewhere where the Treasury Department wouldn't be able to track a transaction. As far as the NSA was concerned, he would have to avoid telephones and the Internet. But before he flew out of the U.S., he needed to get to one of his safety deposit boxes, where he had stored cash, bearer bonds, a counterfeit passport, and other false ID. The closest one was here in New York City. But he couldn't do a damned thing until the bank opened on Monday. He used the driver's cellphone to make a call. He left a coded message for a pilot he'd had on retainer for years. He ordered the man to pick him up at a small air strip outside Drew, New Jersey at noon on Monday. Two hundred thousand dollars would ensure the man's silence. Once he landed in Honduras he would be home free. He would have the balance in his Swiss account transferred and would live like an exiled king.

APRIL 29

CHAPTER 52

At 12:30 a.m., Irving Gold looked out through the interior glass wall of his office and noticed a lobby guard move through the newsroom with a small gang of people in tow. Gold smiled at Gallagher and said, "Mickey, I think you're about to see once again that it is infinitely better to be lucky than smart."

Gold recognized some of the men with the guard—David Hood, for sure. Some of the others had been in the video he'd just watched. He rose from his chair and walked around his desk to open his office door. The guard tried to explain, but Gold cut him off.

"Welcome to *The New York Times*," Gold said. "My name is Irving Gold. I am Editor-in-Chief." He pointed at Gallagher. "That's Mickey Gallagher, one of our best reporters. I watched your tape, Mr. Hood. I am very anxious to talk with you and your friends. Why don't you all follow me to our conference room?"

Including Gold and Gallagher, seven men and one woman took seats at the conference table.

"Mr. Gold, Mr. Gallagher," David Hood said, "if you watched the entire video, you should recognize every person here except my father, Peter Hood, and Detective Jennifer Ramsey, of the Bethesda Police Department. Detective Ramsey is investigating the deaths of my wife and children. Next to Detective Ramsey is Montrose Toney, one of the men hired to kill me. Mr. Toney has been held incommunicado for the past several days. I'm sure you found his appearance on the video eye-opening." Hood then pointed at O'Neil. "That is Detective Dennis O'Neil of the Chicago Police Force. He will be happy to expand on the comments he made on the video. Next to Detective O'Neil is Manny Segal, another hired killer—known professionally as Paladin—whom Bishop paid to eliminate eight men in the last month. Messrs. Toney and Segal are here under duress, but they've agreed to answer any questions in return for their freedom. That's the deal I made with them."

Gallagher stared dumbfounded at Hood. "Let me get this straight. You'll turn two psychopathic murderers loose?"

"They're going free," Hood said. "I gave my word. It's Rolf Bishop we want. I'd make a deal with the devil to get that bastard."

"I think that's already happened, Mr. Hood. That video just about did it."

"I want him finished. If *The New York Times* writes about all that Bishop has done, there will be no way for him to ever recover."

"Okay, Mickey," Gold said, "let's get down to business. My first question, Mr. Hood: Why should we believe what these two killers, or any of you, for that matter, tell us?"

"We're here to allow you to challenge every claim we've made," O'Neil said. "We want you to print every detail of this story. The destruction of the myths around Bishop is the only way David will ever be safe from him and his hired guns. And it's the only way we can bring down that son of a bitch."

"Where do you think Toney and Segal can go after you turn them loose?" Gallagher asked. "The cops, the Feds, maybe every client they've ever had will be after them."

Gold guessed from the change in Toney's expressions, from surly to suddenly mournful, that he hadn't thought all of that out.

"What do you want to ask us?" Hood said to Gold.

"You claimed on the video that Bishop had hired assassins to murder men who'd served under him in Afghanistan. To hide his drug business. If you let Toney and Segal go free, how will you prove your claim?"

"Toney and Segal's testimony would be challenged in court by any competent defense attorney, anyway. But what they tell you doesn't have to meet in-court testimony criteria. You ask them questions; they answer. You quote them in the paper. All we want you to do is quote them."

Gold considered what Hood had said. "Let's do this. We'll hear you out and then decide."

David nodded.

O'Neil looked at Manny Segal, jabbed him in the ribs. "Okay, Manny," he said. "It's time for you to hold up your part of the deal."

Segal shot O'Neil an evil look. "I'm not saying a goddamned thing," he said. "I've changed my mind."

Everyone gawked at him until Peter said, "Why don't we take a break? I think Mr. Segal is just a little nervous. Mr. Gold, do you have an office you could lend me for a minute? I need to make a call to a friend out on Long Island. He'll want to know about Mr. Segal's decision not to cooperate."

The assassin went pale. Before Gold could answer Peter, Segal said, "I was hired by Rolf Bishop to kill some men he served with in Afghanistan."

Gold stared at the little killer with complete disgust. "Lady and gentlemen, I'll record the rest of our conversations. Are there any objections?" Gold looked around the room and then nodded at Gallagher, who pressed a button on a recording device in the center of the table.

Gold then asked David, "How can you prove Bishop was involved with drug smuggling while he was in Afghanistan?"

David lifted a briefcase off the floor and placed it on the table. He opened it, unloaded files, and slid them along the table toward Gold. "These are copies of originals I stored in a safe place. They show cash deposits into a Swiss bank account. The total is just under twenty-three million dollars. The balance in the account, including nearly a decade of investment earnings, is now in excess of forty-one million dollars. I know the deposits were payments for drug shipments Bishop sent to a customer in New York. I won't tell you who that customer was. But I *can* tell you that much money in a Swiss account ought to raise an awful lot of questions."

Gold grimaced. "Without testimony from that customer, you got zilch."

"Ask yourself some questions. 'How did a Colonel from a

dirt-poor family amass that kind of wealth?' Oh, and don't forget Bishop has not paid taxes on that money, on the original amounts or on the earnings. I suspect he's used some of that money to make large cash *political* contributions. Unfortunately, I have no proof of that, either."

"You've told us you'll turn two killers loose and you won't reveal who bought narcotics from Bishop," Gold said. "How do you justify these decisions?"

Peter answered this time. "Don't get us wrong. We've agonized about it. But Bishop has to be stopped now. He can do a lot of harm while the authorities plod through the legal system and investigate our accusations."

"If they investigate your accusations," Gold said.

"There's that," David said.

"With his resources, he could have every person who represents a threat to him wiped out," Ramsey said. "He's already proved himself capable of doing that. By the time the legal system dealt with Bishop, there would be no witnesses left to testify against him."

"I can't write a story about Bishop based on innuendo and conjecture," Gold said.

David said, "I understand that. But you *can* write a story about what happened at The Plaza Hotel tonight. And you *can* publish the claims made on that video. It wouldn't be the first time your paper put out a story based on fluff. And you know damned well there's more than fluff in this case."

Gold smiled. "I'll give you that, Mr. Hood."

He turned to Gallagher and told him to write a rush story for page one of the next day's edition. He then called down to the pressroom. "Stop the presses!" he barked. Then he turned to Gallagher and said, "You've got three hours." He looked at David. "I'm going to ask you a bunch of questions. Your answers will, hopefully, flesh out Mr. Gallagher's story."

The question-and-answer session continued for hours. Gold took notes for a follow-up story. It was nearly 3 a.m. when he finally relaxed and leaned back in his chair. He looked at Gallagher, who had long since joined them again, and asked if he had any questions. The reporter shook his head. Gold then turned to the others in the room. "So, where do we go from here?"

"That video has made every one of us a target," David said. "Even though my dad wasn't in the video, he's too close to me to be safe. And Detective O'Neil's role in this mess—maybe Detective Ramsey's, too—is now common knowledge, so they're in just as much danger as the rest of us. We can't go back to our homes. I think we need to vanish for now."

"I know where you guys can stay for a few days," Gold said. "Why don't you let me make some arrangements? I've got a place—"

David held up a hand. "You might be adding your name to the hit list."

"Let me worry about that," Gold said.

David looked at the others and saw no disagreement. "Sounds great," he said. Then he turned to look at Segal and Toney. "As much as I hate to do this, you guys are free to go."

They didn't make a move, as though they couldn't believe David. It took about five seconds for the reality to hit home and then they bolted out of their chairs and out of the conference room. Toney shouldered Segal out of the way and took the lead to the bank of elevators. They both looked back several times, as though they expected to be pursued.

Peter stood up and moved to the conference room windows.

"You okay, Dad?" David asked.

Peter waved off David's concern. "Back's just a bit stiff from too much sitting."

Peter looked out the window, down at the street in front of the building.

He heard Gold ask, "Where do you think those guys will go?"

"Toney may be able to find cover for a while," David said. "But probably not for long. Segal will more than likely skip the country. He must have money put away."

Peter stared down at two taxi cabs parked in front of the building while the conversation at the table behind him became just so much background noise. He saw two men rush from the front of the building. Despite the twenty floors between him and the street, Peter was sure it was Toney and Segal. The difference in the sizes of the two men was obvious and telling.

He watched Segal dive into one cab; Toney entered the other.

Then four men appeared, seemingly out of nowhere. The men split up; two got into each of the cabs.

Peter sighed with satisfaction. Joey Cataldo had come through. Peter didn't feel bound by his son's commitment to Toney and Segal. It was Old World vengeance, without New World remorse.

"Rolf Bishop is about to be dog meat," Gold told David. "He won't be able to hide anywhere. The media won't give him a moment's peace."

O'Neil snorted. "Anyone with the kind of money Bishop has can do just about anything he wants."

David chuckled. "I didn't tell you my banker friend in Zurich froze all of Bishop's accounts on the suspicion the money there was from narcotics. By now, he's probably already informed Interpol and the American and Swiss authorities. Rolf Bishop will never see any of that money."

CHAPTER 53

The impact of the stories in *The New York Times* and in other media was spectacular. Despite the sterling reputation Bishop had built, there was so much cynicism around the country about the nation's political and governmental leaders that it was easy for everyone to believe the worst about him. The discovery of the body of Bishop's driver drove the final nail in the coffin of the man's reputation.

David Hood went from relatively unknown businessman to folk hero.

News commentators raised questions about the President and his administration.

David, Peter, Jennifer, and Dennis holed up at Irving Gold's beach house on Long Island. When Peter heard about Bishop's driver's murder, he noted that, according to the Medical Examiner's time-of-death estimate, it must have happened shortly after the State dinner ended.

"I'll bet Bishop killed the driver because the CIA had ordered the driver to bring Bishop back to D.C."

"I don't think so, Jennifer," O'Neil said. "Bishop's going to ground. He needed the car because he couldn't take the chance a cabbie would recognize him. He had to assume he would be big news very quickly. He's probably holed up somewhere and has already dumped the government car."

Ramsey said, "Let's assume he dumped the car very quickly after he murdered his driver and he's somewhere in the city, say, within one mile of his ultimate destination. It's unlikely he left himself too long a walk to wherever he's holed up, especially late at night in New York City."

Peter looked skeptical. "Okay, if you're right, and if the car is spotted, then all the cops have to do is draw a one-mile radius around the car. Bishop should be inside that radius. The problem is that in New York, there could be hundreds of thousands of people inside a circle with a one-mile radius. And what if he left the vehicle two miles away from his safe house?"

"But why would Bishop hide out in New York when he should get out of the city and the country as fast as he can?" David asked. "He's a marked man as long as he stays in the States. And there won't be many places he can go outside the U.S. where he'll be welcome. He's got to buy his way to some third-world country with which we don't have an extradition treaty."

"But how can he do that if all of his assets are frozen over in Switzerland?" Peter asked.

"That's it, Dad!" David shouted. "That bastard must have other assets hidden away somewhere. He's too smart to put all his eggs in one basket. He must have other accounts. Or a safety deposit box."

O'Neil finished David's thought. "And at least one of those accounts or safety deposit boxes could be here in New York. He might be hiding out here until the banks open on Monday."

"Gotta be a safety deposit box," Peter said. "Activity in a bank account is too easy for the Feds to track."

After a prolonged silence, David said, "Well, that was fun. Now what do we do? The police, even if they buy it, can't watch every bank in the city. Oh, and by the way, we haven't heard anything about charges being brought against Bishop yet, so the cops won't even get involved until that happens."

"I've got an idea," Ramsey said. "If the local police find the car, we might hear about it on the police scanner here in Gold's house. Once we know where the car is, we can get on the Internet and pull up a map of all the bank branches within eight blocks or so. We could split up and watch at least some of them."

"That could be a huge waste of time. What if your eight-block assumption is off?"

"What the hell," David said. "They'll probably never find the car anyway. But it's still worth a try."

CHAPTER 54

Ramsey and O'Neil watched a baseball game on Sunday afternoon when it was suddenly interrupted. A well-known national television commentator announced that the U.S. Attorney General had authorized the appointment of a Special Counsel to investigate accusations against CIA Deputy Director Rolf Bishop. Also, the city of New York had issued an arrest warrant for Bishop in connection with his driver's murder. They cheered the news so loudly David and Peter ran in from the kitchen.

The ringing telephone interrupted their reverie. David grabbed the receiver, but before he could say anything, Irving Gold yelled, "Did you hear the news? The heat's been brought down on Bishop."

"We heard," David said.

"The whole town's crawling with cops. Every one of them wants to be the guy to find Bishop."

"Our theory," David said, "is Bishop's holed up somewhere until the banks open tomorrow morning. He may not know his Swiss accounts are frozen, but we think he must have an account and/or a safety deposit box in the city."

"Sounds reasonable," Gold said. "But there must be hundreds of banks in Manhattan alone. How the hell can Bishop be tied to one particular bank?"

"I don't have a clue," David said.

APRIL 30

CHAPTER 55

David was too hyper to go to bed until nearly 3 a.m. And even then he slept fitfully. He dreamed of Carmela and the kids, something he'd done many times since they'd been killed. In these dreams they were either on a beach or in the family room in the Bethesda house. Carmela laughed while the children played. They seemed happy together, but David always woke from these dreams drenched in sweat. And the lingering memory was that the dream never included him.

Bishop also invaded his subconscious. In another dream that never varied, Bishop chased his family and he chased Bishop, and the longer the dream went on the closer Bishop got to Carmela and the kids. The scene was in dark, sinister woods and dozens of pairs of yellow eyes dispassionately watched the chase. The aftermath of this dream was even worse than the other.

At 5:15 a.m., David awoke in a panic, soaked in sweat. He felt as though he'd lost his family all over again. His heart raced. And in that moment of fear, a thought struck him with such clarity he was amazed he hadn't considered it before.

He rubbed sleep from his eyes and crossed the room to where his briefcase lay on a chair. He retrieved a legal pad from the case and found Willy Muther's telephone number in Zurich. After only two rings, a woman answered. *"Guten Morgen. Banque Securite Swisse. Kann ich Ihnen helfen?"*

"*Herr Muther, bitte.*"

"*Einen Augenblick, bitte.*"

David waited while the receptionist connected him to Willy's office.

Willy's secretary picked up the phone. "*Herr Muther's Buro hier.*"

"Hedwick, it's David Hood."

"Ah, *Herr* Hood, it is good to hear from you. Are you in Zurich?"

"No, Hedwick. I'm in the United States. Is *Herr* Muther in? It's vital I talk with him."

"*Ein moment, bitte. Ich verbinde Sie.*"

Muther came on the line almost immediately. "David, it's good to hear from you again so soon."

"It's my pleasure, Willy. I only wish I could be with you in your lovely city."

"Well, when you do get to Switzerland you must allow me to treat you to dinner. The information you shared with me about *Herr* Bishop was quite useful. From the news on CNN, it looks as though your CIA Deputy Director is in real trouble. But why didn't you tell me about your family? I am so sorry."

"Thank you, Willy," David responded. "*Herr* Bishop is, as we say in the U.S., going down for the count."

"That is good news, David. Because of the information you gave me, I reported to our Swiss banking officials that I suspected the monies in Bishop's account came from criminal activity. The authorities have concurred in freezing the account. If an investigation proves that Bishop's money was earned from the drug trade, you will receive a five percent reward."

David was surprised. "That's great news, Willy. But if you don't mind, I need your help on another matter. And I need you to put a rush on this, too."

"Of course, David."

"Remember, you told me in addition to the original deposits made to Bishop's account back in the early '70s, there were also a number of more recent fund transfers?"

"That's correct, David. More than forty such transactions occurred. The first one in 2007."

"Can you tell me what banks those monies were transferred

from—begin with the most recent and work backwards?"

"Absolutely!" Muther said. "Hold on for just a minute."

Muther came back on the line. "We have the information. I'll send it to your email address."

A few minutes later, Muther's message hit David's email account. It included dates of wire transfers into Bishop's account in reverse chronological order, along with the amounts of the transfers and the originating banks. The banks were all located in large money-center cities. The first six transfers originated in Atlanta, Dallas, San Francisco, London, Munich, and Bangkok. David wondered what businesses had generated the cash in these transfers. More for the Attorney General to look into. A New York bank—Manhattan Merchants Bank—handled the seventh transaction back. David read down the rest of the list. Manhattan Merchants Bank was the only New York bank from which transactions had occurred. There had been three earlier transfers through that bank in the past seven years.

By 6 a.m., David knew exactly what he would do. But he couldn't waste time explaining his strategy to the others. He knew they would want to join him and he couldn't put his father in any more jeopardy. He knew in every fiber of his body Bishop would be at Manhattan Merchants Bank when its offices opened for business at 9 a.m. He wrote a note which he took into Dennis O'Neil's bedroom. The note read: I couldn't sleep, so I drove to the hospital to see Gino. He dropped the note on the floor by the door, then carefully slipped O'Neil's service revolver from its holster draped over the back of a chair. At the last second, he noticed O'Neil's cellphone on the chair seat and grabbed it.

David slipped out of the beach house's back door and padded out to the garage. He would borrow one of Gold's automobiles and head toward the city. He quietly opened the personnel door to the garage and saw there were two vehicles inside—an old but beautifully maintained red 1976 Datsun 280-Z sports car and a new Mitsubishi SUV. David opted for the SUV. The keys were in the ignition. He got behind the wheel, opened the garage bay door with the remote clipped to the sun visor, and started the engine. As he shifted the SUV into DRIVE, Jennifer Ramsey walked in front of the vehicle, her arms akimbo, legs spread. She ran around to the passenger side of the Mitsubishi, opened the door, and slid into the seat.

"What do you think you're doing?" David asked.

"Taking a ride?" she said, her tone cheery.

"Not with me you're not."

Ramsey's tone suddenly changed. "Cut the bullshit!" she hissed. "I heard you moving around your room. You can't be up to anything good at this time of the morning. I'm going with you. That's all there is to it. Now, do you plan to sit here all day?"

David, jaw clenched, gave her an icy stare, but decided there was nothing he could do to get rid of her short of dragging her from the car. He started the car, drove out of the garage, and sped away.

In the city, David used O'Neil's cellphone to dial Gino's hospital room. Despite the hour, Gino answered the phone with his old gusto.

"You sound great," David said.

"No thanks to you or any of my other friends. Where the hell have you guys been? You forget I was in the hospital?"

David loved hearing Gino give him hell. The man was a master at guilt trips. He could tell from the old man's voice he would be all right.

"What are you doing up so early?"

"I think I figured out a way to track down Bishop. My friend in Zurich gave me information about bank transfers Bishop made into his Swiss account from foreign banks. Some of those transfers came from a bank in Manhattan."

"You give that information to the police?"

"No, not yet. It's a long shot. The cops would probably ignore me."

After a few seconds, Gino said, "You're on your way to that bank, aren't you?"

David hesitated and then said, "I know what I'm doing, Gino."

"Listen to me, David," Gino said. "I understand how you feel and I'm the last guy in the world to tell you that revenge is wrong. Hell, I live for it. But the last thing my daughter would have wanted is for you to spend the rest of your life in prison for the murder of an S.O.B. like Bishop. His time is up anyway. Call the cops and tell them where you think they can find him."

"I'm sorry, Gino. This is something I have to do myself." David cut the connection. He stared at Ramsey and saw the shocked look on her face. "When we get to the bank," he told her, "you stay with the car. You understand?"

Ramsey's protest was cut short by David's unflinching look.

Gino thought about calling Joey Cataldo. Have him send some of his New York City men to the bank to intercept David. But those men might not know what David looked like. He could call the cops, but some trigger-happy cop might shoot if he saw Bishop, and hit David by mistake. Besides, he thought he could get to the bank by the time it opened. Gino pulled clothes from the small closet in his hospital room and dressed. Although he was slightly less robust and definitely paler than he'd been before his heart attack, he still looked impressive in the dark blue suit. He put on the fedora and sunglasses Paulie had brought him. When he walked out of the hospital room, Rizzo jumped to attention and blurted, "Don Bartolucci, you should be in bed."

Gino gave him a dirty look. "Whatsa matter, you want me to stay in this place forever? You'd be happy if I died in this place?"

"No, no, Don Bartolucci," Rizzo said, his face flushed with embarrassment. "Of course I'm very happy you're ready to get out of here."

"Good," Gino said. "Now I want you to take me for a little ride."

On the ride into Manhattan, Gino used Paulie's smart phone to check on the bank's address. He was relieved to discover Manhattan Merchants Bank had only one location.

"I got a quick appointment here," Gino said when they arrived at the bank at 9:05 a.m. "Paulie, drop me off. I should be back out in five or ten minutes."

Paulie looked anxious. "I should go with you," he said.

"You'll make someone a great mother some day." Then he casually added, "You have an extra pistol? I feel naked without one."

"Since when do you carry, boss?" Paulie said as he double parked the car fifty feet from the bank entrance and turned on the emergency flashers.

Gino glared back at Paulie.

"Look in the glove compartment."

Gino took out a pistol, checked the safety, ejected the magazine, and replaced it.

Gino hadn't carried a pistol in decades. Even when he ran the Philadelphia organization, he never needed a pistol. His bodyguards handled the weaponry. But he knew guns. "Nine millimeter Beretta Ninety-two," he said. "Fifteen rounds in the magazine?"

"That's right," Paulie said.

Gino suspected if Bishop did show up at the bank he would be armed and ready to kill anyone who got in his way. He fondled the pistol as though it was something animate, got acquainted with its heft and balance.

The clock mounted on the bank's exterior wall now showed 9:07. He checked for security cameras and noted one each mounted twenty feet above the sidewalk on the two front corners of the building.

"Stay with the car," Gino said. Then he pulled the front of the fedora down, left the car, and entered through a bank revolving door that delivered him into a lobby with a twenty-five-foot ceiling, marble floors, and dark-mahogany counters. He carefully surveyed the expansive lobby, but saw neither David nor Bishop. Then he spotted a sign with a down arrow: Safe Deposit Vault.

David had arrived at the bank just a few minutes after 9 a.m. He'd turned a chair in the waiting area so he could see Bishop if he came down the stairway from the lobby. In the seven or eight minutes he'd been in the safety deposit area, no one had come down the stairs. Then, at a bit past 9:10, David was surprised to see Gino come down the steps. David immediately got out of his chair. Gino was still about fifteen feet away when a man bellowed "You!"

The one word expressed volumes of rage. David and Gino turned toward the safety deposit vault. A man stood in front of a metal barred gate which separated the vault from the lobby. He wore a plaid cap and a mustache and goatee. But David saw through the disguise. It was Rolf Bishop.

David couldn't believe it. Bishop must have arrived at the bank just a couple of minutes before he did and had been in the vault since then with the female safety deposit clerk who now stood beside him.

Bishop pulled a pistol from under his suit coat, dropped the large leather valise he held with his left hand, and grabbed the safety deposit clerk by the neck.

When David reached toward his jacket pocket, Bishop extended his arm and rasped, "You don't want to do that. If I have to shoot one of you, then I'll shoot both of you."

David raised his hands.

"Now take that pistol out of your jacket and put it on the floor."

David obeyed.

Bishop stared hard at Gino. "Now you, *Goombah*, put your weapon on the floor."

Gino spread his arms. "I'm not armed."

Bishop was inclined to kill both men and the clerk, as well. He especially wanted to kill Hood. But he knew his unsilenced pistol would sound like an explosion in the confined space. People up in the lobby would surely hear gunshots. He didn't want anyone to set off an alarm. He ordered the men into the safety deposit vault. Once they were inside, Bishop shoved the clerk at them, shut and locked the vault's metal gate, and extracted the key. He tossed the key across the room, picked up his leather bag, and limped up the stairs. His artificial leg clicked with each step.

David was so exasperated he wanted to scream. He knew Bishop would be gone before anyone could come to their assistance. He looked at the clerk and, without much enthusiasm, asked, "Is there a way out of here?"

The woman whimpered and shook like a frightened puppy.

Gino pushed his way through the others and looked at the gate lock. "You all back up," he ordered. He removed a pistol from the back of his waistband, pointed it at the lock, and fired.

The report of the pistol in the small vault with its metal surfaces sounded to David like a cannon shot. He felt as though someone had punched him in the head. He moved around Gino, raised his leg, and kicked the gate open, breaking the remnant of the lock.

David rushed from the vault, scooped up O'Neil's pistol from the floor, and ran to the stairs. He took the steps two at a time to the main level and paid no attention to the frenzied people there. He sprinted out the front door.

Pedestrians moved in a slow, shoulder-to-shoulder, lava-like mass on 5th Avenue; vehicle traffic was bumper-to-bumper. Emergency flashers at the end of the block had slowed traffic to almost a standstill. David saw a fire engine parked in the middle of the street about fifty yards away. He quickly scanned the area immediately in front of the bank, but saw no sign of Bishop. He turned to his right and to his left. Still no Bishop. Then he heard Ramsey shout his name. She stood on the front bumper of the Mitsubishi SUV about twenty yards away and pointed farther down the street.

David looked in the direction Ramsey indicated, but didn't see Bishop. He raised his arms in frustration.

Ramsey yelled, "In the street, in the middle of the street." Then David spotted Bishop's cap as the man moved between gridlocked cars on 5th Avenue. He fast-walked in a jerky motion, almost skipping. Bishop headed toward the opposite side of the broad boulevard.

Bishop saw a mounted cop stare at him. He had no way to know if the cop recognized him with his disguise, but he knew his face had been plastered on every television screen in the country since the previous evening. He had to assume the officer was a potential barrier to escape. On the move, Bishop smoothly raised his pistol from where he held it along his thigh and slowed his pace just enough to steady his aim. He fired and sent a hollow-point round into the cop's chest. The bullet's impact knocked the officer off his horse. The sound of the shot echoed off the walls of the concrete canyon and the voices and movement on the sidewalks and street abruptly halted for a fraction of a second. Then pandemonium erupted. The wounded policeman's left foot caught in a stirrup. The pistol report, the uneven weight of its rider hanging from the stirrup, and pedestrians' screams, seemed to frighten the animal. It bolted and dragged its rider down the crowded sidewalk.

The panicked crowd surged in one direction until it met resistance and then surged back the other way. The crazed horse knocked down and trampled people while it tried to escape the bedlam.

Bishop saw a mob of people attempt to avoid the animal and then turn and come directly toward him. He pivoted and moved back up the sidewalk ahead of them, only to realize he was about to collide with another mass of hysterical people. He stepped back into 5th Avenue, raised his pistol over his head, and fired three times. The crowd in front of him parted like the Red Sea and he moved through the void.

Ramsey jumped to the street from the car's bumper. She removed her service revolver from the holster strapped to her ankle beneath her slacks. She spotted Bishop's hat bob amidst the crowd and moved toward it.

David watched Bishop cross the street, but he couldn't reach him through the crush of cars and people. He'd been carried by the crowd's surge twenty-five yards away from the bank when Bishop reached the sidewalk twenty yards from the bank's entrance, almost back where he'd started.

Just then, David saw Gino walk out of the bank, right into the middle of the madness. David's heart caught in his throat. He yelled to warn Gino, but his voice couldn't compete with the screams, shouts, and blaring horns. David focused on Gino's face in the hope he'd seen Bishop. But all David saw there was confusion. David yelled again, but his words were smothered by the crowd noise.

Gino suddenly saw the devil incarnate come toward him; the man who'd murdered his beloved daughter and grandchildren. He jerked the Beretta from his suit jacket pocket and watched Bishop move closer while the man looked over his shoulder at someone or something behind him. Then Gino saw, even in the undulating sea of humanity, what Bishop looked at: David, who slowly moved toward Bishop, as though he was walking through molasses. David pushed people out of his way, but couldn't make much progress. Then he suddenly broke through the crowd. Bishop turned and aimed his pistol at David.

Gino was about to shout at David when he saw Jennifer Ramsey launch herself in front of David, just as Bishop fired his pistol. She collapsed to the sidewalk.

Bishop turned back toward the bank. He was only ten feet from the entrance when he looked into Gino's eyes, then looked down at the pistol in Gino's right hand, pointed directly at him. Bishop raised his own pistol.

Gino fired a round at Bishop, who spun around and dropped to his knees. His pistol clattered to the pavement. He didn't know where the bullet he'd fired had hit Bishop, but he sensed it hadn't been a kill shot. He advanced on Bishop, whose left hand still clutched the handle of his leather valise. Gino crouched over and, in a husky whisper, said, "That was for Carmela." He put a round into Bishop's stomach. The man sagged and screamed. "That was for Heather." Then Gino grabbed Bishop's chin with his left hand and placed the barrel of the pistol against the man's forehead. "And this is for Kyle." He pulled the trigger.

The melee outside the bank deteriorated into mass hysteria. People screamed and shouted, pushed, and ran like stampeded cattle. Gino calmly pulled Bishop's valise from his hand and walked away. He looked for Paulie and saw his car was blocked by the jam of vehicles backed up because of the accident at the end of the block. He walked down the block and turned the corner. Out of sight of the bank's security cameras, he stepped into an alley, took off his hat, and dropped it into a trash bin. He used a handkerchief to wipe down the Beretta and dumped it in the bin, too.

After he walked away from the alley, Gino called Paulie on his cellphone. "I'll meet you on 42nd Street, around the corner from 5th Avenue."

"We going home?"

"Back to the hospital," Gino said. "We just went out for a walk."

At Gold's place out on Long Island, O'Neil and Peter raptly watched the Action News helicopter coverage of the aftereffects of a shooting that had occurred outside the Manhattan Merchants Bank. The telephone rang. Peter answered it, and was relieved to hear David's voice.

"Where are you?" he asked.

"I'm in an ambulance with Jennifer. Bishop shot her."

CHAPTER 56

It took three hours of surgery to remove the bullet from Jennifer's chest. The round had just missed her aorta, but had collapsed a lung. When she awoke in recovery, still groggy from anesthesia, she saw a hazy image in front of her. It took a minute for her vision to clear enough to recognize David seated at the foot of her bed.

"I know I'm not in heaven," she rasped. "You're here."

"Ha-ha," David said. "Glad you still have a sense of humor."

"What happened?" Jennifer asked.

"Bishop shot you. Someone shot Bishop. Killed him."

"Who?"

"No one knows. TV news says witnesses claim it was either a man or a woman, somewhere between five feet and six feet tall, weighing between one-fifty and two-fifty."

Jennifer saw nothing but a blank expression on David's face. Then, for a beat, she noticed a glint in his eyes and knew in that instant that David knew who had killed Bishop.

Paulie returned Gino to St. Joseph's Hospital by 11 a.m. He went into the hospital and stole a gown and slippers. Gino changed clothes in the back seat of his car and then leaned on Paulie as he returned to his room.

"Where have you been, Mr. Bartolucci?" a nurse demanded.

"Outside getting some air. Did you miss me?"

The nurse glared at Gino. "Did you unplug yourself from the IV?"

"Yeah, I couldn't drag the damn thing around with me."

"You need to get back into bed. It's almost time for lunch. I'll come in a second and hook you up."

Gino rubbed his hands together. "Oh good," he said. "I can't wait."

MAY 1-JUNE 10

CHAPTER 57

The next morning, Paulie Rizzo drove Gino home to his wife in South Philadelphia. Gino had been so focused on his quest for revenge that he'd ignored her since Carmela's death. Now they would mourn the loss of their daughter and grandchildren together.

Dennis O'Neil caught a flight from New York to Chicago. He drove directly to his office, went to his desk, and typed a letter of resignation. He walked into the Chief of Detectives' office and laid the letter, his department-issued sidearm, and his badge on the man's desk. Then he cleaned out his own desk and made a list of the things he had to do before he moved to Bethesda, Maryland. The job David Hood had offered him with Security Systems, Ltd. was just too good to pass up. He took a cab to his house in Brookfield, greeted only by a small antique clock striking 6 p.m. That night. he slept like a baby.

Peter spent a couple days in New York, spelling David at the hospital where he watched over Jennifer Ramsey. But he soon felt like he was intruding and informed his son he would return to Philadelphia.

Jennifer was in the hospital for eight days before the doctors were satisfied infection was no longer a big concern. David visited her every day, although his visits were frequently interrupted by representatives of the NYPD, the Federal Bureau of Investigation, and the Central Intelligence Agency. Everyone wanted to know who had killed Rolf Bishop. David's standard reply was, "I would love to have killed the bastard if I'd had the chance. But someone beat me to it. I heard the shots, but because of the crowd of people between Bishop and me, I couldn't see a thing. After Bishop shot Detective Ramsey I gave her first aid. I didn't have time to notice anything else."

David explained how he received information from a Swiss banker about Bishop's New York bank.

"Who else came to the bank with you?" an FBI agent asked.

"Just Detective Ramsey. She thought I was on a wild goose chase, but wanted to ride along for the hell of it."

A New York City investigator asked, "Mr. Hood, were you armed?"

"Of course not," David lied. "That would be a violation of New York City law."

Day after day, the various investigators questioned David, but couldn't uncover a thing that helped them in their investigation. They finally departed with promises to be back in touch. David wasn't worried.

After the hospital released Jennifer, David returned Irving Gold's SUV to his Long Island home and rented a car. He drove Jennifer to his father's house in Philadelphia where he and Peter helped nurse her back to health over the next few weeks.

Despite hundreds of man-hours put in by the police and the Feds, not one witness to Bishop's murder could give a clear description of the shooter or a coherent account of what had happened. One witness swore she'd seen a man wearing a hat and a suit stand over the dead man and appeared to talk to him. But she couldn't give a good description of that man.

The only pieces of hard evidence the authorities had were the bullets in Bishop's body, Bishop's pistol found on the sidewalk next to his body, and the bullet in the female cop's chest.

The investigators interviewed several bank employees. Some remembered seeing David Hood. A couple saw Hood and several other men walk down to the safety deposit vault. A couple others thought they saw Hood and another man leave the bank through the 5th Avenue exit. But no one could identify the other man. The investigators thought they caught a break when they learned Hood and a second man had been locked in the safety deposit vault. But when they tried to interview the woman who managed the vault, she became hysterical and had to be hospitalized. The bank's security cameras clearly showed David Hood enter the bank alone. The second man came in later. But none of the lobby cameras provided a good picture of his face. Hood claimed he didn't know the identity of that man and never got a good look at his face. There were no cameras in the safety deposit area.

David never mentioned to anyone the two million dollar reward that would come to him from Switzerland. He also never mentioned the bag Gino took from Bishop's dead hand and later gave to him.

David and Peter became closer than ever as they worked together to nurse Jennifer. David found it ironic that something good could come from the evil perpetrated by Bishop. David asked Peter to come live with him in Bethesda. Peter thought for a day about David's proposal. "Only if I can return to Philadelphia if I ever feel like I'm in the way," he said. "Let's give it six months. After that, if we're still talking to one another, I'll sell the place in Philly."

After Jennifer had recovered enough from her wound to return to

Maryland, David drove her and his father to Bethesda. After he dropped Jennifer off at her apartment, David and Peter stopped at the cemetery where Carmela, Heather, and Kyle were buried. David cried as he never had allowed himself before.

The two million dollar reward paid from Bishop's Swiss bank and the ten million from the sale of the bearer bonds in Bishop's leather bag all went into a trust for the widows and children of Bishop's victims.

PART III

NOVEMBER 24

CHAPTER 1

"Can you believe that lucky bastard in the White House survived the Bishop fiasco?" the Senator from Kentucky said under his breath. "And they called Reagan the Teflon President!"

The Senator from South Dakota laughed and hoisted his glass in the air. "To the President," he toasted. "May he outlive his enemies and survive despite his friends."

"I'll drink to that," the Kentuckian said. He drank a half-inch of scotch and placed the glass down on the white tablecloth. He leaned forward and whispered, "Anything new from the Senate Intelligence Committee?"

"Shit!" the South Dakotan cursed. "That bastard Bishop made Saddam Hussein look like a rank amateur."

"I've seen the briefs. Some hero!"

The Senator from South Dakota scrunched up his eyes. "Have you heard anything about whether that fellow Hood will bring a lawsuit against the government? After all, Bishop had already been nominated to the CIA position when he had Hood's family murdered."

"From what I've heard, that's not Hood's style. Actually, I expected his father-in-law, Bartolucci, to sue the city of Philadelphia, but apparently he didn't want city lawyers to look into his past activities any more than they already had."

"I guess not."

"One thing did come out of the investigation that was kind of interesting," the Senator from Kentucky said. "The Intelligence Committee interviewed all of Bishop's assistants, clerks, you know, all his support people. One guy mentioned a call that came to Bishop's office a couple days before Bishop got shot. Some cop from Bethesda: Cromby . . . Cromwell. That's it. Cromwell called and said he had information about Hood. He put the call through to Bishop, but didn't know what the guy told Bishop. Turns out the cop may have given Bishop information about where to find Hood in Philadelphia."

"What an asshole! Anything happen to the cop? Should have been fired, at least."

"Yeah! His boss tried to fire him, but the union intervened. The District Attorney down there started an investigation, but now that's irrelevant. Somebody whacked the guy. Put a bullet in his brain."

NEXT YEAR

JULY 16

CHAPTER 2

Jennifer Ramsey knew David's wife and kids had loved Cape May, New Jersey. How could she not know it? David mentioned it often enough. The beautiful Victorian village off the tip of New Jersey catered to families, bird watchers, and history buffs, he'd told her more than once. Jennifer didn't care if she ever saw the place. Every time David brought up the subject, she felt as though someone twisted a dagger in her gut.

She and David would take in a show every once in a while; maybe have dinner once or twice a month. Jennifer felt as though they connected on those "dates." But then the damned weekend would come around and he'd retreat deeper within himself. She tried to get him to spend weekends with her—in D.C., Williamsburg, Alexandria, Rehoboth. Anywhere but Cape May. To no avail. And every time he visited Cape May, he became melancholy. He'd return to Bethesda more depressed, more withdrawn. His visits there rekindled the anger and depression he couldn't seem to get past. Instead of healing the hole in his heart, the memories the visits generated seemed to tear him apart.

Jennifer had never been more frustrated. There was no one she could talk with about it, so she bought a diary. A red, leather-bound volume that became her sounding board. And every time she pulled it from the nightstand, self-contempt wrapped a cloying cloak around her. What kind of life do you lead? she asked herself over and over. You're in love with a man who doesn't know how you feel and couldn't care less about you, and now you talk to a goddamn book. It was another Thursday night. Another sleepless night. He'll leave Bethesda after work tomorrow and drive down to Delaware. Take the ferry from Lewes, Delaware over to Cape May. She read what she'd written the past Monday:

We've become friends over the past twelve months, but the friendship has cost me in ways he'll never understand. David seems oblivious to how I feel about him. I'm tormented with the desire to put my arms around him, to make his demons disappear. But all I am to him is a wall against which he tosses his pain and sorrow.

I don't know if it's accurate to say my soul is hurting. Can souls feel pain? And now David appears to have spiraled even further downward, into a state of depression that frightens me beyond any fear I've ever known. I've held off saying the words, but the thought has been with me for months. There is no question in my mind David is suicidal. He can't seem to get past the death of his wife and children, or to see that life could still be wonderful.

I love him with all of my being.

Jennifer slammed the diary closed and tossed it in the nightstand's open drawer. She shut the drawer and nearly toppled the bedside lamp to the floor. "One last try," she groaned. "I'll give it one last try. I can't go on like this."

The clock radio showed 11 p.m. There was no doubt David would still be awake. She knew he rarely went to bed before midnight. She dialed his home number.

"Hello."

"Oh, I'm sorry, Peter," Jennifer said. "Is David there?"

"Hi, Jen. Why are you up so late?"

"I could ask you the same question."

"Huh," Peter grunted. "I suspect neither of us can sleep for the same reason."

"Is he still up?"

"Of course! God forbid he should get a good night's sleep."

"Can I speak with him?"

"Certainly."

Jennifer expected David to come on the line. But a few seconds passed and then Peter said, "Think how you'd feel if you blamed yourself for the deaths of your brother, wife, and children."

She'd heard from Peter about the murder of David's brother, Tommy, and how David blamed himself. And she knew David had been the target of the killer who murdered Carmela, Heather, and Kyle. More blame. "I'd feel like crap, Peter."

"Don't give up, honey. You're just what he needs."

Peter's words sounded to Jennifer like the plea of a desperate man. She didn't have the heart to tell him that giving up was exactly what she planned to do. If her plans for this weekend failed. She honed her argument while she waited for David to pick up the phone.

"Hello, Jen," David said in a desultory tone.

Afraid she'd lose her resolve if she got diverted into small talk, she blurted, "Are you going to New Jersey this weekend?"

"Yes, well I planned—"

"What time will you leave?"

"About four o'clock. Why?"

"Swing by my place and pick me up. I'll go with you."

"Whoa, Jen," David said. "I don't think that's such a good idea. I mean—"

"One way or the other, I'm going to Cape May. You don't pick me up, I'll follow you in my own car. It's about time I found out what's so special about that place."

Jennifer heard David sigh. Then a five-second silence.

"I'll see you at four," he said, and hung up.

JULY 17

CHAPTER 3

Thank God for the radio, Jennifer thought while David parked the car against the side of the elevated blacktop boardwalk that separated Beach Drive from the sand and the Atlantic Ocean beyond. She'd barely been able to get fifty words out of him on the two-hour drive and seventy-five-minute ferry ride. He was obviously angry she had insisted on joining him. Not an auspicious start to the weekend.

David fed the parking meter and hopped up on the boardwalk. He left her standing in the street beside the car. Well, this was my idea, she thought. She jumped up on the boardwalk and rushed to catch up with him.

The blacktop ribbon ended about fifty yards ahead where groups of people stood and looked at the setting sun. Thirty yards of sand continued from the end of the boardwalk to the shoreline and a huge black rock jetty. Across a shimmering bay, maybe a mile wide, stood a red-topped, white-walled lighthouse. The fiery setting sun seemed to lean on the shoulder of the lighthouse. Layers of pink radiated from the ball and cascaded into the sea.

David stepped off the walkway to the beach and set off diagonally toward the jetty that extended into the pounding surf.

Jennifer tried to keep up, but the deep sand sucked at her sandals. She stopped to kick them off and then hurried to the rocks. Wet from the surf and greasy with lichen, the rocks were treacherous. She placed a foot on one, only to skid off the surface. She fell between two giant, squared off boulders and skinned both shins and an elbow.

"Damn!" she shouted. She looked up at David, but he either hadn't heard her or had ignored her. "You bastard!" she muttered. "If you think you can get the best of me . . . . "

Jennifer extricated herself from the space between the rocks, retreated to the sand, and walked away from the shore until she found a dry spot. She mounted the jetty, then, with mincing steps, wound her way to where David now sat, Atlantic Ocean to his left, the Delaware coastline in the distance.

The sun set, inch-by-inch, behind the lighthouse. Despite the drama of the enormous red globe as it descended toward the water, Jennifer couldn't help but question why she had come here. She looked over at him and somehow knew his thoughts: How he used to come to this very spot at sunset with Carmela, Heather, and Kyle.

Tonight, while nature put on a spectacle, Jennifer came to the conclusion she had wasted her time. The longer she stayed around David, the worse her heart would break. She blew out a shuddering sigh and turned back toward the sunset. This was probably all she would get out of this weekend. What an idiot you are, Jennifer Ramsey, she thought, as tears streaked her cheeks.

The sun finally touched the horizon and seemed to dissolve in the water. Tears now flowed down her cheeks. Jennifer sat there, mesmerized by it all, yet bereft of spirit and hope. Then she spontaneously applauded nature's show. While her tears flowed, she clapped in appreciation of the sunset.

"What!" David said.

Jennifer jerked around and stared at him. His face was a collage of confusion, anguish, and anger. Jennifer felt a shaft of sympathy pierce her heart. She sensed the emotion that coursed through him and was suddenly concerned she'd disturbed him. After all, this was the place he'd come with his family. Their place. A lump formed in her throat and she felt like an interloper. She should never have pushed herself on him. If he couldn't love her, if he couldn't see how much she loved him, that she'd risked her life for him, she would just butt out.

David saw the tears in Jennifer's eyes; teardrops spilled down her cheeks. As though he'd been struck in the head, a flash of bright light seemed to go off behind his eyes. And in that instant, a thought penetrated his cocoon of self-pity. He'd become so absorbed with his memories, with himself, he hadn't had room in his heart for anyone else. He and Jennifer had become friends. They'd had dinners together over the past year, and even talked occasionally on the phone. She'd been a wonderful listener. She'd invited herself along on this trip to Cape May on the spur of the moment and he'd treated her like an intruder. With overwhelming clarity, the thought hit him that he'd been a royal asshole. He'd treated this wonderful woman like her role in their relationship was to be a sponge that absorbed whatever he poured on her. He'd given her nothing over the past twelve months; only took.

David felt warmth envelop him. It was almost as though Tommy, Carmela, Heather, and Kyle had wrapped him in their arms. He smiled at Jennifer and saw her face suddenly metamorphose. Her wrinkled brow and trembling mouth were replaced by laughing eyes and a sparkling smile. A deadness he'd carried within him too long started to dissipate, like oppressive hands had suddenly released their grip on his heart.

"Pretty spectacular sunset, wasn't it?" he said.

"What?" She daubed tears with her fingers.

David stood up and brushed the sand off his jeans. He reached out a hand to her and smiled. "You hungry?"

"Yes." She took his hand and looked into his eyes as she stood up. They walked along the top of the jetty until they found a place no higher than three feet from the sand. And jumped down to the beach.

They meandered along the beach for a while, hand-in-hand, in a comfortable silence; listened to the waves break on the shore and gulls cry overhead.

"Are the sunrises as beautiful?" she asked.

David stopped, turned toward her, and gently swept back a few loose strands of her hair. Maybe there was good in the world, he thought. Good that eventually defeated evil.

"Jennifer, you're going to love tomorrow's sunrise."

THE END

To My Readers:

Thank you for reading "Ultimate Betrayal," my seventh novel. Writing this book was an adventure for me as it brought back memories of experiences I had in Vietnam and allowed me the opportunity to research a variety of subjects, including the War in Afghanistan, CIA organization, and narcotics trafficking. "Ultimate Betrayal" was inspired by both personal experiences and historical events.

If you enjoyed this novel, you might want to read my other books, including "The Pythagorean Solution" (my first novel, released in 2003), "Shell Game" (a financial thriller released in 2012), and the 4-book *Danforth Saga* ("Evil Deeds," "Terror Cell," "The Nostradamus Secret," and "The Lone Wolf Agenda," all released between 2004 and 2013).

I would appreciate you writing a brief review on Amazon.com of any of my books which you have read. I value your opinion. The link to that site is: www.amazon.com/author/josephbadal.

I am currently working on my first mystery novel, "Borderline," and the fifth book in the *Danforth Saga*, "Death Ship."

Thank you for your support of my work.

Joe Badal
http://www.josephbadalbooks.com
badalbooks@gmail.com

ABOUT THE AUTHOR

Prior to a long finance career, including serving as a senior executive and board member of a NYSE-listed company, Joseph Badal served for six years as a commissioned officer in the U.S. Army in critical, highly classified positions in the U.S. and overseas, including tours of duty in Greece and Vietnam. He earned numerous military decorations.

He holds undergraduate and graduate degrees in International Finance (Temple University) and Business Administration (University of New Mexico). He graduated from the Defense Language Institute, West Coast, and from Stanford University Law School's Director College.

Joe now serves on the boards of several companies.

He has had six suspense novels published, including "The Lone Wolf Agenda," which was released in 2013, and which was named the top Mystery/Thriller novel in the 2013 New Mexico/Arizona Book Awards competition. His next novel, "Ultimate Betrayal," will be released in April 2014. He also writes a monthly blog titled *Everyday Heroes*, and has written short stories published in the "Uncommon Assassins" and "Someone Wicked" anthologies.

Joe has written dozens of articles that have been published in various business and trade journals and is a frequent speaker at business, civic, and writers' events.

"EVIL DEEDS"
DANFORTH SAGA (#1)

"Evil Deeds" is the first book in the *Bob Danforth* series, which includes "Terror Cell" and "The Nostradamus Secret." In this three book series, the reader can follow the lives of Bob & Liz Danforth, and of their son, Michael, from 1971 through 2011. "Evil Deeds" begins on a sunny spring day in 1971 in a quiet Athenian suburb. Bob & Liz Danforth's morning begins just like every other morning: Breakfast together, Bob roughhousing with Michael. Then Bob leaves for his U.S. Army unit and the nightmare begins, two-year-old Michael is kidnapped.

So begins a decades-long journey that takes the Danforth family from Michael's kidnapping and Bob and Liz's efforts to rescue him, to Bob's forced separation from the Army because of his unauthorized entry into Bulgaria, to his recruitment by the CIA, to Michael's commissioning in the Army, to Michael's capture by a Serb SPETSNAZ team in Macedonia, and to Michael's eventual marriage to the daughter of the man who kidnapped him as a child. It is the stops along the journey that weave an intricate series of heart-stopping events built around complex, often diabolical characters. The reader experiences CIA espionage during the Balkans War, attempted assassinations in the United States, and the grisly exploits of a psychopathic killer.

"Evil Deeds" is an adrenaline-boosting story about revenge, love, and the triumph of good over evil.

"TERROR CELL"
DANFORTH SAGA (#2)

"Terror Cell" pits Bob Danforth, a CIA Special Ops Officer, against Greek Spring, a vicious terrorist group that has operated in Athens, Greece for three decades. Danforth's mission in the summer of 2004 is to identify one or more of the members of the terrorists in order to bring them to justice for the assassination of the CIA's Station Chief in Athens. What Danforth does not know is that Greek Spring plans a catastrophic attack against the 2004 Summer Olympic Games.

Danforth and his CIA team are hampered by years of Congressionally mandated rules that have weakened U.S. Intelligence gathering capabilities, and by indifference and obstructionism on the part of Greek authorities. His mission becomes even more difficult when he is targeted for assassination after an informant in the Greek government tells the terrorists of Danforth's presence in Greece.

In "Terror Cell," Badal weaves a tale of international intrigue, involving players from the CIA, the Greek government, and terrorists in Greece, Libya, and Iran—all within a historical context. Anyone who keeps up with current events about terrorist activities and security issues at the Athens Olympic Games will find the premise of this book gripping, terrifying, and, most of all, plausible.

"Joe Badal takes us into a tangled puzzle of intrigue and terrorism, giving readers a tense well-told tale and a page-turning mystery."
—Tony Hillerman, *New York Times* bestselling author

"THE NOSTRADAMUS SECRET"
DANFORTH SAGA (#3)

This latest historical thriller in the *Bob Danforth* series builds on Nostradamus's "lost" 58 quatrains and segues to present day. These lost quatrains have surfaced in the hands of a wealthy Iranian megalomaniac who believes his rise to world power was prophesied by Nostradamus. But he sees the United States as the principal obstacle to the achievement of his goals. So, the first step he takes is to attempt to destabilize the United States through a vicious series of terrorist attacks and assassinations.

Joseph Badal offers up another action-packed story loaded with intrigue, fascinating characters and geopolitical machinations that put the reader on the front line of present-day international conflict. You will be transported from a 16th century French monastery to the CIA, to crime scenes, to the Situation Room at the White House, to Middle Eastern battlefields.

"The Nostradamus Secret" presents non-stop action in a contemporary context that will make you wonder whether the story is fact or fiction, history or prophesy.

" "The Nostradamus Secret" is a gripping, fact-paced story filled with truly fanatical, frightening villains bent on the destruction of the USA and the modern world. Badal's characters and the situations they find themselves in are hair-raising and believable. I couldn't put the book down. Bring on the sequel!"
—Catherine Coulter, *New York Times* bestselling author of "Double Take"

"THE LONE WOLF AGENDA"
DANFORTH SAGA (#4)

With "The Lone Wolf Agenda," Joseph Badal returns to the world of international espionage and military action thrillers and crafts a story that is as close to the real world of spies and soldiers as a reader can find. This fourth book in the *Danforth Saga* brings Bob Danforth out of retirement to hunt down lone wolf terrorists hell bent on destroying America's oil infrastructure. Badal weaves just enough technology into his story to wow even the most a-technical reader.

"The Lone Wolf Agenda" pairs Danforth with his son Michael, a senior DELTA Force officer, as they combat an OPEC-supported terrorist group allied with a Mexican drug cartel. This story is an epic adventure that will chill readers as they discover that nothing, no matter how diabolical, is impossible.

"A real page-turner in every good sense of the term. "The Lone Wolf Agenda" came alive for me. It is utterly believable, and as tense as any spy thriller I've read in a long time."
—Michael Palmer, *New York Times* bestselling author of "Political Suicide"

"THE PYTHAGOREAN SOLUTION"
STAND-ALONE THRILLER

The attempt to decipher a map leads to violence and death, and a decades-long sunken treasure.

When American John Hammond arrives on the Aegean island of Samos he is unaware of events that happened six decades earlier that will embroil him in death and violence and will change his life forever.

Late one night Hammond finds Petros Vangelos lying mortally wounded in an alley. Vangelos hands off a coded map, making Hammond the link to a Turkish tramp steamer that carried a fortune in gold and jewels and sank in a storm in 1945.

On board this ship, in a waterproof safe, are documents that implicate a German SS Officer in the theft of valuables from Holocaust victims and the laundering of those valuables by the Nazi's Swiss banker partner.

"Badal is a powerful writer who quickly reels you in and doesn't let go."
—Pat Frovarp & Gary Shulze, Once Upon A Crime Mystery Bookstore

"SHELL GAME"
STAND-ALONE THRILLER

"Shell Game" is a financial thriller using the economic environment created by the capital markets meltdown that began in 2007 as the backdrop for a timely, dramatic, and hair-raising tale. Joseph Badal weaves an intricate and realistic story about how a family and its business are put into jeopardy through heavy-handed, arbitrary rules set down by federal banking regulators, and by the actions of a sociopath in league with a corrupt bank regulator.

Like all of Badal's novels, "Shell Game" takes the reader on a roller coaster ride of action and intrigue carried on the shoulders of believable, often diabolical characters. Although a work of fiction, "Shell Game," through its protagonist Edward Winter, provides an understandable explanation of one of the main reasons the U.S. economy continues to languish. It is a commentary on what federal regulators are doing to the United States banking community today and, as a result, the damage they are inflicting on perfectly sound businesses and private investors across the country and on the overall U.S. economy.

"Shell Game" is inspired by actual events that have taken place as a result of poor governmental leadership and oversight, greed, corruption, stupidity, and badly conceived regulatory actions. You may be inclined to find it hard to believe what happens in this novel to both banks and bank borrowers. I encourage you to keep an open mind. "Shell Game" is a work of fiction that supports the old adage: You don't need to make this stuff up.

"Fiction Master, Joseph Badal has another winner in "Shell Game." Take a roller coaster ride through the maze of modern banking regulations with one of modern fiction's most terrifying sociopaths in the driver's seat. Along with its compelling, fast-paced story of a family's struggle against corruption, "Shell Game" raises important questions about America's financial system based on well-researched facts."
—Anne Hillerman & Jean Schaumberg, WORDHARVEST

Made in the USA
Columbia, SC
30 July 2017